UNEXPECTED
FORTUNE

E. Adrian Dzahn

To Emily and Liz

CHAPTER 1

"DID I SAY THERE WAS something wrong with him?"

It was Adelaide's brusque voice. When my granddaughter first came to live with me, the summer before she began law school, I had inwardly dubbed it her 'gruff' voice, connecting it to the loose T-shirts, jeans, and sneakers she invariably sported—not that her clothes were ever dirty or rumpled. But only her brushed long hair, auburn like mine had been, and her unassuming frame betrayed a feminine side. Just yesterday I learned of the tragedy that underlay her indifference to male gazes, and I silently redubbed the voice her 'brusque' one. Yet now it connoted mere puzzlement.

"If there's nothing wrong with him, then why not accept the invitation?" I said.

"I agreed to go for coffee instead."

We were standing in the entryway abutting the living and dining rooms, a space large enough only for a small chair and the vanity, which contained a prodigious quantity of mail—bills, journals, advertising circulars, the occasional correspondence. I should mention that the vanity was in truth simply a narrow mahogany table. Over a half century ago—in 1936, to be precise—as newlyweds furnishing the apartment, Marjorie and I had attended an estate sale off Central Park West. A mirror sat atop the table, along with the label *Vanity*. After whispering in my ear that it was not a true vanity, Marjorie courteously inquired of the seller whether we could purchase the 'vanity' without the mirror. He assented, and having been so amused by his pretense, Marjorie continued to call the piece the vanity, and the children and I came to follow suit.

"Did you try on the robe?" Adelaide asked. "I can return it on my way to class if it doesn't fit or you don't like the color."

"If you have a few moments, I will do that now. By the way, Millie dropped off a letter from your mother—it was inadvertently put in their mailbox. It is on top of the middle pile, I believe."

Without dawdling but carefully, my ankle still a tad tender, I made my way to the bedroom. For my birthday yesterday, Adelaide had given me a lovely dark-brown robe with deep pockets. Embarrassed, I had scolded her that one's seventy-ninth merited no attention—after fifty, birthdays should be noted only at the ten-year mark, if then.

I returned to the entryway wearing the garment. Tying the belt closed, I said, "It fits fine. Your stop at Macy's killed two birds with one stone, encountering your classmate—"

"Is the color okay? They didn't have blue."

I assured her brown was preferable. "Your grandmother always chose pale colors that showed every drop of tea."

Adelaide was no longer listening—she had retrieved Olivia's letter and was reading it. Her posture unwittingly telegraphed her alienation from her mother: no repairing to the privacy of the bedroom for secret girl talk, no eager exchange of confidences. Ironically, *I* was my granddaughter's confidante.

"She's coming for a visit in December," Adelaide said. "She wants to know if the twenty-second would be all right."

"I'll be here."

Showing no sign of appreciating the humor—my weakened ankle kept me from venturing even as far as the delicatessen on Lexington, much less embarking on distant travel—Adelaide replaced the letter in the envelope and set it back on the vanity. I debated returning to my chair in the living room and resuming reading. It was rare for a scholarly journal—and this one in particular—to feature a portrait, and I could not call this the most flattering of Henry James that I had seen, and I had seen no small number.

Instead, I hobbled to the windows. The river was a patchwork of grays, greens, and browns. Red car lights formed a chain along the Queensboro. Roosevelt Island, what we had used to call Welfare Island, had changed greatly since the war; having housed primarily hospitals, now it was home to a substantial resident population.

The skyline, too, was greatly altered. During my early visits to Marjorie in this very apartment, her father had pointed out the marble and granite quarries across the river. Since those years, countless buildings sprouted up. Of course the construction of the United Nations building was one of the more distinctive changes, a wafer of glass not quite visible from our window. How hopeful we had been then of reaching the elusive goal of world peace, despite Stalin's iron rule over the Soviet Union and Eastern Europe.

The principal attraction for Adelaide and me—and no doubt for virtually anyone else positioned by these panes—was the water. The river changed color and texture almost continuously, a dark-green tint giving way to a deep aquamarine when the sunlight hit just so, or a purplish blue when twilight arrived. The river also showcased a variety of watercraft, from large commercial vessels coming down through Long Island Sound to local barges, pleasure yachts, and simple sloops. I hoped Adelaide would dress warmly; November was in full force.

On the other hand, Manhattan's aura as a modern-day bazaar had not changed from when, in 1929, I first set foot in the city, albeit for just one day. Like Paris and London, New York had a claim to the pinnacle, the preeminent metropolis, the center of not just the business world but the cultural world.

Marjorie's mother some years later spoke of Manhattan as an analogue to the Roman Forum, where people of importance convened. During college I had felt that the borough was the locus of a *Renaissance*, a Florence or Bruges, propagating the world's most fertile creative and scholastic impulses. Perhaps those sensations belonged to Youth, and this septuagenarian organism could no longer enter into such feelings of awe and wonderment.

"There's leftover meat loaf," Adelaide said, pausing in the doorway.

"I will manage my lunch just fine—I still have half of the pastrami, piled with 'the works.' My dear, I was just reminiscing about our early years in this apartment, which your grandmother's parents ceded to us when we married, purchasing 4-D for themselves. Bit by bit over the years, I paid them back, concluding the indebtedness with a lump-sum payment upon my own father's death. Although of course Cecil refused to charge any interest. 'What for? Marjorie will inherit it all after Claudia and I die.'"

Adelaide smiled before disappearing down the hall.

Yes, my in-laws' generosity was unstinting. I suppose having a daughter softened a man. And the time I voiced surprise that they showed no disappointment in her choice of me over Edward—a stockbroker and dyed-in-the-wool New Yorker—Marjorie surmised that her father considered it a feather in his cap that he could allow his daughter to marry for love, not from pecuniary necessity.

I was glad not to have disappointed her parents, to have had a career that allowed her a comfortable existence—and a career that they viewed with pride. Her father lived long enough to see me become a respected faculty member at a respected university, with tenure a not-unlikely culmination of my career's trajectory. To have earned his respect was no small source of gratification.

My thoughts returned to my elder daughter's impending visit. Although here only last March to deliver a lecture on Virginia Woolf—not a favorite with me—Olivia would appear changed. Once one's children reached middle age, seeing them after an absence was a double-edged sword. The outer edge smote many foes—possible parental achings, doldrums, the 'rut of routine,' some would say, but I never considered routine a rut, much less a foe. In any case, the sword's inner edge was having to bear witness to time's fingerprints on their faces and movements, which was far worse than a mirror on one's own. Was that because their youth mesmerized us not merely with an illusion of *their* immortality but of *ours*, which now we must relinquish?

Of course, the doldrums were no longer a problem, to the extent they could have been called doldrums, which was *Olivia's* view, not mine. It was only natural I should have gone through a period of grief after Marjorie passed away, and my retirement following in relatively quick succession had compelled some adjustment of perspective. So the fact that I had been unable immediately to embark on my "magnum opus," as Olivia liked to call it, despite my having had the free time to do so, should not have been alarming: the freedom to write had been thrust upon me unexpectedly. I *did* eventually begin working on the book and, indeed, made considerable progress. Adelaide's coming to live with me a year ago July was all the disruption of routine I could be said to have required.

And far from being a puppy loose in a museum—my initial fear—Adelaide was a quiet companion. I appreciated that she did not bring law school classmates home, and when on rare occasion the television set was on, I was as likely the culprit as she. In many ways we were more compatible than her grandmother and I had been. Certainly more so than I and my own children—at least Richard and Marcia. Although

4

it was only of late that we began to share tidbits about our personal histories, our perspectives on the world were much aligned. If it weren't for her inattention to literature, Adelaide could have been what people sentimentalize as a 'soul-mate.'

According to my watch, this was the time she could be expected to be brushing her teeth, right before departing. Her backpack had already been placed by the door. Today's classes were Admin and Con, short for Administrative and Constitutional Law.

The legal world was no longer a dark labyrinth to me. At the dinner table, Adelaide expounded upon her courses without reservation. A far cry from that first summer when she moved in, each of us groping for topics the other might deem interesting, hoping to smooth over our awkwardness. Once her classes began, the awkwardness vanished, for she readily responded to my inquiries and even made specific reference to the fact that explaining to me what she had been taught during the day helped her to "remember it better." It was a maxim among teachers, I said, that instructing another can crystallize vaporous, indistinct thoughts.

As a consequence of more than a year of discussions, certain legal concepts were now familiar to me. I knew that when a lawyer 'deposes' a witness, the lawyer is not ousting a monarch from his throne but, rather, taking a witness's testimony under oath. Of course I had heard of 'taking a deposition' before—I almost had had my own deposition taken when an aggrieved associate professor sued the tenure committee for our refusal to promote her to a full professorship. The lawsuit was quickly settled or dismissed, and at that time it was a matter of personal pride on my part to know as little as possible about the litigating profession. Among the many sins of lawyers and judges, the primary one was the butchering of English prose until it was deprived of all poetry.

My vulnerable ankle began to throb under the slight pressure of standing, so I hobbled gingerly back to my chair. Again, I checked my watch.

Yes, the law provided us with interesting dinnertime conversation—and a few fireworks as well, especially her Evidence class. Just last week she told me about 'privileged communications,' communications a person was required to keep secret even if forced to take the witness stand in court and directly asked what the defendant had said. There was the attorney-client privilege and the spousal privilege and several others. If I were permitted a pun, the priest-penitent privilege was the canonical example. A priest was prohibited by this privilege from telling the jury the substance of a parishioner's confession. The legal Einsteins who formulated this rule believed it should apply even to a man who confessed that he had murdered a child—or a *roomful* of children. That a priest should remain mum was repugnant to any moral code and incomprehensible to any rational creature.

Adelaide's argument in defense of the rule, which did not sway me, was that "society is better off in the long run" by encouraging people to confess to their clergy, compared with how it would fare if criminals were discouraged from seeking atonement. Supposedly atonement made the criminal a better person. To my mind, allowing murderers to obtain absolution from a priest for the hereafter was a less worthy goal than locking them up in the here and now.

And it was not the priest alone who was required to conceal the confession!

So was the murderer's wife, physician, and therapist. Only the *jury*, it seems, was kept in the dark as to what had transpired at the crime scene—the very people charged with deciding the facts and rendering a verdict. The logic of such a scheme cannot be fathomed. Dickens's loathsome Mr. Bumble was correct on one point: *The law is a ass.* Alice's voyage down the rabbit hole had more logic to it. And yet, according to my granddaughter, the highest encomium from a professor was to be told one "thinks like a lawyer." Heaven spare us!

Adelaide returned to the entryway and put on her bulky dark parka. Although her face shared many of Nathan's unremarkable features and would not likely launch a thousand ships, with makeup it could attract admirers. Even without makeup, if it showed a little vitality, shed its deadpan aspect. Much as Olivia and I had quarreled over Adelaide's frame of mind, I did silently concur that Adelaide's demeanor was somewhat impassive. I—but not Olivia—knew the cause of the lackluster mien.

Olivia herself had always attracted men's gazes, with her full figure, bright eyes, and wide, ready smile. During her college years she had brought home no small number of nice young men prior to Nathan. Yet her self-confidence could intimidate a meeker soul. More than a few of our sex prefer a quietness like Adelaide's.

Pretending to peruse my journal, I surreptitiously watched my granddaughter complete her preparations for battling the day: pocketing her keys, doublechecking for her gloves. "When will you be going for coffee with Carson?" I called out. "I need you to pick up a book at the library."

She stepped onto the living room carpet. "I can stop on my way home today."

"It will take me some minutes to look up the exact title. I will give it to you later. No rush."

"We're going Thursday." There was no enthusiasm, no eagerness in her voice. There never was.

CHAPTER 2

THE WALL-TO-WALL CLOUDS and gray dreariness reminded her of Seattle, especially the winters. There, though, the heavy cumulus clouds often held on to the moisture across Puget Sound and the city and dumped it only after hitting the Cascades. But in New York, a dense overcast meant rain. With any luck, it wouldn't start for another ten or fifteen minutes so Addy could walk to the farther subway stop. On a few nice spring days last year, she'd walked the entire way from school to Francis's, a great workout with her heavy backpack. She liked being outside, and exercise felt as necessary as eating. And on the streets of Manhattan, where so many other pedestrians walked quickly and purposefully, she never stood out.

A sign on the deli Francis claimed had given him food poisoning said *Closed for Repairs*. "The pastrami was the culprit," he'd insisted, despite her explaining that symptoms could take twelve, eighteen hours to develop. And refused to let her make a doctor's appointment to rule out something more serious. "Dr. Conti will give me a dressing down for eating pastrami in the first instance." At least he didn't fight her on drinking the juice and soup. But now they always had to go to the deli over on Lexington—no, *she* had to go. What a character.

The moist air felt nice cooling her face—Addy realized her mother's upcoming visit was making her tense. Would Olivia get on Francis's case again about staying in the condo? Carp about the unused rooms weighing on him? Last spring Olivia had seen how they'd converted the master bedroom into his office. The guys in 9-F, grateful to Addy for storing their perishables when their refrigerator conked, happily helped her move the furniture. They also helped her move Olivia's childhood bed down the hall to Millie and John's because their grandson sometimes stayed over. Francis had gotten so absorbed in arranging the books on the shelves that he barely took a break except for his nap. "It's my first office since retirement," he'd said, practically beaming at the desk and computer and bookcases.

His remaining in New York wasn't the only thing Olivia nagged about—Addy living there bothered her too. "You were always such a nature lover. You liked to go hiking and camping."

"There's the Catskills," she'd answered, not admitting the actual reason she liked the city. Sure, the architecture was interesting and the history—buildings dating to the 1700s and earlier, old schools and churches. But it was the constant flux, the constant presence of people. You could look out the window at two in the morning and see traffic and pedestrians. Had she ever been the *only* person? That early Sunday morning, running over to the twenty-four-hour pharmacy for Francis's cough medicine, she'd passed easily a dozen joggers and dog walkers.

She waited at the curb for the light to change and waited while an ambulance pushed through the intersection. Huge black plastic trash bags lined the sidewalk, leaving little room for pedestrians. The next block had fewer bags but more litter: along with the cigarette butts and bits of newspaper, she had to step around orange peels, brown glass shards, a large Styrofoam cup, and the top of a cardboard box saying *Candy Corn.*

"I'd forgotten how dirty New York is," her mother had complained. Compared to Seattle, sure, but Manhattan was twenty-two square miles of more than a million people eating, drinking, working, playing. *All* social species—ant colonies, beehives—had their messes. What surprised Addy was how much got carted away. She hadn't said any of this.

Yes, with people and noise everywhere, you tuned out most of it. And no one paid you any attention—you could be caked in mud. The man on Madison with a parrot on his shoulder got some smiles and double takes, but that was all.

The constant swarm of people minding their own business was *soothing.* She'd never have been able to explain that.

THE NINE O'CLOCK HAD JUST LET out, and the halls were crowded. Like the traffic, the noise formed a cocoon. The classes themselves required concentration, which was good. And she had a job lined up for next summer, a big relief. Though the interview with Joe, one of the partners, had been weird. Most of the half hour he had railed against "the Harvard and Yale boys—think they run everything." Addy left his office believing he couldn't have formed any impression of her at all and was surprised when his secretary had called.

A girl in her old Crim Law study group smiled as they passed in the hallway; Addy gave a perfunctory smile back. She hadn't joined a study group this year—having finally gotten the hang of law school, she preferred studying alone. Carson had been in that group. He was a year ahead—had he flunked the course the first time? She had been so surprised, standing by the directory at Macy's, to hear her name. What was she doing there?

"Buying a robe for my grandfather."

He was shopping for a new umbrella. It was raining, and all he wore was a suit, no coat or parka. She couldn't remember ever seeing him in anything else, though—maybe he was clerking somewhere. Instead of continuing on, he asked if she wanted to go to dinner sometime.

"I fix dinner for my grandfather." What about coffee? Feeling on the spot, she'd said yes.

Good-looking guys usually ignored her, and that was fine. If she ever fell in love again—a *big* if—it would be with a sort of maverick, not someone trying to be charming and cool. Damn, why hadn't she gotten his phone number so she could call and make some excuse.

FORTUNATELY, THE CON LAW CASES were interesting, having to do with the Reconstruction Amendments. Afterward, she nabbed an empty carrel at the back of the library to eat her sandwich and review the Admin cases.

At least her mother had seen that the living arrangement was working. Not that Francis had jumped for joy when Addy'd proposed moving in. The opposite—he'd sounded annoyed.

"Do you believe I am already at the stage of requiring nursing care?"

No, she'd stammered, she'd had no medical training—she just wanted to rent a room. It hadn't occurred to her he might object, given the size of the apartment and that she was his granddaughter. True, he'd never been all hugs and kisses like Grandma, but he talked to

Olivia on the phone practically every week. Actually, it was the coincidence of her mother's calling right then that convinced him the idea of moving in was Addy's alone and not part of some plot.

"Your daughter happens to be sitting in my living room as we speak." Olivia's response must have been something like 'What's she doing in New York?' because Francis's expression immediately softened, and he answered, "We are working out arrangements for her to live here while she attends law school."

He handed Addy the receiver, and she told her mother about being accepted and that she'd only heard the week before and hadn't gotten around to telling anybody. Olivia tried not to sound disappointed—she probably had wanted Addy to go to the U and live nearby—saying only, "Now I'll never convince him to move here."

Why should he? Instead of Addy paying rent, groceries, and utilities—she'd saved a fair amount from her college library job and had planned to look for parttime work—he wanted her to do his shopping and cooking, a deal too good to believe.

Besides, Francis was a creature of habit, and moving to Seattle would upset him more than just about anything. During her last visit, Olivia had told him he was too steeped in memory, and he'd asked sarcastically, "Who are we without memory? Insentient organisms, that is all." Later, he'd joked to Addy, "Men react to middle age by having affairs and buying sports cars; women immerse themselves in silly psychological theories."

Who would Addy be if she no longer remembered? It wasn't a question she'd ever posed, not even during those first two years. Maybe that was the crux of her problem.

Those slumber party debates in middle school and high school—did God exist, did the soul survive after death—Addy had never joined in. Was that because she hadn't been raised in a religion? Or did she lack some basic emotional component? Maybe it was part and parcel of her self-realization in fifth grade: she was a tortoise, not a hare.

Then came Zach. It had snuck up on her, happened so fast, and she *did* have an almost-religious feeling. Their connection was 'right,' special not just to them but in some objective, external-world way. They were 'meant for each other.' Was that just biology talking?

Suicide had crossed her mind, yet there was no way she could inflict that on Olivia or her brothers, especially after seeing how hard Nathan's death had shaken them all. So Addy continued the slog of everyday life. Besides, millions of people suffered losses like hers without having the good things she had: food, shelter, health—the list went on. Her misery wasn't unique or outrageous. And with all the other things she was fortunate to possess, the tortoise had its shell.

CHAPTER 3

IMMEDIATELY UPON ADELAIDE'S DEPARTURE, I began to dust the living room, no simple endeavor, a fact I had only come to appreciate upon Marjorie's death. The shelves and tables in particular were laden—I suppose one could say 'adorned'—with photographs, framed birth announcements, silver and porcelain dishes and bowls, and all manner of bric-a-brac: an imitation Fabergé egg, wooden figurines, scrimshaw, glass wren, ivory letter opener, carving of a Chinese monk, miniature bronze horses, plus an assortment of small decorative receptacles. Several items might have been valuable heirlooms; others were whimsical purchases from estate sales.

I could have boxed them all up, I suppose, but there was a comfort in handling each object, each frame, wiping the dust from each photograph. And, in a nod to my youth, Marjorie had put on display the handful of mementos I had brought back from England: the Sherlock Holmes–style pipe, the small silver cup engraved with images of Pip and Joe Gargery, the brass medallion each boy was given at the program's conclusion, and the painted wooden doll purporting to be a likeness of George Eliot.

The largest frame on the credenza held a black-and-white photograph taken at Olivia's high school graduation. I was the only one over six feet, Richard at fourteen not yet his full height. Marjorie stood beside me, her lovely reddish hair worn midway down the nape of her neck, a style popular at the time. Her hair never did turn gray but in later years acquired a nice coppery tint. Come to think of it, she may have had it colored at the hairdresser's. Olivia of course commanded center stage in the photograph, beaming proudly in her gown and mortarboard. And Marcia, at eleven or twelve already vying for an alluring pose, not to her credit.

The top shelf of the rosewood bookcase was easier to dust—the Memorial Shelf, I dubbed it, housing photographs of Cecil and Claudia in their wedding picture and Claudia, a few years later, holding a baby Marjorie. How ancient these sepia prints seemed. And a copy of my parents' wedding picture as well. My teaching awards, from the early years of my career—busy but heady days. A new PhD with an assistant professorship and all that it entailed—exposing eager young minds to the complex delights of great literature, learning to put together syllabi and assignments and examination questions, writing essays for publication. Marjorie in a whirlwind of her own, Olivia and Richard still quite young. The war interrupted our routines, as it eventually did everyone's, but five years later we picked up where we had left off.

To reach the lower sections of the rosewood bookcase, I had to sit on the green chintz ottoman. One shelf contained the grandchildren's birth announcements, each in its own little frame. *Olivia and Nathan Cohn announce the birth of their daughter Adelaide Rachael.* "Quite a mouthful," I had quipped to Marjorie. Back in college I had been apprised of the tradition of Jewish people selecting a name sharing at least the first letter, sometimes more, with a deceased relative's name—possibly as a ritual of remembrance. Poor Nathan, a good, hardworking man, earning a comfortable living but not the riches he might have accumulated by cultivating better-endowed clients instead of traipsing off to Indian reservations. Once he was paid with a woven blanket, and another client tried to pay with chickens, live chickens! I suppose the fellow became another of Nathan's pro bono cases. Yet Marjorie and I had never worried he would allow his family to fall into poverty.

By now sufficient time had elapsed to render it unlikely Adelaide would return for a forgotten item, so I put down the duster, held on to the bookcase to rise, and walked carefully to the vanity. The lilac envelope was addressed in a strong, flowing hand. Olivia adhered to the dying convention of writing longhand, whereas I, stodgy in so many ways, preferred the keyboard. In its caprice, Age had spared my fingers.

Dear Addy,

You were out when I phoned Sunday, and I decided to write for a change. I always think of you when the lindens do their lovely melt from green to burgundy to purple to gold and brown. For all the abundance of vivid fall colors in New York and New England, we are not without our beauties. Do you remember the photos you took with your first camera?

I had seen Adelaide's camera only briefly, when she was storing her belongings in the closet in Richard's old room. She had come across the microscope and asked if Richard had used it. No, I told her; even by then, his desire to see foreign places was leading him toward the successful career in international affairs he was later to achieve. Marcia had used the microscope during her brief fascination with colored stones, a fascination that I had hoped would mature into an interest in geology, but alas, the interest became jewelry.

The old walnut has gone bright yellow. The Steller's jays have arrived. I remember you marveling at how blue they are—when you were only four! I wish they were as abundant as the crows.

I am planning a trip to Palo Alto in December and then to Taos. I would like to visit you and Grandpa too. I would arrive December 22nd. Would that be convenient? When do your exams end? Perhaps you will humor me one afternoon and stroll along Fifth Avenue. It must be thirty years since I have seen the Christmas window displays.

If on the rarest of occasions Olivia prompted in me a most unfatherly professional envy, it vanished at the sight of such things as *Fifth Avenue*, the spelled-out number. How nice to have had one's children maintain certain traditions in the face of the tsunamic tide of slang and neologisms. Which was not to say I rejected all changes in language—that would have been foolish. Language evolved and would continue to evolve, developing new words and usages and discarding some of the old. I was only sorry to lose those forms of speech and written expression that pleased the eye or ear or imagination. And I remained proud of my wariness toward fads such as 'women's literature' and 'minority literature' majors. "It seems *I* am the minority viewpoint here," I often exclaimed at faculty meetings.

So Olivia was engaging in a cross-country tour and visiting Adelaide's siblings as well. My memories of my grandsons were vague. Elliot was the computer wizard, and Michael, some sort of visual artist. They must have been at Marjorie's funeral, but being in such a state of confusion, I would not have known which young man was Marcia's and which two were Olivia's. Richard's daughters were a blur as well— I may have confused one of them at the time with Adelaide.

15

I returned to the kitchen to reheat my tea, to "zap" it, as Adelaide would say. The microwave was the sole modern amenity she introduced to the common living quarters, although she had come to appreciate that I was in no sense a Luddite, making good use of my computer and printer. Adelaide's room had a computer and printer as well, in addition to a stereo setup that played CDs. *Plus ça change, plus ça change.* A quiet puppy in a mausoleum.

Back in my office, I sat at the computer and pulled up the chapter about writing styles. No sooner had I settled into my chair than the telephone rang.

"What a coincidence—Adelaide and I were just discussing your letter."

"That's what I'm calling about," Olivia said. "To make sure she got it. Are the dates okay?"

"They are fine. Is something wrong? You usually call on Sundays."

"I just want to get the tickets now—they're advertising good deals."

"Well, as long as I have you on the telephone, I will try out my ideas on you, ideas I have been fleshing out in my opus. Do you have a few moments? The section preoccupying me is Henry James's penchant for lush and elegant language. Modern writers, even those who do not eschew a broad vocabulary, take little delight in the complex sentences that celebrate the rhythms and patterns of ornate speech. I am coming to the man's defense."

"I think part of the criticism of James, Dad, is that—"

"The modern preference for short sentences and simple language is born of a *culture*, my dear, a culture immersed in both the written word and spoken. Newspapers and magazines are ubiquitous; our shelves *teem* with books; and spoken word is equally omnipresent, through television and radio, the people around us, and through the telephone. Contrast that, if you will, with an agrarian society, a rural region short on written works and where the only form of literary interpretation is the Sunday sermon. In those circumstances, James's digressions, his elaborations and circumlocutions, have a musicality that levitates us out of the routines of field and farm. We are transported; we marvel at the clever turn of phrase and *le mot juste*, the well-sculpted paragraph. Who complains that Beethoven's symphonies are too long? Do we wish Bach would rush from opening chords to coda? Quite the opposite: we bask in the diversions of melody and harmonies. Why should Henry James rush *his* work to a conclusion?"

"The main criticism that people—"

"It is no accident that the writers who employed a more ornate style hailed from the South, from less densely populated areas. If you want to compare oratory and rhetorical skills, I would pit a Black Southern preacher against the most educated, white New England Episcopalian any day of the week! Brevity may be the soul of wit, but wit is not the sole delight in the pantheon of literary pleasures."

"Valid points, but—"

"I do not dispute that Hemingway deserves a place in the canon. Nor do I contend that James should be *everyone's* cup of tea. But he should not be summarily dismissed because of so-called prolixity. The literature professor's primary goal should be to expose the student to *a range* of works and *a range* of ways to experience them. Indeed, it was this completely reasonable attitude of mine—that literature should not be straitjacketed—that played a not unprominent role in that lawsuit against our department. My vote to reject the tenure candidate was based solely on the insularity of her focus: all her publications offered only a single lens for reading literature. One can disagree with self-styled feminist criticism without in the least endorsing discrimination."

"Listen, Dad, I'd love to talk longer, but I have a class at eleven, and I just wanted to make sure my travel plans are okay with you."

"Your travel plans?"

"To visit in December."

"Yes, yes, it will be a lovely Christmas present for you to visit."

After we hung up, I did not immediately resume work, as a trip to the bathroom could not be further delayed. Plus, my attention slithered onto other paths. Had Olivia faced discrimination in her ascent to full professorship? The climb had been protracted, to be sure, for she took time away from her career when her children were young. However, she subsequently became a prodigious publisher—Nathan had teasingly dubbed her 'the Mozart of Beaux Arts.' Yes, poor Nathan, a heart attack in his early fifties. I would have liked to have gone to the funeral, but Marjorie was bedridden with influenza, and Dr. Conti cautioned against leaving her alone, advice which in retrospect was quite on the mark, since her lungs, we were to learn, were severely compromised organs.

Fortunately, my nap refreshed me so I could proceed apace with my work. I combed the draft for phrasing that might cause hard feelings where I was taking certain doctrines to task. Through much of my career I had maintained an energetic correspondence with fellow professors, former students, critics, and others and had been the recipient of effusive pages from dozens of students—many of them female—eager for my opinion on this idea or that. One postdoctoral young lady had included my name quite prominently in the acknowledgment section of her first publication. Her essay on James so missed the mark, however, that I could not take the tribute as much of a compliment.

Over the decades, alas, I had winnowed these friendships down to a mere handful, likely owing to my "lack of tact," as Marjorie put it. It was true: I had been rather ruthless in my criticisms of the 'ists' and their brethren—the Marxists, feminists, Freudians, and later, the deconstructionists. I used to joke to my students, although in all seriousness, that "a novel should be approached as an 'open book,' without preconceived ideas as to the experiences and wisdom it might offer." Myriad were the ways a great novel could transport us across boundaries we may not even have known existed. You turned the title page and read *Call me Ishmael,* or *I am an invisible man,* or *It was the best of times, it was the worst of times,* and you were launched on a journey. But the 'ists' did just the opposite: they approached a reading experience armed with a battery of questions and interpretative stances before even glimpsing word one. The feminists have superseded them, but years ago the Freudians were the worst offenders. X symbolized Y; A meant B—utter rubbish. Perhaps their silliness simply reflected the silliness of the psychology profession as a whole.

I glanced at my watch. Adelaide should be near the end of her Administrative Law class now. That she was a serious student could not be gainsaid—I had found her grade report in the side desk drawer. When she went for coffee with the young man on Thursday, would she wear something more becoming than her usual blue jeans and loose-fitting sweater? She had donned some nicer apparel for her summer job, although in several of the neighborhoods she visited, armor would have been preferable.

CHAPTER 4

CARSON STOOD TO PULL OUT her chair, saying, "I realize this is politically incorrect, but they drilled it into us at Miss Andrews' cotillion classes."

Addy set her backpack on the seat between them and slid out of her parka, folding it over the pack. "Sorry I'm late. I had to stop by the library to get something for my grandfather." She glanced at him briefly before sitting and opening one of the menus. "What are cotillion classes?"

He sat too. "Ah, the disadvantages of not growing up in Norwalk high society with its quaint Old-World customs. Cotillion is a preparation for the debutante party, for coming out— 'coming out' in the *Old World* sense." He watched expectantly for her to smile. "Proper boys and girls from good families brush up on the niceties of table manners and the fox-trot and waltz."

"They still do that?" Addy rested the menu on the table.

"I don't know—that was years ago."

The waiter appeared, and Carson gestured for Addy to speak first. She ordered just tea, despite his encouraging her to try a pastry. He ordered two scones—one butter, one raspberry.

"You have to taste each; the place is famous for them." Instead of responding, she shifted awkwardly in her seat. He asked her if she'd landed a summer job.

"Yes. At Engel Klein."

"Don't think I've heard of them."

"They're small. Three partners and six or seven associates, I think." She kept her eyes on the table.

"What kind of work do they do?"

"A little of everything. I don't really want to do litigation. Maybe I'll only have to write briefs, not go to court." She unfolded her napkin and placed it on her lap.

He did the same with his own napkin. "Is that where you clerked last summer?"

"No. I worked at a poverty law group. Volunteered, actually."

"Then you can't have crushing student loans."

"No, I don't."

At least she looked up at him. Her eyes were a darker brown than her hair.

"Me neither," he said.

She looked back at the table. "I'm incredibly lucky. My great-great-grandparents set up a trust that pays for my education. Not just mine—everyone's."

"*Everyone's?* Will it pay for mine?" Carson used what his sister called his 'impish' smile, though Addy didn't look in his direction.

"I mean in the family," she said. "It paid for my mother's and aunt and uncle's, plus my generation's—my cousins' and brothers'. It pays for both college and graduate school."

Carson whistled softly.

"So I'm really lucky."

"Was your great-great-grandfather a Rockefeller?"

"No one famous. He got a patent on some machine part used in train engines."

"You're *old* money."

"The trust only pays for school tuition. I'm not saying that isn't a lot—obviously it is. I just mean apart from that, we're typical middle class, I guess. I'll need a job when I graduate."

The waiter showed up and unloaded Addy's tea and Carson's coffee from the tray and placed the dish with the scones in the center of the table. Carson pulled the plate closer and used his knife to divide each scone in half, then pushed them toward Addy. She gingerly prodded at one of the scone pieces with her fork. He watched how her hair traced the outline of her cheek when she turned to look at the back wall, the one without mirrors.

"Anyway, I'm glad I ran into you," he said. "I miss those old study sessions. What a joke Dim-Bulb was. 'Is mental state an *el*ement of the crime?' '*Lisssst* the elements, *lisssst* the elements.' Where did you grow up, middle class and blissfully distant from cotillion classes?"

"Seattle."

"The West Coast! I just accepted an offer from a firm in San Francisco. Midsize—about forty partners, a million associates. Wynken, Blynken, and Nod. That's why I'm in a suit. One of the partners is in town for a deposition, and if he has time, I'll meet him for drinks after. Just a social thing, but I decided to dress professional."

"Is that where your family is—San Francisco?"

"No. Lucy, my sister, is up in Hartford, and Louise, my mother, retired to Florida. That's everybody—my father passed away some years ago."

He expected her to do one of those sympathetic frowns, but she said simply, "My father died when I was in high school."

She ate another piece of scone, and he waited to see if she wanted to say more, but again she just gazed toward the back of the room.

"I picked the Bay Area because computer tech is where the money is. Besides, good-looking straight men are in high demand."

"I visited my brother in Palo Alto once. It's nice. He has flowers that look tropical and a palm tree more like the coconut kind than the ones in Seattle. But I don't think it bears fruit."

Her manners were impeccable, and she moved with that complete lack of self-consciousness you saw in people exposed to good breeding since early childhood. The loose sweater and jeans had to be camouflage—or the insouciance of the true upper class. Her assertion to the contrary had to be just more camouflage.

"You said Engel Klein does a little of everything?"

She actually smiled for a second, sheepishly. "When I asked that during the interview, the partner said, 'Whatever walks in the door.' Though I got the impression it's mostly trusts and estates."

"I'm surprised you didn't like poverty law—I had you pegged as a legal services or ACLU type, before I found out you were old money." Carson leaned forward. "Remember your answer about that rich old crook's sentencing hearing? His lawyer argued for leniency on the grounds that the crook wasn't *all* bad—he'd sat on the board of some charity for the blind and—I don't know—one for the deaf and probably the mute. So the court should excuse this one itty-bitty embezzlement. And *you* said that showing leniency on account of his sitting on boards wasn't fair to poor defendants—they didn't have that option but might do charitable things every day, like—I forget—helping a neighbor mop a flooded basement? Fix their car? Something like that."

"I think it was the longest answer I've given in any class."

"It was the longest you gave in *that* class. You never talked much in the study group either." Carson laughed. "Sure pissed the old boy off."

She laughed too—briefly, as if she hadn't meant to let her guard down. "All I remember is bracing for a follow-up question and being relieved he moved on to someone else."

Encouraged, Carson joked, "Made me start wondering if that's why *I* helped the less fortunate. I used to tutor disadvantaged kids, so maybe it wasn't all *noblesse oblige*—maybe subconsciously I was piling up mitigating circumstances in case someday I get nailed for embezzlement." His smile in the wall mirror was charming—why wasn't she charmed?

"One thing I liked about his class was he showed how things that made sense in theory didn't necessarily work in real life," Addy said.

Carson leaned back and mimicked the professor's deep voice. "'But what are the *real-world implications* of the exclusionary rule?'" She wanted to smile—he could tell! "So what made you bail on the poverty law group? They just stick you in the library doing research?"

"No, I just didn't feel as committed as—as people willing to put in longer hours. I was the only one who left by six. I *had* to leave—to get dinner ready for my grandfather. Plus, he was always worrying. They sent me to interview clients and witnesses in Harlem and some rough parts of the Bronx. It was in daylight, so I didn't mind." She frowned at the table. "I guess it was the lack of dedication—why I didn't apply there again. They need people who do more than just put one foot in front of the other."

"That's the best way to move forward. But I know what you mean—being surrounded by the gung-ho crowd. Remember that battered-woman case? Not the one where she killed him—I was all for that. Where the two of them were charged with manslaughter for their daughter's death, and the wife got off using the battered-woman defense?"

Addy shook her head.

"I gave my two cents, and the group tried to cannibalize me." Her continuing to give a blank look, he changed the subject. "So you planning on climbing the partnership ladder?"

"I thought I'd see what a private firm is like. Maybe someday I'll work for a nonprofit."

"If *I* get sick of the rat race, I'll go in-house. Get stock options, and if the company takes off, the sky's the limit. What are your vacation plans? Skiing in Aspen?"

"My mother's coming to visit. She likes New York at Christmas."

"The Cohns celebrate Christmas?"

"Her side of the family is Protestant. We weren't raised anything, but we exchange Christmas gifts."

"You're not even technically Jewish. It's the mother that counts." He did his impish smile again. "You know why that is, don't you? Because with any child on the face of the earth, you never really know who the father is."

She poked at the remaining scone flakes on her side of the plate. "Another possibility is that people subjected to pogroms and rape needed a rule that all children belong."

"I'm sure you're right. In any case, your family shouldn't object to my Aryan good looks." Addy's manner barely deviated from the deadpan. Her lack of coquettishness left him at a loss—flirtation was usually reciprocal, or at least acknowledged. "So what do you do for fun," he asked, "if you don't ski or volunteer for noble causes?"

"I don't have much spare time. I look after my grandfather when I'm not doing schoolwork."

"He live in Manhattan?"

"Yes, East 70s."

"An invalid?"

"No—he just can't walk long distances. I do the shopping and cooking."

"That's nice of you."

"He lets me stay rent-free. And I have to shop and cook for myself anyway, so it's not really extra work."

"No rent, no tuition—you *are* living the good life. Is the apartment rent-controlled?"

"It's a condo. I think it used to be a co-op. It's a pretty old building."

"And you're old money." Now Carson found a silver lining to her looking away from him—at the table, the walls—he could watch her without awkwardness. "Your situation sounds better than mine. Last year's roommates graduated in June, and I had to find some place quick and grabbed the first thing that came along. But it's only till summer. So besides your mother and your grandfather, who else makes up the extended Cohn clan?"

"My grandfather isn't named Cohn—he's my mother's father."

"You mentioned having brothers. And an aunt and uncle?" She nodded.

"Who are they?"

"You want their names?"

"Yes."

"Really?" When he continued to smile at her, she said, "My brothers are Elliot and Michael."

"Which one has the palm tree in his yard?"

"Elliot. Michael lives in Taos—he's married to Patty."

"Keep going."

"That's all."

"Aunts, uncles, cousins?"

She recited aunts', uncles', and cousins' names and asked about his family.

"I already said: I have a sister, Lucy, in Hartford, and my mother, Louise, in Florida."

"No aunts, uncles—"

"Like proper WASPs, we Smiths are an emotionally cold species when it comes to family. If I have distant relations, they've been happy to keep their distance. Speaking of cold, I know the weather will be terrible, but right after Thanksgiving, a brigantine, an eighteenth-century vessel—will be mooring for a few days in Brooklyn. Would you like to see it?"

"I've never—"

"I'll take that as a yes. I belong to this group of old-vessel aficionados. *We're* not old—not all of us—the vessels are. The newsletter lists when and where they dock and are available for boarding. Once a replica Dutch schooner actually took us out for a couple of hours, up the sound past Stony Brook. Surrounded by blue sky and blue water for miles. Only one other activity leaves you with that same sense of peace."

She didn't smile back. "What's a brigantine?"

He gave a rundown of the one-masters, the sloops and some typical small yachts; the two-masters, from ketches to brigantines; and vessels with three or more masts, which were technically 'ships.' Before the era of steamships, he explained, navies as well as pirates wanted speed and more men available for fighting, so they tried to stick with fewer masts and keep the sails uncomplicated. But for ocean crossings—trade—stability and room for cargo were the priorities, so hulls were larger, more sails were necessary to move the weight, and consequently more men were needed for the rigging.

Whenever Carson paused, fearing he'd talked for too long, Addy asked more questions, so he went on and described different sail shapes and how they could attach fore and aft or athwart, port to starboard. Only when the check came did Carson look at his watch. "Shoot. I didn't mean to eat up half your afternoon." He snatched at the slip while Addy reached inside her backpack for her wallet.

"What's my share?" she asked.

"My treat—since you're only middle class."

SMALL PUDDLES LEFT OVER FROM the rain filled the sidewalk crevices and gave the pavement a cobalt sheen. Carson accompanied Addy to Lexington and watched her cross. There was no sashay in her walk, no strut, nothing to draw attention. He waited until the auburn hair disappeared down the subway stairs before turning west.

Clouds lay thick and low. It wasn't yet dusk, but the streetlamps had come on, exhaling an otherworldly, misty glow that could let you shut out the cars and dumpsters for a second, shut out the buildings and signs and sidewalks, even the noise, and let you pretend to be in a softer dimension. The autumn air, the strange lighting, the sense of approaching darkness stoked dim and distant memories.

He was nine, concealed in the small shadowed entryway of a barbershop, watching reflections in the second-story panes above the sign *Miss Andrews' Studio*. The chandelier made the pale walls and silvery shadows seem a world apart. Always one window was open, even in cold or rain, and the piano notes sounded clearly. From his dark recess, Carson could see the dancers come into view above the sills. The girls wore pastel-colored dresses—yellows, pinks, lavender—and their hair, which at school was in ponytails or loose down their backs, now was piled high on their heads. Even to the livelier music they glided gracefully, like skaters. The boys in their dark suits moved solemnly, and when the music stopped, everyone clapped politely. The girls would tilt their heads; he guessed they were curtseying. Precious ornaments, delicate and refined, like crystal. Cherished and protected.

He took the tie out of this pocket and put it on before taking the stairs down to the BMT. The train came after a minute, and while it sped along, Carson's thoughts reverted to Addy and her shy directness. Arriving at the store with ten minutes to spare, he looked over the new rack of three-piece wools before punching in.

CHAPTER 5

"ALLOW ME JUST FIVE MINUTES." I hung up the telephone and did my best to scurry to the bathroom. After finishing there, I dabbed aftershave on my face and hobbled to the front hall in time to hear the knock on the door.

"Hello, Francis."

Even in her late sixties, Millie was a handsome woman. Her silvery hair, once blond, somehow augmented the warm gentility of her disposition. A more subdued Marjorie—not that Marjorie was ever brash or strident, or even what I would call vivacious. But today Millie's smile showed hints of weariness. John's recent back surgery assuredly had burdened her with additional tasks and responsibilities. Before Adelaide had moved in, whenever Millie stopped by for my grocery list, she appeared as someone refreshed after a long nap. Now we rarely saw each other; she left our newspaper outside the apartment door.

I ushered her into the living room. "Despite my gladness that Adelaide has relieved you of your former chore of shopping for me," I said, "I miss our erstwhile conversations, however brief they used to be."

She sat on the sofa. "Yes, it's a shame we lead such separated lives. And I've come to ask *you* a favor."

"Me? How flattering—the conceit that *I* could possibly be of use. But I am happy to oblige in any way I can. Would you care for a cup of tea?"

"No, thank you." She looked at her hands in her lap. "I told you about my grandson Robert—the sick one?"

"With cerebral palsy, yes."

"I wish that was all! The poor boy has more physical problems than you, me, and John combined. He wasn't expected to live this long—he'll turn eight in a few months. A congenital heart defect, difficulty walking, no speech—the list goes on." I followed her gaze to the window. The clouds had darkened. Would Adelaide get home before the rain resumed? She refused to use an umbrella—said her parka had a hood. To my mind that was insufficient.

"His younger brother just started preschool," Millie said, "and Cheryl is returning to work part-time. So John and I will look after Robert several hours two afternoons each week. His lack of mobility, it seems strange to say, makes it easier; we don't have to run after him. He can't stand up or walk by himself and needs help going to bed and the toilet, and needs to be changed if he has an accident. He wears special diapers called pull-ups."

How unlike Millie to ramble on like this! Usually her conversation concerned things of mutual interest—like a play or concert she had attended. She examined her hands again. "However, on Thursday afternoons, I take John to his therapy activity class—a whole group of them with back problems. The camaraderie is *such* a mood booster—he hates to miss it."

"Yes, you have mentioned that."

"That's right—I tried to get *you* to sign up, even without back problems. Well, I plan to find someone who can watch Robert on Thursdays, but nurses' aides all want to be paid for four hours—that's their minimum. And they're not cheap. So I'm going to try ordinary sitters—experienced ones, not teenagers. Unfortunately, they can be undependable." She looked over at me. "I was wondering if you'd be willing to be on call. What I mean is: If the sitter gets sick or caught in traffic, could you come down and watch Robert? At most it would be for two hours. I'd give him lunch beforehand and take him to the bathroom, although I'd show you how to do it in case he wanted to go again. This would only be in an emergency—if the regular sitter gets delayed or cancels at the last minute."

I fixed my mouth into an obliging smile while mentally groping for an excuse. Millie was well aware of *my* limited mobility, so why did she not consider it an obstacle to sitting for Robert and all that that would entail? But perhaps the need might never arise, I told myself—the sitter could turn out to be dependable. And if on one occasion Millie asked me, I could feign illness. John could miss a single class.

"I would be happy to be 'on call,' as you put it, although you would have to show me all the particulars."

She rose from the sofa and came and gave me a hug. "Thank you.

You've taken a load off my mind." Her perfume was lilac or perhaps lavender. Marjorie had never worn perfume but kept sachets in her dresser drawers. They imparted a delicate odor that had blended perfectly with her own scent.

After Millie left, I considered that the load lifted from her mind lay heavily on mine. I had not even fed my *own* children when they were young, or if I had, that was a good forty or fifty years ago. And how on earth would I help the boy walk, having difficulties of my own? Was there really no one else in the building better suited to handle the child?

I accomplished little on my book, my opus, before hearing Adelaide at the front door.

She had removed her coat and was in the process of hanging up her scarf when I came into the hall. Dressed in jeans and a loose sweater, alas. I scanned her face for some sign the date had been a success but saw nothing out of the usual.

"Is it raining again?" I inquired.

"No, but looks like it's going to. Here, I got your book."

"Why, thank you."

She thumbed through the mail on the vanity and then we repaired, as we often did, to the kitchen to have tea.

"How was your meeting for coffee?"

"Okay, I guess."

She put the kettle on, and I sat at my usual spot, facing the calendar.

November's picture was the famous Caillebotte, the triangular building in the rain. After I had mentioned that Marjorie used to buy a wall calendar from the museum to jot down all her appointments and activities, Adelaide volunteered to continue the practice.

"First dates—or the beginnings of friendship—are often a little awkward," I said. "Are you in any of the same classes?"

"No. He started law school three years ago and got permission to stretch his coursework out over four years—I think he's doing research in some PhD program. He's graduating this spring and moving to San Francisco."

"Oh. Is he from there?"

"No, Norwalk. His family is very wealthy—into debutante balls, that kind of thing. He used the phrase 'high society,' though maybe he was being sarcastic."

My reflexive reaction to such news was disdain, but I wanted to give the young man a chance as he had shown some interest in my granddaughter. "Does he 'put on airs,' as we used to say?"

"It was weird—he wanted to know who all my relatives are: brothers, cousins, aunts, and uncles. I don't know why."

My disdain quickly melted into sympathy; no doubt the young man was nervous and eager to keep the conversation flowing smoothly, hardly an easy feat with a shy young woman.

"So that was the end of it—the end of the friendship? The *possibility* of friendship, I should say."

"No. We're going to see an old sailing vessel that will be mooring in Brooklyn in early December. It's a hobby of his: visiting brigantines and schooners and caravels—I forget what they're all called. Anyway, it sounded interesting, so I said I'd go."

"Isn't such an activity better suited to the summer?"

"If you want to see a particular vessel, and it's only here in the winter, you don't have a choice."

We chit-chatted about minor things until Adelaide poured our cups and sat opposite me, and I said that I had had an awkward discussion of my own to relate. Describing the conversation with Millie, I concluded thus: "Obviously she thinks me capable of it, but I don't mind telling you, in all candor, the thought makes me quite uncomfortable. How can a seventy-nine-year-old care for a boy who cannot talk and barely walk? But I did not feel in any position to say no—not with her having done my grocery shopping for several years."

"I don't have classes Thursday afternoons; I could watch him. It seems a shame for her to have to hire someone for such a short time. And I won't charge anything—like you say, we owe her a lot."

"*We? You* don't owe her anything."

Adelaide gently blew at the steam rising from her cup. "Maybe she could bring him here, and we could both watch him."

Bless the girl! "That might be preferable," I said, "although I would want to move your grandmother's vases and antiques out of harm's way. In any case, if you were to help me, that would put my mind more at ease."

"Let me go talk to her." Adelaide rose and left without trying her tea.

Some minutes later she returned to report that Millie had suggested we try sitting with the boy for one afternoon before committing to a steady schedule.

"An eminently reasonable plan, eminently reasonable."

AT DINNER, ADELAIDE INQUIRED AS to whether any children's books remained from when her mother and aunt and uncle were children. She said by way of explanation that Robert might like being read to.

"The shelf by the piano contains children's books. We certainly could attempt to entertain the boy with stories, depending on his level of comprehension. I am trying to recall the ones *I* enjoyed as a child, beyond the traditional fairy tales and Bible fare, before my 'literary awakening,' one might call it." Adelaide tilted her head in that questioning way.

"I suppose I have never mentioned my awakening to you, although it was the most significant event of my childhood. Until the age of ten, my dear, I was nonchalant about literature—I say that because of the sense of discovery that ensued. Yes, the *enthrallment* of reading came as a surprise. *Twenty Thousand Leagues Under the Sea* was my 'maiden voyage.' I felt as if I were actually exploring the oceans and Atlantis and the Antarctic, the coral reefs, the enormous maelstrom. And then *Treasure Island*: in my own mind I *was* Jim Hawkins, thirsting to discover hidden treasure. The magic of entering through a portal into another world, of forgetting my surroundings, appeared nothing short of miraculous. The alchemy of great storytelling turned me into Robinson Crusoe and David Balfour—yes, my favorite novels in those days were tales of adventure, of voyages to foreign lands brimming with mystery and terror and splendor, that was what captivated and entranced me… often to my detriment."

"Why to your detriment?"

"I mean that facetiously. One night my mother awoke and glanced up the staircase—my bedroom was in the attic—and noticed a strip of lantern light beneath my door. She came up and scolded me: I would have trouble waking to start the fire. She was right. My father was quite

32

annoyed, particularly when I overslept a second day for the same reason, and was sorely tempted to give me what in those days was called 'a good licking.'"

"He used to whip you?"

"My dear, corporal punishment was not at all uncommon, at least in southern Indiana, although my parents never resorted to it. Of course, I rarely gave them cause. Yet, as I say, my father *was* sorely tempted when I failed to start the fire so my mother could begin breakfast preparations in a warmed room. We had no central heating, no furnace, until after I had departed for college. The stove—not like that one, my dear, but a cast-iron, what they called a potbelly—was our only form of heat except when we laid a fire in the hearth. I used to do my homework by lantern light—just like Abraham Lincoln, yet a full century later. And used the lantern to read in bed. Oh, how I loved those adventure stories, Adelaide. Strange characters and animals and landscapes—exotic jungles and tropical islands. I cannot claim to have appreciated at the time all the humor and complex emotions and antagonisms among the characters, caught up as I was in the exotica, if you will. Which is not to say I derived no pleasure from works with more familiar locales, such as Twain's, which I read as a teenager in the upper room. Yes, the seeds of my becoming a professor of literature were planted way back then, for I had experienced *enchantment*."

"That must've been nice, to have a direction when you were only—"

"By high school, my tastes had altered: I was thrilled to travel not to the foreign and exotic but into *myself*, to peer into my own thoughts and emotions. I identified with David Copperfield and to a certain extent Huckleberry Finn and Lord Jim. Yet that profound identification with a literary character was never so consummate as it was with Jude. *Jude the Obscure*—you haven't read it? No matter. A young man in rural England, a young man without means, without an academically inclined community, yearns for education and scholarship, which always loom unattainably out of reach, much like Tantalus's grapes. What Jude felt *I* felt; what *he* craved, *I* craved; what *he* viewed as insurmountable obstacles—poverty and a rural background—*I* viewed as unsurmountable obstacles. Yes, Jude was the character who moved me most keenly and most deeply, who embodied my own frustrations and desires."

"But that wouldn't be good for Robert. What about *Tom Sawyer*?"

"Your mother reported similar experiences among teenagers reading *The Catcher in the Rye*. I was much older when Salinger's work was published; plus, not growing up in an urban environment, I had a very different reaction to Holden's cavalier attitude toward school. Yet the sense that a character has felt what you, the reader, feel is a huge palliative to loneliness, to the sad sensation of apartness. You don't agree?"

"It's not that—I was just remembering in high school, the kids organized a protest for more diversity in authors. I didn't really understand the issues and was timid anyway, so I didn't join in. But now I get it: they wanted characters to identify with."

"You espouse a legitimate point of view, provided the authors are not second-rate. To have that experience of keen identification, one must read a writer of some merit. And I do not want to leave you with the impression that such keen identification with characters is the *sine qua non* of great literature. I am not sure if I identified with *anyone* in *Wuthering Heights* and only somewhat with Eliza Bennet. More so Adam Bede, to be sure, and Pip."

Clearing the table, my granddaughter left me to my ruminations. Poor Jude, frustrated as both scholar and lover. Fate proved much kinder to me; neither academia nor marital happiness presented unscalable walls. But in my penultimate year of high school, how could I have envisioned the future that was to unfold? My life's trajectory was not 'foreseeable,' to borrow a term from Adelaide's law studies.

"Is that why you specialized in Henry James?" she asked over her shoulder, stacking the dishes in the sink.

"James did not write *Jude*—that was Thomas Hardy. Quite a different writer. My love affair with James, so to speak, came later, in graduate school. James does not address the struggles of rural people; what fascinates him are contrasts between well-to-do Americans and Europeans. European society, you understand, is steeped in traditions and class distinctions dating back almost a thousand years. With those traditions comes a certain sense of duty. We Americans have a strong individualistic ethos. Or put differently: we believe in the individual's power of invention, his right to 'go it alone'—to *shed* tradition. I suspect James's observations resonated so strongly with me because of my studies in Cambridge, for whatever traditions were waning then had not entirely disappeared, and—"

"I thought you went to college here?"

"I am talking about my senior year of *high school*, when I went to Cambridge, *England*. I suppose I never mentioned this either. I studied in England my last year of high school. Hard to imagine, is it not, a boy from rural Indiana in that hallowed land? We were not technically university students, but our classes were held nearby, and we could attend certain lectures. The beautiful lawns and libraries and magnificent architecture were at our disposal. An unparalleled nine months, simply unparalleled."

"Must've been exciting."

"It was all Miss Perry's doing, my teacher in the upper room. She encouraged me to apply to a number of programs, most of which rejected me. I did feel like a lost cause. But this particular program, for whatever reason, accepted me. A number of slots had been reserved for foreign students, and I met boys from as relatively nearby as Canada and as far away as Australia and Hong Kong and India. Together we explored the campuses, marveling at historical connections dating back to King Henry III, Oliver Cromwell, Isaac Newton—so many famous people had stepped where we stepped."

"Your parents must've been proud."

"All the wonderful things Miss Perry did—if the seed was already within me to become a professor of literature, she helped it to germinate; she nourished it, coaxed its growth, enriched the soil. How did we get on this subject?"

"Henry James? But I'm going to have to go study—"

"Yes, James trained an American perspective on Europe and the British Isles—the English, in particular. Some of his characters are forced into mental straitjackets by their sense of familial duty, believing they must suppress their own natures entirely. Therein lies their tragedies: the characters forge their own prison bars through a perverse morality. Whereas in Hardy, it is *ex*ternal circumstances, by and large, that control each character's fate."

"I'd like to hear more, but I've really got to study."

"Do not let me keep you, my dear; I have things to attend to as well." Yet in the kitchen I remained, trussed to my chair by memory. The Liverpool piers smothered in gloomy fog, the gray buildings as foreboding as a scene from Dickens. Being hurried from one drab cavernous room to another, showing our papers and searching for our bags in a miasma of smoke and salt-sea smells and damp, dank air. The train then quickly leaving behind factories and squalor, the scenery becoming meadows and farms interspersed with quaint towns one knew boasted a centuries-long heritage. The sun rising to the enchanting names on the signs: Crewe, Newcastle-under-Lyme, Stoke-on-Trent. Resisting falling asleep, despite the body's wish.

And then Cambridge! The greenest of green lawns, and everywhere you turned, the architecture stunned. King's College Chapel, with its vaulting height and magnificent ceiling. Classical structures recalling the Roman era, stone pillars, Tudor buildings, brickwork that charmed. And the dark wainscoting in libraries, even taverns, all of it beguiling the teenage imagination. But most thrilling of all: stepping on the sacred soil of Shakespeare and Dickens, the Brontës, the land of George Eliot and Thomas Hardy!

This royal throne of kings, this sceptered isle,
This happy breed of men, this little world,
This precious stone set in the silver sea
This blessed plot, this earth, this realm, this England
This land of such dear souls, this dear dear land.

AS HAPPENSTANCE WOULD HAVE IT, the first Thursday we were scheduled to watch Robert, the boy was readmitted to the hospital, his heart and other problems laying him open to frequent infections. Secretly relieved, I applied myself assiduously to my work. Later in the afternoon, the telephone rang briefly, leading me to suspect Adelaide had picked up one of the extensions. She hung up the hallway receiver just as I emerged from my room.

"That was Carson. I hope you don't mind—I invited him to dinner Saturday night."

"But wasn't *he* the one to telephone?" The young man's breach of etiquette surprised me, especially in light of his high-society upbringing.

"He asked me to go out, and I said I was cooking for you. I should've made some other excuse, but once I said that, it seemed rude not to invite him."

My surprise quickly changed to indignation. "Please do not assume you must decline engagements in order to cook for me; I am perfectly capable of looking after myself. You should call him back and accept his invitation." The very last thing I desired was to interfere in her romantic life!

"It'll be a shorter evening this way, and maybe I can get some studying done after."

I would have argued that now she would have *less* time available for studying because she had committed herself to preparing a dinner worthy of a guest, but my own curiosity about the young man got the better of me. Yes, my curiosity was piqued. At the same time, I silently vowed not to become a nuisance and even to absent myself whenever a plausible excuse arose.

CHAPTER 6

DESPITE IT BEING A SATURDAY, the firm where Adelaide was to work over the summer had asked her to attend a short meeting in the afternoon. I expressed concern that she would be rushed in the dinner preparations, but she said it was "no big deal" and, indeed, had matters well in hand. The oven gave forth a pleasing aroma.

I surveyed the rarely used dining room, the table set for three, the china resting on copper-colored linen mats I hadn't seen for years. Where had Adelaide found them? Neither the light-gold wallpaper nor the brass chandelier was in any way ostentatious. The only other furnishings were an old mahogany wine cabinet, a white-oak sideboard, and a large painting on the wall—a wedding gift from a cousin of Marjorie's who had imagined himself quite the collector. Titled *Country Supper*, the picture was of peasants at a long plank table dining jovially on hams and pheasants. I seemed to recall the artist lived in the 1800s, yet the work resembled a Brueghel more than a Renoir. A visitor once inquired whether it was acceptable for him to drink to excess like a figure at the far end, prompting from Marjorie the comment that the *tone* of the painting was convivial, not boisterous.

Although I had never been versed in the visual arts, I was certain she was right. Like our dining room, the picture evoked tasteful comfort, not hedonistic abandon.

I tidied the mail stacks on the vanity, brought my slippers and whatnot into my bedroom, and stored my array of pill containers in the medicine cabinet. Adelaide remained preoccupied with additional dinner preparations, so I stayed out from under her feet. You see, Marjorie, I have not forgotten all you taught me.

My granddaughter was not a fussy cook and did not assemble the marvelous—one might say 'sublime'—feasts her grandmother was famous for, but she could perform a decent job on a roast. And perhaps decades of fine meals had led me to a point of satiety, for if I were compelled to be deprived of one sensory organ, the palate would be my choice. Others in the family would feel differently, I suspect, for Olivia continued to reminisce about repasts her mother had fashioned.

I did worry that Adelaide would not dress suitably for the occasion. As six o'clock drew near, I was relieved to see the loose-fitting, bulky sweater and blue jeans give way to a nice brown and more form-fitting knit top and black pants. Her hair was newly brushed. The aromas and table set for three imparted a warmth the dining room had not exhibited in years. A Bordeaux awaited on the sideboard alongside three stemmed glasses. The little wooden bowls filled with nuts and crackers had been moved to the coffee table. Adelaide had vetoed using the crystal decanter, and thus I made no mention of lighting candles, fearing she would find such a gesture, at best, premature.

I staked out a position at the credenza as if engaged in examining photographs. By standing, I would not have to lift myself from a chair in order to shake the young man's hand, rising being no longer a quick and simple feat. The doorbell rang, and presumably Adelaide pressed the buzzer. Searching my mind for conversation topics, I lit upon the scenic beauty of Connecticut, where Marjorie's uncle had owned a summer home. Although my trips there had been limited to weekends, Marjorie took the children for the entire month of July, enabling them to enjoy the delights of lake swimming and boating. I utilized their absence to work long hours, catching up on articles and making significant progress on the coming year's class preparations.

I heard a rap on the door and the sound of voices. My emotions were a mix of excitement at a dinner guest and curiosity and perhaps a dash of gratitude. I peered up from the photographs as Adelaide ushered the young man into the room. The gratitude vanished of an instant. Howsoever I had pictured him, Carson's appearance in the flesh surprised me, and not in a good way. As tall as I, he moved with a gallantry that served as a veritable clarion call announcing his youthful handsomeness. His physique was not as muscular as a football player's, perhaps, but his movements proclaimed *My body is at my command.* The sports coat without necktie and the shirt unbuttoned at the top displayed an unimpeachable combination of formality and casualness for dinner with a young woman's grandfather, and what disposed me against him still further was the impertinence implicit in the practiced ease with which he offered his hand to one so many years his senior. That this blond Adonis, who no doubt attracted young women like flies to honey, had chosen my shy granddaughter as his conquest of the hour—that she represented some challenge he simply could not forgo—enraged me into committing the unthinkable. Unable to smile and shake the outstretched hand, unable to banish in an instant my fury—having no alternative recourse, in other words— I begged his pardon and feigned an old man's urgent need to use the bathroom.

It took several minutes for me to compose myself in order to greet the swine politely. And, in fact, I did need to use the bathroom. Appearing gracious during this visit seemed a futile endeavor, but I nonetheless resolved to rally and be polite for Adelaide's sake. Once the gigolo had departed, however, I would not hold my tongue. Perhaps she had read *Washington Square* and would recognize an allusion to Morris Townsend. Whether this Carson fellow would prove a fortune-hunter or a simple Lothario keeping count of his conquests, I could not tell, but in either instance, he would have to turn his attentions to other victims if Francis Wallace had anything to do with it!

When I reentered the living room, the young people were seated half-facing one another at the opposite ends of the long sofa, each holding a glass of wine. I noticed a third poured glass sitting on the coffee table and went directly to it, taking a large sip. Carson smiled a little less, perhaps apprehensively. Was he wondering what to expect from an old and infirm dotard? He would find out. Easy, Francis, easy. Even the slight asymmetry to his nose no doubt contributed to his masculine attractiveness.

"I can't believe the view you have—all that river. It's incredible."

Because his comment appeared addressed to me, I responded, "Yes, we are quite fortunate that no other structure has been erected to block it."

"I was just telling Addy how windy it is. A woman's hat blew right into the street, and I held up my hand to stop traffic so I could get it, and a poor cabbie thought he'd nabbed a fare."

Adelaide rose, telling me she wanted to carve in the kitchen, thereby compelling me to engage with the young man one-on-one, *mano a mano*. Doubtless he expected to be complimented for his good deed as though his actions were on par with Sir Walter Raleigh's. I did not for a minute assume the incident was anything more than a fabrication designed to show him in an admirable light. Why was my ordinarily sensible granddaughter wasting her social graces on this swinish swain? Was she hoodwinked into believing he felt a serious interest in her?

"Does Addy play the piano?"

"I don't believe so."

"I studied the violin until my parents couldn't stand it, which wasn't very long."

Fortunately, further chit-chat was precluded by Adelaide's announcement that dinner was ready.

The scoundrel's manners: bringing his and Adelaide's wineglasses to the table, waiting to be seated until she had been, promptly folding his napkin in his lap—in other circumstances I might have noted these gestures with pleasure. But his smug confidence extinguished any positive impression.

No one spoke as my granddaughter passed around the platters— she had not only carved the roast in the kitchen but dished out the potatoes and vegetable mix into serving bowls. I could see the mix contained carrots and onions, sprinkled with some kind of spice, perhaps rosemary. If Carson found the meal too homespun for his tastes, so much the better.

"Addy says you used to teach English literature."

"I was a professor of English and American literature, yes."

"I thought about being a teacher—but not college level or even high school."

"Then you are talking about a distinctly different calling."

He rose and retrieved the wine bottle from the living room and went around the table refilling our glasses. "She's lucky she has you to discuss the classics with. I had a hard time getting through most of them, except *Moby Dick*." With his unctuous self-deprecation, Carson relinquished the part of Morris Townsend in favor of that of Uriah Heep.

Adelaide remarked that she didn't read as much fiction as she should, to which I responded how could she, being overwhelmed with her studies.

"My sister loves fiction," Mr. Heep simpered. "She's one of the people who actually *buys* the tabloids in the grocery checkout lines."

When no one reacted to his pointless remark, he said the food was really good, and Adelaide murmured that it was "nothing fancy."

For a moment the room was silent. I exulted in the thought that our guest was uncomfortable. Adelaide asked if he had had a nice Thanksgiving, and he said yes—that since their mother moved to Florida, Lucy and he had taken up the tradition of dining at a country inn near Hartford, telling me, in an aside, that his sister lived there. Adelaide gave an account of our recent tradition: a full spread for just the two of us on the Thursday, and a week's worth of leftovers extending the holiday.

"Don't you have an aunt up in Wilton?"

Adelaide said yes but that her aunt Marcia spent Thanksgiving with her husband's side of the family. I kept my eyes trained on my plate. Later we would have a good laugh about this awkward evening, for Adelaide was certain to reach the conclusion that this Carson was not worth her time.

She turned her attention to me. "Francis, you said you specialized in Henry James because he wrote about differences between English and American culture, and *you* noticed them too, your year in England."

"That was not the *only* reason, my dear. James's use of language played a role. Quite an important role."

"How so?"

I rested my fork on the plate. "He was a master of words and phrases and sentence structure. Reading James is akin to listening to music, a pleasure in its own right, almost without regard to plot and character. Yes, thank you, just half a glass. And possibly another factor influenced my partiality. Henry James was generous to acknowledge the contributions of the *literary critic*. He characterized the literary critic as a *help* to the artist. A 'torchbearing outrider' and 'interpreter'—he even used the word 'brother.' *Many* writers, you may be aware, excoriate literary critics—we have been likened to vultures feeding on a living animal."

"But you were a professor, not a critic," my granddaughter protested.

"At the university level," I explained, "teaching literature *is*, in many respects, literary criticism. The professor shines a torch on literary gems that may not shine of their own accord in his students' eyes. You will excuse the stale metaphors—a poet I am not. No, indeed, which may explain to some extent the awe in which I hold great writers. The great writer is both a *truth-sayer* and *poet*, truth-sayer and poet. He—or she—molds language to give us understanding. But to continue: in illuminating beautiful writing or the ways in which an author moves the reader without resorting to melodrama or cumbersome symbolism—without hitting him over the head, if you will—the professor is thereby implicitly praising that author's work and criticizing those who do *not* employ masterful writing or subtlety."

I carefully sipped my wine—Carson had filled the glass quite full. Adelaide saying something to him I did not catch, I asked her to repeat it.

"My brother Michael and I used to hide the books they assigned us in high school so Mom couldn't quiz us about them. We always missed those kinds of things—the symbolism and themes."

Our guest made the silly comment that he had had a professor who thought everyone was a Christ figure, "like Hamlet and Oedipus and I forget who else. He would've called Judas a Christ figure if there was a play about him." He looked at me sheepishly. "Is there?"

"Since Sophocles pre-dated Jesus by several hundred years," I observed, "your professor was not likely to have included Oedipus among his Christ figures. Adelaide, I am certain your mother was just trying to encourage you to be a careful reader. And I hope that when leisure time presents you with an opportunity to read a work of fiction, you will approach the work with the excitement of a voyager about to set sail across a vast uncharted sea, *not* with the dread of an apprentice fearing correction or rebuke. Reading should be an adventure even if the story is not *about* adventure, in the ordinary sense. The *last* thing I would want—and the last thing I wanted for my students until they had finished a work and were ready to examine the art and the craft of writing—is to turn reading into a test. Literature can offer pleasure, joy, knowledge—so many things. And, I should add, provide a life-buoy; yes, a veritable life-buoy. Here I go again with the stale metaphors." I waved the bottle away. "No, no, thank you, I have had enough."

The young man made some quip about a professor—a law school

professor, evidently, as Adelaide understood his meaning—and I allowed the young people to enter into a private digression, leaving me to my meditations.

In truth, I *was* initially drawn to James's novels by a common interest in differences between English and American culture. But the attraction became so much more. His love affair with language became *my* love affair, the word as an instrument to convey not merely meaning but tone, atmosphere, aura—its sound and allusive properties augmenting those effects. And yet another factor was at play, one that redounded neither to James's credit nor to mine.

Simply put: Timing, or Circumstance, or even Chance. Mr. Taft, my graduate program advisor, had very much wanted me to apply for an assistant professorship position at the university once I received my degree. I, too, wanted to remain, in light of the respect in which I held many members of the department as it was then constituted. Moreover, I had begun dating Marjorie. Relocating to a university in another city hence would have upset numerous apple carts.

In a casual conversation, Mr. Taft intimated that the department had been on the lookout for someone to teach James and, to a lesser extent, Twain and Melville. The proverbial word to the wise was sufficient, and I selected James and his conceptualizations of familial duty as my dissertation topic. Perhaps if the department had been looking for a Conrad or Trollope scholar at the time, or—God forbid—a Samuel Richardson, I would have chosen some aspect of *their* works for my dissertation and subsequent specialization.

Despite this somewhat mercenary spur to selecting Henry James, however, I quickly became infatuated with my mail-order bride. And Mr. Taft became as much an object of my gratitude as Miss Perry. Quite a few years my senior, and of the 'old school,' he expressed no dismay at my leaving the assistant professorship to join the War Department. In his mind, it was an act of submission to a greater duty.

Hearing my name, I looked up.

"Addy says you grew up on a farm and went to a two-room schoolhouse—is she kidding me?"

"That surprises you?"

"You don't sound like someone who grew up on a farm."

"I moved to New York City when I was sixteen to attend college, and except for a few years in Washington, DC, I have been here since, so it stands to reason my diction, and accent even, should mimic those born in this environment."

"You didn't have indoor plumbing growing up, did you?" my granddaughter asked.

"No, we obtained our water from a well."

"Or refrigerator?"

"We didn't have *electricity*, my dear—what use would a refrigerator have been? We had ice boxes, to keep the ice cold, ice that was delivered."

The young upstart again appeared not to believe me and said, "We just read a case in Antitrust from the 1880s. They had electricity then."

"In *cities*, yes. People talk today about a cultural divide between those of us in urban areas and those living on farms—back then, the divide was not merely cultural; it was akin to the chasm between pre– and post–Industrial Revolution societies. The cities were supplied with sufficient electrical power to operate *machinery*. But farms had no municipal power source even for incandescent lights! Vacuum cleaners, refrigerators, simple fans were conveniences that for agrarian populations lagged decades behind their city counterparts. The automobile and tractor—*those* were the significant advancements for us. And they only arrived on farms in the late teens and early 1920s."

Suitably abashed, Morris Townsend was without a ready reply.

How pleased I had been that my parents had acquired electricity and indoor plumbing by the time I brought Marjorie home! And acutely conscious of the impression our main room must have made on her: the large, unadorned space with exposed rafters; the modest pine table and chairs; the hearth in the far wall with its old log rack; the pots and pans hanging from beams; the cast-iron stove. Yet she took delight in it all and even marveled at the items on the mantelpiece: the candles and brass candlesnuffer, the school awards signed by Miss Perry, the copies of my publications—no, those came later, after we were married. Upon our return to New York, Marjorie described the farmhouse to her parents as "charmingly homespun." I suspected Claudia would have used the word 'primitive.'

"It's pretty impressive," Carson said, "going from a farm to become a professor at a first-class university. Actually *living* 'carpe diem,' not just having it as a philosophy."

"'Carpe diem' has never been my personal philosophy. Quite the contrary, I have been accused of a caution that pays too *much* heed to the future. But I do not renounce that aspect of my character; I believe that planning and assiduous work toward a distant goal is a virtue. Those who seek immediate gratification are hardly icons worthy of admiration."

Seeming perplexed, the young man mumbled, "I guess I always heard the phrase used differently."

"By Latin speakers?"

"When I went into Engel Klein today," Adelaide said, looking my direction, "Joe wanted to know if I could work part-time."

"But they hired you for *full*-time—"

"Over the summer I'll work full-time, but he means now—could I put in ten or fifteen hours a week during the school year."

"Billable?" Carson asked. He misinterpreted my expression as signifying an unfamiliarity with the concept and proceeded to unnecessarily lecture me. "'Billable hours' means work you do just for one particular client, so you can bill them for it. Other things—like interviewing job applicants, staff evaluations, or even just reading to stay current in your practice area—that's not time spent on behalf of a particular client, so you can't ask them to pay for it. Ergo: the firm doesn't value it as much. 'Billable hours' is the name of the game."

"Adelaide acquainted me some time ago with the term's meaning." I returned my attention to her. "Won't that be difficult: working part-time in addition to your studies?"

"I'll just be reviewing documents for this one case of his. Maybe you read about it—I guess it's been in the papers. The Scottish fortune—the search for heirs?" Adelaide looked at us questioningly, but we each professed ignorance. "I can at least tell you what's in the press; that won't violate client confidentiality."

CHAPTER 7

"LAST SPRING A WOMAN NAMED Violet MacDonalde died at the age of a hundred and four. She lived her whole life in a village in Scotland. Never married. For the last thirty years, a local couple took care of her. Her father had left her a bunch of stocks that did really well, and her estate's now worth—I don't remember the pounds, but in dollars—around fifty million."

Carson whistled. "Don't tell me: she left it all to her cats?"

I was pleased Adelaide simply continued on with her narrative.

"Her will divides the estate into two parts. The first twenty-five million is split three ways: among the caretaker couple, her church, and some local organization helping unwed mothers."

"And the cats get the *remaining* twenty-five mil." The young man was so enamored of himself as to be insufferable.

"The second twenty-five million goes to her sister, Mary, or gets divided among Mary's heirs. Mary emigrated to the US back in 1904. Violet lost touch with her in 1913. It's our job to find Mary. Or any heirs." Had Mary simply disappeared, I inquired?

"Her last letter was in 1913. Violet never saw or heard from her after that."

"Wow, a true-life mystery," Carson said. "Maybe a murder mystery."

I opined that the case sounded interesting but more suited to a detective agency than a law firm.

"We are working with a private-investigation firm—Drecker?"

She looked at Carson, but he gestured that the name meant nothing to him.

"They specialize in tracking down heirs. We oversee their work and vet the claimants. A lot of people have come forward saying they're Mary's descendants. Most are probably frauds, and Joe says usually we could make them prove lineal descent, but Violet put all sorts of requirements in her will, in terms of the way she wanted the search handled."

"Can't they run DNA tests?" Carson asked. "Violet must've left *some*thing behind, some of her cells—like on her clothes. Or they could exhume her. The DNA could—"

"Mary was adopted, so there wouldn't be a biological connection to Violet."

I peered over to see if any potatoes remained. Adelaide must have noticed my glance because she passed the dish to me. There was enough for three more helpings. If the gigolo was done, we would have leftovers tomorrow.

"I didn't realize people could adopt kids in those days," he said.

"It wasn't through government agencies," Adelaide responded. "People did it privately, and there weren't laws regulating record keeping like there are today. The Scottish law firm handling the estate couldn't locate any information on Mary's biological parents. It wouldn't matter—Violet's will specifies Mary's 'descendants' don't include relatives like siblings, nieces, nephews."

"In point of fact," I told the young people, "adoption was quite a common practice in earlier times. Remember, women dying in childbirth was hardly a rare occurrence until the last half century, and not infrequently children lost both parents—fathers from accidents and disease, there being no antibiotics. Many, many people were called upon to rear their orphaned nieces, nephews, and cousins. Dickens novels are replete with orphans, Oliver Twist, of course, the most famous. But the Brontë sisters' works also feature orphans prominently—Heathcliff, presumably, and Jane Eyre. And consider Eliot's *Daniel Deronda*, which, although not centering on a true orphan, focuses heavily on the inquietude of an adopted son. But, my dear, before I forget: the terms used in Great Britain for lawyer are 'solicitor' and 'barrister,' depending on the nature of the legal work."

"Have the private investigators turned up anything?" Carson asked.

"A few things, but I don't think I can tell you—it's not public. It *is* public that Violet herself hired some investigators back in the twenties, after her parents died, and learned a little about where Mary lived and worked, but nothing specific after her last letter, in 1913."

"Tell me," I ventured, "with so much time elapsed, isn't the task rendered so much the harder? I am reminded of Mark Twain's essay on James Fenimore Cooper. You may recall that Cooper's books about

America's frontier days—*The Deerslayer, The Last of the Mohicans*—were quite popular. Twain, however, took issue with Cooper's invention of improbable events. If memory serves me well, one involves a group of Indians concealed in a tree overhanging a river, waiting to board and commandeer a slow boat passing underneath. A few Indians began the assault by leaping down from the branch, but the boat had already glided past, so they landed in its wake. Remarkably, that misfortune did nothing to dissuade the remaining Indians in the tree from contributing their own efforts, and one by one they, too, tried to jump onto the boat, although predictably missing by an even greater distance. Your case provides an analogous situation: whatever detectives seventy years ago could not unearth will not be unearthed by detectives jumping in the water today."

As was her wont, Adelaide gave careful consideration to my comments before replying. "There are fewer living witnesses, for sure, and fewer records in some places. Joe was saying something about there being fewer phone books."

"There were considerably fewer *telephones*, my dear. We did not have one when I was growing up. Cities had telephones in the 1870s. Yet farmers had to wait a good decade or longer after World War I."

"Anyway, we're hoping phone books will help us now," Adelaide said, "tracking down possible descendants." Carson asked how widespread the publicity was, and Adelaide answered that until recently, when her firm put notices in American papers, the publicity had been "pretty much confined to the UK."

At this, Morris Townsend almost spilled his wine laughing. "Notices in newspapers for someone named MacDonald to inherit twenty-five million dollars? Twenty-five million people will answer! Old MacDonald had a fortune, *E-I-E-I-O*. And an oink-oink here and an oink-oink there. No wonder there are a lot of claimants!"

Displaying the patience of Penelope, my granddaughter explained that the initial newspaper notices did *not* mention the reason the firm was searching for Mary and her descendants. Unfortunately, however, some tabloids had recently gotten wind of the size of Violet's estate and certain details that the investigation had unearthed, so now stories were coming out about *the search for an heir to a fortune.*

Nonetheless, the number of claimants was not as large as it might have been, owing to two facts. First, Mary had a middle name, Agnes, eliminating all descendants of Marys with a different middle name. And second, the spelling of MacDonald was unusual—there was an *e* at the end—*M-a-c-D-o-n-a-l-d-e*.

I could not recall *ever* seeing such a spelling. The young people admitted the same.

"Where did Mary last live?" Carson asked.

"What's been disclosed so far—like I said, I can't tell you everything—what's been disclosed so far is that she came through Ellis Island in 1904. Her intended destination, according to the immigration papers, was a family in West Virginia. But she met someone on the ship who ended up hiring her as a governess for his kids, in upstate New York."

"Did she write to anyone else—friends, her mother and father?" Carson asked.

"Not that Violet knew. Mary was estranged from both parents, and they had no other siblings. Violet wrote almost every month, but in one of her letters Mary complained she didn't have the luxury of leisure time to write as often."

The young man smirked annoyingly. "Maybe Mary wasn't crazy about ole Sis. Maybe that's why she crossed the Atlantic—to say good riddance to the whole damn clan."

"Mary may simply have had a thirst for a life with more opportunities than her provincial town in Scotland could offer," I rejoined. "What others deem rancor or defiance or rebelliousness may be a pioneering outlook, an eagerness not so much to reject an old way of life as to embrace a new."

"But she was fifteen and—" Adelaide began, before the brash young man, taken with his own thoughts, broke in.

"Whatever her feelings, Mary still managed to crank out letters, so the fact that she stopped completely in 1913 suggests she died. Either way, the odds are she's dead now, right? How old would she be?"

"Around a hundred and five—she was born in 1888. The other thing is," Adelaide shyly added, "and it's been in the press: when she left their village for Glasgow, which is where she sailed from, she was five months pregnant. And not married. The child would be almost ninety and might have children and grandchildren. So the search isn't just for her."

Not surprisingly, the ensuing discussion centered on the terrible sorrows and travails that used to attend out-of-wedlock births. And undoubtedly still did in certain areas. Adelaide rightly criticized the stigma attaching to the mothers—noting the irony of the stigma *not* attaching to the fathers, who usually were the ones initiating the forbidden liaisons. Carson said the stigma was particularly blameworthy for extending to the children. I could not quarrel with that. For my part, I described how the plight of the unmarried mother was never more elegantly limned than in Hardy's *Tess of the d'Urbervilles*.

"What's the kid's name?" Carson asked.

"Her letters never actually say. She doesn't even give away the baby's sex, just says things like 'We have done some traveling.'"

"Poor girl," I murmured. "She must have been afraid of the letters falling into the wrong hands and bringing shame—*further* shame—on the family."

"What happened to the child's father?"

"The rumor in the village was he was one of the boys who came up from Glasgow to help with sheep shearing, but we're not looking into that; Violet's will specifically excludes anyone related to Mary's child on the father's side. And from things Mary told her, Violet believed Mary wasn't in touch with him, though she stayed in Glasgow three months before sailing."

I opined that Mary may have harbored a hope that the young man would do the honorable thing. Perhaps he fashioned himself Sherlock Holmes, for Carson now began an interrogation of Adelaide as though she were a suspect in a crime.

"Is there a birth certificate for Mary's baby?"

"No one's found any. It's complicated. Birth certificates aren't always available to the public even after a person has died. And they might be stored only at the county level, at least for a while. Even if they make it to a state's centralized records—like at a Department of Health—it can be a hassle to get copies. You might need a court order, and they've all got backlogs."

"And no MacDonalde baby listed on the ship's manifest?"

"No. Mary was eight months when she sailed, and the crossing took six days, so it's *possible* she had the baby before they landed."

"Did they check for a MacDonald with the typical spelling? You hear about officials at Ellis Island pushing immigrants to Americanize their names—change Gobbledygook to just plain Gobbledy."

"The return address on Mary's letters to Violet kept the *e*. And we can't track down every MacDonald without an *e*—there are tens, maybe hundreds, of thousands."

And so on. Eventually I was able to interject my own questions. "Where did you say Mary lived upstate?"

"A small town—Joe didn't mention it."

"But they put a notice in the local newspaper?"

"In papers around the whole area."

"And there are *no* official records with the *e* spelling?"

"Not that could be her or related to her. But a lot of old county and city records were never centralized or entered in a database. And like I said, we can't check out everything—especially with the conventional spelling—because it could go on forever and cost a ton."

How could I be castigated for telling the young people about *Bleak House* and its lengthy and labyrinthine court proceedings? "Jarndyce versus Jarndyce similarly centered on heirs to a large fortune, but by the time the lawyers had finished with their shenanigans, the estate was entirely depleted—there were no funds left to be distributed!"

Adelaide's smile showed she immediately grasped the ironies. "That's why we can't check for MacDonalds without the *e*."

"Do you want me to open the bottle I brought?" Carson asked, prompting Adelaide's assent. His dexterity in removing the cork was no virtue, given his age.

"How did people travel back then anyway? Horse and buggy?"

"Over long distances, by railroad," I said. "We did not have the highway system that exists today, and the 'horseless carriage,' as it was initially dubbed, was not nearly as ubiquitous as now."

"Did your family have a car when you were a kid?" Adelaide inquired of me. "Yes, the famous Model T. But it was not used for frivolous errands. Few roads in our area were paved, and repairs were not a simple matter."

"Good thing trains were the main mode of transportation," Carson told her. "It made your great-great-grandfather's patent all the more valuable."

So the scoundrel knew about the trust! Did he labor under the illusion Adelaide someday would inherit a large sum of money? Should I disabuse him of the notion? No, I would discuss this later, alert her to gold diggers, to the Morris Townsends of the world.

The gold digger sprawled back in his chair. "I wonder if *I* could pose as a MacDonalde."

To give due seriousness to Adelaide's employment, I inquired as to her role in the case.

"Reviewing records, I think. After newspapers carried the story, like I said, people named MacDonald have contacted us. The spelling is without the *e*, but they claim some older-generation relative dropped it. We have to sift through documents to see if there's a link to Mary. Some are obvious frauds—they say things that are inconsistent with facts in her letters that haven't been made public."

"So the letters still exist?" Carson asked.

Adelaide briefly touched fingertips to mouth. "I probably shouldn't have said that."

"We won't say anything to anyone," Carson assured.

I sighed. "With the advent of typewriters, and now computers, penmanship has become a lost art. So many people do little more than scrawl illegibly. In my day, children were taught how to shape each letter, both the uppercase and lowercase version, and had to practice for quite a long time to master the correct forms. The boldness of the stroke, the absence or extent of flourishes, could reveal a great deal about a person. But, my dear, not to cast aspersions on your abilities, what training have you had to enable you to determine whether a document is genuine?"

"I'm just doing the initial screening for anything relevant—a lot of the documents don't prove anything. If I do find something relevant, it goes to a professional document examiner."

"Who probably charges five hundred bucks an hour," the smug young man interjected.

Adelaide's graciousness compelled her to smile. "Yes, law students and junior associates are way cheaper." She rose and began to clear the dishes.

I rose too and paid a visit to the bathroom. I returned to find her in the kitchen wrapping the leftovers and talking with Carson, who stood at the sink elbow-deep in suds. Apparently a high-society background did not preclude manual labor. I left them alone and repaired to the living room. His coat folded over one arm, Carson came to say goodbye and proffered the usual pleasantries about enjoying meeting me and this and that. He urged me not to rise, and I took the fellow at his word.

After seeing him to the door, Adelaide came into the living room and asked if I wanted tea.

"No, thank you, my dear. I hope your evening went as smoothly as could be expected."

"I guess. He was nervous."

"I didn't perceive any nervousness. What did he have to be nervous about?" Dare I say that, to the contrary, the young man appeared at ease to an extent one might call presumptuous?

"You were a professor at a prestigious university. It can be intimidating."

"I am capable of talking about all sorts of things. The weather, didn't we?" *Besides,* I was sorely tempted to add, *I am the one of humble background—he is the one boasting membership in society's upper echelons!*

My granddaughter examined the hem of her sweater. "You seemed not to like him."

Her statement took me by surprise—I had not thought my behavior uncivil.

"I wouldn't say I *dis*like him. At most, I don't see the areas of common interest between you."

She shrugged. "Not sure I do either."

AFTER SWALLOWING THE FIRST OF my nighttime medications and washing it down with a sip of water, I peered at the reflection in the bathroom mirror. No Dorian Gray deceiver smiled back. Yet the seventy-nine-year-old visage did not displease me, the pinkish tint in my cheeks resulting, no doubt, from the slightly increased consumption of wine.

As I considered Adelaide's confession that she harbored reservations about pursuing a friendship with the shallow young man, the face in the mirror gave a small smile. And yet some of the merriment faded as I found myself mulling over Olivia's contention that her daughter suffered from a depressed frame of mind. Her indifference to Carson thus could be seen as another manifestation of her general mental state. I preferred to believe she had come to see the young man clearly, my own perspicacity lighting the way. I swallowed the last of my medications.

CHAPTER 8

LOOKING OUT THE LIVING ROOM windows, Addy considered how Carson's view of the MacDonalde case—that it was a fun mystery—was far from her own. Mary's story was *disturbing*. A person shouldn't just disappear into oblivion. Obviously, Mary hadn't disappeared to the people who had known her after she'd emigrated, but if she had survived long past her last letter, then it was *Violet* who'd receded into oblivion, at least for her sister.

In high school, Michael had brought up the Holocaust at dinner one night, and Olivia had said something like 'Why talk about these things? We know there were tortures and killings on a huge scale, but to describe them again and again—what's the purpose?' Had her mother been upset at Michael or at his teacher?

Addy remembered her father's response, "We need to bear witness," but didn't get his point and had silently sided with her mother. Now, though, she understood.

Only a narrow strip in the middle of the river was dark, the rest ringed by the lights on the drive and bridges and island. How much of the city was lit up in1904 when Mary arrived? Did it look frighteningly immense?

IN UNCLE RICHARD'S OLD ROOM, Addy put on only the bedside lamp. It was a cozy space, the furniture a warm wood, the curtains a nice brown. Undressing, Addy again tried to imagine what Mary MacDonalde must have felt landing on a different continent and not knowing if she'd see her family again. Had she been bitter? Or had the fear of the unknown crowded out everything else—fear of the people she'd live among, the work she'd be forced to do, whether she'd starve? Nathan's grandfather had emigrated from the Austro-Hungarian Empire at thirteen. All Addy had had to worry about at thirteen was algebra tests and whether she'd disappoint her teammates. The coach never subbed anyone in for her during games, so either she was good at sweeper or no one else wanted the position.

How weird, that Carson remembered her answer in Crim Law. She didn't expect anyone would—and definitely not him. He wasn't sympathetic toward minorities or the poor or anybody who had it rough. *Now* she remembered what he'd said in the study group that upset the others. The jury convicted the husband of starving the child, but the wife had presented evidence she was a battered woman, so she was acquitted. Carson had said something like: 'The wife should've been tossed in the brig too.'

Addy got into bed, and her thoughts returned to the MacDonalde case and things she'd learned at the meeting that weren't public. Mary's child was a boy and named Brian, and in 1908 the two moved out west. Violet had learned about Brian from her investigators, so why hadn't she specifically named her nephew in the will? Because she wanted any half siblings to share equally in the estate? Or figured Mary was in the best position to divide up the inheritance? Addy wondered if she should sign up for the Trusts and Estates course next term.

A light went off across the alley, leaving the room in darkness. Had being fifteen been an *advantage* to Mary, not a handicap? Francis had been excited to travel to England at that age—he talked about wanting adventure. Addy had looked forward to going away to college, her mother encouraging her to "broaden her horizons." Her father, if he'd been alive, would've done the same. But Mary's departure had been a banishment. Maybe by the time she'd crossed the Atlantic she'd begun to love the child inside her. Was she glad he'd be an American, or did she wish he could've been raised in Scotland?

A college professor once said you couldn't know what it was like to be an American until you lived abroad. It made sense, learning from contrast. Wasn't that the first lesson of falling in love: who you were wasn't fixed or permanent? You became someone new and couldn't return to who you'd been.

Addy turned on her side. If she'd mentioned earlier in the day that she wasn't interested in Carson as a boyfriend, Francis might not have been so testy. In the study group, Carson used to play the gallant suitor—opening doors, helping the other girls off with their coats. A few acted annoyed and some flattered. Addy was just embarrassed, like he was a parody of old-fashioned manners. Maybe it was that and his silly jokes that made it easy for her to relax around him—she didn't have to take him seriously.

CHAPTER 9

A FULL BLOCK AWAY THE rectangular sails were visible, flapping angrily in the wind, kind of like her hair shooting every direction. Crossing the parking lot, she could see the upper reaches of the bare masts. Carson separated from the crowd and walked toward her, hands in his peacoat pockets. He had on a dark-green wool cap and a navy-and-green plaid scarf.

"I got your ticket already. You warm enough?"

"I'm under three layers."

He seemed pleased and for a moment she thought he was going to take her arm, but he just motioned toward the crowd on the pier. They walked with heads lowered against the wind to the mass of coats and parkas. The other visitors—most of them men—shifted their weight or walked in place to keep warm. A few smoked cigarettes.

"This used to be a sloop," he said. "One mast. It probably got converted to a brigantine for ocean crossings."

She looked up at the upper reaches of the masts, tilting back and forth while the vessel bobbed. She could see now the spars—or were they yards?—weren't actually bare but held rolled up sails. "How old is it?"

"Mid-seventeen hundreds, according to the newsletter. I don't know when she was converted."

"Was it a war ship?"

"Ones like this weren't fitted for guns. She could've brought provisions and ammo to the warships, though. All the different sails and rigging on bigger vessels are designed to increase speed. The windjammers—triple masters and four- and five-masters—could cross the Atlantic in two weeks hauling heavy cargo like lumber and guano. I'm not joking—it was the hot-selling fertilizer of its day." They thought the line was starting to move, but it was just people walking to keep warm.

"Last year Lucy and I boarded a brigantine that had gone all the way from Boston around Cape Horn and up the West Coast to Vancouver Island—your neck of the woods. Then she sailed to the

Sandwich Islands and back and forth to China. That was a busy trade route, the Native Americans and Chinese."

Addy was surprised. "What did they trade?"

"The Native Americans, furs—sea otter, mostly. The Chinese traded silk, porcelain. It was a global economy—the silk could wind up in Europe. This one, she was definitely for cargo. And not people cargo. I won't take you to see a slave ship. Once was too much for me."

"My dad was given a piece of fabric, kind of a small quilt, from a tribe he did work for, and they said it was a hundred years old. My mother swore it was silk. So it could've come from China?"

"For sure." Carson looked about to say more, but a man in a dark watchman's cap was yelling something, and people formed a single line. The man right ahead told them, "Only twenty at a time."

"If we get in the last group, we can stay longer," Carson whispered. "Are you freezing?"

"I'm fine. I'd rather not be rushed."

She was perfectly content to fight the cold by shifting her weight and patting her gloved hands together. When the wind died, Addy again looked up and noticed how the interweave of rigging resembled a kind of cat's cradle, ropes running from the tops of the masts and across yards and attached at dozens of places near the deck or along the sides. Some of the smaller ropes, she realized, were ladders. "A lot of experimentation must have gone into the rigging," she said.

"Hundreds of years' worth. Make that thousands—when was the Trojan skirmish? The Greeks had pretty sophisticated vessels." Carson pointed to the mast tops. "The upper sails are furled, so you can't tell, but even the squares are cut at different angles and rigged differently. Every one has a name. I don't mean Fred and Hortense. If you only have one sail per mast, they're the foresail and mainsail. But adding sails higher, you have the topsail and gallant, and some vessels have a skysail and moonsail. Behind the foresail versions are the mainsail versions and mizzenmast version, if you have a third mast. It helps the crew know what the officer's shouting so they can act on a dime."

"Who did that: supervising the sails?"

"Could be the third mate, though might've started with the captain, who was in charge of charting the course. He could relay it to the first mate. You're right: it's no mean feat to orchestrate." Carson cupped his hands around his mouth and mock shouted, "Shorten the main topsail, me laddies!"

"How many sailors would be on a ship like this?"

"We can count the crew berths below. Plus, you had the captain and three mates, and the purser and steward—he was like the captain's manservant—and the ship's surgeon and a carpenter and cook. Maybe an employee of the company that was shipping the cargo. Like a small village. They were at sea for months."

When it was their turn to board, Carson went first, grabbing the railings as if hoisting himself, and Addy did the same. The gangway swayed a little, the dark water just below sloshing roughly. It was also a help to see what Carson held on to after boarding because the vessel lurched more than she'd expected.

The first thing that amazed her was how beautiful the wood was; even the floorboards were polished to a shine. And wood was everywhere: sides and steps and railings and storage cabinets. They lingered at the rear of their group, which was heading slowly toward the bow. Carson kept up a steady stream of terms, descriptions, explanations. The sheer number of different objects amazed her: iron gadgets, spools of rope in different sizes, brass fixtures, boxes and crates, hooks and chains and poles. She repeated the names, hoping to memorize them—hawser and capstan, belaying pins, jacklines and leeches, windlass, bowsprit, binnacle, braces, shrouds—although she didn't repeat 'buttocks.' Everything had a function; everything was important.

The man in the watchman's cap approached, and Carson asked if the crow's nest had been added. Addy looked up at the barrel-like structure at the top of the main mast. The man nodded brusquely and went by.

"These old vessels didn't usually have a crow's nest," Carson said. "Not the kind a man could keep watch in."

"Why would there be crows in the middle of the ocean? I could understand seagulls."

"The Vikings took them for navigation, on the theory that if they released them, the crows would head for the nearest land. Could be an old yarn. I always thought of being perched up there as heaven or hell. Hell if you're in rough waters, heaven on a calm, clear night."

Carson knew so much history, like the improvements the Portuguese and Dutch made to navigation and who traded what when. He explained how on a long voyage, you had to expect equipment to break or tear, so all the tools and materials needed for repairs had to be on board. She was pretty sure he was being sarcastic when he said that sails had been made of linen or hemp until cotton became cheap, "thanks to slavery."

They ascended wide stairs toward the bow. Again, Addy was impressed by the beauty of the woodwork, the banisters and deck boards. "The fo'c'sle, short for 'forecastle,' leads to the crew quarters." He gestured at an opening in the floor like a trapdoor.

The watchman-cap guy approached. "You have to wait to go below until the others come up."

Carson turned to Addy and smiled, saying nothing. Feeling awkward, she asked if when he was young, he fantasized about being a sailor in the days of brigantines.

"Sure—who didn't? Most people, I guess."

When it was their turn, Carson gestured for Addy to go first. She carefully descended the wooden rungs, landing in a narrow hall. Carson came down easily a moment later and pointed aft. "The galley—kitchen—is that way. Those stairs are probably to the hold, where they kept the cargo. This way to the crew's quarters."

She followed him into a fairly large room, where the windows on either side ran at an angle to meet at the bow. The broader part of the room, taken up with triple-level bunk beds, was lit by lanterns hanging from ropes.

"Probably a large table was there, and chairs, and over there maybe the footlockers. This was quarters for eighteen men."

"It's nice there's daylight."

"Not much. Let's go aft. You'll like the great cabin, the captain's quarters."

They climbed back up to the fo'c'sle and headed toward the stern. Walking was getting easier, though Addy still followed Carson's lead and held on to parts of the vessel to keep her balance. Two sets of stairs, one port and one starboard, rose to a high, broad platform.

"This is the quarterdeck. And that one is the poop deck—it's not for what you think. In fact, the head, the restroom, is in the bow—that way, it gets cleaned automatically by the oncoming waves."

A large vertical wheel took up the center of the quarterdeck, and Carson said she should "take the helm." She ran her hand along the lovely wooden handles, then moved to the table nearby, which held a broad glass case containing a small telescope, a compass, a leather-bound book, an ink well, and a quill pen.

"This is where the captain would strut his stuff. Usually, only officers were allowed on the quarterdeck except for whoever was helmsman."

"The helmsman wasn't an officer?"

"He could be one of the sailors. He took orders from the captain or the second mate. When the vessel was going in and out of port, they'd hire on some local to navigate—could be just a fisherman if he knew the harbor. Imagine it: a big vessel approaching, and all these little boats tearing out to meet it, kind of like taxis racing for a fare. First to get there negotiated a fee to bring her in safely."

In a weird way, Addy was reminded of her Contracts course, how there was a huge and complex set of rules about the sale of goods and services *plus* a culture of customs that had been fine-tuned over centuries, and she was seeing only the present, not how the rules and customs developed. The thought of how little of the world, of history, of nature a person could learn used to overwhelm her. Zach had joked that Plato's students had it easy because there wasn't much required reading to graduate from the academy. He was amazed she could concentrate on assignments that even she thought were boring.

"Let me show you the captain's quarters. It will make you drool."

The "great cabin," as Carson called it, was beautiful. Large windows spanned the entire width of the stern and for several yards along the sides. The wooden frames and sashes and pieces between the panes were a rich red-brown mahogany, so were the ledges and the window seats and maybe even the shiny ceiling beams. The floor was covered in thick dark Persian carpets. The port side forward of the windows contained a bed and large chest of drawers with brass handles and a little table supporting a white enamel wash basin. The enormous mirror in a mahogany frame reflected a large portrait on the opposite wall of a somber man in a uniform. The table in the middle of the room was half covered with nautical maps. Everything else on it was elegant: the hourglass with a pewter base, the quill pens, the magnifying glass, the flat brass plate with intricate etching.

"What's that?" she asked.

"An astrolabe—to navigate by the stars. Eventually sextants came on the scene, they worked better."

Addy wandered over to the built-in cabinets and shelves. She suspected the books were put there for show, leather-bound volumes with gold-colored lettering on the spines. She tilted her head to read *Celestial Measurements* and *Navigating the Cape of Good Hope* and *Islas Malvinas*. There also were technical titles, an almanac, a Bible, a copy of Plutarch's *Lives*, and an *Iliad* and *Odyssey*.

Carson took her to the officers' quarters and poop deck, and they returned to the gangplank. What amazed her the most, she told him, was how everything on the vessel—every sail, every piece of wood, every line, every metal loop and hook—was functional. Even the tiny or peculiar-looking parts had a purpose and were necessary to the voyage. Now she was reminded of her Evidence class and how what initially had seemed like arcane and arbitrary rules turned out to be carefully constructed solutions to real-life problems. Even if, as Francis was always saying, "the cure is worse than the disease." Still, no rule was random.

The entire way home—walking to the subway, waiting on the platform, riding the train, walking to her building—neither of them said much. As he held open the outside door, Carson asked if she'd been bored.

"No, it was really interesting."

"Maybe next time we'll go in warmer weather." She nodded uncertainly.

CHAPTER 10

MILLIE ARRIVED ALONE THURSDAY, ENGENDERING in me a small hope that this impending visit, too, would be cancelled. However, the hope was immediately quashed by the tote bags that she proceeded to unload in the space we had cleared in the living room. All manner of paraphernalia erupted from the Vesuvian receptacles: a blue plastic container labeled *Wipes*; a tissue box; a package of little garments that seemed a cross between diapers and underwear; toy cars and boats; a plastic policeman; what looked like robots; a plastic facsimile of a red barn; plus a thick wad of sketch paper, box of crayons, and green lunchbox emblazoned with a picture of an astronaut.

"He likes to color," she explained while unfolding a cotton blanket and placing a large blotter of sorts upon it. To the blotter she added the wad of paper.

Barely had she concluded the preparations when John came in holding the boy by the hand. The child managed to walk, but his legs bent inward terribly so he had to lean on his grandfather and proceed slowly. Having had no clear picture of what to expect, I should not have been surprised, yet Robert bore no resemblance to any images my mind had conjured up. For one thing, his head looked a little too large for his body, lending his already thin frame an additional aura of frailty. His hair was dark and unruly. When Millie helped him to sit on the blanket, his legs projected at an awkward angle. He redistributed his weight slightly, and his back slumped so as to suggest an accustomed position, although to me it looked far from comfortable.

"Robert, this is Francis."

He looked up directly at me. His dark-brown eyes were wide and the lashes long, with almost a feminine beauty. I nodded in greeting. He said nothing.

Adelaide entered the room smiling at Robert as if she knew him. Squatting a few feet away, she said, "I'm Addy," receiving in return only his mute gaze. Her pointing to his sketch paper and asking if he liked to draw elicited a guttural noise. She opened the crayon box and pushed it toward him. She rose to sit on the chair nearby, her ease with the situation surprising me until I recalled her saying she had babysat for many years.

John headed for the hall, but Millie murmured she would stay a few minutes. Positioned a trifle awkwardly on the green ottoman, she proceeded to chatter about John's progress in rehabilitation and some of the activities of his group. I watched how Robert maneuvered himself onto his left side, his left arm lending support and his right hand within easy reach of the papers and crayons. He began to draw. Although not entirely lacking in coordination, the boy was not up to the fine and nimble dexterity required for delineating forms, whether of persons or objects. Yet he seemed intent on his work.

"Can you imagine," Millie was telling us, "the PT tried to interest John in macramé. Macramé! 'I'd sooner walk on coals,' he said. The point is for him to improve his posture, to exercise the stomach muscles. The macramé is just some diversion while they sit. 'Why can't we play gin rummy?' he wanted to know." She laughed good-naturedly in a manner reminiscent of Marjorie, whose store of good humor was bottomless.

The boy grunted, and Millie asked if he was thirsty. He bobbed his head, and she poured juice from a container into a yellow plastic cup. I was about to ask if it was grape juice, which I had learned from bitter experience stained carpeting, but seeming to anticipate my concerns, she said it was a "no-spill cup." It had a top and an unusual spout. The boy grabbed the cup around the base, took several sips, and placed it nearby on the blanket before returning to his art.

"How old are you?" Adelaide asked, but Robert did not even look up.

"Seven and a half," Millie said. She lowered her voice to inaudibility and made exaggerated movements with her mouth so we could comprehend her. "He wasn't supposed to see his third birthday."

Adelaide asked if he went to school, and Millie shook her head and spoke in a half whisper. "What is so frustrating is that his hand—the right is the only one he can control at all—he doesn't have enough control over the fingers to sign. They tried; they tried so hard." Resuming in her normal voice, she told the boy, "Robert, Francis and Adelaide will help you with anything you need. Grampa and I won't be gone long." The boy made no acknowledgment of being addressed. "I told you: Francis and Adelaide aren't making Grampa and me leave. Grampa has a doctor's appointment. Francis and Adelaide wanted you to visit with them until we get back."

We sat in silence until Millie mouthed, "I'm hoping he'll stay dry until then." A look of alarm must have crossed my face because she hastily added, "He's in pull-ups, so you don't have to worry. With us he's toilet trained, but I didn't want to put you to any bother."

"It wouldn't be a bother," I murmured.

Adelaide walked Millie to the door, the two of them conferring in low voices. Robert continued to draw, shifting position slightly from time to time, finishing one picture and beginning on another, exchanging one colored crayon for another. In truth, I was peeved that Millie had made caring for the child sound so simple. What if he cried or threw things? Or tried to hurt himself—intentionally banging his head into the corner of the table? I imagined a frantic call to the ambulance.

On her return to the living room, Adelaide brought me the academic journal I must have left on the vanity and retrieved for herself her Administrative Law book. She sat on the floor beside Robert and began her homework. Once or twice he looked up from his drawing to watch her read. I admired her ability to concentrate and, seeing little choice but emulation, attempted to become absorbed in an article positing that Isabel Archer's commitment to her marriage was the capitulation of feminism. Good heavens, where was it writ that sacrifice or the fulfillment of duty is noble when performed by men but capitulation when performed by women? How I wished Henry James were there to share in some brandy and a hearty laugh.

"Excuse me, Adelaide." I gestured at the boy. "Perhaps he requires a tissue?"

She gently tapped his shoulder. "I'm going to wipe your nose. Is that okay?" He made no protest and then resumed his coloring.

Some minutes later, when the boy put down his crayon and sat more erect, Adelaide asked if he wanted some crackers. He bobbed his head, so she retrieved a small plastic bag from the side pouch of one of Millie's bags. He took a cracker from her, bit in, and chewed carefully, all the while watching her face. She handed him the yellow cup when he was done, and he managed to drink some. She offered him a second cracker, which he ate, again drinking juice to wash it down, again watching her.

While they were thus engaged, I inspected his drawings. Sadly, even stick figures seemed beyond the poor boy's abilities. Blobs of color—red, green, blue—were interposed willy-nilly, as best as I could discern. On the other hand, he varied the colors and shapes, and the patterns were not displeasing. Whether they signified objects or landscapes, we would never know. I harbored no doubt that the sheets, if passed off as sketches by one of the famous abstract painters of the day, would fetch a pretty penny—unless, of course, they were considered too pleasing to us *hoi polloi*.

The boy resumed coloring, and Adelaide noticed the mess of crumbs without my having to point it out and promptly cleaned it up. As she did not seem eager to return to her studying, and I had no interest in a silly screed depriving Isabel of the respect that was her due, I initiated conversation.

"Recently I was mentioning Miss Perry, my teacher in the upper room—back in our two-room schoolhouse. My guardian angel, if you will. One moved into the upper room at around age twelve, although I began before turning eleven because I had already been reading at what was then considered a high school level. Do not confuse that with *comprehending* at a high school level. The wisdom that comes from maturity and experiences does not allow for many shortcuts. But where was I?"

"Miss Perry."

"Yes, yes. She loved the classics—George Eliot, Dickens, Melville, Conrad, the Brontës. Twain, too, was among her favorites. I suppose she saw in me a kindred spirit. Dear Miss Perry. Unmarried women in those days were called 'Miss'—a sign of respect, not disrespect, as certain feminists would have it. Like so many unsung heroes—heroines, to be precise—Miss Perry was of a long tradition of spinster school teachers. I will concede that the word 'spinster' carries somewhat negative connotations. But these legions of unmarried teachers truly were heroines, not only because they taught us to read and write but because they enlightened us to so much else—the arts and sciences and history. It is difficult to impress upon younger people how to earlier generations with little access to books and cultural activities, teachers were a veritable lifeline.

"Remember: radios did not become common until the mid to late 1920s, and the variety of programs we have today was then simply unimaginable. My family never owned a phonograph player. People created live music when they could—singing, playing fiddles and other simple instruments, and a few families had means enough to buy a piano, but that was rare. The only instrument of heft in the community was the church organ—among the more fortunate churches. Contrast that with *your* experience: you can turn on the television and perhaps see a Shakespeare play or documentary about the American Revolution or even a film version of, say, *Anna Karenina*. A panoply of riches. We had no exposure to things apart from what we learned at school or at church. So when I say these teachers were a lifeline, a cultural lifeline, that is no exaggeration."

Adelaide handed Robert the blue crayon, which apparently he had been searching for, while asking, "Were any other professions open to women back then, besides teaching and nursing?"

"Not as they are today." Veritably, tears came to my eyes. "You must forgive this display of emotion, these feelings of deep gratitude. Even if Miss Perry were still alive, I would never be able to sufficiently thank her, never repay my debt. I owe all my successes to her."

Robert stared up at me—I must have appeared quite overcome.

"She might deserve *some* credit," Adelaide said genially, "but you obviously deserve most. I doubt all her other students went on to college and became professors."

"I seem to recall the Hamill boy—he was three years younger—I believe he obtained a degree in what they now call the agricultural sciences. It may have been denominated 'husbandry' back then. The other children I knew either remained on the family farm or else took a job in town. Certainly you are right: one's inner nature affects one's choice of vocation. What I wish to emphasize is what an outsize role Miss Perry played, not simply in my choosing a vocation and realizing my goals, but in my coming to recognize my own inner nature."

Robert made some grunting sound, prompting Adelaide to empty the crayon box and group the colored sticks in a half circle within his reach.

"I will never forget that summer, my dear, after my first year in the upper room. Summer is not entirely vacation time on a farm the way it is for children in urban areas. We enjoy the pleasures of swimming and fishing and other recreations, to be sure, but our chores do not diminish; indeed, we work harder than in winter. Not only must the animals continue to be fed and their quarters cleaned, but crops require continual tending, harvesting, and proper storing. And for me, at least, the end of the school year meant a three-month hiatus from my studies, from what I loved. Not the mathematics and science, perhaps, but the literature and history."

"I guess they didn't have summer school back then."

"No, although the children of the day laborers—immigrant families, primarily—would avail themselves of whatever instruction they could come by, eager to adopt all things American. In any case, Miss Perry detected my despondence and pressed upon me three books I could return when school began again: *Treasure Island*, *Twenty Thousand Leagues Under the Sea*, and *Robinson Crusoe*. This was a monumental gift; the nearest library was twenty-five miles away! Ah, Adelaide, these volumes opened up a universe—as I told you: my awakening. The richness of description, exotic places, strange characters—how could a boy not thrill to journey along the ocean depths? Of course, in subsequent years, literature brought me on a voyage into *self*-discovery, into the human mind and spirit. David Copperfield, Jude, and later Stephen Dedalus and Proust: these were my travel companions in the lands of yearnings and ambition, loneliness and desire, the quests for meaning and love. My university professors taught me the building blocks of literature—eloquence and imagery and the like—but my choice of profession redounds back to Miss Perry and the respect for great literature she instilled in me."

"I'm going to get him more juice." Adelaide rose and went toward the kitchen.

My goodness: their covers remained imprinted in my mind! A terrifying brown eddy in a dark-blue sea. A sunlit turquoise expanse and small roan patch containing one wind-blown palm. Peg-legged Long John Silver leaning menacingly over a map on a table.

Walking home that early-summer day, my chest throbbing with excitement, I was the child in a fairy tale bringing a bag of gold.

Picturing my parents' joy and delight, picturing their faces lit with excitement to behold such riches. Immediately upon arriving, I stacked the three books—tomes they seemed!—on the table. My mother being the first to appear, I showed her each volume and told her what Miss Perry had said about the authors. My father came in not long after, wiping his forehead with his kerchief. Espying the books, his expression denoted puzzlement, perhaps consternation. Right away my mother explained that they were on *loan* from Miss Perry—that I was not expected to pay for them, just to return them when the school year began anew. I awaited his smile.

"Is something wrong?" Adelaide had squatted beside Robert to offer him the juice, but her question was addressed to me.

"Not at all, my dear; I was simply recalling a less than happy memory. I did not realize my face was such an easy read."

"What memory?"

"Nothing of significance." I readjusted myself in the chair. "I told you about my year in Cambridge, its pleasures and delights. But they were not unalloyed. I was not costing my father one red cent, you realize? The scholarship covered tuition, room and board, books and study materials, *and* transportation. Yes, he was deprived of my weekend and before- and after-school labor, but remember: the Depression had not yet begun, and he had already made financial gains that would last a lifetime. We needed only *two* hired men then, and a girl came out from town to help with the laundry Mondays and Tuesdays."

"Your father didn't want you to go?"

"Why dwell on such things? I have had more than my share of good fortune. And on that precise point I was telling you about Miss Perry. Not just for those three books am I indebted to her; she subsequently steered me to many, many others. When I was older, she loaned me *Jude the Obscure*, which, as I have said, was life-changing. But these small acts—small for her, momentous for me—and her assistance in procuring me the year in Cambridge and applying to college, these acts pale before the most important gift of all."

Of course Robert had to pick that moment to whine and pump an arm up and down. Adelaide offered him more crackers, but he shook his head angrily. No, the juice was not his Holy Grail either. At her asking if he needed to use the bathroom, he emitted what could only be described as a yelp. One by one, she lifted toys that lay beyond his reach. Not until she held up the large red barn did he quiet. She put it beside him, and he opened the red plastic doors and extracted no small number of plastic animals: a pink pig, a brown-and-white cow, a brown rooster, orange hen, and more.

The boy thus absorbed in his toys and Adelaide's attention no longer divided, I resumed the discussion. "The most important gift of all I received from Miss Perry was not anything tangible, but a lesson, a precept, if you will, a catechism, a *value*. Never stated explicitly but inculcated all the same. It was this: literature is *important*. It is not a frivolous or idle pursuit. Literature is *worthy* of serious study."

Adelaide laughed—my granddaughter laughed! That she should greet this heartfelt pronouncement in such fashion took me aback. My reaction did not escape her—my visage *was* an open book—and she hastened to explain, "I never realized anybody thought literature wasn't important. Mom drilled it into us since—"

"Yes, yes, undoubtedly you were raised in a different milieu."

The affront instantly dissipated, her reaction completely comprehensible in light of her own personal history. From Miss Perry to me to Olivia to Olivia's daughter: culture is passed down as assuredly as genes. There was solace to be had in that.

"Do not fault my parents, my dear. They were farmers, and my childhood and youth pre-dated the modern conveniences of electricity and indoor plumbing.

"To them, to the entire *community*, the highest virtue was pulling one's own weight in the demands of day-to-day living. An ethic born of necessity. As I have said many times, there were always chores to be done: tending the crops, milking the cows, the daily feeding and caring of hogs, chickens, or other livestock. Waste products had to be removed, wood felled and chopped. Rain, snow, extreme heat, storms, droughts had to be contended with on their own schedules, not ours. Leisure time was a scarcity for my parents, and reading was considered an activity for leisure time. Even perusing the Bible was less important than contributing to the tasks necessary for survival. If the roads were impassable due to a storm, if a barn caught fire, if *any* disaster hit, the minister wasted no time exchanging his robe for overalls and pitching in in whatever way was needed. So do not suppose I denigrate that ethic—it sustained me as well as my family."

"I didn't—"

A troublesome sound came from the boy, and from the glances Adelaide and I exchanged, I could presume she had drawn the same inference.

"Perhaps it is just gas," I opined, striving for optimism.

"I'm not sure. Robert, do you want to go to the bathroom?"

Her petition, so meekly made, again elicited a vociferous reaction: a shriek that sputtered cracker bits out past the blanket onto the carpet.

"Okay, okay," she said, "we'll wait until Grandma and Grandpa come home."

The boy hushed, and in some act of Providence, Millie and John rapped on our door not five minutes subsequent.

"It was a short session," Millie said, looking happily at the youngster. "The regular PT has the flu, and the fill-in put them through a different program. How did it go?"

Adelaide recounted the boy's activities and suggested he might need changing. John nodded, the odor no doubt having corroborated her claim. Then, to my great consternation, Adelaide told Millie that watching Robert was "no big deal," and she would be happy to watch him every Thursday "for free."

Was she certain? Millie asked. And they would insist on paying Adelaide *some*thing.

"No, you shopped for Francis for a few years, before I moved in. I really don't mind. I got some studying done. But I'll do it at your place so Francis won't be disturbed."

"Nonsense," I said, surprising myself most of all. "We will both watch him here. That way Adelaide and I can spell each other if one of us needs to tend to something." Why such a ridiculous speech should have issued from my mouth I could not say. Buyer's remorse was sure to afflict me.

CHAPTER 11

DESPITE MY CAUTIONING THAT HER examinations loomed, Adelaide again accompanied Carson on a Saturday outing to see an old ship. She telephoned afterward to say they would bring back Chinese food. When we "rang off," as I had heard British people say, I did minor straightening up—primarily stowing away my various and sundry medications in the medicine cabinet—but did not concern myself with making the apartment pristine. However, I exacted a solemn promise from my worser self to behave in a manner beyond reproach.

They arrived toting two large paper bags. Having set the table—with both chopsticks and forks for the young people, only a fork for myself—I asked Carson to select the wine, gesturing at the rack, a true antique from a monastery, I told him, and one of Marjorie's favorite finds. If he preferred a chilled wine, there were several in the refrigerator.

Once we were seated, the food dished out, and the wine poured, the discussion quickly homed in on the MacDonalde case. Carson asked what would happen if all of the claimants turned out to be frauds—who would get the $25 million designated for Mary and her heirs? Adelaide said that portion would go into a trust, administered by Violet's church, for poor children around the world.

I opined how gratifying it was to see that the desire to do good deeds still arose—that not everyone was driven by the desire to make money.

"Agreed," Carson said glibly before asking Adelaide, "how long will your firm keep looking? If you go on forever, you'll use up the estate, like Francis said happened in that book."

"I'm not sure. There was a deadline, but they got an extension."

"The novel is *Bleak House*," I said. "One can hardly bemoan a result in which the money is put to good use. I am speaking of if no heirs are found."

"We do hope we can find out what happened to Mary and her descendants."

Carson lowered his chopsticks—he was as proficient with them as Adelaide—and again had the gall to lecture me. "The Scottish courts are probably like ours and favor 'finality,' especially in probate. You want the beneficiaries to not worry some undiscovered heir might pop up years later and make them fork over the money." He then offered the ill-informed opinion that because no one had filed a death certificate in New York State, we could assume that Mary and her child did not die here. His ignorance risked my granddaughter being misled.

"It would depend on where and *when* they died," I said. "Some rural communities in the early nineteen hundreds were less than assiduous at recording births and deaths with governmental offices. *Churches* were often the repositories of such information."

Adelaide responded that she believed cities and towns were required by law to record deaths and file death certificates with the Department of Health.

"That may be, my dear, but the law is not always adhered to. In 1918 and '19, when the Spanish influenza spread like wildfire, the sheer *magnitude* of the epidemic threw customary practices into disarray. Government offices and businesses closed; entire *towns* were quarantined. Thank you—I will have some more. So record keeping became quite a low priority."

"How do you disprove people's claims they're related to Mary?" Carson asked.

"They need to come up with *some* evidence—they can't just allege it," Adelaide said, abruptly standing. "There are photos of Mary—I can show you; they're public. If someone has other photos, that could do it."

She disappeared down the hall, returning with a photocopy of what must have been a sepia print of a young woman. The face was quite pretty, despite the serious expression; the hair, swept back and pinned behind in a very becoming manner, was neither very dark nor very light. The high collar reminded me of the dress my mother wore to church in winter, although my mother's lacked a lace trim.

Carson leaned over my shoulder, so I handed him the page. "Did Violet say how tall Mary was?" he asked.

"Five six. Light-brown hair, blue eyes."

He handed the photocopy back to her. "This has been in the press?"

"Yes, and the description."

"Why not simply publish each claimant's *name*," I suggested. "Won't the people who know the claimant's family history—for example: relations, friends, neighbors—won't they come forward to denounce the fraud, if in fact a fraud is being perpetrated?"

Carson subjected us to his clever smile. "Not if they want a cut of the booty. You wouldn't turn in Addy if she pretended to be an heir, would you?"

Fortunately, her speaking obviated the need for me to formulate a courteous response. "Most claimants sign our standard nondisclosure agreement. We—Engel Klein, the Scottish firm, and the claimants—we all agree not to disclose the claimants' names or the information they provide us."

"Why enter into such an arrangement," I inquired. "Wouldn't a claimant desiring to conceal his or her identity be considered suspect on that account alone?"

The young man's clever smile only expanded. "You know the media frenzy that descends on lottery winners. They can't leave their house because TV cameras have staked out the block. Long-lost relatives show up expecting handouts. You want to be anonymous when you inherit Fort Knox."

"Adelaide, tell me: Aren't ordinary people deterred from making false claims by fear of the consequences? Isn't it *illegal* to perpetrate a fraud?"

Again, the whippersnapper could not hold his tongue! "Prosecutors don't bother going after crimes like that. For twenty-five mil, you can't blame somebody for trying to put one over."

When she *was* allowed to speak, Adelaide gave an informed and informative answer. "The Scottish attorneys want the nondisclosure agreement too. We ask claimants questions that give things away. I'm making this up, this example, but say Mary lived in Alaska for a year. If we interview someone and ask if Mary ever lived there, and the claimant tells the press we asked that, then other claimants are tipped off to say she was there. Not that there's any real penalty if a claimant does talk to the press."

"It seems to me that your task is rendered the more difficult, my dear, by the custom of wives assuming their husbands' names, for Mary may have gotten married after 1913 and dispensed with MacDonalde altogether."

"We're checking for marriage certificates."

"She might've kept MacDonalde even if she got married," Carson said.

"That was hardly the custom back then, young man."

His disputatious nature knew no bounds. "I can see a reason. Her kid probably asked questions about the father, and Mary probably built him up. He was a brave soldier or great doctor, things like that. Changing their names would seem disloyal."

"You are imputing a good deal of duplicity to Mary," I deigned to point out. "It is far more likely she would have wanted to adopt her husband's name upon marrying so she would share a surname with *subsequent* children. And life would have become simpler for *all* if her eldest child then shared the new last name as well."

"I'm just saying she could've felt stuck in a story she'd told—that's human nature."

To be lectured to about human nature by someone one-third my age!

"The only fictions she likely felt obligated to continue," I said, "were that she had been married to a Mr. MacDonalde, he was the child's father, and he did love or would have loved the child— depending on when Mary said she was widowed. Certainly one can sympathize with Mary's need to lie about the circumstances of the child's birth and paternity, given societal attitudes at the time, but she had no need to spin elaborate yarns in its wake."

The recalcitrant young man merely shrugged and mumbled something about Mary "feeling stuck."

Adelaide interjected the observation that Mary was carrying a large emotional burden for a fifteen-year-old. "Were there many therapists back then, Francis?"

"In that period, the word for 'therapist' or 'psychologist' was 'alienist.' A person sought counsel from an alienist. They were not nearly as plentiful as they are today; we took more responsibility for our state of mind. But tell me: What days do you anticipate going into the office? Remember that Robert will be coming on Thursdays."

"Who's Robert?" Carson asked.

Adelaide explained about the boy and then assured me she could do much of her work here at the apartment. "They're making me my own set of copies of the documents. Which reminds me—I need to get a briefcase to carry them; my backpack won't work. Maybe I'll hit Macy's again."

"Their collection's lousy," Carson broke in. "I was looking myself that day I ran into you. You know where you're better off going—there's this shop…"

So now he was an expert on department stores as well as the Scottish courts! While he overwhelmed her with details about this store and that, I went to my office and returned with my own briefcase.

"Your grandmother gave this to me at my tenure party. A trifle weather-beaten and engraved with *my* initials, not yours, but you are more than welcome—"

Adelaide's delight was undisguised. "It's perfect!"

"Nice leather," Carson said, massaging the flap. "*F. W. Jr.* Your father's name was Francis?"

"Yes, but he went by Frank. As a child I was called Frankie—to avoid confusion. Of course, as a young man, I found the moniker a trifle juvenile and reverted to Francis."

Her mouth still fixed in a smile, Adelaide murmured that it looked like something a writer would use and did I really mind if she could borrow it.

"Borrow it? You can *keep* it, my dear. When would I have occasion to use it again?"

"You never know."

I laughed. "Yes, I do know, and the answer is 'Never.' Keep it, with my blessing."

After further inspection, her smile never retracting, she rested her new acquisition on the floor by the vanity.

CARSON DEPARTED, AND WHILE WAITING for the kettle to whistle, Adelaide regaled me with descriptions of some of the absurd claims put forth by impostors hoping to win a share of Violet MacDonalde's estate—impostors who had trumpeted their implausible accusations to the press. One woman maintained that Mary had never actually emigrated to the United States but took refuge in a shepherd's humble quarters on the Isle of Skye, a fabrication easily put to rest by immigration documents. Another claimed to be Mary's grandson by dint of Mary's marriage to a Swiss undertaker in Geneva, an impossibility again put to rest by documents.

And a third contended that Mary had changed her name to McGillicuddy and opened a haberdashery in Vermont. That claim as well crumpled in the face of scrutiny.

Engel Klein paralegals were not without a sense of humor. Their file cabinet drawer labeled *Claims with Confirmed Documentation*—which was empty—had no moniker as yet, but the drawers containing the files of claims still under investigation—officially labeled *Open Claims*—had been dubbed the 'Limbo' drawers. The third set of drawers, officially labeled *Disproved Claims*, was nicknamed 'the Graveyard.'

"Think how many file cabinets—*rooms* of cabinets—would have been required if the MacDonaldes had adhered to the conventional spelling," I observed.

"The proverbial search for a needle in a haystack."

"Violet might not have tried looking for Mary or her descendants, then."

Certainly the unusual spelling proved serendipitous for my granddaughter, providing her with unanticipated gainful employment.

CHAPTER 12

OVER THE NEXT FEW WEEKS Adelaide burned the midnight oil, her attention monopolized by her studies. She refrained from indulging in diversions—not merely the one of visiting ships but of extended mealtime conversations. I flattered myself that she was a 'chip off the old block,' showing the same dedication to career that I had shown at a similar age. The ability to say, 'For the nonce, I will put aside my customary leisure activities to devote all my energies to the pressing tasks at hand,' is a quality essential for achievement.

Fortunately, she was willing to take a break from studying to accompany me to my annual physical examination. Dr. Conti declared my state of health "excellent" for a seventy-nine-year-old, my ankle's recovery from the sprain as complete as it could be. Alas, the muscle or tendon would always be subject to reinjury, both twists and sprains. But if that infirmity were the sole limitation other than mild arthritis, I had much to be grateful for. In light of certain "lab values," the good doctor rebuked me for certain dietary indulgences, which it was his professional duty to do, much as it was my unprofessional duty to meekly listen and ignore his proscriptions.

And before you knew it, Christmas season was in full gear. Adelaide shifted from studying for examinations to taking them.

"HI, DAD, GOOD TO SEE you." Standing in the doorway and clad in a black wool coat and red hat, her face widened in a smile, Olivia momentarily reminded me of Marjorie, although their coloring was so different, my daughter's hair and eyes being quite dark. She hugged me warmly. "Go sit down; I'll just hang up my things."

"How was your flight?"

"Smooth, but the Van Wyck was a mess, and the cabbie kept switching lanes. Go, sit down."

"Are you hungry?"

"No, I'm fine."

We repaired to the living room and stood taking stock of one another. She was dressed in nice—almost elegant—black slacks, a black sweater, and a bright-red scarf. The flush in her cheeks imparted a certain energy above and beyond her usual momentum.

"You look good, Dad—you've put on weight."

"Adelaide takes the credit, I suppose. And *you* are looking well. Not at all like someone who has just endured a cross-country flight."

She laughed giddily, girl-like. "I was able to doze. When does she get back?"

"Around four. It's the last exam of the term."

"Great! And I won't be presenting a paper, so we can have a true holiday." Olivia scanned the room. "I don't see any more changes."

"Not since your last visit. The big change, as you know, was converting the master bedroom into my office."

"And you're still pleased with it?"

We each took a seat: Olivia, on the sofa; I, in my chair.

"Quite."

"And Addy still prefers Richard's room? It's so small."

"The desk and bookshelves are arranged to her liking."

"You still use this old blanket—it's faded. I can pick you up a new one."

"I prefer the old, the familiar. Tell me, how are your sons?"

"My treat, the same color, fabric, everything."

"It's not the expense—I mean it when I say I prefer the familiar, faded or not. You visited your sons, correct?"

"They're doing well. Elliot is totally absorbed in his work—you know: computers. He didn't say anything about a girlfriend, but his roommates are nice. Michael is driving a taxi twenty-five hours a week to pay the bills while he does his sculptures. If that's what you call them. I should say his 'art.' Mostly copper now; some stone. He has to keep them outside. One is the size of my large rhododendron bush. They have a nice community in Taos, sort of an artists' colony. And Patty is six months along, already inflated like a beach ball. She's petite, so it really shows."

Olivia had risen, and throughout this little speech, she strolled around the living room, picking up and putting down various *objets d'art* familiar to her from childhood: the reindeer antler, the ivory letter opener, the glass wren, the tusk dagger. You would never have guessed she was fifty-five or fifty-six—more likely *forty*-five—the way she moved gracefully, with almost a sashay to her step.

"How is your opus coming along?" she asked.

"Oh, the sacred cows I am slaying! The tragic-flaw theory, the protagonist-antagonist theory, the feminists and Freudians and Marxists and deconstructionists—I believe I have never met a theory I didn't dislike."

"That's a lot of windmills." She bent to peer at the photograph collection on the credenza.

"You needn't humor me."

"I'm not. Actually, I'm impressed; you are taking on quite a lot. What's wrong with the tragic-flaw theory?"

I threw my hands in the air in mock exasperation, not at Olivia—for truth be told, we loved literary sparring—but at the simplemindedness of literary theorists. "Did Esther have a tragic flaw that precipitated her orphanhood and later sorrows? Did Tess have a tragic—"

"Some would say Esther's sorrows are pathos, not tragedy."

"Fiddlesticks. The very critics with whom I quarrel. You know I do *not* subscribe to the nonsense that 'all responses to a literary text are equally valid'; there *is* a text—words on the page—and there *is* a reader—whether you label him the ideal or ordinary reader or what have you—whose reactions are *reasonable* in light of the text and, one might say, reasonably anticipated by the author. In that vein, Dickens anticipates our sadness at Esther's misfortunes—no tragic flaw is necessary. As I have said more times than you can count: therein lies the *miracle* of literature. A writer has myriad ways to move us to sorrow and anguish and laughter and knowledge. Why must critics—including your beloved Aristotle—devise these narrow theoretical constru—"

"Tess had a tragic flaw," Olivia said, examining Adelaide's high school graduation photograph. "She was too timid. She only made half-hearted efforts to confess to Angel, which led him to believe he was entrapped. And while I don't necessarily *agree*, some people make the case she had a weakness for lux—"

"Balderdash! Angel deserted her for the simple reason his ego was bruised: because *he* was not the one to vanquish her maidenhead!"

Laughing, Olivia put down the photograph. "Dad, *please* don't use 'maidenhead' in your book. It will peg you as an old fogey."

"I *am* an old fogey. And proud of it, as they say."

She walked to the window and gazed out at the river. "Will you let me read a draft at some point and play devil's advocate?"

"Nothing would please me more."

And I meant it; Olivia was an astute reader. Yet how could she label timidity a flaw? It was part and parcel of Tess's *nature*. People do not share equally in traits, even at birth. Perhaps Olivia was being judgmental regarding that trait because she herself had never known timidity.

All of a sudden, my daughter was sitting beside me, on the green ottoman, tapping my arm. "Dad, do you ever consider not working so hard? You have a long and distinguished career behind you. Why not relax and enjoy the golden years?"

"How can they be golden without your mother?" I quickly added, "Working on my book *is* enjoyable. I am not doing it to pay the bills."

"Enjoyable but demanding. Isn't retirement a time to discover new interests, find fun hobbies, maybe even socialize a little?"

At this remark a laugh escaped me. "John, Millie's husband—down the hall—they enrolled him in some rehabilitation program for his slipped disk. Exercises, you know. But as an adjunct to the physical therapy, they teach the patients crafts. He brought me a sample of origami—oh, we had a good chuckle."

"So crafts aren't your thing. Didn't you start a stamp album with Richard—"

"The commemoratives, yes. It was a way to make history interesting. He took quite an interest until the travel bug—"

"Do you still have the album?"

"I doubt it. No, I do not see myself developing a passion for philately. Or coin collecting. I am not a hobby person, my dear, any more than I am an arts-and-crafts person. Besides, writing my book is more than enough of a daily activity. I see no reason to give it up. I am not—what is the phrase they use nowadays? 'Cognitively impaired'? In my youth, we simply said 'batty.'"

"Just don't push yourself too hard. Or try to meet deadlines."

I made a sweeping arc with my arm. "You deem these working

conditions difficult? Protected from the elements, heated in the winter, cooled in the summer? Comfortable—even luxurious—furniture, surrounded by lovely art. A stone's throw from the kitchen and indoor plumbing. The most arduous part of my day is taking a shower. How can you conclude I am *not* taking it easy?"

My daughter shook her head as one would at a mischievous child. "Stress can be mental."

"I assure you: I have not agreed to any deadlines with any publisher. I have not so much as *spoken* to a publisher. Literary criticism is not a genre that garners advances."

She rose again and paced slowly back and forth behind the long sofa. "I'll warn you, Dad: I haven't given up on convincing you to move to Seattle. Like I've said before: you would have your own quarters—bedroom, bathroom, even a small study. Separated by a hallway from the rest of the house."

"I appreciate the offer, but over the years I have become an unalterable city person."

"Seattle is a city!"

"A *large-city* person, then. The cultural attractions of Seattle, whatever they may be, cannot measure up to what Manhattan, alone, has to offer, almost at my fingertips."

She placed one hand akimbo. "When was the last time you set foot in a museum? Or went to a concert? Twenty years ago? Thirty?"

"Your mother dragged me to some Japanese exhibit at—"

"That's my point—you had to be dragged."

"What would I do in Seattle?"

"What you do here: your work, go for walks. I could take you on drives to many beautiful places: Mount Rainier, the Olympic Peninsula and Hoh Rain Forest, the San Juan Islands. We have two mountain ranges and a bevy of waterways—lakes, Puget Sound, rivers, the ocean."

"A bevy! You always were the poet in the family."

"Just to mix more with people would be good for you." The hand moved from her hip to her other hand, where she fiddled with her rings—the wedding band and engagement ring. She was much too young to be a widow.

Of a sudden, it dawned on me that *Olivia* might be feeling a certain loneliness. Nathan gone now six or seven years, her three children far away, living by herself in a place that had once housed five. The push for me to move to Seattle was not about *my* loneliness but about hers.

Although my daughter's plight tugged gently at my heartstrings, moving nonetheless was out of the question. Aside from the enormity of effort required—packing up books, deciding what to do with the artwork, the furniture, not to mention the contents of the storage locker—in addition to all this, the timing was inconvenient. Adelaide was in the middle of her law studies. Strange as it might seem to an outside observer, my companionship was a comfort, an anchor, if you will—I provided that modicum of human interaction Olivia was so certain people required. And more than once my granddaughter expressed gratitude after she had wrestled in solitude with some thorny homework issue and then found clarity and resolution upon presenting the issue to me. *She* was the one to unravel the skein, but I provided the sounding board. Ah, Francis, what mixed metaphors you weave. Thankfully I stuck to professorial tasks and never fancied myself a poet.

After one more turn around the room, Olivia seated herself on the sofa, again fiddling with her rings. "What are Addy's classmates like?"

"How would I know?"

"They never come over?"

"No, she does not parade them through."

"Does she mention them? Is she dating anyone?"

"Not presently. She has had a young man over to dinner, but I believe she's decided he's rather shallow, in terms of character. And he will be moving away soon." I was tempted to make a Morris Townsend allusion—Olivia would have enjoyed it.

To my astonishment, my daughter again jumped up, resuming her circuits around the room, picking up and putting down objects handled not ten minutes previous. The sway in her walk returned until she once more sat abruptly. She flashed a nervous smile and took a deep breath.

"Dad, I've been delaying breaking some news. I have a rather significant announcement." Her dark eyes glowed intently, reminding me of the preteen Olivia.

"Well, what is it?" As if Marjorie had taken possession of me, I braced myself for the name of a fatal condition.

"I am planning to remarry."

I let out my breath. "Anyone in particular? Or is this simply a general change of mindset?"

She laughed. "Yes, someone in particular. His name's Tony Esposito. He's a clinical psychologist. We met through mutual friends some years ago but only started dating last January. His wife died from ALS."

"A terrible disease."

"Yes."

"Does he have children?"

"A daughter, Rhoda. She lives down in Portland—Oregon."

"I have no glass to raise in toast, but congratulations."

"Thanks."

"How has Adelaide reacted to the news?"

"I haven't told her yet. Just Elliot and Michael."

"So *this* is the reason for the cross-country excursion."

"And to see you all."

"You don't expect some objection from her?"

Olivia considered her words carefully. "I think she'll warm to Tony once she meets him."

So she assumed Adelaide would object. I was skeptical that her carryings-on would have much impact on her daughter. Instead, I asked, "Short for Anthony? Antonio?"

"Antony," she murmured. We shared a smile. "But I'm way too old to play Cleopatra."

Olivia proceeded to fill me in on assorted details. Tony had been raised in Los Angeles but had lived in Seattle since attending graduate school; he maintained a clinical practice, taught at the community college, and served on various professional committees. His daughter's partner was stationed in Germany but due to be discharged shortly. When Tony and Olivia married, they would reside in Olivia's home and sell his. *None* of these plans, she stressed, altered her willingness— nay, her *eagerness*—to have me move to Seattle and live with them. Tony was "completely on board" and looked forward to meeting me. I said I looked forward to meeting him as well.

Our conversation wandered on to other subjects, winding around to Adelaide's job at Engel Klein. I explained that it would become full-time over the summer and it was my understanding that a 'summer clerkship' was the most common route to postgraduation employment.

"She hasn't talked about moving after she graduates?"

"Why should she?"

"I just assumed she was here for school—that New York's not a place she'd want to live long-term."

"Because it displeases you for her to live with me?"

"Why would that displease me? And why the tone, Dad?"

I hadn't been aware of the edge in my voice, but in my answer, I recognized its absence. "Perhaps I believe you see us as conspirators undermining your campaign to move me to Seattle."

"Your loneliness worries me. You've become reclusive."

"One man's reclusiveness is another man's cheerful solitude."

"Cheerful?"

"Relatively speaking, yes. We octogenarians do not express our cheer through exuberance. Of necessity it is a subdued emotion."

"You don't turn eighty for almost a year. Anyway, *some*day you'll have to move. It wouldn't hurt for you to start thinking ahead, to when Addy graduates. Oh, before I forget: How would you feel about my inviting Marcia and Ted and Alex down for Christmas dinner? Not here—we'd go out. I left it vague in my last conversation with Marcia—what days I'd be in New York."

"I have no objection. I doubt Adelaide will."

"Great." Olivia jumped up a third time and strode into the hallway, presumably to telephone her sister.

Returning some minutes later, she announced, "Marcia doesn't want to come here, but surprise of surprises: she's invited us up there. She's eager for Addy and Alex to see each other again. It's been since Mom's funeral."

"That will be nice for you. And I will be content to spend the day quietly here—"

"Don't be silly; you'll come too. She specifically asked if you had any dietary restrictions."

"According to Dr. Conti, quite a few. But Adelaide and I studiously ignore his prohibitions. Just the same, I think you would all have more fun without me."

"We wouldn't think of going without you! And Marcia would be insulted—you'd just be feeding her ridiculous resentments."

WHEN ADELAIDE ARRIVED HOME, SHE greeted her mother with a short hug. Olivia looked at her daughter appraisingly but not without warmth. Some of Marjorie's welcoming nature had been imprinted on Olivia, the unharnessed smile that greets friends and family. My granddaughter apologized for not having any dinner prepared, but Olivia expressed enthusiasm for partaking of our little routine of ordering takeout and said she would accompany Adelaide to pick up the food.

In their absence, I reflected further on Olivia's news. Her remarrying should not have been surprising, but was this Tony a good match? The psychology profession had never impressed me. I would have expected Olivia to choose a true physician or perhaps another lawyer or a fellow professor. But her amatory endeavors were no more my business than my living situation, hers.

CHAPTER 13

OLIVIA CONFIDED IN ME IN a moment alone that she had told her daughter about Tony during the walk to the restaurant, and "on the surface," Adelaide didn't seem upset. "We also chatted about Christmas in the city. *I* chatted, but she seemed attentive. Reminiscing about traipsing in the snow with Mom along Fifth to see all the window displays."

"Richard and Marcia used to go too, as I recall."

"By junior high they thought it was too childish. Mom and I never got tired of it."

"Would Adelaide accompany you on such an outing?"

"She says she will."

At dinner I raised my glass and toasted my daughter's prospective nuptials, and Adelaide joined in happily, confirming my suspicion that her mother's connubial doings were not of significant concern. Olivia talked a little about Tony and their early dating—he had agreed to attend two opera performances if she would accompany him twice to a bar featuring jazz ensembles. The jury was still out on whether either of them would experience a change in musical taste, but each was making a sincere effort at expanding his or her artistic horizons.

Exhausted from a week of exams, Adelaide retired for the night early. Olivia joined me in the living room, where we indulged in a routine from decades ago: I sat in the dark-chestnut leather chair, a journal in my lap; and she sat in the burgundy, a book in hers. The burgundy brocade, with its curved back, was the place she'd preferred to all others for ensconcing her then girlish frame, enveloping it as physically as some author's otherworld was enveloping her mentally.

'Where's Olivia?' Marjorie might ask, and someone would reply, 'Have you looked in her chair?' It did a better job of concealing her than the window seat concealed poor Jane from her brutish cousin.

The two nearby lamps were the only ones lit, the farther reaches of the room veiled in a soft dimness. The sounds of traffic barely penetrated, the quiet broken now and then by the crisp crackle of a turned page. For some people, candles and a fire in the hearth dispel the dark and chill of a winter evening, but having grown up with candles and lanterns for light and only a cast-iron stove and fire in the hearth for heat, I was happy to sacrifice such romantic accoutrements for the comforts of electricity and central heating. The stresses of daily life subsided, leaving me in a lovely calm.

THE FOLLOWING DAY WAS A productive one, on all counts. I penned an entire section on Catherine Sloper's transformation into a swan, if 'penning' may be allowed to include the act of typing. Adelaide and her mother toured the holiday displays along Fifth Avenue, interspersing the activity with Christmas shopping, a short visit to the Metropolitan Museum of Art, and a stop at the grocery store.

That evening's dinner conversation flitted to different topics but, not unpredictably, alit on law. I enjoyed watching Adelaide impressing upon her mother the intricate analyses underlying legal principles, the "thoughtful complexity," as Olivia summed it up.

"The law is not without its ludicrous aspects," I felt obliged to point out. "For example, the jury's job at trial is to be the 'trier of fact.' That means deciding among competing views as to who is telling the truth or had the most accurate testimony. One witness said the vehicle went through a red light; another said the light was green. The jury picks the 'truth.' But consider: these jurors are the very same people who believe all manner of advertising, that some cream will remove wrinkles or an item advertised on television is 'the best money can buy.' Why should a cross section of the gullible public be expected to discern truth-saying in *any* matter?"

ADELAIDE WAS AGAIN THE FIRST to retire in the evening, doubtless still feeling the effects of finals week, and again Olivia and I took our accustomed seats in the living room.

"So was the window tour everything you had hoped it would be?"

"The displays are so much more elaborate now, but they enchanted me as a child: quaint little villages, the railroad, the miniature house interiors. And she let me pick out Christmas gifts for her. I must've phrased it right, because she didn't seem annoyed."

My smile could not be suppressed. "It is good to hear someone else intimate that parenting requires a long apprenticeship."

"Yes." Olivia gazed off at the wall and gave a small sigh. "It's hard not to have regrets. I feel like she got the short end of the stick—that as the third child, she was not exactly *neglected*, but not fussed over. I'm talking about when they were young. Nathan doted on her to the extent he could, but he always worked long hours."

"I can't imagine Adelaide harboring resentments in that regard. Has she voiced any?"

"No. She always seems to accept whatever life throws her way, without expectations. Even more so now. I asked how she liked law school; she said it was 'okay'—not that she *enjoyed* it or found it *fascinating*."

"Is that not par for the course? I assume law school is like boot camp or a medical internship: an experience one simply has to grin and bear."

"I asked about her classmates—they're 'okay.' The professors are 'okay.' At the museum, she was very knowledgeable about Vermeer and Van Eyck and Rembrandt, and I said she must be extremely fond of their work to know so much, but she said, 'Not really.' Did she prefer the Impressionists? No—they were 'okay.' It was her answer for everything!"

Olivia seemed to be working herself into a small storm, and I racked my brain to think from whom my elder daughter inherited a personality prone to intense emotions. Perhaps someone in Marjorie's maternal line. And if Adelaide *were* more laconic than usual, was not the likely cause her having just completed a term's worth of examinations? To then be given the third degree—did I dare suggest that the interrogation itself may have been the problem? Marjorie, you handled these issues so deftly!

"And she doesn't socialize with classmates," Olivia continued to cavil. "She doesn't go out, even to the movies with girlfriends. I asked if she likes certain courses more than others, and all I got was 'Not really.' Everything is just *okay*."

"An eminently satisfactory frame of mind."

"For an old man, yes, but not a young woman. Excuse me; I didn't mean that the way it sounds."

"Certainly you did. I *am* an old man, a fact not of disgrace but of longevity."

Olivia leaned forward. "Life goes on, Dad, even at my age. Certainly at hers. Nathan's been dead over six years. It isn't natural for her to grieve like this still—and her lack of enthusiasm for *anything* is a sign of retained grief. Trust me—I know. She was *quiet* as a child and teenager but had things she was enthusiastic about. Photography, nature—she knew all the plants in the yard and what nutrients they needed, how much water. Trees too."

"Without agreeing that she is inappropriately unenthusiastic, and for the sake of argument conceding that she may be grieving, do not assume it is over her father."

"Who, then?"

"A young man."

"A boyfriend? How serious could it have been? I've never even heard of him."

"Serious enough that they planned on moving into an apartment together."

Olivia frowned—I would even say scowled. Did she resent having been kept in the dark? Or was her distaste from having to imagine her daughter *in flagrante delicto*?

"They started dating early on in their freshman year of college," I explained. "They planned to move in together for their sophomore year."

"Moping over a cad who dumped her five years ago!" Olivia's dark eyes shone.

'Cad' was a word from *my* generation, not far in time from 'maidenhead,' and consequently I had the urge to chuckle. However, the gravity of the situation quickly reimposed itself.

"He didn't 'dump' her. He was killed. He had gone home for the summer—his parents live up in Maine. He happened to be at a lumberyard when a former employee—a man with a grudge, what the newspapers often term 'disgruntled'—showed up armed with a rifle and began shooting wildly. At anyone who was there—customers, employees—it did not seem to matter. Zach, the young man, was among the victims. The proverbial wrong place, wrong time."

Olivia's grave expression no longer seemed angry. "How terrible."

"Yes, and the manner in which Adelaide learned of the tragedy was terrible too. The boy had not mentioned to his parents that he was dating her—for reasons I will expound on in a moment. So they did not know to notify her. She learned of his death from an article in the school newspaper."

"My God! When was this—the summer after freshman year? Two years after Nathan. I had no idea."

"I assume she kept it from you precisely because it *was* just a few years after Nathan."

The scowl returned but had no anger in it—if partaking of any selfishness at all, the scowl signified frustration at being deprived of the opportunity to console. A mother's sympathy admitted of no peer, in Olivia's worldview. Perhaps she was right.

"And since then, not a word," she said. "But she told *you.*"

"Only last month. And only because we became embroiled in a tangential disagreement. About safety. I took the position one should take care to avoid certain neighborhoods, and she argued violence can be random and happen anywhere. And in that context the young man's death came up. Your letter arrived the following day, and since you would be visiting, I thought it better to mention it in person. Yes, she assented to my telling you."

"All I ever heard about was classes. Nothing about a boyfriend."

"I imagine *she* imagined that was what one's mother prefers to hear."

"I was never a prude."

The night seemed to emanate its darkness indoors like a spreading miasma. The windows were black rectangles, and only the area near the sofa and my chair fell within the lamplight, leaving the rest of the room in shadow. The sound of a siren approached, then grew faint. How ironic that a harsh noise should be named after honey-voiced temptresses.

"When I gave birth to a daughter," Olivia said softly, "I thought: Finally, there will be another conversationalist in the family. She's the most taciturn of the three."

"She's *reserved.* 'Taciturn' connotes—"

"Resistance, sullenness, I know. All right, Dad: she has a quiet nature."

"Nathan was reserved."

"His name was Zach?"

"I don't recall the last—or perhaps she didn't mention it. As I was saying, *his* parents, as well, were unaware of their dating."

"He's buried up in Maine? Has Addy visited?"

"The funeral had already occurred by the time the article ran in the school newspaper. And she believed a surprise girlfriend would have proved unwelcome news. Evidently they are quite devout and expected him to marry someone from their church."

"What religion?"

I shrugged—a distinctively Adelaide gesture.

Now Olivia's expression took on a woefulness that reminded me of a Renaissance Madonna, a Da Vinci, perhaps. "Poor Addy."

"Not poor Addy," I snapped. "She pulled herself together, finished college, applied to law schools, moved her belongings here— and is quite a companionable companion. She attends class and works hard. She asks for nothing and takes care of herself."

Olivia recoiled as if smarting from a wound. Truth be told, the outburst took *me* by surprise. I vaguely sensed it was unfair, but anger was roiling inside me, rendering an immediate apology impossible.

My daughter rose and left the room. The paintings, even the furniture, loomed accusingly. Yet Adelaide *had* pulled herself together; she did *not* ask for pity. Sorrows of one sort or another befell us all, yet we had to soldier on, continue to execute our responsibilities.

Some minutes later, my daughter returned wearing her robe. She sat near me. "I apologize for my unkindness," I said. "We were discussing a sensitive subject, and I reacted inappropriately. Let me add this: you have obviously provided a model of strength and perseverance in the face of tragedy, and your daughter learned from you and is following in your footsteps."

"It's okay, Dad. But you should think about whether you're putting too much pressure on yourself. To finish your book." She came over and kissed my cheek before bidding me good night.

I DID REFLECT ON WHETHER I was putting too much pressure on myself to finish my opus, whether I had been laboring under some compulsion that had crept up on me unawares. My verdict was decidedly 'not guilty.' Both interest and effort in the endeavor waxed and waned; rarely did I resist a diversion. I was not driven to write the way Michelangelo was driven to sculpt and paint or the way Beethoven was driven to compose. *Teaching* was my profession, my vocation, my calling. A career in academia is a demanding one, and thus I had devoted a great deal of time and attention to my professorial obligations, a fact that on occasion Marjorie was wont to protest. That my professorial obligations had precluded attention to an in-depth book on literary criticism was to be expected.

Once I had retired, true, I threw myself into the project, but with Marjorie gone and little else on my plate, industriousness was a welcome distraction from loss. *Then* Olivia's concerns might have been well grounded. However, that industriousness had diminished of late; I no longer rose each morning with the single-minded purpose of edifying the human race. Some mornings I was lucky to motivate myself simply to turn on the computer and review the previous day's intellectual peregrinations. Which was not to say I *never* got excited about my book. There were days when I forgot to stop for lunch, being 'on a roll,' as one of my students used to call it. Yet that mindset was infrequent.

Why, then, did I not reassure Olivia that I was, in fact, taking it easy? Perhaps the image of the doddering old man, the feeble invalid unable to contribute to his own keep, nettled. Dependent senescence as a well-earned right was not my watchword, not that I begrudged *others* such a state; I could recall as a young man wishing my parents would partake of more leisure. Unfortunately, they did not live long enough to indulge in these so-called golden years. My mother had reminisced about *her* mother, who apparently managed to survive to ninety—the mind, unfortunately, departing a full decade earlier. Grandmother Mildred may have prompted the first occasion on which I had heard the term 'batty.'

Pride—pride, no doubt, underlay my reluctance to tell Olivia that my writing scarcely merited the encomium 'labor.' Plus, if I were no longer employed in any important work, how easy it would be for her to feel justified in badgering me to give up the apartment, to move across the country, perhaps eventually to be eased into a nursing home. No, I would not go gentle into that good ward!

CHAPTER 14

AFTER TALKING TO TONY ON the phone until eleven thirty, Olivia let herself sleep in the following morning. She was still on her first cup of coffee when Addy returned from the basement with a load of laundry. Olivia followed her into Richard's old room.

"Grandpa told me about Zach. I'm so sorry."

Addy sat on the side of the bed and began folding a dark shirt. "It was a long time ago." She did not look up.

"Four or five years is not a long time."

So many questions Olivia wanted to ask. Did the relationship become sexual? Was Zach her first? Did he love Addy equally, or was it one-sided? Did Addy *consider* calling home when she'd found out he'd died—and if so, what made her decide not to?

Instead, Olivia simply said, "Tell me about him."

Addy reached into the basket and took out another shirt, this one forest green. "What do you want to know?"

"Anything. Was he tall, short, fat, thin? Have a sense of humor? What was his major?"

"Geology." Addy pinned the neckline of the forest-green shirt under her chin and stretched out the sleeves.

"Do you have any pictures?"

"A few."

"Can I see them?"

Her daughter methodically finished folding the shirt and placed it on the dark one before rising and going to the closet. Olivia wondered: *Was* it normal to be grieving four years later—grieving for someone you hadn't known a full year?

Was there a 'normal' for grief? Especially for a lover dying horribly and so young?

Better pass boldly into that other world, in the full glory of some passion— God, Joyce was a fool. And yet it *was* better to have loved and lost. Even to have loved unrequited. Olivia couldn't remember the exact words of the French saying, but it was something to the effect of *There is one who kisses and one who holds out the cheek.* True of many relationships but not all, not all. And if you *were* in a slightly uneven relationship, better to be the one who kisses. Young women didn't realize that—they thought happiness was in being the beloved.

Addy sorted through photos in a shoebox and handed a slim stack to her mother. The first three were just scenery—woods or small grassy areas surrounded by woods. Then came one with a green tent and a slender, pleasant-faced young man. Light-brown curly hair, T-shirt and jeans. The next photo was the same, but he smiled more broadly. *His poor mother.*

"Where were these taken?"

"Allegheny National Forest."

"Have you been in touch with his parents? Grandpa said you'd never met."

"I phoned, back when I heard, and someone took a message, but they never called. It's a long story, but I didn't find out what happened till a while after the funeral."

"Grandpa said."

"They're very religious—some Christian Science offshoot. He had to push to go to a regular college, even after getting a full scholarship."

"So he wasn't as religious?"

"*They* hadn't been—not when he was young." Addy sat again on the bed and resumed folding laundry. "Not till his older sister OD'd."

"Oh! Those poor, poor people."

"They thought it was some kind of divine punishment on them, so they joined this very strict church."

Olivia peered closely at the boyish smile, the lanky arms. Maybe it was good his parents found a deep faith. "So you never contacted them after that—you never wrote?"

"Zach never told them we were going together. I wasn't sure they'd want to meet me."

Olivia gazed at her daughter's bent head. "Have you stayed in touch with your college friends? Did any of them hear in time to go to the funeral?"

"No, I'm not in touch with anyone. Mostly we hung out with guys in his dorm. I didn't know them that well."

Maybe she'd misperceived her youngest child all these years—maybe Addy never formed close friendships. Yet she hadn't been a loner—she was included in groups going to movies and sleepovers and seemed to get along with everyone, just as she did at home. But Olivia couldn't remember a *best* friend, someone you talked to for hours. Was Zach her first best friend?

"I'm so sorry for all this, Addy. What a terrible thing—for him, for you, for everyone who cared about him. I'm not sure what to say—just that you *will* recover from your grief. That's not the same as forgetting—you'll never forget him."

Addy was pairing socks and rolling them up. "I'm not really grieving anymore. Like you say, remembering is different."

"Yes, it is. And hard as it may be to believe, you will someday fall in love again."

"If it happens, it happens."

Olivia bit her tongue. *You need to let defenses down so it* can *happen—so you don't scare it away,* she wanted to say. She placed the photos on the desk and with effort made her tone matter-of-fact. "Changing the subject: Does Grandpa ever go out, other than his occasional 'constitutional' around the block? I mean to a concert or the theater? Or even to dinner? Who are his friends these days?"

"He writes to people."

"He never meets an old colleague for lunch? For a drink?"

"He chats with neighbors." In the process of putting the folded shirts in a dresser drawer, Addy didn't catch her mother's look.

"When we were kids, he was always going to department events, dinners with students or former students, other faculty. He and Grandma had subscriptions to the theater."

"His arthritis bothers him—his hips."

"Yet he can walk six blocks for a pastrami sandwich!"

Addy scooped the balled socks from the basket and put them in the bottom drawer. "Not recently—he sprained his ankle a few months ago, and it's taken a long time to recover."

"That's aging for you. But I doubt he has real arthritis—he'd be in a lot more pain. He's been finding excuses for everything since Grandma died."

Addy shut the dresser drawer and looked up at her mother. "What was she like?"

"You remember."

"I remember when we visited—her going crazy hugging us."

"Marjorie Burstingstar, Grandpa called her. 'Let them come inside before you smother them to death.' She was always like that: warm, affectionate. Played the peacemaker when we fought—me and Richard and Marcia. Or when Grandpa was cranky. It was too bad she was from a generation that wasn't encouraged or allowed to pursue careers."

"Did she want a career?"

"I think so. She wasn't a stupid woman by any means. Before I forget, I want to fill you in on some minefields to avoid at Marcia's—things that will start an argument between Grandpa and Marcia. The trust or whatever it's called, for one thing."

"But it's from Grandma's side."

"He's the liaison—the one the trustee consults before paying for something. They send us each a letter a few times a year explaining the payments—like your tuition—but informally they talk to him first just to see if there might be a problem. Grandma used to do it. Anyway, there's a long history of tension between Grandpa and Marcia dating back to childhood, and now it's exacerbated by an argument over the funds. He refused to support Marcia's request that the trust subsidize Alex's first years as a sales trainee. The equipment is complicated, so Alex had to learn a lot before they could send him to do demonstrations. But the trust specifies payments can only be made for 'educational' expenses."

"It was a job, though? Alex got paid?"

"Yes, he drew a salary, not a stipend. Marcia's argument is that he's entitled to reimbursement because his education was on the job—his first two years at the company were like business school, just hands-on, a hands-on education."

"But if he was paid a full salary, not at some internship rate—"

"A salary and sick days and two weeks' vacation. Not as much as he's making now, of course. But he got a raise."

Addy put the empty laundry basket in the closet. "What does Francis have to do with it? I haven't studied trusts, but the little I know, the trustee has to follow the terms that are written. They can't go by what Francis thinks."

"You're right—Grandpa has no legal authority, and he doesn't tell the trustee what to do. It's just that they discuss it before the trustee actually makes the payment. It's meant as a courtesy—Grandpa then tells the rest of us before we get the official report."

"So if the trustee doesn't care what Francis thinks, why does Aunt Marcia?"

Olivia shook her head. "She doesn't believe that Grandpa has no sway."

"Besides, if the trustee violated the terms of the trust and disbursed funds to Alex, he—the trustee—might end up liable for the money if any trust beneficiary decided to sue. I'm not really sure—like I said, I haven't taken a course in trusts yet—but anyway, it seems completely irrelevant what Francis thinks."

"Marcia had her own lawyer look at the documents. He claims there's wiggle room if the employer uses certain categories—'apprentice' or 'intern,' like you say. But they'd have to ask the employer to change Alex's job title—what do you call it? Retroactively. But the trustee didn't go along with it. And Marcia's convinced it's because Grandpa said not to."

"It's not only *us* who could sue," Addy said. "Any of our heirs too, if the trustee violated the terms. I'm not saying we—"

"*Now* no one imagines it, but Tony says people feel differently when things go bad. What if the stock market crashes like in '29? A member of the family counting on the funds for school and then learning there isn't enough left—even *harmonious* families can fall apart in stressful circumstances."

"What about harmonious families?" Francis smiled genially from the doorway.

"I was just telling Addy to avoid mentioning the trust at Marcia's."

"Ah, the trust. Marcia puts the blame squarely on me, Adelaide, although I have no legal authority *whatsoever*. The trustee makes the decisions. In any event, perhaps it is time you all ousted me from the position of family liaison. It was your mother's doing, Olivia, my taking it on, but I really should not play any part in it."

"We'd never agree on a replacement, Dad." Olivia turned to Addy. "Francis would approve paying for any *legitimate* school—academic *or* trade. Virginia went to culinary school. Aunt Marcia is just being silly—she claims Francis is refusing because it's *her* child." She whispered so Francis wouldn't hear. "This isn't about the trust—it's unresolved childhood issues."

"Is she hard up for money?" Addy asked.

Olivia laughed. "She should be, the way she spends it. No, they're not hard up. Ted's an orthodontist in suburban Connecticut. And her beef about the money is just one beef among *dozens*."

"In Marcia's book, Adelaide, I was a distant and unloving father. She doesn't understand that I grew up in a time when working long hours was what fathers *did*. Hard work, in those days, was the primary manifestation of love for one's children, one's family. No one expected more. My own father could barely muster suppertime conversation. Playing games—physical affection too—would have defied his comprehension."

"Marcia's good at holding grudges," Olivia said.

"About the only thing Marcia has *not* accused me of, Adelaide, is cheating on their mother. A professor does not lack for opportunities to cheat, I should mention."

"Would you like some tea?" Addy asked. He nodded, and she sidled past him in the doorway. Olivia said she would go put on coffee. Francis, looking lost in thought, didn't step aside for her.

"I am reminded of an incident at a faculty cocktail hour some years ago," he said, smiling at the floor. "A young assistant professor— who, by the way, was quite attractive—she delivered quite a declamation against pornography—a veritable tirade, it was—to those of us gathered round. *Playboy* and the other magazines were a degradation of women. In jest I responded that pornography deserved some credit for saving many marriages: better that the mind should wander than the body. Such a shrewish look she threw me!" Noticing now the thin stack of photos on the desk, he went over and picked them up. "What are these?"

"You never saw them? That's Zach."

"She never showed me."

"You never *asked*?"

"Why would I pry?"

Olivia moved to the door and quietly closed it. "Dad, I'm curious: Does Addy ever seem afraid? Living in New York is a strange choice for someone who lost a loved one to violence. *I* grew up here, but she grew up in Seattle, which is ridiculously tame in comparison."

"She's not the one who's afraid. I told you we had an argument— her trekking up to the Bronx last summer for her job. *I* was the one who worried. Thankfully, her position there ended, and her job next summer is in Manhattan and in a vastly safer neighborhood. But as I mentioned, she voiced the opinion that violence is the luck of the draw; it can happen 'anywhere to anyone at any time.' Naturally, I rejoined that, as you suggest, different regions and neighborhoods have different crime rates, an indisputable contention. I do not recall exactly how the conversation then progressed, but it came out about the young man."

Olivia rested a hand on the doorknob. "Do you mind if I use your phone to call Elliot and Michael? We can wish them Merry Christmas tonight. With the time difference, I don't want to call in the morning."

"By all means. I cannot approve charging the calls to the trust, you realize."

ADDY WOULDN'T RECOGNIZE SEATTLE, OLIVIA told her daughter at dinner: construction was everywhere downtown, old-time businesses had closed, new ones were cropping up. Nathan's cousin Ruthie had gotten married, and his nephew Donald had had a bar mitzvah. No firm date had been set for her and Tony's wedding, but it would be in February.

"We have room for all of you. Elliot has volunteered his old room for Rhoda and Pat, and he'll take the futon sofa. Dad, you'll have a bedroom *and* bathroom to yourself."

"That would be quite an excursion for me. Perhaps it will suffice if Adelaide is my representative."

"Nonsense! The airports have wheelchairs that can take you from the entrance right to the plane, and we'll meet you with a wheelchair in Seattle."

Francis smiled off at the wall. "I am reminded of Grandfather Smallweed, always carping to have his position in the wheelchair readjusted. *Shake me up, Judy.* But the house will be crowded. Your sons and Tony's daughter—"

"It will be fine."

"And Marcia and her family. Do you recall when you were young, Olivia, Marcia shouting at me that I was a 'stuffy old professor.'"

"Vividly. I said she should be glad you weren't always correcting our grammar the way Miss Goldman did—our English teacher in junior high, Addy. Good grammar was the holiest of holies; literature was secondary."

Francis raised his fork in the air. They watched him swallow. "Among literature professors, I rank as one of those *more* prone to grammatical errors. And as one with more limited vocabulary. You look skeptical. Indeed, a dictionary is my constant companion. Perhaps that is why I remain in such awe of wordsmiths like Henry James. And I cannot shake certain grammatically-incorrect phrases that we commonly used during my childhood. When I was still teaching, I felt compelled to employ a student to proofread each syllabus before it went to the printer's. Stuffy old professor!"

"You're not going to restart old arguments tomorrow, are you?" Olivia said.

"The sobriquet 'stuffy' implies an elitism, insinuates that I hold myself above others. Nothing could be further from the truth. Good heavens—consider my origins, growing up on a farm and knowing hard work since the age of four. Yes, four, gathering eggs and other simple chores, and by the time I was eight, I was bringing water to the cows, chickens, hogs. At ten or eleven, milking the cows. Every spring, the job of feeding the newborns fell to me: the calves and piglets. That would be *before* heading to school.

"My point, Adelaide, is that anyone who has done farm chores has engraved into the core of his character an enormous respect for those who continue to perform such work. Farm labor is not for the lazy or squeamish; it requires physical exertion and endurance and fortitude. Even a form of courage, I might add. Especially to a child, the vicissitudes of weather and unpredictability of animals can be quite frightening. So my invocation of humble beginnings is no Uriah Heep hypocrisy."

"Dad, would you like some peas?"

"There are peas too? Yes, I'll have some. Quite a little feast—I may not require any Christmas dinner tomorrow."

"Marcia's a good cook," Olivia gently chided. "Don't exacerbate tensions by not eating when you're there."

"What tensions?"

ELLIOT WASN'T HOME WHEN OLIVIA called. She reached Michael and after a few minutes handed Addy the receiver.

"Good luck tomorrow," her brother said. "You remember how obnoxious Alex is—he can run *faster* than anybody, throw a football *farther*, beat anyone at arm wrestling."

"That was when we were kids."

"A tiger can't change his stripes."

CHAPTER 15

THE DOOR WAS WIDE OPEN before he reached the landing. Carson stepped across the threshold and kissed his sister on the cheek, wishing her Merry Christmas.

"Come on in." With her usual crisp grace, Lucy took the wrapped box and placed it on a nearby table and held out her hand for his coat. Her hair, pulled back into an elegant clasp, was dyed darker than usual, and the color set off her pale complexion, as did the wine-red blouse and matching slacks. Real velvet.

"Finally, a day off!" she said.

"I'm racking up overtime, so I don't mind."

Carson sat on the foyer bench and removed his shoes and left them neatly in the row beside the six or seven pairs of heels and flats. At the far end were black boots he recognized as Cole Haans. He rose and surveyed the living room appreciatively. The stylish furniture; the tall, broad windows; the deep-green drapes blending in with pale-pink, green, and white upholstery fabric gave an impression of modern, feminine elegance. Matching chrome lamps on the matching glass end tables could've been a furniture store display.

He wriggled his toes in the plush pale-green carpeting. "Pretty swanky place—I can see why you moved."

"It goes into the bedroom—come look. The only thing I don't like is being half an hour from my salon."

They proceeded single file down the freshly painted hallway. Even in stockinged feet, Lucy moved briskly.

"Aren't there any closer?" he asked.

"I won't give up my girlfriends—the gals who do my hair and the gals with the same Friday slot. Lovers come and lovers go, we say, but your girlfriends are always there for you."

"They're all single?"

Her bedroom was larger than Carson's living room.

"Two are, but husbands come and husbands go." Lucy flashed a smile. "They're a hardworking group and lots of fun. Leanne is a travel agent, and Denise started out as the manicure girl for a *very* wealthy lady—you'd recognize the name. Ashley double-dated once with Harrison Ford."

Carson turned his attention to the row of teddy bears lined up against the pillows. Some were a foot high in a seated position; others were small enough to be cradled by a toddler. Among the shades of brown was a powder-blue with a jockey cap and a red one sporting a black-and-white checked bow tie.

"Is the bowler guy new? What size mattress is this, Luce—a king? You'll probably land a king one of these days."

"He's not exactly a king."

"What, then?"

This smile was coy. "I'll tell you after lunch. Yes, the bowler's new—a gift. You see his cane? Come, let's eat."

On the way to the dining room, Carson paused to read the names of the magazines fanned out across the glass coffee table: *Glamour, Cosmopolitan, Star, True Crime, Vogue, People.* A tabloid-size newspaper blared the headline "BERMUDA TRIANGLE CLAIMS NEW VICTIM."

"Don't tell me you want to read one of my 'trashy mags,'" Lucy called from the doorway.

"I didn't know people still believed in the Bermuda Triangle. I guess the UFO crowd eats that stuff up."

"Not the *real* one—this Bermuda Triangle's south of the Finger Lakes. Women vanish without a trace—they find the cars but no bodies. Three of them, in thin air—poof! You want soda?"

"Water's fine."

The dining room was separated from the kitchen by a white tiled counter, a better setup than in her old apartment. Carson recognized the linen placemats from an upscale competitor's 'Danish' collection— probably manufactured in China from a German design.

"Nice appliances."

"You like them?"

He stepped back into the dining area and looked at the platters of bread and cheeses and cold cuts and salad—undoubtedly fresh from a deli, a good deli. He filled both glasses with ice water from the carafe. When his sister set down the soup tureen and took her seat, he sat too. Raising glasses, they toasted Christmas and the New Year.

"I've got some good news," Carson said. "Next month, they're moving me to Men's Casual."

"What you wanted!"

"Close enough. And I'll help in suits, get my foot in the door."

Lucy's hand with the oven mitt, holding the tureen top, stopped midair.

"Raise?"

"Small but decent."

"That *is* good news. I hope your new manager will be more sympathetic about your schedule."

Carson picked up the ladle. "Already is—he's working on his MBA."

She nodded knowingly, setting the tureen top carefully on another plate.

"When you get your degree and move among professionals, you'll see—your coworkers won't resent people wanting to get ahead."

He was about to say that they'd misunderstood the meaning of 'carpe diem'—he'd looked it up in the dictionary after dinner at Addy's and found it meant grabbing at the *present*, not at life generally. But it had become their motto.

He filled Lucy's bowl and handed it to her. "How's your job? Any chance of another promotion?"

"I don't want another one. I'm happy exactly where I am. The pay's good—I get the exact same as people who finish college. They let me work four ten-hour days and take Fridays off. *And* respect the job I do. That's all I ask. I never wanted upper-level management. Too much responsibility."

He filled his own bowl. "Unfortunately, in law firms, the only job security is making partner. Up or out. Six, seven, eight years you spend crossing your fingers."

"Wouldn't the odds be better at a smaller firm?"

"Sure, but you have to take on more administrative tasks. Like personnel. I'd have a hard time firing someone."

Swallowing, Lucy waved the hand without the spoon. "No you wouldn't—not slackers."

"An *obvious* slacker, maybe not, but what about someone who tries but just can't make the grade?"

"You're doing them a *favor*. It makes them find a job they can do well."

"Still, I wouldn't like it."

Lucy passed him the cheese platter. When he returned it, she used short, quick movements to spear the slices and move them to her plate.

"That's why you never would've made it as a teacher, Car—punishing is not in your bag of tricks. Admit it."

He carefully poked a cherry tomato with his fork; the tines went into the skin without the juice splattering. "Lawyers get paid more—I'll admit that."

"I know a teacher—in *high* school, not elementary—and she can barely cover the basics: food, rent. Forget a real vacation or dinner at a nice restaurant. And if you had little mouths to feed?"

"I don't have regrets, Luce; law's interesting and, as you say, pays the bills. Or *will* pay the bills."

"Speaking of paying bills, have you heard from Louise lately?"

He chewed carefully and drank some water. "No. You?"

"Wednesday."

"How much did you send her?"

"Sixty. I now get *all* the utility bills, so she can't pull crap like they're shutting off the water."

"She tried telling me they're raising the rent."

"Make her prove it."

"Didn't have to—the lease prohibits hikes before July. Then she tried some bit about if she paid cash, they wouldn't raise it next year."

Mid-chew, his sister laughed, quickly covering her mouth. "Did you tell her you'd mail them the cash directly?"

"I wasn't buying it."

Again, he glanced around at the furnishings, nodding approvingly. "It will be nice to have my own place."

"You said you never wanted to live alone."

"That was when I had decent roommates. These two are slobs."

"Living alone has advantages. You pick the furniture, the dishes, sheets, towels—you're the boss."

When Carson was done eating, he folded his napkin and set it on the table and leaned back in his chair.

"So, how's your love life?" Lucy asked.

"What love life?"

"You're not dating?"

He leaned forward and picked up the glass and gently rotated it, watching the water swirl. "Yes and no. Says she's not ready for a relationship."

"*That* line."

"I don't think it's a line."

"What's she like? What's her name?"

"Addy, Addy Cohn. Was in my study group last year. Quiet but really nice."

"You mean gorgeous."

"You might not think so."

Arching an eyebrow, Lucy speared the last tomato dead-on with her fork. "*There's* a change. Why isn't she *ready* for a relationship?"

"I'm guessing her last ended badly."

"You never did tell me why you and Gloria broke up."

"The usual: mutual lack of interest."

Lucy shot him her suspicious look. "She got tired of waiting for you to pop the question?"

"I can't keep secrets from you."

"No, you can't. So what's the attraction with this supposedly unattractive Addy?"

"She's not unattractive, not to me. I ran into her at Macy's and spur of the moment asked her out—more to be friendly than anything. We went for coffee, then she invited me to dinner with her grandfather—she lives with him. By the way, we're in the wrong professions, you and me. Her great-great-grandfather invented some little gizmo that goes in a train motor, became a multimillionaire, and the trust fund he started back in the 1800s is *still* paying out. And it's not a small family—she's got brothers and cousins. It pays for everybody's education."

"And you criticize me for dating men with money!"

"The fund just pays for school—she's not rich. After she graduates, she'll be a working stiff like the rest of us. Though without debt."

"Why don't you date someone else in the meantime—until she's ready?"

Carson cradled the water glass in both hands. "I don't know. There's just something *different* about her. *Genuine.*"

This time Lucy made no effort to cover her mouth. "Genuine? Keeping you at a distance and won't say why?" She rested her fork. "It's probably because you're not Jewish."

"Her mother isn't. They celebrate Christmas."

"*Everybody* celebrates Christmas."

The irony hung heavy over both of them, and neither spoke for several minutes. Gray clouds moved swiftly past, darkening the sky. It was cold enough for snow. He wouldn't mind a thick snowfall on the train ride home. Simultaneously the siblings rose and began to clear the table.

WHEN THEY SETTLED IN THE living room with their coffee, he said, "Now tell me about *your* love life."

Lucy nestled against a cushion, her stockinged feet drawn up on the sofa.

"My love life just *had* to see me last night. But I can't tell you his name."

"Married?"

"Not just that—a judge."

"Jeez, Luce—he'll never leave her."

"No, he won't—he said so."

"Then it's just to pass the time? You could end up in over your head."

"Already am. It's only been a month, but we see each other every chance—he's *very* good to me."

Carson carefully set his cup back down, not knowing what to say. Talk about a situation built to end badly! And she, of all people...

"*Very* good." Lucy extended one arm palm down and studied her nail polish.

"*Now*, but what about in ten years?"

"He deposited two hundred grand in a bank account in my name—my name *only*."

For a second Carson was too stunned to speak. "What happens when the press finds out about the mistress slush fund? His wife can sue to get it back."

"It's from the sale of stocks he owned before his marriage—it was never hers. I had my lawyer examine everything."

Lucy was proud of her achievement, he could tell, and expected him to be impressed. Maybe he was, but he was also bothered. What if she fell for someone else: Could the judge demand she return it all?

"The bank account was his idea," she said. "I told him I worried about old age—what if something happened to my job—and *he* suggested it. And for as long as we're together, he'll deposit the dividends from the stocks he's held on to. He really does love me."

Carson nodded absentmindedly. It wasn't hard to imagine a middle-aged man—even a young man—falling passionately in love with his sister. She was pretty, dressed with style, and lacked the timidity and clinginess that often made men lose interest in mistresses. Falling in love even to the point of establishing a—he smiled to himself—*trust fund*. But why didn't he feel glad that she had secured her future above and beyond her decent pension and savings?

"I know what you think," she said. "That it's built to end badly. But I don't think so." She held out her other hand to admire the polish. "Time will tell."

"Is the money worth giving up marriage and everything?"

"His wife gets the ring and family, true. Which is all she wants, in my opinion. She's cold potatoes in the sack." Lucy turned toward the windows. "I don't need the ring and family. He's kind and sweet and treats me well—it's not just about hopping into bed. I *am* fond of him, I really am. And having a good job, nice apartment, and great girlfriends—what else is there? Not kids—you know that."

"People change."

"It was different for me."

He didn't need reminding. For a moment they were silent.

Then she said, with a gaiety that wasn't entirely forced, "I'll be a wonderful aunt. I'll give lovely presents."

"I'm not proving much of a success making you one."

"Ditch the JAP. Find someone new when you get to California."

"Don't call her that." He could have said more, would have liked to, but the heaviness of having cost Lucy her childhood weighed on him. He would never forget her arms cradling him to sleep.

CHAPTER 16

TRAFFIC WAS LIGHT CHRISTMAS MORNING, and the cab took Park, so for a few minutes Addy savored the quiet Sunday feel of the sun-filled boulevard. The stone and marble building facades, their entrances swept and tidy, were decorated in colored lights and wreaths, and red potted poinsettias dotted the sidewalks. Marcia had called to warn them it had snowed in Connecticut but only a few inches. Addy and her mother kept it a secret from Francis, who was fishing for an excuse to stay home.

They were plenty early for the train. Once he was reassured they could walk slowly, he seemed to get a kick out of being in Grand Central. "Despite living within a stone's throw," he told Addy, "I haven't been here for years. There are changes, yes, but so much is still the same. The glittering chandeliers, the constellations above, the shiny floors, all the marble and brass, the archways and balustrades—it evokes a sense of magnificence. Even at rush hour, when thousands of people are hurrying hither and yon, this chamber emits a regal splendor."

Her mother leaned close and murmured, "It's a shame he never got to see the Parthenon or Notre-Dame or Rome, so many other places. Grandma wouldn't fly, and he didn't feel right going without her."

The train was pretty empty. Olivia sat with Francis, and Addy put the shopping bag with the presents on the seat beside her. Once they emerged from the tunnel, the city turned gritty: old brick buildings with zigzagging fire escapes, shabby stores and offices, graffiti-filled playgrounds. The Harlem River looked green-gray in the morning light. The Bronx was dismal too: miles of tenements, soot-stained factories, burned-out buildings.

"Pelham," the conductor shouted. What a contrast: spacious lawns, trees, shrubs, nice houses. Mount Vernon, New Rochelle, Larchmont—the names had become familiar during Addy's year and a half in New York, but she'd never been up this way. Not far past the Connecticut border, a light layer of snow covered the yards. By the time the conductor called out "Norwalk" and they were in the city itself, only the cars parked in shade had snow on their roofs.

The other passengers rising to get off were nicely dressed, but nothing about them suggested the high society Carson had talked about. Maybe families like his used some kind of livery service or had a personal chauffeur who took them everywhere.

The platform had been shoveled and sprinkled with something crunchy. Aunt Marcia emerged from a large fancy car and gave a small wave. Olivia, all smiles, waved back, and Addy, her mother, and Francis continued at their snail's pace, Francis leaning on Olivia and murmuring about his ankle.

"I thought you'd send Alex to get us," Olivia said, hugging her sister.

"You think I can't drive on a sprinkle of snow?" Marcia's eyes were dark like Olivia's, but her hair was lighter, and she wore it fuller.

"I thought you'd be busy in the kitchen."

"The roast is in, potatoes peeled. I made the squash casserole last night—it always tastes better reheated. We're not eating until two—more than enough time to throw together a salad." Marcia hugged Addy. "Can't remember when I last saw you. Too many funerals for one family. Hi, Dad. You're looking good."

"'Flattery will get you nowhere,' as they say."

"Yes, well, why don't you climb in. Give me that."

Marcia took Addy's shopping bag and put it in the trunk, and Addy helped Francis into the back seat.

"I'm looking forward to seeing your new house," Olivia said.

"New? We've lived here six years."

"Do you have a long driveway?" Francis asked.

In the rearview mirror, Marcia's eyebrows were furrowed. "Long driveway? No."

"Is it gravel?"

"It's paved. What possible—"

"He's worried about his ankle," Addy said. "He sprained it, and it took forever to heal."

"We have a door from the garage directly into the house," Marcia said drily. "You won't have to take a single step outside."

"That's quite reassuring. In September, poor Adelaide had to be my legs for a number of days."

"Only two days—you got a crutch."

"A poorly constructed one."

In no time they were on winding roads, passing through woods and alongside fields. Norwalk was rural, not suburban, Addy thought, the lots being so large. A stately white colonial was followed by a Hansel-and-Gretel cottage and then a red-brick townhouse with wrought-iron railings, all of them well maintained. Francis also seemed absorbed in the scenery. He hadn't mentioned needing to use a bathroom.

"I don't regret the move," Marcia was telling Olivia. "Norwalk's a nice area, though Rye was closer to things." She pointed to a one-lane road. "My friend Betsy owns three horses. And the Larsons have an Olympic-size pool. Of course, Westport is where Paul Newman and Joanne Woodward live. Weston and Wilton are smaller and don't have *any* poor neighborhoods, not that *I've* ever seen. Norwalk's older—has a real downtown and all that goes with it." She took one hand off the steering wheel to gesture. "Why am I complaining to *you*—you *like* cities."

"Every place has its pluses and minuses."

"There will be six of us at dinner—Mindy isn't coming. Her stomach's upset."

"They've set a date?"

"Not yet. She's nice enough and not too nice, if you know what I mean. You're always hoping your kid will reach a little higher. He's technically in sales, but he has to know how everything works: TVs, radios, sound systems, those little portable things the kids carry around. And be able to explain it to the customers. Electronics are *complicated*. Anyway, somebody's got to be home minding the kids. Unless you want to toss them in day care and don't mind how they turn out."

Olivia forced a smile—Addy remembered how proud her mother had been when her committee was able to offer grad students more childcare options.

"So what's new with everybody?" Marcia called into the back seat, turning the car so sharply up a steep a hill that Francis gripped the armrest.

"I'm the one with the big news," Olivia said. "I have a beau—a man I've been seeing, and we're getting married."

Marcia looked over to see if her sister was joking. "Good for you! What's he like—besides smart?"

"His name's Tony. His wife died a few years ago, and he has a grown daughter—"

"What does he do? For a living, I mean."

"He's a clinical psychologist and teaches at—"

"Our family sure could use one. Does he do the whole couch bit?"

"You're thinking of psychoanalysis. He does a different kind of talk therapy."

"Already you lost me. But you're happy, right?" Again, Marcia looked at her sister.

"Yes."

"Maybe I should remarry too," Marcia said as though seriously considering it. "Maybe I could shoot Ted. Of course, divorce is safer. But so darn expensive."

They drove along a winding road and after a few minutes pulled into a driveway leading to a wide pale-brick house with gleaming white shutters. The front lawn was large, and where the sunshine didn't hit, it had a silvery sheen. A stone birdbath stood in the center. Off to the side was an arbor, just a weave of twigs now, and a wrought-iron bench. Carson's phrase 'old money' came to mind, but the house wasn't a mansion, and the property didn't look large enough for things like stables, just maybe a tennis court or pool in the back. As the nearer of the two garage doors rose up automatically, Marcia stopped the car and turned off the motor.

"The path's dry—let's go in the front."

The air smelled of pines, and the sky above the treetops was a nice blue. Bits of deep green in the ivy and frost-hardy bushes broke up the brown of the lawn and bare tree trunks and leafless shrubs. Addy took a deep breath and held in the fresh, cool air.

Ted greeted them when they came in, hugging her and Olivia and shaking Francis's hand. Her uncle hadn't changed much since Addy had seen him at her grandmother's funeral—he had a kind of bland handsomeness.

"Let me take coats. You're all looking great. I'll give the grand tour when you've had a chance to relax. Addy, you were how old when I last saw you?"

"Seventeen?"

"It's been that long? You look nineteen!"

Marcia ushered them into the living room, a spacious area with nice furniture. Olivia murmured, "This is beautiful," adding, "it should be featured in *Better Homes and Gardens*." Marcia rolled her eyes but was obviously pleased.

"I would not mind using the facilities, if I may," Francis said.

"I'll show you," Marcia told him, "while the rest of you fill Ted in on the wedding."

"Wedding?" Ted looked at Addy.

"I'm remarrying," Olivia said.

"Congratulations! Who's the lucky guy?"

While her mother talked about Tony, Addy meandered around the living room, which was less cluttered with knickknacks than Francis's. The paintings on the walls were Constable-like landscapes of river valleys and woods.

"Alex should be back any minute," Marcia said, coming in.

Francis reappeared and asked if it would be possible to have a short nap "in some out-of-the-way location? I slept quite poorly last night. I don't know why."

"You can use the guest room."

"And where is that? Are there many steps?"

"No steps, relax."

"I'll show him," Ted said. "I'm going to duck into the den for a few minutes to get some bills paid before I start on the wine. Who knows what mistakes I might make—a decimal point here or there could put us in bankruptcy."

HER MOTHER AND AUNT TOOK their coffee to the far end of the living room. Addy sat on a bench set in the recess of a bay window and paged through a yachting magazine.

Marcia's voice traveled. "Is Dad getting dementia or what? He acts like he's *ninety*-something, not seventy-whatever."

"Seventy-nine. Addy says his ankle injury took forever to heal, so he's always worried about re-spraining it."

"Does he get to be that liaison thing until he dies? Or until he starts losing his marbles?"

"We don't know if he *will* lose his marbles."

"If he does or dies, you become it, right?"

"Only temporarily—until we select someone else."

"Richard doesn't want to—he's never in the country. Where is he anyway—Istanbul? I haven't seen any of them since Mom's funeral. His kids are such brats."

"Copenhagen. I get a Christmas card—that's all."

"Well, you should know I'm considering challenging Francis—his refusal to pay Alex any kind of tuition equivalent. I've already taken a copy of the papers to Ted's lawyer. Your kids and Richard's have gotten several hundred thousand dollars, if you add it all together. Why should Alex be left out?"

"Look, *I* didn't write the rules. Dad didn't either. Go argue with our great-grandfather. And you're free to contact the trustee or whatever he's called. Why do you have to bring this up today?"

"I'm mentioning it to *you*, not him. Maybe before you go back to Seattle, you can cram some reason into his skull so he won't oppose us when my lawyer goes to the trust people."

"All he ever does is give his honest opinion when they ask. He's no lawyer and has no power—they decide it. I think he'd be *relieved* to get out of being liaison. The only reason he agreed to do it is because Mom asked him."

"Asked? She pleaded. Though why she had to—"

"He didn't know how sick she was."

"He *should've* known—he lived with her, for God's sake."

"She hid it," Olivia said, a little more softly. "From *all* of us."

Olivia had cried openly at Nathan's funeral and then at Grandma Marjorie's. And lots of times afterward. Sometimes a routine task like opening the drapes in the morning would start her. But Addy had never seen her mother quietly sad like she was now.

"You remember how grumpy he always was. How is that love?"

"He can be a curmudgeon, sure, but who doesn't have moods?" Olivia fiddled with her rings.

"*Mom* didn't. What's the point of talking to you—you'll defend him no matter what."

"That's not true. I admit he can be curmudgeonly. But he can also be friendly. Mom saw that side of him. So did I."

"It's *my* fault I didn't? He never showed it to me!"

"Look, you and Richard have some legitimate complaints. Dad wasn't perfect. Still, he and Mom had a strong marriage."

"She was a saint as far as I'm concerned."

A car door slammed, and moments later, Alex came in wearing a royal-blue parka. He walked with that side-to-side stride Addy associated with athletes.

"How's Mindy?" Marcia asked as everyone exchanged hellos.

"Threw up twice."

Olivia squinted sympathetically. "Does she have the flu?"

"Don't worry, Sis—it's not contagious. A bun in the oven. I'm going to be Grandma Marcia in July."

"Why didn't you say!" Olivia beamed at both Alex and Marcia as both she and Addy gave congratulations.

Through Alex's back-and-forth with Marcia, Addy learned that he and Mindy would be moving soon to Queens or Staten Island because his company was transferring him to the flagship store in Manhattan, and he didn't want an hour-and-a-half commute.

"You working?" he asked Addy. "No, I forgot, you're in law school."

"I'm working part-time at the firm where I'll work over the summer."

"What kind of cases do they have?" Marcia asked.

"A variety. Some wills and trusts and—"

"Trusts?" Marcia clapped her hands gleefully. "Maybe *you* can become our liaison."

Addy shifted in her chair. "It should be someone who can't receive any benefits so there wouldn't be a conflict of interest."

"You won't be getting money after you graduate," her aunt said.

"Yes, but someday I could have kids—they'd be beneficiaries, or potential. It's just better if someone totally impartial does it."

Marcia rose and picked up the empty coffee cups. "Like Francis is impartial?" She headed toward the kitchen. "Your mother has always been his favorite, so whatever she asks for, she gets. She hasn't had to deal with getting turned down."

Alex quickly picked up the *TV Guide* and leafed through it. Olivia looked at the floor.

When Marcia returned, Olivia told her, "If you had more than one child, you'd know that *all* siblings see parental slights that aren't there—it's normal rivalry. Elliot and Michael and Addy may have had different senses of who was favored and who wasn't, but I have always loved each with all my heart. I wouldn't even know how to measure and compare."

"Cute speech, but Richard agrees with me."

"Dad and I just have more in common."

"*Mom* loved us equally. What did she and Richard have in common?"

"Dad would be crushed to hear you say he didn't love us equally—you have no idea."

"It would bruise his ego—he'd finally have to admit he isn't perfect."

"You think he thinks he's perfect?" Olivia peered at her sister, then looked away as if mulling something over. "Perhaps for your sake more than his, forgiveness would be a good thing."

"*My* sake! What a laugh. I'm going to make the salad. No, I don't need help—why don't you socialize. Alex, you can bring out the cheese rolls for everyone to nibble on. And tell your dad if he chops some of that cord, we can light a fire later."

CHAPTER 17

THE CREAM-COLORED TABLECLOTH WAS FAR more elegant than anything Addy's mother ever used, and the silverware, too, was fancy. Marcia took the candlesticks away, saying that with all the sunlight they didn't need them. Ted opened a bottle of wine, something red.

Francis looked refreshed, subdued but not unhappy. Ted kept them all amused with stories about teenagers and braces, and Olivia reminisced about Michael losing a tooth when he "briefly, thank God," played ice hockey in high school. Marcia goaded Alex into describing catching a winning pass and breaking his arm in the end zone. People quizzed Addy about law school and whether it was as bad as in the movies, and she said not really.

"The law and academia operate from very different perspectives," Francis chimed in. His description of some of the cases she'd studied forced her to clarify a few things, but when he switched to stories from his time teaching, she was able to get lost in thought.

But again her aunt's voice grabbed her attention. "He wrote a whole book about *that?*"

"There was more to the novel, to be sure, but the nature of the hero's injury played a pivotal role. The student missed it entirely, and I did not relish being placed in the position of having to explain—"

"You should've said he wrote that kind of thing," Marcia told Olivia. "I thought it was all snooty stuff. Mindy gave me one with a sexy picador. I'm done with it—you can take it on the plane."

"I'm in the middle of *two* books right now—I can't start a third."

"Then when you get home. She doesn't want them back." Marcia finished her second glass of wine.

"Bodice-rippers," Ted said.

"Honestly, I have a stack of books waiting to be to read, Sis. I don't want to add any more."

"Your loss."

Ted turned to Addy, "I thought there was no disputing taste—what's the Latin?"

"*De gustibus non est disputandum,*" Olivia said.

"That's never been the rule in the Wallace household!" Marcia smiled and asked no one in particular, "Why am I starting an argument about books with two English teachers at the table?"

"It might surprise you to know, Ted," Francis said, "how unsparingly harsh writers can be in critiquing fellow writers. Henry James hated Dickens's work; Tolstoy pooh-poohed Shakespeare. To my mind, both Dickens and Shakespeare excelled at the forms they chose, which admittedly were not the same forms that James and Tolstoy chose. What makes a work of art great, I used to tell my students, is not the absence of flaws but the presence of virtues, of things of value, of *worth*. Yes, Dickens gives us melodrama and a frequency of coincidence straining plausibility, but we do root for Oliver Twist and Nicholas Nickleby and David Copperfield and Pip; we shed tears for Esther and Flo, and laugh ourselves silly at Pecksniff and Micawber. You cannot employ an identical measuring stick for different types of works."

"Then what makes the books *I* like so terrible?" Marcia asked, smirking behind her glass.

Olivia said quietly, "Just because Dad and I think certain books have more value, more to offer, *doesn't* mean we think people who read one kind or another are better or worse people."

"If you want to talk about *value*," Marcia shot back, "let's talk about my gardener. What *he* does has value. Up on that ladder pruning for *hours*—the size of those trees! And the work that goes into clearing the undergrowth. I don't know what kind of lawns you have in Seattle, but—"

"They're certainly smaller than—"

"We have three acres! Ted, tell her about the beavers—what they did by the creek. Roderigo dealt with *all* of that, hauled away the branches—three runs in his truck! Our sycamore died—I couldn't get my arms around it, it was like a pillar. His brother helped—they chopped it down, dug up the humongous roots, and loaded everything. That's *value*."

"But who pays the gardener?" Ted asked. "I hope you don't think my time at the office isn't important."

"I'm just saying that before we go patting ourselves on the b—"

"Certainly no one can dispute," Francis said, pausing in cutting his meat, "the valuable function gardeners and other manual laborers perform for society or how arduous their toil. But to suggest that reading and understanding literature is somehow a *frivolous*—"

Olivia patted his arm. "Dad, no one's saying it's frivolous—"

"Hell no—pardon the French," Marcia said gaily. "Entertainment is what keeps us going. Is it the Jehovah's Witnesses who ban dancing and singing and everything fun? I'm the last to complain about fun. Ted, open the chardonnay—the zin's too sweet."

"I think it's the Adventists," Alex said.

Keeping his eyes on the tablecloth, Francis continued, "Literature is not mere entertainment. It is an important, worthwhile pursuit. It *teaches*."

"Mom's talking about fiction."

Francis looked puzzled. "Fiction is truth delivered through poetry."

"I didn't realize you specialized in poetry," Ted said cheerfully. "I thought you were a novels man. One of my patients wants to be a poet. I told her to find a rich husband."

"I distinguish between poetry and *poems*," Francis said. "You are right: I did not teach poems. But poetry can arise in any form of fiction. Shakespeare's plays are poetry. Not because of the rhyme and meter—although many adhere to schemes common in poems—but because of the way he uses language. You understand the difference between *de*noting and *con*noting?"

Ted laughed. "You got me there—no—"

"*De*note is to give the spare meaning of a word—what one might call the dictionary definition. *Con*note is to infuse words with more than literal meaning—to impart tone, aura, music, value, memory, allusion. Instead of the *Tomorrow, and tomorrow, and tomorrow* stanza, Shakespeare could have written simply, *Time passes too quickly, and we die and become nothing*. But what a barren statement that would have been! It imparts nothing of the dismal blend of emptiness and regret Macbeth is feeling, the senselessness of human strivings, the relentless march of time, the imminence of death. But Olivia is the Shakespeare scholar here."

"I'm on vacation," she said. "The food is delicious. What's in the potatoes?"

"Shallots, garlic, enough butter to drown an—"

"So I use the term 'poetry,' Ted, to mean the use of language in any nonliteral way. That includes not only the works of traditional poets—Blake, Wordsworth, and the like—and of the dramatic poets, such as Shakespeare and Milton—but also novelists. Dickens, Conrad, Hardy, George Eliot—they were all poets to me."

Marcia said to Addy and Alex, "We're about to get the poet-and-soothsayer speech."

"*Truth*-sayer," Olivia whispered.

Francis continued to address Ted. "A great writer is both truth-sayer and poet, truth-sayer and poet. He shows us truths about ourselves and the world through story and an alchemy of language."

"That's a contradiction in terms," Alex said. "How can it be the truth if it's fiction?"

"It is only a contradiction," Francis answered, "if you are expecting the truth to be revealed through reportage. Certain truths are better illuminated through story, fictional story. Olivia, I recall the paper you wrote in high school—"

"Really, Dad? Are you going to embarrass me?"

Marcia leaned toward Addy. "I doubt he remembers my *appendicitis* in high school. Taken to the hospital in an ambulance."

"Your paper on *Lord of the Flies*, if I recall correctly, had as its central thesis that the book conveys to the reader the horrors of violent mobs—something to that effect. And you were right. Among other things, the book puts us in the shoes of the hunted in a society run amok. And does so in a way that a newspaper account cannot."

"Why didn't you become a writer, then," Alex asked, "instead of just a professor?"

"My imagination is *impressionable*—I am easily captivated by an able writer's creation of another world—but it is not *creative*. I cannot conjure up fictional worlds. Better I should play the role of 'torchbearing outrider' and 'interpreter'—those are Henry James's terms."

"Saved by the bell!" Marcia cried out. The hallway phone had rung, and Ted rose to answer it.

"But to return to your question about truth," Francis said to Alex, "literature gives us facts that history books omit. If you want to understand what it was like to actually *live* during the eighteen hundreds, for example, you are better off reading Jane Austen's novels, not some historical treatise. If you want to know what it was like to go away to sea, read Melville."

Ted's normally soft-spoken voice carried from the hallway. "Is it bleeding? Wrap ice cubes in a towel and hold it against the jaw. Do you have someone who can drive you to my office?"

Marcia said to Olivia, "Like clockwork. It's a holiday, Ted gets a call—an emergency that can't possibly wait."

Ted strolled back to the table but remained standing behind his chair. "There have been a lot lately. I'm sorry to have to run out like this. Save me some dessert—no one's German chocolate cake competes with Marcia's."

"Lately?" she said. "Try two years."

Ted addressed those on each side of the table. "Most orthodontists want to be the only game in town. I wish there were *more*—then the emergencies would be spread around." He looked at his wife. "But our income would take a hit."

"Go, go—don't jeopardize our income." Ted took his plate and glass to the kitchen.

Alex asked Addy, "Do you watch the Seahawks? Sonics?"

"I don't really follow sports. I used to play soccer but don't even follow that."

"I played soccer a couple of years—we made it to the championships. But I liked football better. Played varsity."

"He couldn't have done basketball instead so I could've watched games *in*doors."

"Ma, you know I'm too short."

AFTER THEY'D CLEARED THE TABLE and Addy and Olivia helped load the dishwasher, Marcia said she had a splitting headache and would go upstairs to lie down "for twenty minutes, max." Alex was absorbed in a football game on TV, and Francis seemed content reading a magazine, so Addy asked her mother if she wanted to go for a walk. Surprised, Olivia immediately said yes.

The frost covering the lawn when they'd arrived had melted, but the air was still cold. In Seattle, grass stayed green in the winter—here it was a brown stubble. Beyond the birdbath, at the end of the lawn, was the woodpile. Addy could barely make out the neighbor's house through the thick woods.

The street was a quiet offshoot, the houses set far apart and surrounded by large shrubs and groves of trees, giving the feel of a wilderness. The only sounds were rustlings in the leaves and underbrush, the crisp air and sunshine adding to the calm beauty. Addy and her mother walked in the middle of the sidewalk-less asphalt.

"This is such a lovely area," Olivia said, "but too isolated for me. Grandpa wouldn't call this isolated—not compared to where he grew up."

"What were his parents like?"

"I don't remember. I'm sure they must have visited, maybe when I was a baby. I was young when they died."

"You never visited them?"

"No, we never went to Indiana. I always had the impression—I don't know if it's true or not—I always had the impression that they didn't like my mother."

"But she was so friendly."

"There was *some* tension."

Addy bent down and scooped up a pine cone. Were close families the exception, not the rule? Carson's family wasn't close. Zach never would have moved back to Maine. And look what Mary MacDonalde's parents had done.

Around the bend they passed another house, a nice brown clapboard that blended in with the bare-branched woods. The road rose and dipped, and they went up a dead end, coming upon old railroad ties. Addy couldn't imagine a train barreling through this silence.

ALEX WAS BY THE SIDE of the house chopping wood when Addy approached. Olivia gave him a little wave and went indoors. The logs already cut were split lengthwise and stacked loosely, the inner pulp a dark butterscotch.

"I can help carry them," Addy said.

"Nah, it's no big deal."

"After I graduate and get a job, I'll pay you the equivalent of half my tuition, the amount I'm taking from the trust. It will have to be over time, maybe a few years, because—"

"Forget it." He raised the ax with both hands and brought the blade down hard on the block of wood. The cracking noise and shards of pulp shooting into the air startled her. "He can do anything with the money he damn well pleases. What pisses me off is he's insulting *her.*"

Pressing his boot hard on the cleaved piece, Alex maneuvered the ax blade back and forth until the halves broke completely. The innermost part was a dark rust. Did that mean it was too moist to burn? Addy remembered a time camping when the fire crackled loudly, and her father'd said it was because the tinder was too damp. Alex bent over and grabbed one of the halves and tossed it aside. He used his boot to position the second half.

"I'd feel better sharing," Addy said and started toward the house. She couldn't tell if she heard him correctly, if he'd muttered 'Like I'd take it?'

CHAPTER 18

OLIVIA'S DEPARTURE FOR SEATTLE, MARKED as all loved ones' departures are by that sense of Time's inexorable passage, insinuated a silver lining into its cloudy melancholy: Adelaide and I resumed our routine. Our first guest-free morning, I spent several productive hours at the computer weaving a thread of "thwarted ambition" through the works of Conrad, Dickens, Hardy, and Eliot. Pip and Jude affected the reader so differently; the same could be said for Eustacia and Miss Harleth.

Upon entering the kitchen for a cup of tea, I found my granddaughter in the process of storing the dried dishware in the cupboard.

"Mom's visit went okay, don't you think?"

I concurred. "But tell me: How do you feel about her remarrying?"

"Good."

"I, as well, see nothing to fault. Of course, we do not know Tony, but they are hardly children."

Adelaide put on the kettle. "You heard they might honeymoon in Kenya?"

I sat in my accustomed seat at the table. "No, I hadn't. That must be Tony's idea. Paris, Vienna, or London would be more to your mother's taste." Was I wrong about who would wear the proverbial pants in the marriage?

"Actually, she's excited about it. Though I guess you're right—it's a change. She didn't go on most of our camping trips."

"Having grown up on a farm in the years before electricity, I confess to being mystified by the allure of 'going camping.' I have no desire to revisit such primitive experiences."

Adelaide opened the tea-bag canister—a quaint tin of Marjorie's originally containing French hard candies, if I recalled correctly. "Don't you sometimes miss being surrounded by nature?" she asked.

"If I did, I could walk to Central Park. Yet growing up on a farm *formed* me—molded me in ways that urban environments have never altered. I learned the importance of hard work and of pulling one's own weight. Of not shirking responsibility or succumbing to lassitude. And my upbringing allows me a perspective about characters in literature often lacking in literary scholarship. In fact, I was addressing just such an issue recently, in a chapter in my book—my 'opus,' as your mother teasingly calls it. Have you read *The Return of the Native*? Well, no matter—I can explain my point."

My granddaughter cocked her head in that way signaling curiosity, so I did not fear boring her. "The story concerns a young woman from a vibrant seaport who is compelled by circumstance to move in with her grandfather on a rural and remote heath. Quite the opposite situation for you—New York City is a vibrant seaport and hardly rural or remote. In any event, to Eustacia, the young woman, such a desolate and unpeopled landscape is tantamount to exile. She grieves over her separation from city life, from theater and literary discussions and musical recitals. Not to mention a society of others likewise drawn to intellectual and cultural pursuits. On the heath, her neighbors are farmers, sheep ranchers, itinerant peddlers."

The kettle began its murmuring just as I rose from my chair. "Allow me to read a passage to you. I won't be a minute." I repaired to my office as swiftly as my ankle permitted. "Ah, here it is," I said, sitting back down. "This is Eustacia's plaint, the articulation of her intellectual loneliness, and I quote, *But do I desire unreasonably much in wanting what is called life—music, poetry, passion . . . and all the beating and pulsing that is going on in the great arteries of the world?*"

The kettle whistled, and while Adelaide filled our cups with hot water, she agreed that solitude could "be hard on people when it's not their choice."

"And amplifying the wretchedness of Eustacia's plight was the expectation that in time she would stifle all personal ambition and longings in service of her role as a dutiful wife." I wagged my finger playfully. "Thomas Hardy was a feminist long before it came into vogue. But he has been misunderstood—his *heroines* have been misunderstood—which is what brings me to my point. In an early scene in the book, a party is given where mummers—who were essentially actors—will be performing a skit. Gatherings of this sort were infrequent—as I said, this was sparsely settled countryside with little in the way of entertainment. Eustacia was not among the invited guests, but being keen to attend, she persuades the mummers to allow her to don a boy's disguise and join the troupe *incognito*, as it were."

My granddaughter brought the cups to the table and sat across from me. Having her full attention, I continued.

"A former colleague wrote an essay condemning Eustacia's disguising herself as a boy and mummer, calling it a form of *rebellion*. She was eager to violate social boundaries, he claimed. *Rebellion* he termed it! Yet nothing could be further from the truth! Light-years from wanting to *rebel* against society, Eustacia yearned to *join* it, was *ravenous* for it. Don't you see: from his perspective, arising no doubt from his upbringing—I believe he was from Boston—my colleague failed to perceive an essential element of Eustacia's spirit. She was starving."

I pondered whether to mention my colleague by name when I took aim at his contentions in my opus. Marjorie was firmly of the opinion that only those people with whom I agreed should be explicitly named in print—those with whom I disagreed should be referenced along the lines of 'Some scholars have argued.' I understood her reasoning: written criticisms sting worse than spoken.

"Yes, my dear, to those in rural isolation, even something as unrefined as a school pageant or poetry recital presents a diversion impossible to resist. When I was growing up, everyone within a ten-mile radius who could manage the transportation attended our school events, be it by automobile, horse-drawn conveyance, bicycle, on foot—the rain proved no impediment. Of course, the pageants were always held in late spring, long after the snow had melted, although the mud could be troublesome."

How exciting it was, at seven years of age, to be initiated into that privileged group of pupils charged with readying the room for the performances! On hands and knees, we scrubbed and buffed the floorboards until they shone like yellow marble. The lower room was converted into a makeshift backstage, the desks pushed up against the outer wall, and the inner wall, separating the two classrooms, lined with desks on which we arranged props, costumes, and copies of the readings. The two Indian headdresses had more than a hundred feathers each, the younger boys fighting among themselves and pleading with the teacher for a chance to wear them. We had navy-blue cavalry uniforms with gold-braided cuffs and brass buttons, mutton-sleeve gowns and corsets, elaborately plumed hats. Someone had donated a large bearskin that was utilized for a wide variety of animal roles. Smells of glue mixed with the smells of paints and turpentine. The potbellied stove was covered with a red-checked cotton tablecloth and held the water pitcher and cups for any performers whose throats were rendered dry by stage fright.

By the shores of Gitche Gumee,
By the shining Big-Sea-Water

The telephone rang, and Adelaide rose to answer it, taking the receiver into the hall.

Once the rooms had been readied, we hurried home for supper and returned with our families in tow. Daylight would persist another few hours, but the angle of the sun's rays cast an aura of evening. The lanterns we used as stage lights glowed yellow, leaving the rafters and upper reaches beneath the slanted roof indistinct in the penumbra. So important I felt, leaving my parents behind among the others in the mere audience, while *I* passed through the jury-rigged drapes into the lower classroom.

And as the murmuring grew louder, signifying the arrival of more people, our sense of excitement grew. None of us looked the way we ordinarily did, either by virtue of being costumed or clad in church clothes. I recalled the Shelby twins in braids just like Heidi wore in the illustrations. Jacob Meyerdorf sported a sombrero for the Alamo siege reenactment.

Fiercely the red sun descending. Something-something *along the heavens.* Parting the curtain and stepping out onto the makeshift stage, I was stunned by the number of faces! During my moment of terror, they seemed to smile as one. Every seat was occupied; people on the benches squeezed close. Those standing in the back, too, watched expectantly. Miss W., off to the side, nodded, which was my cue. And the clapping afterward—a resounding thunder.

"Was that your mother?" I inquired as Adelaide returned to hang up the telephone.

"Someone from Engel. The MacDonalde case notebook is ready for me to pick up. It has all the background information."

"I have been reminiscing about the recitals of my youth, poems by John Greenleaf Whittier and Longfellow, even Sandburg, who was at the time quite modern. I always garnered a great deal of applause, but that may have been more in appreciation of my eagerness to perform than any oratorical talent."

"I'll probably go soon—to Engel."

"And yet I never considered a career in the theater. For one thing, it was not deemed honest work. Of course we were quite mistaken. But of no moment; before long, my sights were aimed elsewhere. And academia provided a deep sense of fulfillment I could not have foreseen."

"I should be back in an hour."

"And I believe I can state with utter confidence that the world did not suffer on account of my forgoing a career in the theater. Indeed, I may have performed a public service by selecting a less visible profession."

CHAPTER 19

THE TABLE OF CONTENTS LISTED a timeline, photographs, a *Summary of Physical Traits*, and the dates of Mary's letters to Violet. Many of the tabs for the letters contained the notation *NR* for 'not relevant,' meaning they wouldn't help in finding Mary or her heirs, so Addy wasn't supposed to waste time on them. The second-to-last tab in the notebook was labeled *Inves* and contained the investigation reports Violet had ordered. The last tab was Violet's obituary.

The *Summary of Physical Traits* looked like it had been drafted in Scotland and annotated at Engel. At the time of emigrating, Mary was five six and her weight was *9 stone 12*—someone had handwritten in parentheses *138 pounds.* She looked thinner than 138 pounds in the photo, but that was taken before she'd gotten pregnant. *Blue eyes, light-brown hair, left-handed. Singing voice high alto.*

Behind the tab for the first letter was a photocopy of its envelope, the postmark blurry. *Miss Violet MacDonalde, Grier House, Glynnis-on-Tay, Scotland.* The capital letters had small flourishes, making them a little hard to read. Had Violet watched for the carrier and intercepted him before her parents saw the mail? Or had their parents known that the sisters corresponded? In small villages like Glynnis-on-Tay, was the mail actually delivered, or did you have to pick it up at the post office?

The timeline ran from January 1904 to October 1913. According to the first footnote, most of the information on Mary's whereabouts came from her letters, not the investigators Violet had hired. The second footnote said there were only two official documents: an immigration record and the ship's manifest. These established that a Mary Agnes MacDonalde, age fifteen and a citizen of Scotland, sailed in a second-class cabin from Glasgow on 4 January 1904 on the SS *Empress of Wales.* The *Empress* docked in Lower Manhattan on 11 January 1904, letting off the first- and second-class passengers. Joe had told Addy that typically only those in steerage were ferried to Ellis Island for inspection, but according to her first letter to Violet, even though she'd had a second-class ticket, Mary had been required to join the third-class passengers on the ferry. The letter didn't say why—maybe Mary hadn't been told.

The page after the tab labeled *Immigr* looked like it had been photocopied from an old yellowed chart that had originally spread across two pages.

SS EMPRESS OF WALES

MANIFEST OF ALIEN PASSENGERS FOR THE UNITED STATES IMMIGRATION OFFICER AT PORT OF ARRIVAL

The columns below were long and narrow and filled with dense writing—Addy had to squint to read the headings. *Name, Age, Sex, Married or Single, Occupation, Citizenship*—she couldn't make out the ones near the page crease. The final right-side columns were titled *Height, Hair Color, Eye Color, Birthplace*. The footnotes summarized what Violet and the estate solicitors had learned.

Although the immigration records indicated Mary would live with and work for a Mr. and Mrs. Thomas Ferguson in Aracoma, West Virginia, Mary had gone with a Dr. Beebe to upstate New York. The envelopes Violet received until 1908 bore a Clopes, New York, postmark. *Clopes, south of Syracuse in Onondaga County, lost most of its residents during the Depression and ceased as a postal designation in 1938.*

Despite having learned that Mary had had a son named Brian, the early investigators were unable to find a record of the boy's birth or any baptismal, confirmation, or school records for a Brian MacDonalde or for *any* MacDonalde.

They did locate a cemetery where Dr. Beebe, his wife, two sons, and a granddaughter were buried—the most recent tombstones dating back to 1922—but found no living, related Beebes or any other person mentioned in Mary's letters when she lived in Clopes. And they came up empty looking for marriage licenses, driver's licenses, and death certificates for Mary and Brian.

In 1908, when the boy would've turned four, Mary moved clear across the country, to Washington State, of all places—not to Seattle but the town of Wapato, near Yakima in Eastern Washington. A Mr. and Mrs. Fredric Williams, who owned a fruit orchard, hired Mary as governess for their three children.

Addy took her uncle Richard's US atlas off the shelf and leafed to the Washington page. She had gone through the Yakima area on a camping trip with her father and Michael and now found it hard to imagine fruit orchards thriving in the dry, rocky yellow-brown hills. Maybe somewhere in the Yakima River valley there was rainfall or irrigation, but she remembered only high prairie and desert, a harsh, dust-covered, treeless country. The weather could be as brutal as anything in the Midwest: nasty winds and sweltering heat in the summer and nasty winds and bitter cold in the winter.

In the fall of 1913, Mary left Wapato, planning to return to Clopes. She made it as far as Spokane, where, in October, she mailed the last letter Violet ever received.

Did something awful happen—did Mary and Brian die on the trip back east? Or was Carson right: the sisters became estranged, and Mary stopped writing? Did Mary send letters that Violet never received?

The typed versions of the letters were much easier to read than the copies of the handwritten because Mary's script was sprawling yet compressed a lot into a small space. The first letter, mailed from New York, was written on the ship, and because it was labeled *NR*, Addy only skimmed it.

Sea calmer & appetite back. Breakfast ate porridge, plaice, ham, toast & marm… Our section nice but stateroom small. 6 of us, 3 bunks. They are all Finns. Littlest sleeps above me… Their soap odour makes stomach worse… We reach America tomorrow. I will be glad for land. Why do many young men yearn for sea?

The second letter, labeled *R*, was dated *25 Feb 1904*. Addy wasn't sure exactly what in it was considered relevant to finding Mary.

In Clopes in north New York state. State big as all Scotland. Find Syracuse in atlas & look 30 miles SE. Kind gentleman on ship, Dr. Edw. Beebe, asked me be children's governess. W Virginia rugged & no place for lady. Family helped during my convales. The city New York is 200 miles away! Picture 100 Edinburghs together & 10 times higher. Saw my first Coloureds, Dr. B calls them Negroes. Many have skin lighter than your photographs. They wear clothes like ours & no strange pins or face rings…

Much more snow than Glynnis. Winter not as dark, true blessing. The children love to sleigh. Beebes have two boys and two girls. Mrs. forgives my foolish mistakes. Their gallon smaller than ours & I questioned milkman. I do not like hair styles. Purchased three ribbons from my wages, green, red, and your favourite brodie blue. I see no tartans except Campbell & Gordon. Lost thistle pin on ship and look for another.

Both letters were signed *Your loving sister Mary.*
Addy read just a little of the letter dated April 1904, tagged *NR.*

Spring has come. I want to go into town… Morgan would make quite a fuss if asked to sweep parlour. No rules here, if they had butler, would be made to shoe horses!

At some point the sign-off in the letters changed to simply *Your sister Mary.* In late 1907, she wrote, *I cannot match your letters in length. By day's end, I am too tired to hold the pen. But we are well enough.*

The second letter labeled as relevant was dated in May of 1908 and began with Mary's new address: *Williams Ranch, Parker Heights, Wapato, Washington, US.* Mary gave no reason for moving. All the subsequent letters sent from Wapato were labeled *NR.* The final letter, the October 1913, mailed from Spokane, said only that Mary was leaving Washington and heading east, probably to Clopes *because it is familiar.* The reason for the departure was simply *Circumstances.*

The paralegal's summary behind the *Inves* tab said that during the 1920s, Violet's investigators had located and interviewed five people who had known Mary or may have known her. However, their information was vague or else had to do with Mary in Wapato. Those who may have known Mary or her son after 1913 lived in upstate New York not far from Clopes, which was encouraging, except that none actually knew her personally or were even sure of her or her son's names.

Out of curiosity Addy paged back to the early letters from Wapato that were labeled *NR*—she wouldn't bill her time. The Williams's house was *quite fancy yet use well water* and *Mrs W like Mrs. Shelby but without double chin. Keeps good table, quite proper.* The orchards were irrigated by ditches and grew a variety of fruit: pears, cherries, apples, and peaches. The entire household became involved in picking *except Mrs.* The cherry trees must have been taller than the others because when Phyllis climbed too high in the oak tree, Mr. Williams had to *fetch the cherry ladder.* Phyllis was the middle child; the boy, Jack, was two years older; and the youngest was named Julia.

Addy found some of the descriptions interesting.

From ranch we can see valley orchards. Hills opposite called Rattlesnake Range. More dangerous than adders. Also coyotes, like Celtic shepherd but wild, & mountain lion. Mrs W won't go walking, Mr W & Jack go everywhere. Bushes called sagebrush, very dry, Mr W says why many more stars at night. Jackrabbits big as hares.

To Addy, the letters from Washington were more enthusiastic than the ones from Clopes. It was sad, though, that Mary never mentioned Brian. Wouldn't Violet have wanted to know how he was doing, what he was like? Wouldn't Mary's parents? Or did the fact that Mary was adopted keep them from caring about a child they'd never met?

Though Joe had told her to get up to speed on Mary's relevant history, Addy wasn't sure the notebook had told her much. She felt guilty even billing for half an hour.

CHAPTER 20

THE RECTANGULAR SHADOWS LOOMING ACROSS the river and Roosevelt Island signaled the sun was close to setting. I returned to my chair just as Adelaide joined me, dinner on her mind, I presumed—it was certainly on mine.

"Have you begun studying for next term's classes? You look weary."

"Just reading for the MacDonalde case." She sat on the sofa—one might say *collapsed* on it. "Luckily, someone typed up Mary's letters, because her handwriting is a mess. And most of what she writes isn't relevant to tracking down heirs. Things like differences between Scotland and here—the trains, the size of farms and houses and rooms, different words we use for things."

"Even if not, strictly speaking, relevant, Mary's idioms and colloquialisms, the ways she expressed herself, could be quite interesting. Even *charming*. Yes, the legal profession and academia operate quite differently. Scholars do not recoil from tangential byways. How much material must you digest?"

"It's hard to say what I need to know until I start reading the questionnaire answers and documents."

"Questionnaires?"

"I told you: that's how we vet the claimants. The questionnaires ask basic stuff like 'What's your date of birth?' and 'Where do you work?' and then things like 'How are you related to Mary?' And we ask for copies of driver's licenses and birth certificates and death notices, records like that."

"Those inquiries seem appropriate to the task at hand. The lawsuit in which I was almost deposed is another story. I was required to fish from my files materials that no one in his right mind would ever care to read: notes from tedious faculty meetings, calendars, memoranda— all assembled and copied and collated and sent to stupefy who knows how many people. Why should any human being have to expend a single *minute* of his precious life on God's green earth learning that on such and such a date, I met with a graduate student at three, an undergraduate student at three thirty, and attended a faculty meeting at four—a faculty meeting the substance of which I could not possibly recall? Proust's prolixity has been decried, yet the trees felled to keep his oeuvre in print serve the cause of an important literary experience.

"In any event, if you should find your mind benumbed in the course of reviewing all these materials, I am more than happy to provide modest assistance—for example, by combing Mary's letters for details that seem irrelevant to you and your colleagues but which might carry significance to someone closer in age to her."

"Thanks; I appreciate the offer, but I'm not allowed to share the information with anybody—Mary's letters or the claimants' information. It's all confidential except for the parts that are made public by the Scottish firm."

"Whom would I tell?"

"That's not the point. I'm not *supposed* to."

A smile undoubtedly animated my countenance. "I am reminded of how, during my years in academia, *I* was accused of being a stickler for rules. However, never did I advocate adherence to rules for their own sake—outside the confines of the War Department, of course. Ideally, rules serve a purpose. And much of the time, society functions better if we habitually observe them. But have I never jaywalked? Inadvertently littered and then not retraced my steps to retrieve the discarded wrapper? Paid a compliment that was not God's honest truth? No, like all but the most saintly, I have strayed over the line. Never in ways causing serious harm, I would like to think. No, Socrates was never my model as regards obedience to rules. I would *not* drink hemlock in deference to an unfair verdict. Nor can I honestly predict that I would drink hemlock in deference to a *fair* one." No slight pivot toward me to acknowledge the humor—instead, Adelaide rose and went to the windows.

"Let me ask you this," I said. "If I were, say, your husband, could you share the information with me, in light of the spousal privilege? And are you sure there is no grandfather-grandchild privilege? Well, I will not burden you with assurances of my ability to maintain confidences. But perhaps there are newspaper articles I could review for a fuller picture of Mary's travels and whatnot?"

At this remark, Adelaide turned with a wry smile. "The newspapers are *filled* with misinformation."

"Perhaps that is a boon to you all: it will lead claimants astray; they will postulate scenarios that could not possibly be true."

"That's happened."

"Such claims presumably end up in what your firm refers to as the Graveyard drawer?"

"Yes, but we haven't said so publicly." She resumed gazing through the pane.

"In addition to reviewing questionnaire answers and records, will you also be interviewing claimants?"

"I don't know. Joe has associates and another law student working on the case."

"Well, as I said, if I can be of use in any way—even as a sounding board—please do not hesitate to ask."

ON THE FRIDAY BEFORE SCHOOL was to resume, Carson prevailed upon Adelaide to visit a museum exhibit on wooden ships. I was relieved to learn he would not be able to visit with us afterward. Her absence that day, alas, subjected me to a temptation beyond my powers to resist—Eve stood more of a chance against the serpent.

Adelaide's room was dim, the only light coming from the alley the window faced, so I turned on the desk lamp. As if the devil himself had feared I would prove recalcitrant, he had positioned the notebook from Engel Klein smack in the middle of the desk.

Skipping over the explanatory material preceding Mary's letters and skipping over the letters themselves, I homed in on the material behind the tab labeled *Obit*, which I should have anticipated was Violet's. Underneath her name was written *4 February 1889 to 15 June 1993*.

Our eldest and cherished congregant, Violet Elspeth MacDonalde, daughter of Gregor Owen MacDonalde and his wife, Fiona Reed MacDonalde, left us Tuesday last to join our Lord.

A brief description of Gregor Owen MacDonalde's accounting

business and his wife's father's position as an elder in Angus County followed. Violet had attended Saint Oda's School for Girls, where she was awarded *honours* in *Geography* and received *Commendations in Ornithology, Nomenclature, and World Service*. Were these courses or projects or competitions?

The list of charities to which Violet devoted her time and money was extensive: organizations helping the poor and infirm, plus schools, museums, theaters, and—during the years of the two World Wars— hospitals in Edinburgh, Glasgow, and Perth. I hypothesized that two of the organizations listed—Saint Andrews Home and The Residences—provided services to unwed mothers, whom we used to call 'wayward women.'

The obituary ended thus: *Violet was an exemplar of the duteous daughter, kind neighbour, and generous benefactress. Ad vitam aeternam.*

My initial reaction, of course, was deep respect for Violet's generosity and charitable service. But my second reaction was indignation: for such an extensive biographical account to make not a single mention of her sister! Of course, Violet did not compose the obituary herself—or so one presumed. But in light of the small community in which she lived, surely the persons preparing the eulogy were familiar with Mary's existence. Did they feel awkward expressing ignorance of her fate? Nonetheless, did she not deserve mention? A simple *Her sister, Mary Agnes, emigrated to the United States in 1904?*

I looked out Adelaide's window on to the alley. At midday, sunlight would penetrate, but now the gray stones opposite cowered in shade. The same stones, the same shadows, I had looked on forty years ago, when my son had occupied this room. So much changes in this world; buildings are torn down, and new ones are erected; people are born and age and die. Yet this particular vista, with little to recommend itself, was changeless.

That Violet had lived a busy and productive life could not be gainsaid. Was her choosing a life of service a consequence, somehow, of the disgrace her sister's ill-timed pregnancy occasioned the family? Or of Mary's banishment? Did Violet's parents appear the greater victims—to Violet, at least—such that tending to their needs supplanted tending to her own? But would they not have preferred Violet marry and produce grandchildren? Marjorie, how your face lit up when Nathan telephoned to announce Elliot's birth—I believe it was Elliot—yes, yes, he was the eldest. And even if Violet had possessed none of Mary's physical attractiveness, surely she must have had suitors—Morris Townsends, if nothing else. And Catherine Sloper did have beaux who were decent men.

I left off such musings and returned to the beginning of the notebook. A footnote stated that behind each letter of Mary's was a short summary of its relevant information. Certain Scottish idioms had been paraphrased, and other material had been deleted due to *illegibility or excessive descriptions*. I shuddered to think if lawyers had been put in charge of translating *War and Peace*. Certainly Tolstoy's masterpiece would have been rendered shorter, but at what cost! And poor Proust, his life's work reduced to plot summaries. The choice of the word 'illegibility,' however, was not unwarranted.

And—my goodness!—her description of the ocean voyage included every morsel of food consumed, although certain items caught the eye, like ox tongue and sago pudding. Her comparison of the quarters for the second-class and third-class passengers was instructive.

Saloon dining room pleasing. 1st-class they say fit for King. Steerage crowded, dirty, foul smell, men women children penned like sheep. In storm, hatches battened down making air putrid, some sneak on deck than breathe below but when allowed up, there is much singing & fiddle play. ... Dr. Beebe says German ships worse, no privacy, straw mattresses not true beds. Men & women together, porridge thin, mouldy bread, little water. There's never a bad that couldn't be worse... I let Swedish girl stay when Finns in dining saloon, she taught me many phrases.

In describing the Good Samaritan Dr. Beebe, Mary positively waxed eloquent. Along with most of the first- and second-class passengers, he disembarked when the boat docked in Manhattan, but somehow—Mary did not say—they reunited for the trip upstate.

The train ride was summed up in a spare sentence or two. Allowing Mary the benefit of the doubt, I concluded that the state of pregnancy—the discomfort and tiredness accompanying the latter months—accounted for the brevity of her recitation. As for the arrival in Syracuse and ride to the town of Clopes, their destination, the only features Mary was moved to write about were that the carriage was *closed* and the roads were *broad*. She subsequently made reference to her convalescence, which I speculated was a veiled allusion to her confinement.

Several letters had little to offer of cultural or historical interest. One dated in July of 1904 merely noted:

Glynnis never so hot, but dresses more comfortable & stockings too. Dr. B took me in open carriage to cousins. Farm has 20 dairy cows. Fences, not walls between neighbours. Everything large, shops, chairs, tables, doorways. Houses tall but most wood.

I could understand the economy of words, the resort to telegraph-style writing that omitted articles like 'the' and 'an,' but the paucity of detail chagrined me. Eliot, Hardy, Melville would have catalogued more of the unfamiliar sights, sounds, and smells. Mary could have enhanced the portrait of her new home sufficient for Violet to share in the experiences. And if rendering the external world more vivid was not within her powers, could she not have so rendered her internal one? For example, did the largeness of so many things convey grandeur or, instead, an immensity that made her feel overwhelmed? Did Americans seem a people bursting their britches, ambitious and pioneering, or a people squandering their riches, reckless with their natural-resource bounty? Dickens and Twain were able to put national differences in hilarious perspective.

The iceman says I am starting to sound American. Not my accent, because he still teases. They don't say lass or lad. . . . Poor beloved Quince. Will you get another? I see setters & Labs but no Jack Russells, few collies. The Bs have a spaniel with a soft coat. She's a sweet one.

The letters continued in a mundane vein until a 1907 missive, in which three lines stood out.

I understand more about human nature living in a crowded household, something you have not endured. The most vicious sin is envy. Christian charity not always praised, sometimes despised.

I paused to take stock of these accusations. *Two* people had prompted Mary's anger. The Clopes denizen exhibiting envy was the obvious first, but the second was Violet. The line *something you have not endured* had to be construed as a remonstrance. Had Mary begun to feel the unfairness of her exile? Why was *Violet* an object of her anger when, it would seem, Violet was not the cause? And besides, clearly her sister missed her, as evidenced by her faithful correspondence.

The following tab contained the notation *R*, and the letter immediately behind the tab was dated in May of 1908.

Have taken trains almost 3,000 miles. Saw Indians on reservations where could not hurt us. Williams family from Perth many generations ago. Boy & two girls, 11, 9, 4. Well behaved except boy may have bit of rascal in him. He tiptoes to surprise me. Farm is fruit orchard they call a ranch.

That was the extent of her description of a three-thousand-mile journey, and she did not have the excuse of pregnancy this time!

In a subsequent letter, Mary was surprised at how so many conveniences she had come to take for granted in Clopes were lacking at 'the ranch.' There was no indoor plumbing and *no WC*; the *dry closet* was over a small hill fifty feet from the house. And the Williamses had *no gas lamps, only oil,* to supplement candles. *Mrs W* was eager to hear about the modern inventions of the East Coast and wasted no time informing *Mr W* of civilization's progress—I could only suspect these communications were thinly disguised wifely plaints. Most assuredly, Mary would have found southern Indiana amenities at that time quite wanting.

Yet apparently life at the ranch allowed Mary the time to write longer letters to Violet, and the peevish tone of earlier missives had all but vanished. And I enjoyed a moment's nostalgia at the description of swimming in the ditch, not unlike my own childhood experience in a creek. *Such fun to let current take us along, get out & run path to do again.* Yes, even a twenty-year-old—despite the burdens and responsibilities of motherhood and being a governess to three additional children—could become a child at heart when circumstances permitted.

I also took vicarious pleasure in Mary's first ride in a Model T automobile, which the family had nicknamed 'Bessie.' *Mr W soaked shirt turning crank, ride bumpy, hair flew out bonnet. Lucky road damp from night shower. Only two pair goggles, Mr W buy more.* The automobile was acquired in the fall of 1909 from the Midwest, and all the neighbors came to see it, which to my mind signified Mr. Williams possessed considerable financial resources. My parents lacked the means to pay for either a Ford or Fordson until after the Great War.

However, much as I found many details sparking reminiscences, whole paragraphs were devoid of interesting observations—perhaps to Violet too. Which peaches shipped well (the 'slappy' did not) and which fruit was picked when, and where the fruit pots were set to boil in the servants' kitchen and the jams and jellies prepared—this was the fodder of tedium.

But good things come to those who wait! My careful perusal produced an unexpected reward in a letter dated December 1909.

No one to take apples to Spokane, fear mobs, went ourselves. 5 days by carriage but 2 in Bessie. Like Bedlam! Working men crowds, signs, speeches, police. Rushed to lodgings. From window could see hungry men in rags, unshaven, marching. Mr W says all scoundrels, concerned for safety. He gone to evening bus. appointmt, Jack sleep, I went to Wobblies hall. Crowded but people kind.

Mary had snuck out from under Mr. Williams's protection to see the world firsthand—how Eustacia-like!

Such speeches, conditions terrible for miners, loggers, long days, rough work, much danger. Low pay & job sharks take poor man's last dollar. A girl speaker younger than me! What a talker! Servant girls have rights, "entitled to limits on drudgery". Tears in my eyes. Arrested many times. I tucked pamphlets in muff & read every one in lodgings.

In later missives, the young Scotswoman described additional trips in the company of Mr. Williams and his son, Jack, their purpose being to expand the geographic scope of the fruit sales. The three drove to Pendleton and Portland, in Oregon, and twice drove as far as San Francisco. Mary's talents as a travel guide, however, continued to prove wanting. Portland was summed up as *on a large river*. The cable cars in San Francisco did thrill her and the boy, and Chinatown was *unusual,* but Mr. Williams would not permit her to taste the food. They were permitted to *buy Oriental toys for the younger children.*

Yet again my patience was rewarded! As she had in Spokane, Mary used her time away from the company of Mr. Williams and Jack to attend labor rallies. *Cruel conditions for men on wharves. Stories same copper mines, gold, silver, iron. Capitalist injustice goes round world, working-class in slave bondage.* Continuing at some length in this vein, she concluded one letter thus: *No longer believe in upper & lower classes. We are all humankind, lucky & unlucky.*

My goodness, my goodness: *We are all humankind.* It would be nigh impossible for Adelaide and her generation to appreciate the radical transformation that had occurred in Mary, for nowadays it was a given that race and class and ethnicity do not signify a person's character, abilities, or potential. But in the early 1900s, the accepted wisdom was that race, class, and ethnicity molded us. Talk of 'blood lines' was common, as was talk of 'natural differences,' various traits being assigned to the Irish, French, Poles, Jews, Germans—*every* group. Culture and circumstance took a back seat to biological inheritance in terms of molding whom we became. And among the British, including the Scots, such beliefs ran deep—even such venerable figures as Winston Churchill spoke of the 'British race.' So nothing less than a heresy had occurred in Mary's breast.

Her attainment to enlightenment inspired in me an especial admiration, coming as it did neither from education nor catechism but from *experience.* For a simpler soul than she, the abrupt eviction from a life of comfort into a life of labor might have whetted a determination to reclaim her former position; after all, having been raised by a prosperous gentleman, she must have felt keenly the implied insult of subordination. Yet Mary refused to view her life's trajectory as a downward arc and instead adopted the philosophy of strangers— impoverished ones at that. From whence did this fearlessness derive? Ah, Jude, if only *you* had had some of the young émigré's spirit, if only *you* had channeled your disappointments into righteous anger, perhaps your sorrows would have been the less. But would the transformed Jude have been the same man who had loved Sue and was loved by her?

The next few letters led me to infer that Violet had expressed opposing political or social views, for Mary wrote, in early 1913, *How do I explain the wide world to someone not ventured beyond the village of her birth? Or had to earn her keep? You know nothing of millions living with starvation & choices they must make.* Again, I had to be admiring: Mary was not distressed over her own consignment to the servant class, nor was she righteously indignant over the personal loss of status and income—although such emotions would have been understandable. Rather, her sympathies had *expanded*.

My eyesight beginning to falter, I barely skimmed the remaining letters yet noted another jewel added to Mary's treasure box of wisdom.

To you the Coloreds are to be pitied, but injustices should bring anger not pity. You write Andrew has become a deacon. Remember his sermon about "dark savages"?

I did read the brief, final letter in its entirety, mailed from Spokane in October of 1913. *Circumstances required us to leave. May return to Clopes because it is familiar.* According to Adelaide, at this juncture, for all intents and purposes, Mary's trail went cold.

CHAPTER 21

SHE SQUIRMED HER WAY ON top, her breasts dangling. They finished within moments of each other, and Lucy bent forward, the dark-tinted hair draping her face. The phone rang.

It rang again before she whispered, "That could've been *very* bad timing."

"Are you going to answer?"

"I better, in case it's the plumber." She reached and lifted the receiver. "Hello? Oh, hi!" She mouthed *Carson*. "Hold on one sec—I want to grab my coffee."

She laid the receiver on the bedside table, reached for tissues, and carefully un-straddled the man. He rose and went into the bathroom. She threw the tissues in the wastebasket and put on her panties.

"I'm back. What's up?"

"Saw in the obituary page Mrs. Henderson died. And apparently *he* died last year."

"How? They weren't that old."

"Doesn't say. She passed away *peacefully at home surrounded by her children.* The picture looks from around the time we knew them."

"Save it." Lucy pulled on a lavender kimono-like robe, nestling the phone between her shoulder and jaw. "Are you going to send a card? Who would you send it to?"

"It says *Amanda Henderson of La Jolla.* I guess I could address it 'To the family of'—see if I can find out where she lived."

"I doubt their kids ever heard of us. Still, we should do *some*thing. Does it mention a charity to donate to?"

"Parkinson's Foundation."

"I'll send it in both our names." She remembered Mrs. Henderson in pale blue, and the striped scarf, and her gracefulness even grabbing a line.

They chatted a few minutes, until the bathroom door opened and steam floated in. "Listen, Car, I'll have to call you back—the plumber just buzzed."

She smiled at the man as he put on his boxer shorts. His physique was nice, more muscular than that of your typical forty-five-year-old. No accident, their meeting at the gym.

"Carson saw the obituary of a woman we knew, Mrs. Henderson. Her husband died last year. They were nice to us when we were kids."

Before pulling on a T-shirt, he made an expression signaling interest if she had more to say.

"One summer practically every Sunday our parents dropped us at Hammonasset Beach—the state park—so they could go hang out with friends. Carson and I usually walked around or sat on the piers. The Hendersons saw us get out of the car once and heard Louise say they'd come back for us at eight—it was probably not even noon! They could smell rot, the Hendersons, and asked if we wanted to go out on their boat." Lucy gave a short laugh. "It's not like we were warned against strangers."

"That was nice of them."

"Yes, it was, very nice. The *Sprightly Spirit*—she was thirty-eight feet and had four berths and the cutest little galley kitchen. Carson got used to going below deck on the very first trip. He'd ask a million questions about the sails and steering, and after that, whenever we were there the same day—six or seven times—they took us out. And I mean *out*! To Long Island, way up around the tip—the North Fork, not Montauk. Hours each way—once, it was almost sundown when we got back."

The man finished buttoning his crisp white shirt. "Nowadays, they'd get called on the carpet, charged with kidnapping. Times have changed."

"Do you want a bite to eat?"

"No—I'll pick something up in the sandwich shop. I hate these mediations—either both parents are fit or neither." He stepped into one pants leg, then the other.

"Built to end badly," Lucy said.

After pulling up his pants and zipping his fly, he gave a puzzled look.

"When Carson was in kindergarten, he came home all proud—the teacher had praised him for an answer about the 'Three Little Pigs' story. 'What did the first two pigs do wrong,' and he said their houses were 'built to end badly.' We always joke about it: certain situations are 'built to end badly.'"

The man came over and held her shoulders. "I hope ours isn't."

"Not if it's up to me."

After a long, deep kiss, he said, "I'm sorry I haven't met your brother. Maybe someday." He scanned the room. "You don't have any pictures. I never saw any in your old apartment either." He sat on the bed and reached down for his socks.

"We didn't own a camera growing up. I have Carson's class picture from third grade." Lucy sidled to the dresser, opened a drawer, and took out a manila envelope.

The man finished pulling on the second sock and took the envelope from her. He removed the glossy eight-by-eleven sheet, studying the faces for a family resemblance. The photographer had managed a fairly close shot, cutting out the legs of the children in the front row in order to capture all the faces clearly.

"I give up."

"Back row, far right."

The bandage wrapping across the thin forehead almost blocked one eye completely. "What happened—was he in an accident?"

"Daddy got drunk."

The man's mouth tightened. He stared at the photograph a moment without speaking. "When you said your father was mean, I thought you were—exaggerating."

"Carson was his punching bag."

"Punching bag," the man repeated. "Did he ever hurt *you*?"

"No. Or Louise, as far as I could tell."

He handed the picture back. "What could Carson have possibly done to provoke—I don't say 'deserve,' obviously—"

"Existing." Lucy sucked in one cheek, creating a dimple.

"Exis—and your mother—what did she do when—"

"Poured them each another drink."

The man stared at Lucy in disbelief. Her expression didn't waver.

"Didn't his teachers notice? No one called Children and Families?"

"Usually the bruises were on his chest, arms, legs—that was one of the few times he got hit in the face. Louise told everybody he was accident prone."

The man reached down and mindlessly straightened his socks. "What about the family doctor?"

"Doctor? What doctor?" Lucy laughed harshly, slipped the photograph back into the envelope, and dropped it in the open drawer. "No one thought twice about it, not in those days, not at *our* school. We didn't live in the tony part of town." She watched the man shake his head. "You wonder why *I* didn't tell someone? Because by the time the cops finished checking out my story, Carson and I'd *both* be dead."

"That wasn't what I was thinking." The man rested his hands on his knees. "Did you have to see it, see him get hit?"

"Someone had to shout for the bastard to stop. And ice the bruises."

"Good God—how long did this go on?"

"Till the SOB croaked. Middle of seventh grade, Carson in fifth."

Again, the man pulled at his socks. "I didn't realize. I'm sorry."

"So it shouldn't surprise you he's moving to San Francisco. This area holds bad memories."

The man said nothing until he'd finished putting on his shoes and lacing them. "Yet you didn't leave."

"We never came up this way, so no bad associations. And I was never beaten." She examined the nails on her left hand. "The only time we left Norwalk was in the summer, like I said, when they visited their friends. Even if the Hendersons weren't there, we had fun, wandering around the boats and marina shop. This one place had nets hanging from the ceiling and huge wood steering wheels and heavy ropes and portholes built into the side of the building so you could see the harbor."

"Do you ever go back—to Hammonasset?"

"No. One memory leads to another." She raised her head and appraised his reflection in the closet mirror. "You look quite judicial, even without the robe."

He glanced down at his abdomen. "I need to lose weight." He picked up his tie from the chair back.

"I don't even go back to Greenport, on the North Fork, though that was all happy memories. Carson does—had a girlfriend whose parents lived near Riverhead, and he loved visiting."

"We all deal with things in our own way."

She examined the nails on her right hand. "Yes, but you see: people *can* overcome their circumstances. Carson and I have."

"Yes, yes—you definitely have."

Lucy went to him and began tying his tie. He let her, and when she was done, he said, "You even drink alcohol. Most people I've encountered—sons and daughters of alcoholics—avoid it like the plague. Or drink too much themselves. You've avoided both extremes."

She stepped away and squinted at the knot. "That would be admitting what they did wasn't their fault—'the liquor made them do it.' Carson and I drinking in moderation proves it wasn't the liquor."

"You really should go to law school."

She moved close again and readjusted the tie. "I don't like losing, and you say it goes with the territory. If there was a way straight to a judgeship . . ." She stepped back. "I'll have to do something in their memory—the Hendersons. It wasn't just that they were nice—they were role models. We needed that."

He looked at her tenderly. "I'm sure they were a help, but I can't see you ever following in your parents' footsteps."

Lucy laughed giddily. "I might not be as nice as Mrs. Henderson, but I'm no Louise!"

CHAPTER 22

"THAT'S RIGHT—IT IS THURSDAY again already. Shall I help you straighten up?"

"I think I'm done." Adelaide pushed the green ottoman to the side.

Einsteinian physics may be a subject for more brilliant minds, but as any septuagenarian knows, Time passes with breakneck speed once one has passed the seventy-years-of-age mark. Only yesterday, it seemed, Robert had spent the afternoon with us, yet now he was due again.

As we awaited his arrival, I remarked that it was difficult to ascertain how much conversation he understood. "Does he simply develop expectations—that if he grunts, someone will offer food or crayons or toys?"

"He understands words. When I asked if he wanted crackers, he acted frustrated."

"But I wonder if he heard the word 'cracker' or merely saw you holding it?"

We heard rapping at the door, and Adelaide went to answer it. She returned holding Robert by the hand, Millie following with the tote bags. It pained me to see the odd, knee-knocked angles of the boy's legs, but whatever discomfort he felt was not made manifest on his face.

Again, the child spent a good deal of time drawing with crayons, taking breaks for crackers and juice. However, when he grunted and shook his head more violently, Adelaide quickly divined his wishes and brought him the red barn and plastic farm animals. The menagerie I could now see contained *two* pink pigs, one brown-and-white-spotted cow, a brown rooster, an orange hen, plus two gray geese, a roan horse, and three yellow chickens. His good hand moved the animals around, possibly in obedience to some story his mind had fashioned.

Bored with her studies, perhaps, Adelaide set down her book, leaned on her side facing the boy, and began moving toys too. He continued his own activities, not distressed by her participation, and I watched the recumbent mimes, their individual thoughts no doubt quite disparate.

"It amuses me," I said after a bit, "how the animals are pretty shiny things. I seem to recall a children's movie on the television that struck me the same way: the fictional—or in this case, 'pretend'—farm was many light-years away from a real farm. Creatures on a real farm—human creatures as well—live amid an abundance of dirt, sweat, and manure—there is little one would deem pristine. In rainy weather, a slog to the barn or shed is a slog through mud; in summer, if rain has been scarce, a mild breeze is sufficient to spread dust on everything. And especially in summer, everyone sweats—and never hastens to wash up."

Once or twice in the course of my rumination—to use a farm-derived word! —Robert paused in his play to regard me. I could not decipher the meaning of his stare.

"The Saturday-night bath ritual would amuse you, Adelaide. The timing, you understand, was in anticipation—and preparation—for attending church Sunday morning. For hot water, we had to carry in well water and heat it on the cast-iron stove. Filling the tub, no mean feat, was done only once. The custom—and this is the amusing part—the custom was for my father to enjoy the first bath. Which had a certain justice and *in*justice to it.

"On the one hand, he toiled the most in dirt and grime and therefore was the most in need of cleaning. And the most deserving, you could say. Yet, being the filthiest of the three of us, he sullied the bathwater to an extreme degree. Particles of mud and bits of leaves and hay and twigs floated all around. Nonetheless, he went first, and my mother, second. She did make an attempt, when I was quite young, to scoop out the larger particles of dirt before my turn came, and I can remember huddling nearby, wearing only my towel for warmth, while she bent over the tub edge with the dipper. By the time I was eight or nine, of course, I performed this rudimentary filtering myself. But it was not until I went to England, my dear, that I luxuriated in the pleasures of an indoor shower and bathing in unused water. Of course, my British classmates had no end of fun at my initiation into what they called 'proper civilization.' And the ubiquity of indoor plumbing there was the tip of the iceberg; my classmates were wont to point out how the English surpassed us in any number of measures: civility, manners, decorum, and in historical and cultural knowledge. We were, in comparison, rustic pioneers. But their teasing was not malicious."

"Are you sleepy?" Adelaide asked the yawning boy. He nodded, and she took the small pillow from the bag and set it down and draped the blanket over his shoulders when he reclined. As she gathered up the plastic farm animals, she said, "Mom doesn't remember ever going to Indiana."

"No, she never went."

"Or meeting your parents."

"Perhaps not. They came for a visit shortly after Richard was born, but she was quite young."

"They didn't visit again?"

"Once before, they had come, for the wedding. Which was soon after I received my degree."

"How come not more often?"

"You are inquiring about events I have not reflected upon for years, my dear, for years. I suppose that unlike Marcel Proust, I am not prone to indulging in nostalgia. In any event, I believe the wedding may have prejudiced them against the city. What I mean is: they were not used to large affairs. Over two hundred guests attended. New Yorkers, for the most part. None of my extended family could make the trip, or even Miss Perry. And despite Cecil's and Claudia's and our own efforts to make my parents feel comfortable, still—it was an unfamiliar environment."

"Had Grandma met them before you got married?"

"Yes, one time, yes, the two of us traveled by train to Indiana. Marjorie had written them after I had announced our engagement, quite a long letter, filled with details about her and her family. And once we were settled in after the honeymoon, she wrote another, apprising them of this and that—my job, her routine, little details she thought they would enjoy knowing. But it did not seem to make a difference."

Adelaide cocked her head in that way she had. "They didn't like her?"

"I don't know that they *dis*liked her. They were 'easily intimidated,' is how I would phrase it. At the reception, my mother told her—

apropos of what, I am not sure—she said, 'We are not schooled people.' Marjorie of course quickly responded with something along the lines of 'You are family, which is all that matters.' But my mother was easily put on her guard. A simple person, really. She had no wish to appear unkind, and your grandmother was quite cognizant of that."

I looked down at the sleeping boy, at the rhythmic up and down of his rib cage. Slumber when we are young is all-encompassing, not like the easily disturbed sleep of the old. Now *that* was something to be nostalgic about!

"Was your father uncomfortable around Grandma too?"

"I would simply say they were set in their ways. And that encompassed living as farmers. Which is not to suggest they resisted progress—my father was proud to be the first in our area to own a Fordson. It was not a reckless purchase, mind you—we paid for it in part through the sale of the horses. Consider: a single tractor could plow three or four times the area a team could cover. Plus, horses needed to rest and be fed and given water, and a fair amount of pasture had to be set aside for grazing. Those needs all disappeared with the Fordson."

"I know almost nothing about farming."

I could not help but smile. "You are hardly alone among your generation. Yet farming was the most common occupation for most of civilization's history. And in a similar vein, to people your age and even your mother's, the Industrial Revolution's pinnacle is in the production of household appliances and the telephone and television and computer. While significant, these modern inventions did not provide the immediate relief from arduous moil that farm machinery did. Yes, my father was wise and prudent. During the war years—the First World War—prices were strong because Europe provided little competition, its ablebodied men being—and dying—on the battlefield. And after the war ended, prices remained strong until Europe was back on its feet. That was when my father invested in the Fordson, unlike many of our neighbors, who used their wartime profits to buy large amounts of acreage, and when prices dropped, they lost everything. How did we get on this subject?"

"I was wondering why your parents never visited you and their grandkids."

"We must be careful not to subscribe to the view that every man should have an academic bent. This is a fundamental tenet with me: every individual must decide for *himself* what form of work nourishes the soul, if you will allow me to wax poetic. I would no more criticize the farmer than I would tolerate criticism of other ways of earning a livelihood."

Robert stirred—perhaps I had inadvertently raised the volume of my voice. He opened his large eyes with the long lashes and for a moment peered at the carpet and chair legs as if trying to recall where he was. Young fellow, well I know that struggle to awaken!

CHAPTER 23

WINTER KEPT ME HOUSEBOUND—I should say apartment-bound— both on account of my increased dislike of bitter cold and my fears of slipping on ice or slush and thereby exacerbating the weakness in my ankle. Adelaide had no such concerns for herself; no matter how inclement the weather, she intrepidly bundled herself up in coat, scarf, hat, and gloves and braved the elements, some days walking a considerable distance.

The resumption of her classes lent a not-unwelcome predictability to our days. I certainly never made it a habit to enter her room during her absence, yet if a break from concentrating on my opus would prove restorative, I might resort to the young Scotswoman's history.

On this particular day, I took the opportunity to turn to the tab labeled *Inves.*

The first page behind the tab was a letter to Violet's solicitors from the *George T. Small Agency* in 1923, describing the enclosures as *two potentially positive interviews.* A teacher in Syracuse had some years earlier taught at a school in Clopes and recalled a boy with the last name MacDonalde. He would have been about nine or ten at the time, in her estimation, and her tenure at the school was from 1913 to 1915, so those dates more or less comported with the age of Mary's child. However, the child had not been in this teacher's class, and she did not remember his Christian name. Nor did she know anything about the boy's parents or the current addresses of others who had taught at the school, which had closed in 1918, so the door was shut on locating additional witnesses.

The second interview was with a retired foreman at the Seneca Broom Factory, who recalled *a young woman with MacDonald spelled funny* who worked *one of the treadles* during his years there, 1910 to 1916. Her first name may have been Mary *or Cherry or Martha.*

A year and a half later, the George T. Small Agency sent another letter, this one stating that *no further leads were discovered* following up on the school and broom-factory witnesses and the Beebes. *However,* Mr. Small ventured to *suggest further inquiries based on the enclosure.*

The enclosure ran to several pages and covered the interviews of three witnesses. The date, time, and location of each interview was punctiliously noted, causing me wry amusement at how a just-the-facts rendition could be so verbose. Distilled to its essence: in May of 1925, the investigator interviewed three siblings in Wapato, Washington: Jack Williams, Phyllis Williams Baker, and Julia Williams White. They ranged in age from twenty-eight down to twenty, respectively. Their father had died in 1921, and their mother, Margaret, was *non compos mentis*—whether that was a medical diagnosis or the investigator's assessment was unclear.

According to the report, the three Williams siblings had sold the family *fruit ranch*, and the two elder—Jack and Phyllis—moved to the nearby city of Yakima.

Julia remained in Wapato, on her husband's farm near the sold property. Jack and Phyllis were *not forthcoming*; the investigator also complained they were *not plain-spoken*. I would hazard a guess they simply had better uses of their time than reminiscing about childhood events that had been, and remained, inconsequential to them. They did confirm that a Mary Agnes MacDonalde had come to live with their family around 1908 and departed in 1913. Phyllis disputed that Mary was technically a *governess*—apparently the investigator's word—as the children attended school, and denominated Mary a *house servant*. Mary had had a son, Brian, who was close in age to Julia.

So the child's name and sex were known to Engel Klein, even if not the world at large!

Julia Williams White, on the other hand, was happy to talk to the investigator, but as luck would have it, she remembered little from the years 1908 to 1913, having been quite young. She and Brian had studied the alphabet and numbers and learned to read together up until the time she began accompanying her siblings to school. Brian did not go to school but was tutored at home by his mother. Had he a disability? Was the school a private one requiring a prohibitive tuition? The report did not indicate.

The Williams family was wealthier than their neighbors, according to Julia, and Mrs. Williams occasionally entertained *important people, the mayor and bankers*. Mr. Williams's business interests were more extensive than just the ranch, and he traveled frequently, sometimes to

California, to engage new buyers for his fruit and to cement arrangements with distributors. Yet he remained *a farmer at heart* and would often pick apples and peaches himself. *"It's the Scottish in me,"* he told the children. *"I take pride in what I have produced."* Their mother, who was of German descent, used to scold him for not displaying the dignity of his position, a memory that amused this Julia.

Julia also remembered Jack and Mary going along on some of Mr. Williams's business trips. I suspected that Jack's assistance was required for carrying the luggage and cartons of jam, plus any difficulties with the roads or vehicle, and Mary's assistance was required for laundry and other domestic chores that in those days innkeepers might not provide.

Mary and Brian's departure in 1913 was quite memorable. Julia and her brother and sister returned from school to find trunks and bags on the front porch.

A neighbor took Mary and Brian to the railroad station. The investigator's report concluded thus:

I returned to re-interview Jack Williams and Phyllis Williams Baker. They did not remember Mary's departure as sudden. Jack suggested Julia had had an active imagination as a child. Julia was only nine when Mary and Brian left Wapato.

How this report must have disappointed Violet! Imagine her eagerly opening the letter from her solicitor and reading the enclosure, only to learn that the sole new information the Small Agency had to offer was that Mary's pregnancy had resulted in a son and he was named Brian.

THE MYSTERY OF MARY'S TRAVELS after leaving Wapato, while captivating the imagination, served a practical purpose by furnishing a topic of conversation when Carson came to Saturday-evening dinner, which he had begun to do with regularity. Toward the end of January, as we took our places at the table, he informed us that his sister knew, based on "the rags she reads," Mary had left New York State. Where she went and whether she ever returned to New York, however, had not oozed into the public domain.

Adelaide looked up from carving the roast. "The fact that people know she moved is causing a new bunch of claimants to pop up all over."

"They'll bankrupt the estate, like in the book Francis mentioned."

"*Bleak House.*"

"At least it hasn't come out that *we* know where she lived," Adelaide continued, "up until 1913. So people claiming she lived other places can be discounted."

"And their claims relegated to the Graveyard file," I noted. "And we can infer from the investigative reports that she never *returned* to Wapato, for the Williams family never saw her or the boy again. Adelaide, that piece looks perfectly done—medium rare—just as I like it."

She threw me a peculiar look, notwithstanding the fact that my request was not impolite, for she could still serve our guest first. His face seemed to reveal puzzlement as well. I was passed the platter and slipped the delicious-looking slice onto my plate before relaying the platter to Carson. Resuming carving, Adelaide stopped only when enough of the roast had been sliced for us each to enjoy a second helping. I encouraged her to serve Carson and herself the potatoes and spinach before passing them down to me, to make up for any faux pas I may inadvertently have committed.

We dined for a minute or two without conversation, and indeed I had the good fortune to consume an exceptionally tender piece of meat. Adelaide repeated—apparently having little trust in Carson's discretion—that anything said about the MacDonalde case should not be repeated to anybody besides the three of us. She then inquired of me as to mail delivery between the United States and the United Kingdom during World War I.

"My dear, I was just a young child then and have no idea. I do know that for Violet and her sister, their correspondence had a magnified significance compared with today, for their separation seemed permanent; any reunion would have been deemed propitious. And when Mary moved to Washington State, she had to doubt seeing her friends from Clopes again. Contrast that with how we live now:

your mother was here twice in one year, across three thousand miles. And your uncle Richard circumnavigates the globe—didn't we just get a postcard from Bombay?"

"He's the foreign-service uncle, right?" Carson asked. "Not the linguist?"

"The linguistics professor is on Adelaide's *father's* side. In any event, as I was saying, the frequency of reconnection we have with your mother, my dear, was unheard of when I was young. I recall *my* mother talking wistfully of her brothers and sisters in Kentucky, a mere eighty miles distant. Before the automobile, with no train stations nearby, it might as well have been eighty *thousand* miles, given the slowness of carriages and the delays required for resting and feeding the horses. Plus, there was great uncertainty about whether roadways would be flooded or bridges damaged or other impediments to travel. That changed by the late thirties. Yet I did not have my first license until 1940, before our move to Washington, DC, yes, when I left the university to join the War Department. August of 1940."

"You mean '42," Carson presumed to correct me.

"No, August of 1940."

"But we weren't at war. Pearl Harbor was December '41."

"*Europe* was at war and had been at war since the invasion of Poland, in September of 1939."

"Did you think we'd go to war *eventually*?" Adelaide asked. "Is that why you joined the War Department?"

"My dear, like Churchill and many millions of Europeans, I was afraid the United States would *not* go to war. The British Isles might fall to Hitler, as so much of the Continent already had: Austria and then Czechoslovakia, Poland, France, Belgium, the Netherlands. Looking back through the lens of what we know today, you may find it difficult to comprehend how strong a streak isolationism was in this country. Even in southern Indiana, people dismissed the Nazis as 'Europe's problem'—when England's very existence hung by a thread! The nation that gave us the Magna Carta, and, as you yourself have said, our legal system—and that gave us the writings of Locke and Hobbes and John Stuart Mill, Francis Bacon and Newton, Chaucer and Shakespeare and the greatest novelists of all time—it teetered on the precipice of utter annihilation!"

"We barely covered World War II in school," my granddaughter murmured. "It was always June by the time we got to the Depression."

"You are saying an entire generation has grown up ignorant of the provenance—and providence—of its own well-being! Do not despair—you are hardly alone. I have taught many a student—*graduate* student—who could recite *A horse, a horse, my kingdom for a horse* and spout knowledgeably about King Henry VII's vanquishing of Richard III at Bosworth Field, yet these self-same students were woefully ignorant of the evacuation at Dunkirk and the valor of the RAF, without which there no longer would *be* a United Kingdom. The ideals of the Enlightenment and democracy, a belief in the virtues of education and literature and the arts, and science too—these hallmarks of civilization we take for granted were on the verge of extinction everywhere except the Americas. The sun was about to set on the British Empire and Continental Europe."

As Carson refilled our glasses, images that had lain dormant for decades began to emerge from the peculiar miasma of memory. How those of us in our little corner of the War Department offices, to ignore the pervasive fear, busied ourselves with reading and writing reports, barely pausing to relay a joke. By focusing on the assignments at hand, we pretended that our individual and collective efficiency could keep at bay the horrific events unfolding across the ocean.

"I feel like Cassandra," I had once confided to Marjorie, my tossing and turning having awoken her. "The president campaigns he will keep us *out* of the war." At that time, of course, many details of Roosevelt's covert aid to Britain were not widely known, nor was his personal dedication to opposing Hitler's military might. Marjorie, saddled with the burden of raising two toddlers, had proved the emotional stalwart. "Go back to sleep," was her standard admonishment. "Dwell on the good things just around the corner."

"Excuse me," I said to Carson. "I am afraid I did not catch your question."

"What did you do for the War Department?"

"The higher-ups believed they could make use of my fluency in French and German."

The young man rested his fork on his plate. "You did *code-breaking?*"

"Nothing so glamorous. I translated local news, information that might or might not prove useful."

Shedding neither his awestruck expression nor unctuous tone, Uriah Heep loudly exclaimed, "Still, that had to be *important*."

"I served in the safety of Washington and its suburbs; I was not among the men shipped overseas to face the dangers of combat. And the concomitant dangers of accidents, disease, and natural forces, which took the lives of so many. And after D-Day, when many translators *were* needed at the front lines as the Allies progressed further into France and then Germany, still *I* returned each night to a home and wife and children."

Fawning never pleased me, yet undeterred, the toady insisted, "You were part of the effort that defeated Hitler."

"So were tens of thousands—*hundreds* of thousands—serving in noncombat roles. The men who trained pilots and submariners—"

"He's just trying to say—"

"My point is that encomia should be reserved for those who risked life and limb. By scattering praise too widely, we diminish its value."

Uriah Heep had no retort to that! For the remainder of the evening, his manner showed more deference and less garrulity, a welcome development.

MY QUERY TO ADELAIDE AS to whether she would be performing interviews for the MacDonalde case was prescient; one evening she announced that Joe, her supervisor, had assigned her to interview a claimant living on the North Fork of Long Island. In something of a coincidence, she explained, Carson had wanted to show her boats in the town of Greenport, which was nearby, and had volunteered to drive her.

"He will not attend the interview, will he? You will be discussing confidential information."

"He'll find a coffee shop or some place to study until it's over."

"I thought he didn't own an automobile."

"He'll rent one."

"The Long Island Expressway can be quite a quagmire."

"We'll be going against rush hour."

The thought of her cornered in a vehicle with the wheedling Lothario for several hours did not please me, but I saved myself from an unseemly outburst by changing the subject. "That is quite a responsibility Joe is handing you: interviewing a claimant!"

"I need to study the transcripts of other interviews to learn what to ask."

"I possess no special expertise in the art of legal interviews, but if you were to require a sounding board as you prepare your outline, I would be happy to oblige. I do understand the confidential nature of these things and can promise complete silence about any morsel of Mary's history you inadvertently disclose."

"It *would* be helpful to bat some ideas around, if you won't mention anything to anybody."

"You have my word."

Quite gratified, I was, that she trusted both my ability to keep a secret and the wisdom I could offer. My confidence in the former was greater.

WHAT I PLAYFULLY TERMED MY "induction into the MacDonalde brotherhood"—Adelaide's willingness to share confidential information with me—led to my learning a number of new facts. For example, Violet's will specified that her beneficiaries need not be Mary's blood descendants, and, as a consequence, any adopted child or grandchild was entitled to a portion of the inheritance. And the will explicitly allowed for out-of-wedlock children and their descendants inheriting in the same proportion as those of legal wedlock. This provision was a tightly guarded secret, my granddaughter explained, for if the fact were to become widely known, no end of mischief would ensue: people could claim to descend from a one-night-stand with, say, Mary's son.

Of course, in lawyerly fashion, I countered that Violet obviously did not want to exclude such single-tryst descendants from a fair share of the estate.

"True," Adelaide replied, "and if someone claims they descend from Mary that way, we'll investigate. But we don't want to advertise the idea, because it'll encourage false claims."

Other information she imparted duplicated information I had already learned from the notebook, including Brian's name. But I did not disabuse my granddaughter of the notion she was doling out facts that were new to me.

CHAPTER 24

IN SEVEN MINUTES UNDER THE fifty he'd allotted himself, Carson had dusted and vacuumed his room, mopped the kitchen, and—because his roommates did a poor job when it was their turns to do the bathroom—cleaned the floor and base of the toilet. He was about to grab the sponge to wipe the mirror when one of them shouted, "Your sister's on the phone." He quickly washed his hands.

"I hate to cancel again but can't go see the whaler. He just got back from five days at a judicial conference, and Saturday's the only time he's free."

"Don't worry. I'll skip it because next weekend I'm taking Addy to see a halibut schooner in Greenport."

"Greenport! Will you go for fried clams and corn on the cob and oh, that *chowder*."

Carson brought the extension into his bedroom and closed the door. "I don't know what's open off-season."

"Sounds like she's come down off her perch. How is she in the sack?"

He sat on the edge of the bed. "I wouldn't know."

"She *hasn't* come down. Why are you bothering?"

"Not sure I can explain. Even to myself."

"*I* can. It's rejection, plain and simple. It galls you to be rejected for once."

"She's *hardly* the first."

"Maybe she looks down on you for working your way through school."

"Doesn't know. It's a long story—don't ask."

"Let me fix you up with one of the girls at the salon. Leanne would give you a whopping time under the sheets, and Denise—anyway, soon you'll be in San Francisco and will forget about Miss Stuck-Up Cohn."

"You shouldn't encourage me to stop seeing her. She's working on that case your rags love, the Scottish—"

"The *MacDonalde* case? Why didn't you tell me! Is the Ozarks clan legit? What about the waitress in Anchorage?"

He laughed. "She can't tell us anything that isn't in the press."

"Who's this *us*?"

"Her grandfather, Francis. A strange old bird—I can't figure him out. Sometimes the crank, sometimes the doting grandparent. But like I said, I don't know anything that's not already in the papers. If the claimants haven't gone public—"

"Some haven't gone public? There're people claiming to be heirs keeping it secret?"

"Imagine you were an heiress, Luce—would you want the whole world to know?"

"Yes! Especially the people I detest."

"Louise?"

"She'd camp out on my doorstep."

"Exactly. And the headlines: 'Heiress Shuts Out Own Mother!'"

"Car, don't stop seeing Addy—you've got to pump her for details. You can still date other women—she doesn't have to know. Or tell her—jealousy might light the fire."

When he got off the phone, Carson gave all of two seconds to the idea of making Addy jealous. The last thing he wanted to do was give her a pretext to end their relationship—such as it was. He remembered how he'd handled it with Gloria and Jennifer. Weirdly, it hadn't been a big deal. Maybe because they'd fallen so hard for him, his asking forgiveness gave them a chance to hold the reins. Or they were just relieved all he'd hidden was facts about his childhood, not some infidelity?

It was so different with Addy. For one thing, she hadn't fallen at all—she tolerated him. They talked and laughed, her shyness even went away, but a steel door always crashed down. If he admitted the lies, the door might never go back up.

It wasn't like he hadn't tried to come clean—a bunch of times he'd even settled in his mind on a time and place. Yet he always chickened out. Leaving for San Francisco could seem like a blessing.

CHAPTER 25

"COME IN, COME IN." JOE gestured impatiently with one hand as Addy waited in the doorway, his other holding the phone. "No, they've got to come up with something," he barked into the receiver. "We're not about to take it on faith. Jesus H. Christ."

His suit jacket was off and his shirt sleeves rolled up to the elbow, like during her interview. Though in his sixties and not a large man, he was far from meek, but his volatility seemed more hot air than real anger—Addy could imagine him at home yelling at the TV but not at his family. He had only the one picture of them in his office, over on the sill. The walls were bare except for his City College and Brooklyn Law diplomas, bar certificate, and admissions to district and circuit courts. Other offices she had seen during job interviews had artwork, vases with flowers, and lots of photos—spouses, kids, boyfriend or girlfriend, dogs, even horses.

Of the five firms where she'd gotten a callback—she'd applied to twelve—Engel had the oddest-looking offices. Their main door was something out of a forties film noir, a single wooden panel surrounding a frosted-glass pane. Zach had loved *The Maltese Falcon*. The reception desk was modern, and Joe's office had a fancy conference-call phone. Still, Engel didn't reek of money the way others did. "*Old* money," Carson would say. The one white-shoe that had given her a callback had made her claustrophobic, dark gleaming paneling everywhere, towering bookcases, thick carpets—like you were in a rare-books library. If they'd made her an offer, she probably would have turned them down, not wanting to be a fish out of water. "You just got shown the partners' digs," Carson had joked. "The associates' probably look like a steno pool." Maybe she'd decided on Engel because it wasn't pretentious.

Joe hung up, gestured at a chair, and asked brusquely, "Schedule the Mattituck?"

"Yes, a week from Saturday."

"What's the joker's name—Nagy, Gregor Nagy. I told the Scots it would be an all-day junket—round-trip, almost six hours just for traveling. Get hold of Brittany's transcripts, she asks everything. It's not a deposition—the Scots aren't shelling out for court reporters, let me tell you. Find out where everyone on the line of descent was born, lived, died. Look at Simon's too. He lanced the bubble that fraud in Idaho blew up—that Mary moved to Boise in '22 and married somebody named Gunn. Too bad for the Gunns, their Mary'd been busted for passing bad checks the year before Gunn married her. No *e* on the end, not in the court records. How'd we find out it was the same Mary? He was her probation officer. Son of a gun!"

Addy forced a smile, wondering which secretary to bother for copies of the transcripts.

"You want to ask for anything Nagy didn't send us: copies of Mary's and her descendants' birth and death certificates, driver's licenses, marriage licenses, draft cards—see what Brittany and Simon asked for. The *only* thing he hasn't alleged is the song and dance we keep hearing: Mary or some son or daughter dropped the *e* because it was a nuisance. Does anybody have documentation she legally changed the spelling? Ha! Not a shred of evidence, nothing to show their names *ever* had an *e*! I can't believe how the Scots want to run this thing— we'd be sued for malpractice trying anything like this. The claimants should be litigating against each other—on *their* dime—but the Scots got the estate doing it. *Nicely*, they say, *nicely.* Irv says I shouldn't be looking a gift horse in the mouth—just bill what we can. Great in theory, but those penny-pinchers use a fine-tooth comb on every damn invoice. Remember to hold on to your receipts—train, cab—you have to change trains in Ronkonkoma and maybe Riverhead."

"Actually, a friend is driving out that way to look at some boats and said he could give me a ride."

"You got a friend shopping for boats? What is he, one of those Harvard Club guys? Never mind—none of my business. If he wants to drive you, terrific. I'll badger the Scots to reimburse for gas. What a tight-fisted bunch. The little beauty contest they ran to figure out who to hire, six or seven of us lined up for interviews—couple of small firms, couple of mid, two or three large—one at a time, we go into a room—the three Scotties sitting behind a desk—and we're supposed to put on our dog-and-pony show. A joke! Two minutes into their opening spiel, what they were looking for in a firm, I could tell they couldn't care less about our ideas for tracking down MacDonaldes, just keeping expenses low. Scrooge McDucks, the lot of them. I said I'd send law students on initial interviews—you should've seen their eyes light up. The more of *your* time I bill, the better. And using Drecker—they cost half as much as the big-league investigators."

"Did Mr. Nagy send any documents?"

"Ask the paralegals. I think they've been dealing with his son, not Gregor."

"But he answered the questionnaire?"

"In theory. These clowns come up with all sorts of evasive crap. It's not like a lawsuit, where the lawyers pull the interrogatory information out of the clients and then craft the answers, and if they don't, you move to compel. No, we're stuck with any damn scribbling. Plain stuff—name, address, social—they can't seem to cough it up. Brittany's notes should be in the file, what the son told her over the phone." While he ranted, Joe burrowed in his file cabinet—Addy was surprised he could remember what he was looking for. "She's down in Miami interviewing Mary MacDonalde's grandson—*alleged* grandson. Her parents live there, so she can stay for free. Brad's in Wisconsin—I wouldn't have bothered with *that* claimant—not a document to his name and a doozy of a story—Mary was in a caravan in Montana that got wiped out by Indians and diphtheria. You believe that, and I'll sell you the Tappan Zee. Brad was going anyway to visit his girlfriend, so what the hell—just don't charge your travel, I told him. Yours: we'll put the burden on Nagy to come up with an expert—somebody to testify to the age of the carving. If he does, the Scots will have to decide if they want us to find our own. What kind of expert analyzes the age of tree carvings? It's going to pass *Frye?*"

"What carving?"

"Connie didn't tell you—paralegal with hair out to here? Nagy's main evidence is some tree inside his house—*inside* the house. Has Grandma's maiden name carved into it. I'm not making this up! *He* sure is, or my name's FDR. That carving's proof he's heir to millions. Take the camera—ask Connie how it works, and get some shots—get the inscription up close. And ask her for the tape recorder. I may send you up to Mamaroneck next month, if hoity-toity Mr. Grey-Davison is around. This clown *only just heard* we're looking for a MacDonalde heir. We've been publishing notices for a year, but he's been 'on the Continent'—like there's only one! And he might not 'be able to schedule it so soon'—like we've got all the time in the world. His attorney tried to arrange a meeting in Edinburgh—the Scots had a fit! They don't want to get their hands dirty with claimants."

Addy stopped by the large warehouse-like room housing the floor-to-ceiling gray metal shelves. The top and mid-level shelves were filled with black loose-leaf binders, white labels on the spines. The bottom shelves were a mix of notebooks and white document boxes, also labeled. She walked along the tiled floor to the back of the room, where the paralegals' desks were crammed together. On the wall, a whiteboard with the heading *MacDonalde* contained two columns of names: the left, claimants to be interviewed; the right, attorneys and law clerks assigned to the interview and the date of the interview in parentheses. Not every claimant would necessarily be interviewed, Addy knew—the assignments just represented Joe's thinking of who'd do it if the Scots gave the okay. When they thought a claimant might be legit, they had Engel hold off on other interviews until they had fully checked the claimant out. Joe said it was like trying to plan a bar mitzvah during wartime.

Brittany, Simon, Dan, and Brad were each listed six or seven times on the whiteboard. Addy was listed opposite Nagy and someone named Grey-Davison.

Connie was helpful, providing copies of interview transcripts and explaining how the tape recorder and camera worked. "Look at a transcript: each interview starts with the same formalities after you turn the machine on—who you are, the date and time and location, who else is present. At the end, state the time you're ending it."

One of Simon's transcripts Addy leafed through showed him going through the introduction and then asking the claimant to state her name, how it was spelled, and her address. Then he instructed her to use proper names—Mary MacDonalde, for instance, instead of 'my mother' or 'my grandmother.' Next he asked where the interviewee worked and whether she was married and had any children. Only after this background information did he ask about Mary MacDonalde: how was she related, was she still alive, who her descendants were.

Connie was also helpful about documents, pointing to pages in the transcript where Simon had the witness identify them and read portions out loud.

"Sometimes the witnesses send documents ahead of time, so you know what you'll be asking. Or we get hold of them ourselves, either through Drecker or FOIA or state FOIAs. Financial records and family-court records are off-limits, but you'd be surprised what Drecker digs up. Joe says don't ask them how—we don't want to know."

FRANCIS WAS IN THE LIVING room reading but put down the journal when Addy sat on the sofa and told him some of what she'd learned. "Record keeping varies state by state and county by county, and there's not always a central location with complete information. Back before World War II, it was really hit-and-miss. The hospital where a kid was born might've notified the county, and the county would've sent the parents a birth certificate, but the state agency overseeing the records might just get some notice that a child named X was born on this date at this place to parents Y and Z. And with home deliveries, you had to rely on the doctor or midwife to send in the information. Connie, the paralegal, was saying that the only copies of marriage licenses in some county in the Midwest got destroyed in a flood."

"That does not surprise me. Photocopiers are a relatively recent invention. And before carbon paper and ditto machines and mimeographs, people copied by hand. To get a sense of how time consuming that was, read *Bartleby the Scrivener*. Dickens, too, gives us a sense of the painstaking demands placed on the clerk."

"This is changing the subject, but it's been bothering me. When I told Carson I'd go see vessels in Greenport after the interview, it wasn't to get a ride—I do like seeing the ships, learning about them. But is that leading him on—like I want to date? Should I have said no?"

"As long as you are not dishonest about your feelings, I see nothing wrong with—but tell me: Will it actually be *enjoyable* to see boats in his company? Is it truly enjoyable to go on an outing with someone you are not at all fond of?"

"I don't *dis*like him. He can be funny. And he doesn't go on about high-society stuff anymore. It's just that I know he feels—romantic—

about me, and I don't feel that way about him. Actually, I think that's why I'm so comfortable with him—because I *don't* have those feelings."

Francis leaned back in the chair, his eyes on the far wall, and his mouth widened in a smile. "Your grandmother maintained a similar friendship for a time while she and I were dating. He was a suitor—by that I mean someone who wanted to marry her. She had made clear to me she was not in love with Edward—that was his name—and was candid with *him* about dating *me*. But for whatever reason he was not dissuaded from wooing her and continued to take her to plays and concerts. Why wasn't I jealous? She had admitted to . . . to what you young people call a 'lack of chemistry'—her exact phrase eludes me now. Which also functioned as a tacit admission that with *me*, chemistry was *not* lacking.

"No, chemistry was not lacking. My goodness—how did we get on this subject? I certainly never intended—Marjorie's friendship with the stockbroker, that's right. In an odd way, Adelaide, I *appreciated* his attentions to her. I could ill afford tickets to plays and concerts—other than student productions. Plus, my studies and teaching obligations consumed most of my time. So my thinking went: if she enjoys the afternoons and evenings we are obliged to spend apart, she will not resent the long hours I am required to work. In any event, the young man eventually had to retreat to lick his wounds. But to return to the subject at hand: I believe the difficulty *you* face will be Carson's persistence. Not only is he without a known rival, but he is prodigiously endowed with conceit and no doubt believes his charms will wear down your resistance."

"He's moving to San Francisco in June, after graduation. And I'm pretty busy with school and homework and the MacDonalde case, so I wouldn't go out that often."

"With the situation as you describe it, then no, I see no harm in your agreeing to a date. As long as he behaves like a gentleman."

CHAPTER 26

IT WAS ONE OF THOSE weird January days where the sunshine and temperature in the upper forties made it feel like spring. Addy wore her parka anyway and brought a scarf and gloves because Carson had warned it would be windy by the water.

They'd taken the subway and now were walking to the rental car agency, the only one in Queens with vehicles still available—the ones near La Guardia were out of everything but "monstrosities." He'd insisted on carrying her briefcase—she'd made a pro forma protest, but he said it felt like it was filled with bricks, and he didn't want to spend the afternoon at her orthopedist's. It had a tape recorder and camera, she told him.

"Then I won't slam it against the subway car. You realize you're crazy to go this far for a halibut schooner?"

"Do you think it will be crowded?"

"Doubt it—the North Fork isn't the Hamptons."

There was no sign advertising Hertz or Avis or one of the other auto franchise names at the lot, but the man in the booth seemed to know Carson, and the two huddled briefly. Addy scanned the dozen or so vehicles, none looking new.

Carson came over dangling a key.

"I went with a beater because we can keep it until ten if we decide to stop for dinner."

HE DROVE CAREFULLY, STICKING TO the same speed as most of the other traffic and rarely changing lanes. They passed dense commercial areas and light industry, residential neighborhoods and nondescript woods.

He seemed to read her thoughts. "Have you been out this way before? It's a boring ride till you reach the coast. The ocean side is rough, big waves, what the Jones Beach crowd loves. I'd think twice about taking anything smaller than a thirty-foot. The sound is better for swimming, though it gets some nasty squalls and nor'easters."

"How far out have you sailed?"

"I've crisscrossed the sound as far up as Orient Point—I can show you later. That's not the same as ocean sailing." He looked briefly in her direction. "I've heard the Pacific isn't as rough but nothing for novices."

"Seattle's on Puget Sound, not the ocean. And surrounded by lakes."

This time he asked what her family did for fun, and because the upcoming interview made her nervous, Addy was glad for the distraction. She told him about camping trips with her father and brothers, the trails at Rainier and how the streams were ice cold even in June, and that they once saw a bear, which her father scared off by banging pots and pans. In the early morning she would lie in the tent before anyone else was awake and listen to the birds. Eating huckleberries right off the bush was nice too.

Maybe because of the questions he asked, she ended up talking about in middle and high school a sense of being on the fringes. But that was okay, she insisted; she never felt pressured to conform. Not that she was a nonconformist, like her brother Michael—an avant-garde sculptor supporting himself by driving a cab.

"I never thought of it that way," Carson said, "having to conform."

"Didn't you feel a lot of pressure—all the social rules?"

He glanced in the rearview mirror before answering. "Yes and no. But speaking of bucking the rules, your grandfather—"

"I'm sorry he's rude sometimes."

"Oh, that? He's just being protective. Doesn't trust my intentions."

Addy almost laughed—'intentions' was the kind of word Francis would use.

"What I mean is," Carson went on, "he set his sights on being a professor and went for it. Sometimes you know what you want to do but don't have the guts."

For some minutes they silently watched the scenery, mile after mile of bland landscape, strip malls, factories in the middle of nowhere. The names on the signs sounded Native American: Hauppauge, Ronkonkoma, Patchogue, Yaphank—Carson pronounced them for her. They exited the LIE at its very end in Riverhead, on a road of car dealerships and family-style restaurants. But five minutes later, like magic, they were deep in farmland. Nothing was growing now, but they began to pass hand-painted signs by empty roadside stands advertising pumpkins, flowers, fresh eggs, peaches, bicolor corn, zucchini, new potatoes.

"Poles, Greeks, Italians settled the North Fork," Carson said. "The Greeks and Italians know how to handle seafood."

"Did your family come here a lot?"

"College was when I really explored the place. Had a roommate from Aquebogue."

THE FOUR WAS DANGLING FROM the 214 on the mailbox. Sitting some twenty yards from the road behind a weedy-looking yard, the one-story structure half-resembled a small barn. Carson continued driving, and a few blocks away, they found an open coffee shop where he'd wait until she was done. He drove her back to 214.

The man answering the bell looked about forty and wore a red-plaid flannel shirt, old jeans, and brown boots. He didn't shake her hand when she introduced herself, just led the way into what could've been the interior of a log cabin, a long space with exposed rafters and varnished walls. The few windows were narrow, and the lighting was poor, but Addy could make out a table and chairs and fireplace. To the right, a rough, knotty tree stump about four feet high jutted up into the room between floorboards. Some of the bark had worn away.

"They didn't have the equipment to uproot the thing," the man said, "so they built the house around it. Shored it up pretty good."

He motioned at a couch near the fireplace where an elderly man sat. "That's my father."

The old man turned and smiled. His hair was bright white.

"You're Gregor Nagy?" Addy asked.

"Yeah, that's him," the younger man said.

"You're Dwayne?"

"Yeah."

According to the letter that Dwayne had sent Engel Klein, Gregor was only in his early seventies, but his shock of white hair and wrinkles made him look a lot older than Francis. Addy set down her briefcase and used the low table for the tape recorder, camera, and manila folders. When she looked up, Gregor was smiling. His eyes were a very light blue.

"You're recording us?" Dwayne asked.

"It said so in the letter," she murmured.

Dwayne shrugged. Gregor Nagy said nothing.

Addy found an outlet, plugged in the recorder, and sat in the chair opposite the elder Mr. Nagy. Dwayne took up a position behind the couch, over his father's shoulder. With the machine turned on, she was able to recite from memory the introductory speech adapted from Simon's transcript: her name; the date, time, and location of the interview; and the official Scottish title of the matter. She asked the elder Mr. Nagy his name, and he said nothing.

Dwayne tapped his father's shoulder. "Tell her your whole name."

The old man mumbled, "Gregor Stanislav Nagy." She asked him to spell it, and Dwayne answered for him. Flustered, Addy said that his father should answer the questions, and Dwayne said that that would take all day—couldn't she see he wasn't young anymore.

"Then could you state *your* name and spell it."

Dwayne did as she asked and in response to Addy's questions gave both men's employment history: Gregor had worked in a hand tools manufacturing plant until retiring, and Dwayne had worked for a commercial fishery until laid off "on account of some crock about overfishing."

"When were you born?" Addy asked Gregor.

He blinked his light-blue eyes and whispered, "January 18, 1920."

"What was your father's name?"

"Dominik Nagy."

"What was your mother's name?"

"Mary."

"What was her maiden name?"

"Dad, she wants to know your mother's *whole* name—you remember."

The father tried looking over his shoulder but couldn't turn enough. Dwayne said, "Mary Agnes MacDonalde Nagy. Isn't that right, Dad?"

"Yes." The old man smiled kindly at Addy. She asked him to spell MacDonalde, but Dwayne did it for him, with an *e* at the end.

"Do you have a copy of your parents' marriage license?" Addy asked Gregor.

"All that stuff was tossed years ago, all their papers," Dwayne said. He motioned at the walls. "It's not like there's storage space."

"Did your parents get married here in Mattituck?"

"The story my mom used to tell," Dwayne said, "and by the way, she died in '84—the story that got passed down to her was that Dominik was about to ship out to Europe—World War I was going on—and Mary and him eloped right before. Were gone four days and never told anyone where." Gregor blinked.

"When did Dominik Nagy and Mary Agnes MacDonalde get married—what day and year?"

Gregor continued to sit silent and blink. Dwayne answered, "In 1918."

"You don't remember a month or day?"

Dwayne made an offhand gesture. "Do you, Dad? Remember when your parents got married?"

Gregor still stared kindly at Addy. She tried asking the question as leading.

"So you don't know the month and date your parents got married?" He still stared and blinked. It wasn't until she asked about brothers and sisters that he spoke.

"Had Gwennie, but she's gone now."

"Gwendolyn," Dwayne said. "*G-w-e-n-d-o-l-y-n.*"

"Did she have a middle name?"

The blank stare returned to the father's face. "Who knows." Dwayne said.

"When was she born?"

"Twenty-two," Dwayne said.

"In 1922?"

"Yes."

"Do you know the exact date?"

"No."

"But you know she was born in 1922?"

"My dad and her were two years apart."

"Did Gwendolyn have any children?"

The older man said slowly, "Gwennie died when she was eleven. The polio."

"Do or did you have any other siblings?" Addy asked.

The pale-blue eyes seemed to focus, to fasten on her. "No, just two of us."

Gregor didn't seem to understand most of the other questions, such as whether he knew of any half siblings or other children Mary may have had or where she'd lived before moving to Mattituck. Dwayne said Mary had moved there in her late teens, he'd heard, to work for a family that lived nearby. He didn't remember their name, and he didn't know where Mary had lived before Mattituck, though it was "common knowledge" she'd been born in Scotland. When Addy asked for any records with Mary's name on them, the old man opened his eyes wide but said nothing. Dwayne repeated that his grandparents' papers had been tossed years ago.

Dwayne did produce a copy of his father's birth certificate, which gave Gregor's date of birth as January 18, 1920, in Mattituck, Suffolk County, New York, and his parents as Dominik V. Nagy and Mary Agnes McDon. Nagy.

"When did your mother die?" Addy asked Gregor. He gazed at her.

"In 1937," Dwayne said.

"Was she living in Mattituck at the time?"

The question was directed to Gregor, and Dwayne answered, "Yeah."

"Where is Mary Agnes Nagy buried?"

"Cremated," Dwayne said. "Wanted her ashes thrown in the water near the Statue of Liberty."

Again, Addy asked about records or any kind of document with Mary's maiden name, listing as examples birth and death certificates, a passport, driver's license, social security and voter registration cards, immigration and naturalization papers, even utility bills or correspondence.

Dwayne repeated that everything was tossed long ago. "Even if we did still have stuff," he added, "they might not have the right spelling."

"Why not?"

"People misspelled it all the time. The death certificate probably got it wrong, but my grandfather figured that wasn't worth hassling. Who was going to see it? Not her."

"Do you have *anything* with Mary MacDonalde's maiden name on it?"

"Just the tree," Dwayne said. "When my grandparents were dating, my grandfather carved her name onto the trunk." Addy said she needed to photograph it, and he told her to take all the pictures she wanted. "It's been through some things—spilled drinks, termites—but we cleared them out pretty quick 'cause it's an heirloom."

Addy took the lens cap off the camera and went to where Dwayne was standing with a flashlight. He ran the beam up and down the stump.

"Guests get a kick out of carving their initials. When my grandparents got engaged, he went whole hog."

The bark had worn away, and carvings old and new ran horizontally, vertically, diagonally. *Annaliese, age 6; the Kreuzers 1929; VFW.* The pith was uneven and a deep mustard color where dug out the most; the shallower wood was lighter. For some reason the older carvings were easier to read—*Nell Morse 1933* was more legible than *Amanda Olds 1977.* Addy squatted to read where Dwayne pointed the flashlight beam.

"Like I said in the letter, it was a tradition. Used to be a special knife—don't know what happened to it. Family, *good* friends—not just anybody—it'd be a mess if everybody who came inside could do it."

Dwayne lowered the beam to a spot toward the bottom of the stump. "You might have to bend down."

Still squatting, Addy stooped further and read *Dominik Nagy + Mary A. MacDonalde 1917.* She photographed the carving from multiple angles.

CHAPTER 27

CARSON CLOSED HIS BOOK. THE pepper shaker sat on the check and some cash. "How did it go?"

"Weird. I'd tell you more if I could."

"Lucy will fill me in when it hits the tabloids. You hungry?"

"I brought a bunch of snack bars I'll eat in the car."

He carried Francis's briefcase and waited a few yards away from the rental while Addy changed into jeans and boots in the back seat.

They drove back to the main road and continued east. Pastures spread out on both sides, alternating with woods and clusters of houses. A few clouds lingered in the distance, but overhead was clear sky.

Addy wondered if the photos of the tree would come out well. The *e* at the end of MacDonalde was so blatantly recent, the pulp a brighter yellowish brown and flakier, she'd had to make an effort not to smile when Dwayne first shone the flashlight beam on it. Would Joe hire some expert to come out and look? Would they take samples? When she got home, she'd write the recap. Joe wanted it to be very short and just state the claimant's connection to Mary and what actual evidence clearly supported or disproved the claim. "The Scots" also wanted a sentence with the interviewer's impression of the witness's honesty, but Joe had nixed the "subjective bullshit" and told her to always end with the line *The claimant's manner gave no indication of dishonesty*.

"That's all we need," he'd yelled, "somebody suing us for twenty-five mil because their claim was tossed on our *opining* they were liars!"

"You okay?" Carson threw her a puzzled look.

"Yes—just thinking about the interview. It was uncomfortable. Don't repeat this . . ."

He moved his hand like he was zipping his mouth.

"I think these claimants are frauds. My opinion doesn't matter— the Scottish court will look at the evidence—but it's uncomfortable when you think people are lying to your face. I really don't like it. That's one of the reasons I don't want to do litigation."

Carson said nothing. A few minutes later he pointed to the side of the road. "Vineyards." They were passing rows and rows of what looked like miniature trees with low branches twisted like witches' hands. "Home of some halfway-decent Long Island wines. Want to see if one's open? They might let us do a tasting. Not out of generosity, you realize, but hoping we'll buy a case."

"Let's just go see the boats."

They passed small shops and homes set behind trees and shrubbery and suddenly, not expecting it, Addy faced an enormous expanse of blue-green, waves and whitecaps and a ship on the horizon. Carson decelerated for a few seconds before the view was gone.

"Yep, that's the sound. Look, how about we go to Orient Point first? Just ten minutes more, at the very tip of the island."

The ride continued to be countryside picturesque, and they crossed a causeway bordered on both sides by water and a fringe of reeds. The lagoons on the right broke into open bay and sand and marshland. The distant shoreline was a dusky green.

Carson parked the car in a dirt lot, and they walked along the beach pebbles, the wind gusting but not too cold. "We're on the very tip of Long Island." He pointed. "That's eastern Connecticut, and out that way, past the small islands, Martha's Vineyard and Nantucket and the mighty Atlantic. Three thousand miles of her."

Addy stepped back as the breaking waves sent foam creeping up the sand before it melted away. She found herself transfixed by the currents, like an undulating quilt, obliquely angled swatches continuously rippling and merging. In the midst of these melding patterns, a flat, glassy patch would glide unperturbed, like a still pond.

She stooped now and then to examine a mussel or clam. They found a large dark helmet-like thing Carson said was a horseshoe crab. Limp rags of green and red seaweed stretched along the high-tide mark, interspersed with bits of gray driftwood and brightly colored stones, some purplish, some coral, some almost alabaster.

"Imagine a calm summer night," he said, looking out at the water and sounding almost dreamy, "and you're the sailor on watch. You're perched up in the crow's nest all by yourself. And say there's no moon. Suspended a hundred and fifty feet in the air, you're surrounded by darkness, blackness, no shapes or details. You can't see where the ocean ends and the sky begins. The only sound might be the waves sloshing or rigging hitting the mast. Now imagine, against this complete darkness, the *stars*. Sprinkled all across the sky, *thousands* of them, like shiny confetti, more than you could ever count. Wouldn't the world seem fantastic?" A gull banked right and left in graceful arcs.

"Or imagine a full moon, bronze, gold, platinum—whatever color, she's like sun hitting metal. You can see why people personified her, especially sailors—your night companion, just the two of you keeping watch, making sure nothing goes wrong while everybody sleeps."

Addy also spoke meditatively. "Puget Sound, our lakes, they're really pretty, and the mountains too. All sorts of colors, and not just at sunrise and sunset. But you don't get the same sense of vastness as here."

He moved as if to step closer but stopped. After several more minutes of watching the waves, they went back to the car.

WIDE-BRANCHED TREES AND OLDER WOODEN homes lined the road into Greenport. Quaint touches like porch swings and white latticework, and features like tall narrow windows and slatted shutters, gave the feel of an older, simpler time. Addy imagined in summer wicker tables on lawns and mason jars filled with flowers on front steps. It dawned on her that those images came from Zach's photos of Bickville. "We're River City, Iowa," he used to joke.

They strolled to the docks along a narrow street of antique shops, clothing boutiques, and small restaurants. Dozens of small boats bobbed complacently, their white masts a bright contrast from the tarp covers. No one was around; you could hear the water sloshing.

Spotting an old two-master, they headed toward it. The sails were down and the rigging tied tightly. The vessel was barely half the size of the brigantine, and her foremast almost as tall as the main mast. On the stern was painted *The Scamper*.

A man in a green parka bent over the pier by some dinghies. "Hello," Carson called out. "Ahoy." The man straightened up and smiled. Carson showed his membership card. "She okay for boarding?"

"Suit yourself—you've got her all to your lonesome."

"Great. Are these her dories?"

"Taken from another. I call her 'The Scavenger.'"

A corrugated metal sheet fitted with wire handrails served as a gangplank; Addy assumed it wasn't the original, because Carson had said the vessel dated from the late 1800s. She could feel the swaying more than on the brigantine, even though the water was calmer. Copying him, she placed her hands on gunwales and posts as she followed aft. None of the woodwork or metal fixtures looked polished or elegant. The dark deck was rough and uneven.

He stopped at a huge iron spool and rested his hand on the boom.

"Each of these dories has its own gurdy. You see, halibut hang out on the ocean floor, but you can't pinpoint where. So in the morning, the mother ship lowers a bunch of dories into the water, one or two men apiece, and they spread out and drop longlines. And if a school moves through, you use the gurdy to haul up the catch."

The man in the green parka had come over. "The females can grow to four hundred pounds."

Carson shook his head in wonder. "They had to crank the fish the whole way up from the ocean floor, against gravity, the weight of the water—"

"The power gurdy made a difference," the man said. "Still, a foggy day, you can't see your own nose, trying to keep the dory steady while working the gurdy, a squall comes through with big swells—a lot of men died. They outlawed it by the thirties, the dories."

As he had done on the brigantine, Carson pointed out parts of the vessel—the hatch cover, anchor winch, scuppers. The pilothouse was a small, boxlike room.

When they returned midship, the man asked Addy if she belonged to the organization too. "Or you let him drag you here all the way from the city?"

"I was visiting someone nearby."

"Well, I'll give you a souvenir to take home."

He brought out a Polaroid from under his parka. Noticing Addy's awkwardness, Carson said he didn't want to be in the picture. They convinced her to pose with one arm around the main mast, and when he was handed the photo, Carson said it was great. In the car, he offered to make her a copy, but she said she didn't need one.

THEY STOPPED FOR AN EARLY supper, and he finally became talkative about his own childhood: the summers at Hammonasset State Park and sailing with family friends who owned a boat. "They taught me how to tack, steer, put up the jib, tie different knots." He went to "a small college nobody's heard of," and "the law school admissions police probably put my application in the acceptance pile by mistake."

Both of them were quiet for most of the drive back to the city, until Carson asked where she saw herself in ten years. "Partner putting in sixty-hour weeks? Stay-at-home mom? Working part-time?"

"Haven't thought about it."

Her answer seemed to surprise him. "Why did you become a lawyer?"

"I don't know—my dad was one, it seemed interesting. Why did you?"

"Almost flunked chemistry, so med school was out. I'm lousy with numbers, so forget finance. That left law. You've *never* thought about having kids? I never dated a woman who hadn't already made up her mind one way or the other."

"Have you made up yours?"

"I want to be a dad. Come on: imagine living in a big old house like the ones in Greenport, sitting on a porch swing on a summer night, three or four kids running around in the yard chasing fireflies." He sat straighter in the seat. "But it's not a deal breaker. My wife would have to want them too."

IT WAS DARK WHEN THEY returned the rental car, and the subway was crowded, making conversation difficult. At Addy's stop, Carson announced he would walk her home, even though she said it wasn't necessary. As they approached the small park, he asked her if she wanted to see *Julius Caesar* the next weekend. A little embarrassed, she said she had a hard time understanding Shakespeare plays when they were performed.

"How about a movie, then?"

"What movie?"

"Who cares? The point is a cozy place to smooch. We can sit in the last row so we don't annoy people."

She gave a half laugh. "You'll have to find someone else for that."

"It wouldn't bother you if I did?"

"No."

"You say it like you're being nice."

They moved to the side of a bench to let a man walking a dog by. Addy ran her fingers along the top of the bench back. "I'm trying to be honest."

"Then be honest with the why."

Now she laughed outright. "Are you used to everyone who goes out with you wanting to—to 'smooch'?"

"Not at all. But usually there's clear disgust or someone else in the picture."

"I guess there's someone else."

"You said there wasn't."

In short simple sentences, she told him about Zach. "Ever since, nothing seems to matter. I don't feel about anything like I used to. It's weird to become a stranger to yourself, to lose—I don't know—continuity?"

Carson looked at the bare branches above them. "I don't want to push a lot of psychobabble on you, but not caring about things could be a way of trying not to get hurt again."

"That's what I figured."

"Have you tried a therapist? Lucy had some rough stuff happen and went to somebody. Helped her a lot. She said."

"I don't really have the time. School, working, Francis—keeps me pretty busy."

"Would my taking an oath to be around for the long haul make a difference?"

She shook her head. They walked to her building without talking.

CHAPTER 28

"WHAT HAPPENED!"

Prepared for her shock at seeing my body sprawled on the carpet, I was ready with reassurances. "It is merely my ankle that feels tender. Not five minutes ago. I foolishly had my nose in a book while walking and fell over the ottoman. Some minor abrasions on my arm, but it's the ankle that is painful."

Adelaide squatted and put her arm around my back. "Use just your other foot, and I'll help lift you onto the couch."

"How can you manage—I'm so much larger?"

"I can."

It was not an easy maneuver, the two of us straining, yet she was able to raise me enough that I could rest my derrière on the cushion. "I should stop scolding you for carrying such a heavy backpack," I managed to pant. "It has probably built up your strength."

Adelaide fetched ice cubes wrapped in a dish towel, which I held against the injury, and then brought a glass of water and the container of ibuprofen. Only when convinced I suffered from no greater damage—my bones were all intact and I did not "black out" or "become dizzy" before falling—was she willing to discuss her expedition to the North Fork. Her facial expression while recounting the story of the tree stump interview denoted wry bemusement, and to my inquiries about the remainder of her day, I was rewarded with an overabundance of information about halibut vessels and longlines, details I could well have survived without.

MONDAY MORNING, ADELAIDE TELEPHONED DR. Conti's office and was able to procure an appointment for that very afternoon, a consequence, I explained, of Marjorie having been a dear friend of his mother's. I was compelled to use Adelaide as a crutch, and our pace in walking to the elevator, cab, Dr. Conti's waiting room, and examining room was glacial. Although he believed I had suffered merely a sprain, he had the ankle X-rayed to be sure. The nurse provided me with a *useful* pair of crutches, adjustable for my six-foot-two frame.

However, with one crisis withered, a new one bloomed. Being incapacitated, I firmly insisted on forgoing the trip to Seattle for Olivia's wedding later in February. My granddaughter assailed me with a veritable *legion* of arguments, appealing to my sense of guilt and enumerating the myriad ways in which the trip could be managed without undue difficulty. I was pleased at her performance, revealing as it did the deft marshaling of arguments that is the lawyer's stock in trade; she was well suited for her chosen profession. But I was not to be countermanded.

Number one, I said, I did not relish the idea of burdening people at what should be a lighthearted celebration. Every wedding party relocation—home to church, church to reception, reception to home—Adelaide and her mother would concern themselves with my transportation, ease, and well-being instead of 'abandoning their cares' and fully enjoying the nuptial festivities. And number two: physical discomfort was best endured at home. Dr. Conti did not predict I would be pain free, I reminded her, and I was loath to take palliative medications—in my limited experience, they constituted simply a trade of one set of symptoms for another.

Seeking to curtail the discussion, I did not explain that enduring pain unaided by pharmaceuticals was a source of pride with me. If an injury were severe enough to require *some* medicinal application, I would take a dose sufficient to mitigate, not erase, the pain. All my life I had been able—as had my father and grandfather and great-grandfather—to invoke a certain stoicism in the face of physical discomfort.

"Call me a stubborn old man, if you will; I do not deny it. Yes, your mother will be disappointed, but she has to admit that a second wedding, particularly one occurring in middle age, is not the blushing-bride extravaganza of a first. And *you* must acknowledge my wisdom in having insisted on purchasing refundable tickets."

Of course, Adelaide had no choice but to accede to my wish. Yet she was persistent enough—manifesting her Wallace genes—to extract from me an agreement for a home health aide to visit each day.

Telephoning Olivia to break the news, I was sorry to learn that defections were rampant. Richard would be presenting a paper at some conference in Cape Town, and his wife and daughters each had a reason for not making the trip—school examinations and the like. Nor would Marcia's branch of the family be in attendance, for Alex's nuptials were occurring the very same weekend. His affair was to be quite small—just the immediate families; I surmised that the bride's pregnancy might have prompted embarrassment, although Olivia said that Marcia reported "all sorts of scheduling problems" beleaguering them. Adelaide's brothers, at least, would be in attendance in Seattle, but the younger, Michael, was not bringing his wife, because she was too close to *her* due date.

To her credit, Olivia took the cancellations in stride; she *sounded* like the proverbial joyful bride. "How do *you* feel," she asked, "about becoming a great-grandfather, and twice in one year? Patty is due in March, and Mindy, in August."

"A bit like Methuselah."

The conversation ended on a positive note, Olivia assuring me, with a vibrant laugh, that a small wedding suited Tony and her "just fine."

ALL WAS NOT QUIET ON the law-firm front, however, Adelaide having been chastised by Joe over the Mattituck interview. His copy of the tape-recording transcript contained red markings on "every single page" indicating questions she should have asked or ways she should have phrased the ones she did ask.

One mistake was not scrupulously adhering to the rule of using proper names. She followed up a question about Mary MacDonalde with one along the lines of 'When did she do thus-and-such?' The second question should have been 'When did *Mary MacDonalde* do thus-and-such?' Although in ordinary conversation, the use of 'she' would suffice for a listener to understand the person referred to, Joe contended that a transcript excerpt presented to a court might be deemed ambiguous.

"My dear, we all experience fits and starts at the beginning of our careers, no matter how well prepared we believe ourselves to be. Over time, you will gain knowledge, expertise, know-how—all manner of wisdom. Do not let early missteps discourage you."

"Anyway, the claim's been disproved. Drecker—the investigators—tracked down some document showing Mary Agnes Nagy's maiden name didn't have an *e* on the end, plus she was born in Schenectady."

DESPITE HER NOVITIATE MISTAKES AT the interview, Adelaide continued to be assigned work on the MacDonalde case, reviewing records and questionnaire responses from other claimants. And I, for my part, continued working on my opus. Sometimes a literary problem confounded me, requiring a distraction, so I would steal a peek at Mary's letters. Her metamorphosis from a girl absorbed in how Mrs. So-and-So dressed to a young woman pondering larger causes never failed to impress me, even if I did not subscribe to every political allegiance Mary adopted.

I have read most astonishing pamphlet about injustice to the Negro. Written by a Negro far more scholarly than father. This particular letter went on to describe various and sundry businesses that discriminated against Black people by refusing to hire them or by treating them unfairly as shoppers. A large department store—was it in Spokane or San Francisco or Portland, Oregon, I wondered—permitted them to shop only in the basement sections. A millinery shop did not permit Black women to try on hats prior to purchase. And so forth.

Yet the young Scotswoman also filled Violet in on the lighter side of life on the fruit ranch. Her description of picking fruit with the children held some charm. *The bees are not fearsome. Mr W climbs the ladders with us and makes a game. He says there is great satisfaction working with nature's bounty.* She ended the missive by remarking, *I wish you had come to America with me and learned that true Christianity does not raise brother over brother.* Oh, Henry James, would you have found Mary's conversion to Americanism thus complete?

ROBERT SPENT A PORTION OF his next visit coloring and playing with the farm animals, but when he noticed Adelaide reading—she was trying to finish some assignments before her trip—he paused to watch her. Did her jottings in a notebook strike him as analogous to his drawing? Did he wonder why she stared at a book without appearing to move, or was he used to his parents and grandparents reading? He generally paid me little mind, although this visit I was able to provide some distraction by showing him how I moved with the crutches. It only occurred to me after sitting again that he might assume a pair could be fitted to permit *him* to walk by himself. At least he was able to see that he was not alone in having ambulatory difficulties.

THE EVE OF ADELAIDE'S DEPARTURE for Seattle, she was late returning home, and I tried not to think of misfortunes that could have befallen her. When the telephone rang, I silently prayed it was not the police or a hospital nurse with terrifying news. It was neither.

"Dad, I'm just calling to let Addy know Elliot will pick her up at SeaTac."

"That's fine; that's fine. She's not here yet, but I will convey the message."

"Did I catch you in the middle of something?"

"No, no. It's nothing."

"Because you sound—"

I did not want my daughter concluding I was a worry wart! "It is only that while I have you on the telephone, I thought of mentioning a small victory over a problem in my opus that has been vexing me. But if this is an inconvenient time—"

"No, go right ahead."

"The conundrum was how to characterize Catherine Sloper's change in the years after Morris's departure, how to characterize her metamorphosis from ugly duckling into swan. Because she did molt, or change, or shed a carapace of some sort. And I believe I have hit upon the answer: Catherine acquired self-respect. Courage, too, and independence, but these flowed from her newfound dignity. Self-respect was the source of it, of her capacity to 'discard,' one might say, both suitor and father."

"I thought she *acquired* a carapace," Olivia said. "It wasn't a happy ending."

"No, in her own way, Catherine emerged triumphant. No life partakes of every joy—one can over-romanticize the so-called happy ending. Michelangelo, Dostoyevsky, Beethoven—I suspect none of them would fit our picture of 'the happily married man,' yet they had lives well worth living. And how many happily married men don't secretly covet the life of the artist? Catherine did not have everything, no, but she became useful and respected. And even quite popular among—"

"She was entrenched in bitterness, Dad. Never got past the betrayal."

"Many losses mark us for a long time, but that is not the equivalent of an enduring bitterness."

"Other suitors were decent men who could have given her contentment."

"She did not love them."

"She would not *allow* herself to love them. Her bitterness was a cement wall."

"Ah, your daughter has just arrived home. We will continue this discussion at a later date—after your nuptial vows. Please convey my congratulations to Tony."

Adelaide's cheeks were flushed pink.

"Francis, you can't say anything about this to anybody."

"Good gracious: What has happened?"

"In the MacDonalde case—it's not public."

"You have my word. But before I forget: your brother—I believe your mother said Elliot—will meet you at the airport."

"Great, now listen: they found an official record of an Anne MacDonalde—MacDonalde with an e on the end! Near Elmira, which isn't that far from Clopes!"

"My word."

"It's a record of her birth, in 1962."

"A record of her birth. So that would make her how old?"

"Around thirty-two."

"Has anyone spoken to her?"

"Not yet—they don't know where she is. They're checking phone books, property records—lots of things. They don't have the actual birth certificate—her name popped up on an index."

"But in 1962, Mary would have been well past child-bearing age. She would have—"

"It could be her son's or grandson's kid. Isn't it exciting?"

"Yes, of course. But, my dear, don't you have considerable packing left to do?"

CHAPTER 29

CHARMED AS I WAS BY her delightful Caribbean accent, the home health aide, a stout, middle-aged Black woman originally from Jamaica, in short order dissolved the goodwill with which I initially had greeted her by proving herself a scold. I iterated and *re*iterated to Mrs. Procrustes—not her real name—that the flare-up of arthritis in my hip was not due to any failure to follow the exercise regimen decreed by the physical therapist. The physical therapist, I might have added, was clearly a disciple, if not direct descendant, of the Marquis de Sade.

"An unimpaired person can compensate for a painful right ankle by placing additional weight on the left, but with the resurgence of inflammation in my hip, the crutches are of limited value," I was compelled to repeat like a mantra.

For three full days I was at the mercy of Mrs. Procrustes for tasks I could not perform alone, principally food preparation and bathing. Because each visit had to meet the minimum of four hours—another benefit furnished our civilization by lawyers, no doubt—her visits felt unnecessarily protracted.

Other than tormenting me with advice on exercises I could perform sitting down, her chief form of amusement was watching crime dramas on television. As the sounds penetrated my office, concentrating on my opus became an impossibility, and my only recourse was to join her in the living room.

A fascination with violent crime has always mystified me. Excluding wartime, violence is not a staple of ordinary life except, perhaps, for the poor.

Indeed, Zach's murder was the exception in terms of my own family being affected. In almost eighty years on the planet, I have never been assaulted, robbed, or otherwise subjected to a violent act. *Crime and Punishment* was interesting only for being a psychological meditation, not a story about crime.

Nonetheless, for better or worse, I became conversant in certain criminal law jargon: 'DOA,' 'perps,' 'remand,' and the morbid 'eating one's gun.' At least I drew satisfaction from instructing Procrustes on a thing or two, drawing on Adelaide's tutelage from her courses. 'Man two,' short for 'manslaughter in the second degree,' would be the charge leveled if I were to strangle Procrustes for ridiculing me. Which she did without fail when I donned an old pair of swim trunks before my bath. What she had or had not 'seen before' was of no interest to me whatsoever.

My arthritis subsided on the eve of Adelaide's return, obviating any further need for Procrustes's services, but I was not entirely free of the harpy, as she was coming by in the afternoon to have me sign her 'hours log,' which she had inadvertently left on the vanity. Hence, I had need to accomplish my special project prior to my nap.

Limping on one crutch, I made my way into Richard's old room. The closet door opened easily. And the gray shoebox was in "plain view" on the shelf, within easy reach. I rested the crutch against the jamb and took the box in both hands and carefully arranged it under one arm. With the crutch under the other, I hobbled over and placed the box on the desk.

To my surprise, the top photograph was *not* a picture I had been shown during Olivia's visit. And no Albert Einstein genius was needed to see why Adelaide would have set this one aside. The subjects were clad—that was not the issue; Adelaide and Zach wore the same T-shirts and blue jeans they had worn in the other camping photographs. And their pose was not in the least indecent: he had one arm around her shoulders; she had one behind his waist.

It was her face. Perhaps an artist or art historian could explain what it was about her features that revealed something more than innocent fun, although 'lascivious' wasn't the right word, nor 'salacious.' No, there was no leering or Mae West lewdness or come-hither coyness, no siren or lady-of-the-night coquetry. Nor any Mona Lisa intimation of secrecy, inscrutability. Nonetheless, Adelaide's eyes and smile betrayed an emotion I had never observed in her. Pleasure? Joy? Zach's face certainly imparted a satisfaction, that exultation of early passion. My, my, my. I suppose it would be fair to say Adelaide's expression bespoke a glad abandon. Yes, my granddaughter had ventured far beyond what Marjorie used to call "puppy love" or the tentative intimacies of early courtship.

A trifle embarrassed by my prurient discovery, and suddenly

bereft of curiosity, I quickly did my utmost to return the box to its original position in the closet. If there was consolation to be had, it came from the absence of a like expression on my granddaughter's face in Carson's company.

"A NERVOUS NELLIE! MADE ME call the airlines *twice*. To be sure you arrived, and he didn't trust me, so I had to call again. Up to today he was a slug. Now he's a ninny."

Having risen and grabbed hold of the crutch, I scolded Procrustes for spewing nonsense. To Adelaide I said, "Take off your coat. How is everyone? Was the wedding a success? No one left stranded at the altar?"

"It was nice. The service was at the arboretum, and the weather was great—sunny and mid-fifties."

"And this Tony—is he well suited to your mother?"

"I think so."

"By that you mean she will run right over him?"

"No, he takes her with a grain of salt. He said she was so set on a safari in Kenya for their honeymoon, he's afraid she'll make him carry a spear."

I gestured at Procrustes. "Well, *we* are *not* well suited. She takes sadistic delight in making me move around, and all she has fed me are salads and raw vegetables."

"Saturated fat and processed meats are bad for you," the ogress hissed.

"I've lived to seventy-nine on such poisons."

"Do you want me to fix something?" Adelaide asked.

"Putting your granddaughter to work the moment she walks in the door!"

Fortunately, in short order I was able to review Procrustes's work log and sign it, and she departed. I could then demonstrate my improved facility with the crutch by hobbling to the living room. Adelaide said she would put on the kettle and join me in a few minutes. The return of routine was nothing less than manna from heaven.

While our tea was steeping, Adelaide showed me some photographs, including one taken the previous summer of Tony in sunglasses and a short-sleeved shirt unbuttoned just enough to reveal dark chest hair. The particulars of the ceremony and reception were recounted; a Unitarian minister performed "a pretty secular service," and the guests numbered around forty friends, family, and colleagues. On the other days of her visit, Adelaide, Elliot, and Michael "hit" various haunts from their youth—the schools they had attended, certain parks, and a few fondly remembered restaurants.

"So all in all, it was not a tiresome excursion?" I asked, my tea still too hot to sip.

"No, it was fun."

"A change—travel—is always nice. But now that you have lived in Manhattan, I suppose you would find Seattle, shall we say, a bit of a backwater? It's one thing to visit, but quite another to live day in and day out. And it has been a while since you have traveled, so the sheer novelty—"

"Actually, I'm thinking of taking another trip: up to Maine."

"Maine?"

"Mom thinks I should write to Zach's parents and say I want to come up and see his grave."

My thoughts could not be diverted from the photograph I had illicitly viewed. "Is this the ideal time—are the airports there even operational in February and March?"

"I wouldn't go right away—I'd ask them a convenient time."

"A letter certainly makes sense, yes, as opposed to a telephone call. You can plan exactly what to say, how to phrase it, and they will have privacy in which to react. Yes, yes, I quite agree."

THAT ADELAIDE SOUGHT MY ASSISTANCE in composing the letter to Mr. and Mrs. Henley was quite gratifying. Should she refer to herself as 'girlfriend,' 'close friend,' or simply 'friend,' she asked. My advice was to begin with the term 'friend,' as the fact of her seeking to make the visit to Maine would demonstrate an important, if not special, friendship. After she met his parents in person, she could ascertain how they might react if she were to make further disclosures. In my own mind, the romantic aspect of her relationship with Zach would become at least a question in the parents' minds the moment they read the letter, but I did not inform my granddaughter of that.

The completed missive was a paragon of simplicity, economy, and discretion. Adelaide wrote that she had been *a friend of his in college* and would like to come up to Maine to meet them and visit his grave. Was there a time in the summer when such a visit would be convenient, and could they *recommend a motel or hotel in the vicinity*? The last clause, she explained to me, was to prevent any implication she was expecting them to put her up.

"Your grandmother would have shown the same delicacy, the same concern for mistaken inferences." The sealed envelope remained on the vanity only until Adelaide next departed for school.

CHAPTER 30

MARCH CAME IN LIKE A lion and left like a hyena. April brought showers but also sunny days, windy days, a snow flurry, unseasonably warm days, and a return to showers—the entire gamut, for all intents and purposes. The most significant sign of rejuvenation, of the season of renewal, was the birth of Michael's son, Noah. When a photograph of the baby arrived in the mail, Adelaide affixed it to the refrigerator door.

Yet the mail brought no response from Zach's parents. Perhaps they had moved, and Adelaide's letter took some time to be forwarded. In any event, I was loath to raise the delicate subject with her. We did receive a postcard from Richard showing a seaside view in Cape Town.

HABIT IS HEAVEN'S OWN REDRESS, Pushkin wrote. *It takes the place of happiness.* Although it may be anathema to the young at heart, as we age, habit assumes the role of cornerstone—nay, *keystone*—to happiness. For example, quotidian sounds such as the shower water running when Adelaide readied herself for school, or the sight of the newspaper on the doormat, where Millie would leave it when she fetched theirs, or the scent of my tea as I seated myself in the chair by the computer—these simple, *repeated* experiences afforded genuine and deep pleasure. The eighty-year-old heart can no longer thrill to the splendor in the grass, just as the five-year-old heart cannot know the joys of adolescence and adulthood. Time metamorphoses us into different emotional creatures as radically as the insect is transformed from larva to pupa to imago.

And if ambition pulsed less forcefully in eighty-year-old arteries, work could be oared along by patient perseverance. What remained to be done in my opus divided roughly into two categories. The simplest was the refining of those sections that had already been fleshed out with examples and explanations. Edward Casaubon and Gilbert Osborn, for instance, were the examples I chose for unkind egotism in the brutalization of a younger woman's affections. John Jarndyce provided the contrast: he wished the best for Esther and ultimately curtailed his selfish desires. Possibly I would be grouping Michael Henchard with Jarndyce; I still had to review *Casterbridge*.

The second category of unfinished work required me to select the examples that would shore up the remaining arguments. I had posited, for instance, that Jane Austen and Henry James shared the view that social duties and strictures are guideposts for virtuous conduct. I posited the opposite for Thomas Hardy: he saw social strictures as *destructive* of the human spirit. But shoring up these arguments with examples required reimmersing myself in their works, a more demanding experience.

And alas, my resort to Mary MacDonalde's letters for rest and replenishment was coming to an end, for I had reached the penultimate missive. Penned in September of 1913, it began with a litany of minor complaints, evidencing a peevishness that had all but disappeared from her earlier Washington correspondence. Yet the triviality of her grievances masked a deep frustration, the same frustration Jude had suffered, although in his case the cause was simply poverty. *We women are kept ignorant but are the ones to suffer the consequences*, she wrote. The bias against accepting women into the groves of academe was longstanding, and whether it had been entirely eradicated in the present, I could not say.

ADELAIDE'S ROUTINES IN SPRING WERE more varied than mine: she attended classes and meetings at Engel Klein and spent evenings in her room studying and reviewing documents. We continued on Thursday afternoons to watch Robert, who had become quite accustomed to us; indeed, it surprised me how he began to put down his toys and crayons when Adelaide and I discussed a topic at any length and appeared to listen to all we said. Saturdays, Adelaide might accompany Carson on an outing—visiting boats or a museum, walking along the river if the weather were obliging—and in the evenings, the three of us typically dined on take-out cuisine. Or if for some reason Adelaide declined an expedition, she might prepare a meal at home. In either case, Carson remained a fixture at our apartment Saturday evenings.

On the whole, our dinner conversations avoided controversy.

Adelaide shared any newly public details of the MacDonalde case as well as so-called facts published by the media, which as often as not were untrue. The solicitors neither admitted nor denied these rumors, allowing speculation to run rampant.

We, too, allowed speculation to run rampant, metaphorically donning the ulster, deerstalker hat, and pipe. Carson championed the position that Mary had married after 1913 and taken a new last name both for herself and her child, which accounted for the absence of documents with the *e* spelling. Why had she stopped writing to Violet, I countered, now that she had become—to use the language of the day—a 'respectable woman'? Because it was a marriage that would have displeased her sister, he asserted. More likely, in my estimation, Mary had remained a single woman—a 'single mother'—and simply chose not to look back at a time and place that had occasioned so much sorrow. And we all accepted the possibility that Mary had at some point given birth to a daughter, who subsequently married, and thus descendants with any number of last names could be lurking.

For her part, Adelaide preferred to marvel at the number of people who had no qualms about lying and the lengths they went to in pretending to be heirs. The ones who contrived elaborate explanations for every uncorroborated document impressed her with their diligence; those whose stories did not "pass the red-face test" impressed her with their lack of shame. Virtually every profession and trade offered up an impostor: doctors, lawyers, automobile mechanics, cosmetics saleswomen, plumbers, waitresses, even a mortician asserted descent from Mary Agnes MacDonalde. Most claims were expeditiously consigned to the Graveyard drawer for, as I quipped, although the world had no shortage of dishonest people, the percentage who were especially clever was mercifully small.

And if the MacDonalde case were to offer no grist for our conversation mill on a given Saturday, Carson might expound on some new computer technology he had encountered. Apparently he, too, was versed in electronic mail, which Adelaide had tried explaining to me, to no avail; such "e-mail" would remain beyond my ken. Yet I vastly preferred these topics to his questioning me about growing up on a farm, or what I did during the Second World War, or what I remembered of the violent demonstrations on campuses during the

1960s and '70s. Ordinarily such curiosity did not bother me, but as I supposed it stemmed not from any desire to learn history but rather from a desire to pander to Adelaide, my patience was taxed, my tolerance bankrupt.

ONE SATURDAY IN MAY, ADELAIDE having left for a meeting at Engel Klein, and the weather being warm and sunny, I ventured on a short walk. As Milton said, *In those vernal seasons of the year, when the air is calm and pleasant, it were an injury and sullenness against nature not to go out, and see her riches.*

My ankle fared well, so I perambulated as far as Park Avenue and strolled a few blocks along the broad esplanade. On the return circuit I came upon a small lot corralling a herd of furniture: chairs, tables, sofas, even a bedroom set—an estate sale, I quickly surmised. It was one of those *presque-spirituel* moments, as I liked to dub them, when Marjorie seemed present. So, in the fine spring air, I made my way through the makeshift paths among the furnishings.

Here was a chair like the one by the front door: a straight cane-back, although not with as wide a seat as the one she had selected forty or so years ago. "People need a comfortable spot to sit and remove their galoshes," she had rightly claimed. So much wisdom in her—not of an academic sort but of the needs of our vulnerable species, a kind of interstitial knowledge. How her presence could brighten a room, and how she had infused even difficult circumstances with a sense of solid optimism, a sense that the chaos would sort itself out, events end on a positive note. Not an easy feat in wartime. And how little praise I had doled out for these unheralded virtues! God, give me the years to live over.

"Is this Victorian, Marvin?"

"Absolutely not—try to imagine a lady in petticoats or hoops and bustles trying to park her fanny there!"

"Excuse me, ma'am; please do not remove the sticker."

"How do I know it isn't scratched underneath?"

"Irma, a chamber pot!"

"Can I buy just the table?"

"I'm sorry; it's a set."

"But I don't need all those chairs. What if I buy two?"

"It comes with eight. It's a set."

"I'll leave my number, in case you can't sell any of it."

"I'm not breaking it up."

"Maybe someone will want just the chairs. Oh, I don't really like the table anyway."

What fun you had, Marjorie, mingling in this world. Did that fellow ever sell the mirror he had once attached to our vanity?

THE EXERCISE LIFTED MY SPIRITS, and I returned home eager to share my adventures with Adelaide. But she was nowhere to be found. I glanced anxiously at my watch—Carson would be arriving in less than an hour. But not a minute later, a key sounded in the lock, the door swung open, and Adelaide's face and quick removal of her coat told me she was aware of the lateness.

"We found some significant documents in the MacDonalde case; I'll tell you when he leaves." With no further ado, she took her briefcase into the bedroom. The prospect of an exciting development was icing on the cake of an already full day. I silently resolved to be a gracious host.

Adelaide changed into a fresh blouse—a pale mint-green— and while I selected two bottles of wine for the sideboard, she sorted the mail. On arriving, Carson mentioned passing a new Indonesian restaurant off Third, but as we had no menu available, my suggestion of the German delicatessen carried the day, and the two young people set out.

They were laughing when they returned, about something having to do with law school, and set about distributing the meals—I had already put out the plates and silverware. Carson opened the dinner conversation as he often did, inquiring as to any new developments in the MacDonalde case, and Adelaide replying, "Not really," I felt compelled to look away to conceal my smile.

Our discourse then caromed off a variety of topics, returning to the MacDonalde case on an oblique angle: the kind of clothing Mary would have worn as a young woman. I described dresses with high-neck collars, mutton sleeves, corsets and stays, lace cuffs, ruffled bodices, petticoats, and buttoned boots—items altogether unknown in contemporary fashion. Adelaide asked perspicacious questions about the difficulty of cleaning such garments, prompting me to describe the laborious processes of using scrub boards and rudimentary wringers. Carson glibly remarked that it was ironic that "now that we can just throw something in the washer or drop it off at the dry cleaner's, people actually prefer jeans and other casual, easy-to-clean clothes."

I violated my silent vows to be a gracious host, unable to refrain from educating the young man on the importance of finery in earlier times. "In my parents' and grandparents' generation, a farmer's daughter—or a merchant's—might have one dress for school and one for church and special occasions. A girl would consider herself lucky to own a few ribbons and perhaps a brooch. Contrast that with the drawers full of clothing and jewelry and hair adornments that are the rule today. My daughter Marcia's closet was full-to-bursting in high school—not just dresses, skirts, blouses, sweaters in every conceivable hue but scarves, belts, handbags. Both she and Olivia, and Marjorie, too, owned jewelry boxes *teeming* with all manner of bracelets, necklaces, earrings, and whatnot. My mother's jewelry box, in contrast, contained nine items, including a pair of earrings—I know because, as a young child, I often gazed at the bracelet and necklaces, imagining they were the crown jewels of some foreign royalty. The scarcity of fine things only enhances their importance."

"You're right," Morris Townsend too promptly responded. "We value the things we feel shortchanged in."

"*Shortchanged?* We never considered ourselves shortchanged! Certainly we had to work hard, and our surroundings were spare, but we always had a roof over our heads, and a wood-burning stove and well-constructed hearth that sufficiently warmed the downstairs. A freshwater well and livestock. We ate three solid meals a day and did not lack for clothes on our backs or shoes or boots on our feet. There were difficulties, yes, but—to use a cliché—they built character. Arduous work from an early age has beneficial consequences. Yes, thank you, this wine is a good complement to the food. The baby boomer generation and yours, too, have come of age with the notion that childhood should be a time of *fun*, of *play*, that childhood exists as a special retreat from the demands of life. Yet for centuries—

millennia—society believed that childhood was a period of training and preparation—an *apprenticeship* for adulthood, if you will."

"I think he means that—you once said that school and cultural activities, things that stimulated you mentally—"

"Manual labor does not extinguish mental stimulation, my dear. Manual labor that is simple or repetitive—planting seeds, picking corn, hoeing, and the like—such work allows the mind to run free; one can recite poetry or sing songs; ponder ideas and philosophies; let the imagination roam where it will. The farmer also becomes a horticulturist, a zoologist, a meteorologist."

"But—"

"I will not pretend it was the life for me. Nonetheless, the farmer's exertions demand respect. My father toiled terribly and in inclement weather of all kinds. The relationship between his labors and the food on the table was neither hidden nor attenuated."

"He must've been glad," the young man said, "you were able to become a professor, to not have to, like you say, toil so hard."

"It is difficult for you to comprehend, in this age of reinvention and relocation, the significance of a family farm. My great-grandparents built the house we lived in. My grandfather and father through their own labors added to it. When a home and its contents are passed on to the next generation, they are not mere material possessions; they are imbued with personal history. Understandably, then, it can be a disappointment to know that they will pass into the hands of strangers."

Adelaide cocked her head. "He didn't—"

"Where nature wields power over life and death, my dear, where your very livelihood is threatened by drought, pestilence, blizzards, fire, flooding, it is only natural that literature and literary scholarship appear as idle pursuits. Scholarship *in general* occupies a lower tier, although studies directed toward the sciences—particularly the applied sciences—may be spared somewhat from the more general opprobrium accorded academic concerns. Yet despite our differences—you recall Tolstoy famously wrote, as it is often translated, *All happy families are alike?* His point was that happy families share certain traits, including kindness, helpfulness, fidelity, to name just a few. My parents and I—we were loyal, devoted to the household's well-being and, within the bounds set by the customs of the time, affectionate."

"My upbringing was the polar opposite," Adelaide told Carson. "Reading was more important than eating." She recounted some of her mother's rituals, such as book discussions at dinner, Sunday-evening poetry readings, and periodic visits to the theater. Only her father would give toys as presents; Olivia insisted on books. I will say this for the upstart: he did not join in Adelaide's gentle ridicule. And, in fact, he praised her mother's intentions.

AS SOON AS MY GRANDDAUGHTER returned to the living room upon bidding Carson good night, I asked what she had learned at Engel Klein.

"We found more documents having to do with Anne MacDonalde—remember I said she was born in '62 near Elmira? We tracked down the daughter of the doctor who delivered her. He'd moved there when he retired—near his daughter—and he saw some patients out of his home, and one was Anne's mother."

"Does he remember her?"

"The doctor died a while back. His daughter threw away most of his files, but she kept the maternity, just in case adopted children came looking for information about their birth mothers. She let Brad look through them, and he found the actual record of Anne's birth."

"Anne was adopted?"

"No—this doctor delivered her, and her parents are named MacDonalde, with an *e*."

"And who is her father?"

"His first name's John. I'll show you copies. Remember, you can't breathe—"

"Mum's the word." I sat patiently in the living room while she fetched her papers.

The first document was quite official-looking. "This is the form Dr. Lomond sent the county to record the birth." The page was titled *Application for Birth Certificate (live birth)*. The blanks on the form had been filled in by what was clearly an old-style typewriter, reminding me of the Remington I had used in graduate school, which utilized a font you never saw in electric typewriters or computer printouts.

The child was listed as *Anne MacDonalde*; the mother, *Lynne Lowe MacDonalde*; and the father, *John Patrick MacDonalde*. The date of birth, February 11, 1962, was typed above the space for the parents' address: *Dawes Lane, Treurig Twshp, State of New York*. The signature was completely illegible, but beneath the scrawl was typed *Alfred Lomond, M.D.*

"Could John Patrick MacDonalde be Mary's son?" I asked.

"Not the child she was pregnant with in 1904; he was named Brian. Remember, that's not public. Brian would've been fifty-eight when Anne was born. This John Patrick could be Brian's son or a younger brother or a younger brother's son. Here's the other document."

This form was titled simply *Maternity* and employed a less formal font and format than the birth certificate application—perhaps it was something Dr. Lomond had had printed up for his retirement practice. The entries were not typed but handwritten. Another difference was that no space was provided for the father's name—only the mother's and newborn's. Which, upon reflection, made sense: the father was not a patient, simply a visitor. In the space for the mother's name was written, in quite a florid hand, *Lynne Lowe MacDonalde*, and in the space for the child's, in the same hand, *Anne MacDonalde*.

Spaces below called for the child's height, weight, and sex and had been filled in with brusque strokes. At the bottom, the same brusque pen had written *Feb 11, 1962 3:16 a.m.* and, in the margin, *Apgar* and the number *9*.

We each remarked on the differences in penmanship, and I opined that the names at the top of the maternity form were written by a woman—either Lynne or a nurse or assistant.

Adelaide did not disagree. "Dr. Lomond's daughter said he had a live-in housekeeper who was also kind of an assistant—maybe a nurse or midwife."

"She needn't have been a midwife, my dear. Until recently, most babies were brought into the world without a professional's assistance. And I would wager most still are. Not in this country, of course, but elsewhere. And if this were in a rural area, the presence of Dr. Lomond would have been considered a luxury, possibly even in 1962. I will say this: I dreaded having to grade examinations written with such florid loops. Just look at them! But tell me: Haven't these documents exposed a large set of witnesses to interview? In"—I peered closer—"Treurig Township?"

"There's not much there anymore, according to Drecker."

"Drecker? Oh yes, the investigators."

"They've been reviewing phone books, and there are *tons* of MacDonalds, but all without the *e*. They're also checking into local tax, school, and property records. Dr. Lomond's daughter thought most people went to the established OBGYNs, and her father helped out only if someone went into labor suddenly and their regular doctor wasn't available."

"I recall your Aunt Marcia making these curlicues when she was a teenager, despite my insistence it reduced legibility. I believe she also made small circles for the dots on lowercase *i*'s and *j*'s. Quite a display of silliness."

"Joe said that now we at least know there were people who spelled it that way—so the index entry where we first found Anne's name wasn't a typo."

"Quite an important corroboration," I concurred.

CHAPTER 31

THE DISCOVERY OF DR. LOMOND'S records ushered in no spate of new discoveries, however, Anne's and her family's whereabouts proving as elusive as Mary's. Adelaide reminded me, when I chanced to speak resignedly of the dashing of hopes, that even if Anne were located, her relationship to Mary needed establishing. Yet I found it difficult *not* to assume a kinship, considering both the shared spelling and the close proximity of Treurig to Clopes. Ninety miles or so, with only the tips of the Finger Lakes between them, was the proverbial stone's throw when one considered the size of the country as a whole.

Of course, I scrupulously avoided mentioning Anne at Saturday dinner. Given Carson's repeated reference to his sister's close perusal of the tabloids, we would undoubtedly learn forthwith if Anne's existence became public knowledge.

'BETTER LATE THAN NEVER,' THE adage goes. Adelaide finally received a reply from Zach's parents, suggesting late August as a convenient time for her to visit. The brief missive conveyed nothing further: not why it took so long to answer or why they preferred to delay the visit until August, nor even a banality along the lines of 'We look forward to meeting you.' Of course, many possibilities presented themselves: the Henleys may have been traveling, entertaining other visitors, or undergoing surgeries or rehabilitations of some kind.

"Will you travel by train or bus, or will you fly?" I inquired.

"I'll rent a car."

"But that is no short expedition; the distance must be—"

"I looked it up—I can do it in a day if I leave early."

"But the *amount* of driving—"

"I like driving. Most is highway, so I can relax, listen to the radio." Again her Wallace stubbornness reared its head.

"You wouldn't arrive in Maine until after dark."

"It still stays light pretty late in August. I could stop in Massachusetts if I need to; otherwise I'd stay at the motel they mention."

"What if you were to have car trouble—a flat, say? I would be worried sick the entire time."

"I can call every few hours."

Why did *my uneasiness* amount to so little in her calculations? And was the possibility of engine trouble or flat tire *so* remote that it could be dismissed out of hand? Her intransigence was quite nettlesome.

After several days of useless fretting, I telephoned a travel agent and inquired as to airplane, train, and bus fares as far as Portland. The information was encouraging, and while Robert slept on his blanket between us, I presented the details, volunteering to foot the entire bill, a small price to pay for my peace of mind.

Every argument fell on deaf ears. Exasperated, I found myself asking, "What if I were to accompany you?"

She leaned over to readjust the blanket on Robert's shoulders. "You *want* to? It wouldn't be too uncomfortable—the long ride?"

"If we could make brief stops every so often, to make use of the facilities, I would venture it. Unfortunately, my driver's license expired some years ago—"

"Like I said, I don't mind the driving, but having your company would be nice."

My own offer had half surprised—and half worried—me. However, any incipient buyer's remorse was nipped in the bud by her frank admission. In truth, the thought of Adelaide making the trip alone was far more worrisome than any physical discomfort I might endure in accompanying her. Even if I were a less-than-forbidding bodyguard, the mere presence of a second individual removes the aura of vulnerability of a young woman by herself.

OVER THE NEXT FEW DAYS, I found myself *looking forward* to the trip. Central Massachusetts and Maine presented unexplored terrain for me, and meeting Zach's parents should open a window of sorts on the poor young man himself.

Yet in contrast to my own mood brightening, hers markedly

declined. Had the arrival of the letter resurrected painful memories? Was she beset by second thoughts about the wisdom of probing old wounds? I inadvertently overheard her on the telephone with Carson refusing an opportunity to board a ship and begging off from Saturday dinner, saying she had too much work to do, yet when I managed a casual how-is-school-going, she responded "Fine" and even volunteered that she had done well on an examination.

The downturn in the weather was the likely culprit. Late April and early May had graced us with blossoms on trees and little patches of grass sprouting along the pavement, but a round of dismal rains and wind had followed in quick pursuit. The only blossoms now to be seen were strewn along the gutters.

Adelaide's continued dour mood induced a dour mood in me, and when Thursday came around, I was not thrilled to have Robert visit. To make matters worse, he spilled his juice, thereby demonstrating that the so-called no-spill cup did not entirely live up to its advertising. Nor was *Robert's* mood a sunny one—I would have gone so far as to accuse him of petulance, for when a crayon broke, he threw the stub onto the carpet, where it bounced and lodged under the sofa.

Adelaide gave him a cookie, which quieted him some.

Concentrating on the Forster article proved beyond my powers, so I put down my journal and rose and grabbed aimlessly at the poetry shelves, my fingers nabbing a Blake anthology. Robert grunted, but I paid him no mind until Adelaide said, "Francis, read him something."

"From this?"

"Why not?"

The boy fixed such a gaze on me—his large, dark eyes with their long lashes so beseeching—I paged to the most-anthologized of poems and read,

Tyger, tyger, burning bright,
In the forests of the night;
What immortal hand or eye
Could frame thy fearful symmetry?

A deer suddenly coming upon a newfound field of clover: that most nearly describes the boy's expression—wide-eyed, eager, wondering. I continued reading,

In what distant deeps or skies.
Burnt the fire of thine eyes?
On what wings dare he aspire?
What the hand, dare seize the fire?

Continuing through to the poem's conclusion, I peered up to behold the same eagerness—a craving, almost.

"Did you understand that?" Adelaide asked the boy. "Read him some more."

I followed with "The Lamb," watching Robert as I said the last two lines,

Little Lamb God bless thee.
Little Lamb God bless thee.

If his eyes did not water up!

For the next however many minutes, I went back and forth between *Songs of Innocence* and *Songs of Experience*. Adelaide meanwhile retrieved several other volumes from the poetry shelf. When my throat tired, I asked what she would like to read, and she held aloft a large wafer-thin book.

"*A Child's Garden of Verses*, excellent choice."

In a soft but very clear voice, Adelaide read,

I have a little shadow that goes in and out with me,
And what can be the use of him is more than I can see.
He is very, very like me from the heels up to the head.

Lying on one side with his weight resting partially on the elbow, his favored position while drawing, the boy shifted his transfixed gaze from me to her. She followed up the shadow poem with one about a swing; it was as though he were watching a magician. Why *shouldn't* he understand the words? His comprehension, Millie had often said, was on a par with his age.

Adelaide paged through the thin volume for another selection, but he waved his free arm. "Perhaps he would like you to read it again," I said.

How do you like to go up in a swing,
Up in the air so blue?
Oh, I do think it the pleasantest thing
Ever a child can do!

His delight was unmistakable. She repeated the poem a third time, his rapture never faltering.

"He understands not only the words, but the rhythms, don't you, Robert? Yes, Adelaide, he understands the *rhythms* of poetry."

Stevenson proved an astute choice; the hand on Robert's free arm began to sway to the cadence of Adelaide's voice, although at one point, she flipped past a poem, murmuring it was "sort of racist." Eventually she handed me the volume, asking me to pick one.

"I will try something else." I stood almost too hastily but recovered my balance and made my way to the shelves.

For easily half an hour we took turns reading, Adelaide and I, trading off and resorting to one of my anthologies for some Gerard Manley Hopkins, Coleridge, and Keats. The boy may not have understood everything, but he was acutely sensitive to the meters and rhythms and sounds, qualities in poems that many college English majors are prone to shrug off. Each time I glanced up from the page, he was watching me attentively, spurring me to hone my intonations. It seemed no time at all when the doorbell buzzer went off.

"Millie and John must have forgotten their keys," I said. "The extra set is on the hook in the kitchen."

Adelaide went to the intercom and waited by the door. When it opened, I heard her say, "We're in the middle of watching Robert."

Like a fly in the ointment, in walked Morris Townsend. The mood that had settled over the three of us evaporated of an instant. The boy stared at the intruder, who, for once, was bereft of sports coat or suit jacket, wearing instead a red-and-blue rugby shirt.

"Robert, this is Carson," Adelaide said.

Robert continued to stare while Carson handed Adelaide a paper bag. "Happy birthday. I know it's months from now, but I couldn't pass this up."

My granddaughter graciously thanked him and sat down on the sofa near the youngster. "Do you want me to open it?" she asked. The child grunted, and Adelaide slid her finger under the tape and undid the paper just as Marjorie used to do, without causing a tear. If the paper were particularly attractive, Marjorie would reemploy it for some other purpose, such as encasing a plant pot. The gift was revealed to be a book of photographs of sailing vessels.

Adelaide again thanked Carson and then showed Robert the cover.

"May I?" The gift-giver tugged the book back and squatted beside the boy.

"This is a replica of one of Columbus's ships. It was called a *nao*—a 'carrack' in English. It could carry lots of men and cargo and was pretty stable in rough seas, but it couldn't go shallow. Columbus used the other vessels to get to shore. See all the masts."

The boy stared at each page, oblivious to the fact that the attention lavished upon him had nothing whatsoever to do with *him* and everything to do with his 'benefactor' showing off to Adelaide. The exploitation of the child for purposes of putting himself in a good light seemed a new low even for Carson. Alas, Adelaide's facial expressions gave no indication of seeing through the shameless charade—perhaps her sense of courtesy inhibited a demonstration of annoyance. So for the next five or ten excruciating minutes, Adelaide and I watched Carson play the pedagogue, and his pandering might have continued indefinitely had Millie and John not rapped on the door.

But my need for forbearance only increased! After Adelaide made introductions, Carson's showmanship continued, and Millie and John evidenced through their ingratiating smiles that they saw artlessness in his consummate craftiness. When the charlatan excused himself to fetch a glass of water and Adelaide followed him to the kitchen, Millie clucked that he was "such a charming young man." I changed the subject to John's class and kept it there while they finished packing up Robert's things. And, in point of fact, I—with my weakened ankle—

was the only one standing in the hallway waving goodbye to the poor boy.

Returning to the living room, I picked up the ships book, which I quickly learned contained very little text and was for the most part a compilation of glossy photographs and hand-drawn sketches. Setting what would be appropriately denominated a 'coffee-table book' on the coffee table, I went toward the kitchen. At the sound of voices, I abruptly halted.

"He can survive one night without you. We'll get takeout, keep him company while—"

"It's not that."

"Then what?"

"I'm just not ready."

"Sex doesn't mean marriage. It's a way of expressing affection and friendship."

Adelaide lowered her voice almost to a whisper. "To me it's more."

"Then let's get married. We'll find a minister in the yellow pages. I'm serious."

It was all I could do not to rush in and throttle the gigolo. Indeed, Morris Townsend was a rank amateur in comparison to Carson Smith. And to make matters worse, Adelaide's tone suggested she took his proposal at face value.

"I'm just not ready. I don't feel what I should."

Perhaps Carson realized that the living room chatter had ceased, for he whispered as well. "I'll settle for knowing what you *do* feel."

"Affection, friendship."

"Could you feel more *some*day? Forget it—I withdraw the question."

Exercising the patience of Job, I clumsily tiptoed back to my chair. Yet took myself to task immediately. Why should I have been crowning *myself* with laurels for Patience and Forbearance when the honors most assuredly should have been bestowed on dear Penelope, resistor of false suitors?

FOR THE NEXT SEVERAL WEEKS, I abided the unwelcome suitor by reminding myself of his imminent departure for California. And I acknowledged the possibility that he was playing a positive role in Adelaide's life: serving as a 'rebound boyfriend.' Marjorie had acquainted me with the concept when Olivia dated a love-struck fellow in high school, a member of the varsity wrestling team, I seemed to recall. After my expressing some surprise at her choice of beau—for he was not up to her level either intellectually or in terms of maturity—Marjorie explained that the boy functioned as a 'rebound boyfriend' after the debate-club president had broken up with her. In other words, the new young man boosted Olivia's morale, and when she lost interest in him—an eventuality of which Marjorie was certain—our daughter would be in a better frame of mind for picking a more worthy companion.

Yes, as long as Adelaide to her own self was true, I should have little cause for concern. Yet July could not arrive soon enough.

CHAPTER 32

ONE EVENING, ADELAIDE PROVIDED AN explanation for her low mood of late. Her colleague Brad had, as I knew, enjoyed great success for having tracked down the two Anne MacDonalde documents from Dr. Lomond's daughter, but it turned out other colleagues had scored coups of their own. Brittany had pored over a 1937 divorce decree and found some fact disproving a claim; Simon had identified an inconsistency in an asserted date of birth. Sheena, a tax associate who helped out only rarely, had shown that a claimant's grandfather had died six months prior to his purported marriage to Mary. Adelaide had been assigned a number of claimants—or so she gathered from her name appearing on the paralegals' whiteboard—but either the Scottish solicitors had not yet authorized interviews or else others at the firm, or the Drecker investigators, had disproved the claimants' allegations. In sum: she felt her contributions fell well below those of her colleagues.

I tried to buoy my granddaughter's spirits by noting that she had been at the firm less than a year, and only part-time, and thus was likely considered a trainee, with the expectation that her first years would produce little that was earthshattering. "As for the mistakes Joe has pointed out, do not fall victim to the tendency—although who has not?—of inflating a single instance of failure into a conviction of failure on an epic scale."

Whether because of my pep talk or for other reasons, Adelaide's mood by and by improved. Robert, too, seemed to shed a certain dolor. His love of being read to did not diminish, and throughout the interlude between visits, Adelaide and I would exchange suggestions as to what he might enjoy next. The more lyrical and musical of the poems enchanted him, so we read quite a bit of Gerard Manley Hopkins and Coleridge. The lad was positively smitten with "Pied Beauty."

We discussed branching into stories. Winnie-the-Pooh and Mr. Frog and Mr. Toad appeared to bore the boy, Millie had said—and why shouldn't they? He was almost nine. Without eye problems he would have learned to read, and with better finger and hand coordination, he would have learned Braille and sign language.

"I am trying to recall my own preferences at his age," I told Adelaide. "I latched on to Robert Louis Stevenson's novels and Jules Verne's, but I was a tad older."

"What about *The Jungle Book*?"

"An excellent proposal! Or should we perhaps begin with the *Just So Stories*—I ran across a copy the other day. It had fallen behind all the Kafka."

"Who wrote those?"

"Kipling as well. Yes, let us try him."

Kipling proved an excellent choice. The tale of "Rikki-Tikki-Tavi" so captivated the child that at the part where the mongoose chased Nagaina into the underground nest, tears formed in his large dark eyes. We quickly went through the *Just So Stories* and *The Jungle Book* volumes. Adelaide subsequently bought copies of *Charlotte's Web* and *Stuart Little* and a few works I was unfamiliar with. We took turns, she and I, reading aloud, our styles not so different.

As a measure of our delight in reading to Robert, when Millie informed us that John's rehabilitation was complete and he would no longer be attending Thursday sessions, Adelaide and I expressed disappointment at losing our time with the boy. After a brief discussion, it was agreed that we would host him on alternate weeks, although once summer came and Adelaide began working fulltime at Engel Klein, we would push the time to four o'clock.

AT SATURDAY DINNER, I BROACHED with Carson the subject of the timing of his move to San Francisco. He would leave New York in mid-July, he said, the tenor of his voice dissuading me from further pursuit of the subject. The possibility that he might decide at the last minute *not* to go did suggest itself. Adelaide, for her part, showed no signs of chagrin at his imminent departure but did express disappointment that she could not attend his commencement ceremony—Joe had assigned her to conduct another interview on the same day, down in Trenton.

As it turned out, the Trenton candidate—a sixty-year-old woman married to a Russian émigré with a Dostoyevskian-long last name and the patronymic Ivanovich—produced no documentation supporting her assertions, which had something to do with being the daughter-in-law of Mary's son, who died under mysterious circumstances in Mexico. I could not keep up with the details Adelaide showered upon me and thus accepted unquestioningly that the claim was destined for the Limbo drawer and ultimately the Graveyard.

Meanwhile, Brittany scored another coup: she had spoken on the telephone with Julia Williams White, one of the children Mary MacDonalde had taught during her years on the Wapato fruit orchard out in Washington. "Julia is ninety," Adelaide said, "but her memory's sharper than it was when the investigator interviewed her back in the twenties. Or at least Brittany got more details out of her."

"That is one of the peculiarities of old age, my dear. Childhood events reappear in the mind's eye with astonishing clarity and detail. Yet recalling what we had for dinner the day before is nigh impossible."

"Julia remembers Mary and Brian's arrival, even though she was only four or five. Her parents had been talking about them for a while, she guesses—a lady and her son coming from New York. Julia and her brother and sister had to put on special outfits, and Julia was excited to wear new shoes. They waited eagerly in the dining room, but when Mary and Brian arrived, Mary was taken to her bedroom in the back, and the doctor was called—Mary was sick. Julia remembers meeting Brian as he sat silently in a corner in the kitchen, and she offered him an apple."

"That *is* a vivid recollection. Yet it does not strike me as odd, for the event constituted a dramatic departure from her daily life."

"She remembers Mary being nice and speaking with a strange accent and dressing Julia in hats and hair ribbons. Their departure was sudden—Mary and Brian's. Julia saw their trunks on the front porch; no one had told her they were leaving. There were no goodbyes; they got in someone's car and were gone. Her Aunt Mildred came to stay for a few months, and she smelled like castor oil." Adelaide appeared amused by this tidbit.

"I suppose memories like that—even vivid ones—warrant a certain degree of skepticism. On the one hand, children may be astute observers; on the other hand, they often draw erroneous inferences. But tell me this: Why look into Mary's comings and goings in Washington State when I believe you said she left there in 1913?"

"We *think* she left there—but all we really know is she got as far as Spokane, where she mailed the last letter. Maybe she returned—and if not to Wapato, then the Yakima area. Or maybe she kept in touch with people there. Julia might be a source of witnesses—friends Mary had made. Remember: Mary was there five years."

"*Did* she make friends?"

"Not that Julia remembers so far, but now that her memory's been jogged, who knows?"

"Did Mary visit again or ever run into Julia in the Yakima area after 1913?"

"Not that she remembers. The only time Mary's name came up was when the investigator interviewed Julia in '25."

"In other words, when all is said and done, Brittany's efforts were unavailing?"

"So far."

Sadly, Adelaide exhibited no trace of *Schadenfreude*, whose salutary benefits, I would venture, rival those of many mood-improving medications doled out by psychologists.

THE CONCLUSION OF THE SCHOOL year and Adelaide's embarkation upon full-time summer employment at the Engel Klein firm imparted even greater uniformity to our schedules. Except for the Thursdays we watched Robert, she left the apartment before eight each weekday morning and returned each evening between six-thirty and seven.

The interruption-free mornings proved conducive to progress on my opus, and I veritably sailed through the section on Hardy's respect for manual labor, which was manifested in many characters but perhaps none so paradigmatically as Gabriel Oak, the hardworking sheep farmer. Of course, the reddleman also embodied the integrity and decency inhering in honest toil—even poor Tess was a testament to the laborer's virtue.

Yet, while the mornings flew by, the summer afternoons prolonged themselves unconscionably. The minute hand on the kitchen clock became leaden; the second hand on my watch had to exert itself against some molasses-like ether. I would tidy up the living room, straighten the stacks of mail on the vanity, and refill the kettle, all the while my ears straining for the sound of a key in the lock—might she not have reason to come home early? When she did arrive, I feigned absorption in some minor activity such as wiping the kitchen counter or aligning the magazines on the coffee table, for I did not want her to feel pressure to be convivial. In the early days of our marriage, Marjorie and I sparred on the subject of my unsociability at first arriving home after a demanding day teaching.

On the other hand, freed of homework, Adelaide was able to dawdle longer at supper and impart more details of her day. The largest share of her time at Engel Klein was devoted to reviewing records and questionnaire answers in the MacDonalde case. Although some of the records offered tantalizing or amusing details, most were irrelevant. The questionnaire answers often were long, inarticulate ramblings.

"In regular litigation," she explained to my sympathetic ear, "you can file a 'motion to compel' to force the other side to answer directly or produce specific documents." Alas, however, the Scottish solicitors were adhering to Violet's directives of leniency toward claimants, restricting Engel Klein to a kid-glove approach tolerant of evasive answers. Poor Violet, I mused, going through life naïve as to the number and methodology of mountebanks and scoundrels.

Thus far, Engel Klein had only a single folder in the file labeled *Claims with Confirmed Documentation*: the two sheets pertaining to Anne MacDonalde—Dr. Lomond's admitting form and the birth certificate application. And Anne was not even a claimant!

"If no MacDonalde-with-an-*e* claimant is ever found," I asked, "how does the firm intend to treat all the Limbo claims—will the estate be apportioned among them equally?"

"It's not up to us. The Scottish firm will make a recommendation, I think, but the court will decide."

ON CERTAIN DAYS, ADELAIDE WAS assigned to other cases at Engel Klein, which she appreciated because it gave her the opportunity to work with partners besides Joe. I suspected these assignments may have softened the blow she no doubt felt in light of Brad, Brittany, and Simon being chosen to travel hither and yon on interviews.

Carson remained in New York while studying for the California bar examination, a fact that initially heightened my fear he would renege on his decision to move away. However, my simmering anxiety was put to rest by Adelaide's disclosure that he had visited San Francisco and rented an apartment. And one of the first statements out of his mouth when we sat down to dinner at his next visit was that he had signed a lease.

"It's a landlord's market, so I'm paying an arm and leg for a shoebox. But if you and Addy ever decide to move there, they have *gorgeous* townhouses." I did not grace his absurdity with a response.

"The good thing is: I'm six blocks from the Pacific. Even have a small view—pretty small, but better than nothing."

To Adelaide's inquiry as to whether ships docked nearby, he said the beach was too unsheltered. "But there are piers along the bay near the office, so I can scoot over during lunch. Did I tell you the conference room windows have a view of Alcatraz?" Again, the annoying grin. "And there are a lot of sailing tours. I'll try to find a decent group until I can afford my own boat. My own twenty-two, twenty-four foot—that's the dream."

"How much actual sailing experience have you had?" I politely asked.

"Just some informal lessons when I was young—friends of the family—and in college a little. I was the weird kid who wanted to go away to sea on a whaler when I grew up." Rotating the glass stem back and forth between his thumb and fingers, he watched his wine curve up the sides. "It wasn't the harpooning part that appealed—it was going out on the open sea. That sense of freedom."

"In point of fact," I said, "a whaling or navy ship—or even a *mercantile* vessel—was and is the last environment one could call 'free.'"

The smile never left his face. "I know: you're at the mercy of storms and rough—"

"Perilous storms, yes, but even in calm waters, a ship—particularly in the days of whalers and the like—was a prison-like environment. The living space was cramped; the work taxing and unrelenting; and the captain ruled with an iron fist. I am not criticizing this practice—maintaining order and discipline in such isolated and demanding circumstances is a necessity, much as it is in the military. But the reality of that dictatorial setting was a great deal of physical brutality, not a joyous romanticism. Misconduct was rewarded with a flogging. Perhaps you have read *Mutiny on the Bounty*, the fictionalized history by Nordhoff and Hall? Captain Bligh deviated from the typical captain only in the irrationality of his iron rule, not the iron rule itself."

For once the young man was without a facile rejoinder!

AT LONG LAST THE SATURDAY arrived of Carson's final meal with us. Adelaide had been summoned into Engel Klein to work on a brief, but she expressed confidence she would be done by late afternoon and would pick dinner up on her way home. In deference to the young man's departure, she would let him select the restaurant.

CHAPTER 33

ADDY PHONED RIGHT AFTER HE'D finished taping the last carton of books. She was leaving the office and wanted to know what kind of takeout to get, adding, "I'm sorry your goodbye dinner will be so ordinary."

Kind of like the Titanic sinking was ordinary. "I'll hit the deli on my way over."

"You don't mind?"

"No—you must be beat from work. Should I get you and Francis the usual?" Her yes pleased him—nothing mellowed the old man out like a pastrami with the works.

He surveyed the stacks of cartons his roommates would haul to the PO on Monday—he had to agree to pay not just for the cost of shipment and their "labor" but for "gas," some random amount they knew he'd accept.

The sight of the two open suitcases, neatly piled with shirts, pants, and sweaters, was depressing. *If I really thought this was goodbye, I wouldn't be able to swallow Jell-O.* The only thing staving off some kind of breakdown was the wild hope she'd miss him more than she realized. It wasn't totally crazy—she was nothing like the iceberg of that first date. A college roommate had stuck with a girl who just wanted to be friends, but the minute he shipped to Kuwait, she did a one-eighty and married him on his first leave.

Even Lucy wasn't discouraging, after he'd told her about Zach. "That's horrible. Maybe you just need to give her space."

"It happened four or five years ago."

"You can't set a deadline."

"I know."

"I take back everything mean I said."

No, you couldn't set a deadline. In the meantime, while waiting to find out if there could be a future, he knew he *would* fall apart, do the crying jag, walk around kicking junk on the sidewalk—things he'd done when *he'd* been the one to pull the plug.

And going cold turkey wasn't possible, not this time. He couldn't simultaneously be three thousand miles away *and* accept that it was over. A little two-step instead: get used to the distance by telling himself his absence would make her heart grow fonder and that they'd have some impassioned reunion, and later, down the line, after her absence had become the norm, *then* face the truth. "Denial and self-deception are survival techniques," Dr. Kim used to say. The guy wasn't only a savior; he was a genius—genius alienist.

ADDY LOOKED GREAT WHEN SHE opened the door. Pale yellow suited her, especially with her arms tanned from their last vessel boarding. There was a gentleness, a weird kind of yielding, even if she never yielded.

He came in with bags: one holding the takeout, the other with gifts. "You can unwrap these later, but only one's for you." He put the gifts on the hall table and brought the food into the kitchen.

Sometimes the meal started with Carson toasting "the MacDonalde heirs and heiresses," but tonight he just asked Addy if there was anything new in the case.

"They want me to go to Ellis Island. If Mary went into labor on the voyage—though we don't think she did—but if she delivered on the ship or at immigration, there might be something I could find out. I think it'd be interesting anyway. My father's grandparents came through there."

"But Mary wrote of convalescing in Clopes," Francis said. "Surely that implied she had given birth there, as her letter made no mention of any illness or injury she would otherwise be recovering from."

Addy threw Carson the look meaning *It's not public.* The old man had already let slip the name of Clopes a dozen times, but it still hadn't shown up in Lucy's tabloids. His sister always brought up the MacDonalde case, hoping Carson would spill something, not believing for a minute he only knew public information. Maybe her judge was a sieve.

"But she did go through Ellis Island," Addy was telling Francis, "and that wasn't the typical protocol for second-class passengers, only steerage. They got inspected aboard the ship out in the harbor, and if their papers were in order and they seemed healthy, they got off in Manhattan."

Francis began droning about something. Usually it didn't bother Carson, but tonight he didn't want dinner to drag on and leave less time for a walk. Would Addy like the gift? Would she be willing to visit? He'd pay plane fare and hotel.

"Women of today complain about lack of opportunity, my dear, but compare life on the family farm even as recently as the 1930s. The housewife had none of the amenities we take for granted—vacuum cleaner, gas or electric range, washer and dryer. I was almost *ten* when we were furnished with electricity, and that was only enough to power lights, not refrigerators and stoves."

"And you needed to hire someone to help with the laundry, right?"

"Yes, a girl from town. Do not imagine it was a quick, simple task, washing by hand with a scrub board. You are unfamiliar? A metal ridged board about this big, usually in a wooden frame. You sit with the bundle of soiled clothes beside you and a wide bucket of water in front, and you position the board so as to allow vigorous rubbing of the fabric against the ridges. The word 'scrub' is significant: one must apply repeated hard pressure. Soil, manure, fruit stains—the dirt could be quite ingrained. Imagine the hours consumed washing not only the family's clothing but bed linens, towels, kitchen rags, pot holders— everything." Carson tried to mimic Addy's interested expression.

"And each item had to be rinsed, wrung out, and hung on the line. You have heard the phrase 'put through the wringer'? It was operated by a hand crank and considered quite an advancement—which it was—over wringing with one's hands. You fed the wet clothes into the space between . . ."

She pretty much always looked attentive, though she'd had to have heard this stuff a dozen times. She'd be a dynamite mother.

"It wasn't until the washing machine came along, *and* the electricity to power it, *and* the electric iron, that laundry ceased being a two-day affair. And that was not the end of the housewife's chores! My mother tended the vegetable garden, weeding, hoeing, watering, pruning, picking, *and preserving*—we had to put by provisions for the long winter months. Yet she often said how much easier her chores were than *her* mother's and grandmother's. They owned pigs and cured their own ham and bacon."

"My sister doesn't trust a vegetable unless it's wrapped in plastic."

"Cooking was done daily, and meals were prepared from scratch—some families had to grind their own flour! It was not simply a truism that 'a man may work from sun to sun, but a woman's work is never done.'"

"My dad said that on reservations, the Native American women still—"

"And with those demands, how could the farm wife find the energy, much less the *time*, to engage in intellectual and cultural pursuits? Nor could the men, with the arduous physical labor they were required to perform."

AFTER DINNER, CARSON HANDED THEM each their gift and left a third for Robert. Addy unwrapped hers first. The picture on the box showed the name, *Anjo Doce*, and when she took the model out of the box, she examined it carefully—the masts and sails and rigging.

"A Portuguese caravel," he said, "like the *Santa Maria*."

"It's beautiful."

Francis seemed a little flustered, grasping for words when he unwrapped his present. His model also had three masts and many sails.

"Thank you. This is very nice."

"Did you see the name?"

He squinted at the stern. "The *Pequod*."

"From *Moby Dick*."

"Yes, I remember."

"I'm sure you can guess what's in Robert's," Carson said. "His has old British flags all over the masts and yards—an early eighteenth-century British man-of-war."

Addy collected the paper from the unwrapped gifts. "I'll do the dishes later," she told Francis. "We're going for a walk. I'm taking my key, so don't wait up."

CARSON WAS RELIEVED TO ESCAPE the apartment even if his time with
Addy was probably down to minutes—thirty if he was lucky. At least
the old coot had been civil all evening—but still had to turn away if
one of Carson's jokes amused him. They had parted with a handshake,
Francis looking at the floor.

The evening air was mild. To the west, the sky was streaked pink
but to the east had already darkened. They walked in silence to the
river, crossing streetlight shadows running every which way. The
woman ahead was talking to her corgi. A boy with a basketball slowly
dribbled past. Even in the phalanx of Manhattan, people knew to bask
in the summer night.

The path by the river was crowded. Carson and Addy passed
lovers strolling arm in arm, teenage girls in skimpy shorts and halter
tops, gray-haired ladies wearing fanny packs, joggers, dog walkers, little
kids licking ice cream cones—a "smorgasbord of humanity," Francis
would call it. If nothing else, the old man improved Carson's
vocabulary.

Where the path veered farther from the street, the gentle breeze
dispelled the exhaust, gas, and diesel-fuel smells. Here you got whiffs
of fish and seaweed mixed with suntan lotion and cigarette smoke.
Farther along, the foot traffic thinned, and when the breeze picked up,
only river scents persisted. They stood with their hands on the railing
and watched the lights from the bridge reflecting in blinking chains
across the water. Car and building lights from the boroughs sent
upward glows of purple and indigo. Above, the blue had become a
dusky turquoise. Nowhere was the sky black, not over the sound and
never over Manhattan or Roosevelt Island or Queens.

"Looks like high tide," Carson said.

"It's over the rocks."

A small tug approached slowly, puffs of deep gray rising from the
stack. Behind it was a barge, a long low box barely cutting a wake in
the dark surface.

"I wonder what she's hauling," Carson said. "Can't be much."

"Maybe it's empty."

"You're right—no one's on deck."

Lights danced along the bridge, but where they stood, the milky
texture of the night sky and river gave no reflection. Were Addy and

he and the boatman the sole members of the human race conscious of this piece of indifferent driftwood?

"I don't suppose it would make a difference—for us—if I stayed, looked for a job here?" He watched her silhouette while she watched the river. "Then at least humor me: say you'll miss my charm and good looks."

Her eyes remained on the water, but the corners of her mouth curled up. In the dim lamplight her hair glowed. Again, he looked at the opaque sky. Too bad they hadn't stayed late in Greenport—there you could see millions of stars, like diamond confetti. How did sailors pick out constellations in that glittering crowd?

"You're always welcome in San Fran." He rested his left hand on her right.

She didn't withdraw it. "I know."

"Any possibility the famous MacDonalde case will send you to the West Coast?"

She gave a little shrug.

After a moment, he said, "It'd be cool if she's still alive—people do live to over a hundred. If she found out how much money and manpower—and womanpower—has gone into tracking her down, that would be kind of a happy ending."

Addy turned toward him—not enough to face him but almost—and her hand remained beneath his. "I think she stopped caring about her family. Otherwise, wouldn't she have kept writing to Violet? Especially after the wars—wouldn't she have wanted to find out if everyone was all right?"

"Scotland didn't suffer like London and Coventry. I wonder if Hess landed in Glynnis-on-Tay?"

"But the war could have changed them—her parents might've regretted sending her away. Violet had no way to reach her."

His hand felt on fire. He tried not to apply too much pressure with his palm, to make his touch seem casual. "Bitterness can reach a level where there's no looking back."

"I bet we'll never know."

Another barge, a small one—maybe just a raft—glided by from the other direction. Nothing and no one was on it, but you could hear a sputtering motor. They watched it pass, leaving their band of dark water desolate.

"You planning to stay with Engel when you graduate?"

"I guess—if they make me an offer. I'm not sure they will."

Addy gently eased her hand from under his and pushed back her hair. He couldn't remember feeling this powerless, this ploy-less. Jennifer had once accused him of "putting on a puppy-dog face" to get what he wanted, which was unfair—the hurt in his face was real. Or so he had thought at the time. But maybe he had some shadow personality that was manipulative and conniving. He wished he could connive something now.

A church bell clanged somewhere. You hardly ever heard church bells in the city, just sirens and angry jackhammers. Addy glanced at her watch, and he took the hint and gestured for them to start walking back.

At the no-parking sign in front of Francis's building, Carson strained to hold back tears. Addy's profile and expression showed no extra sadness. He halted by the outer glass doors. Should he kiss her? God knows he wanted to, wanted to hold her in his arms. But even a brief kiss risked souring the goodbye. The worst thing would be for her to feel relieved he was gone. He opened the door, and she stepped into the lighted entry.

"Goodbye, Addy."

"Goodbye."

He could have lingered, could have asked again if she'd write or phone—asked all sorts of questions that would delay their separation. But the stronger impulse was running for cover.

CHAPTER 34

SHE PULLED HER HAIR INTO a band because of the wind, but the sun was warm once the ferry got past the shadows of buildings. Spray from the oncoming waves speckled her face and arms. Most of the other passengers went inside the cabin or took the stairs to the upper deck. Addy remained gripping the railing, Francis's briefcase locked between her shins, shifting her weight back and forth, getting her sea legs. The sky was a lovely cornflower blue and cloudless.

Ahead, a thick mist hovered over the islands and Jersey coast. The towering aqua-colored figure became clearer, the upraised right arm and torch, the tablet, the spiked crown. Addy barely remembered the visit with Grandma Marjorie maybe twenty years before; Nathan's story about his grandfather kissing the ground had made more of an impression. Was this how the statue had looked? No, her great-grandfather would have seen her almost full-face, sailing north from the mouth of the harbor. Manhattan would have had skyscrapers but not as many or as tall. Did Mary MacDonalde, over eight months pregnant and arriving in the month of January, go out on deck—was the sight worth braving the cold and wind? Addy hoped so, for there was an implicit kindness in the folds of the robes, in the figure's fearless stance. Anonymous piers wouldn't have been the same.

Turning a little aft to avoid the wind, she noticed a guy who reminded her of Zach—maybe the light-brown curly hair or the wiry build. Her glance must've lingered too long, because he immediately smiled and came her direction.

"Checking out what the forbears witnessed? A tourist? Allow me to point out over there, that lady is the Statue of Liberty."

She smiled good-naturedly. "Actually, I live in Manhattan."

He smiled good-naturedly too. "Your first trip? My second—this time I brought a decent camera." It hung around his neck. "By the way, name's Sam."

"I'm Addy."

"I'm putting together a scrapbook for my grandmother in LA. Her parents came through Ellis. My old camera was a piece of junk. I could do like the smart folks and buy postcards, but since I fancy myself a photographer, I have to put my money where my mouth is. What do you do in Manhattan? Grad student? Or working in—"

"Law school."

"Now *there's* a path to a paying job. I got a BA in English lit and am stuck filming documentaries for chump change."

The ferry's maneuvers drew their attention; they had entered a narrow inlet, and the wind died. Addy turned to the bow. The mist had burned off, and the immigration center loomed enormous, like a gargantuan fortress. No, not a fortress: the bright-pinkish bricks and pillars and towers and ornamentation made it look like a palace, an immense palace. Three broad white-stone arches dominated the front, their windows several stories high. The roof corners were elaborately sculpted rectangular pillars topped with iron-like cupolas themselves topped with tall spikes. Some of the moldings looked taken from Greek columns. The intricately sculpted cornices and carvings made the massive structure seem gaudy, like a doge's Venetian palace.

"I didn't expect a government building to be so ornate," she said.

"French Renaissance Revival is a casserole. Romanesque, Italian Renaissance. It's not the original immigration center—that was wood and burned to the ground, so they decided on brick and limestone for the replacement." He pointed to a group of buildings similar in style across the inlet. "Those were the hospitals."

"That's where an immigrant would be sent if she failed the health inspection?"

"Depends on the reason. She could have been quarantined on one of the other islands—they were set up for contagious diseases. But Ellis also had wards."

"This person I'm wondering about, I know she went through Ellis Island even though she sailed in a second-class cabin."

"Was she sick? Her papers not in order?"

They turned to watch the ferry pulling up against the pier. Young men tied the lines. With the wind gone, Addy slipped the band off her hair.

"What kind of documentaries are you making?"

"Dull stuff. It's just a gig till I figure out what'll pay the rent while I'm writing the great American novel."

"You're a writer?"

"I see two options. Number one: go to grad school, get a teaching job, and write on the side. Number two: join the family biz and rack up enough dough to quit and write full-time. Vacation packages, that's what my dad and uncle peddle. Pretty mercenary, but at least I'd travel, play the scout. How bad can it be to test hotel beds in Bali?"

Addy picked up Francis's briefcase, and she and Sam followed the other passengers off the ferry. The walkway to the center went by deep-green lawns and colorful flowers and trees in full leaf. Sam stopped to take pictures, and Addy wondered out loud how much of the scenic beauty the immigrants appreciated, given they were weary from the long voyage and worried about the future.

"Not much. There was a battalion of government officials waiting for them. You came off the gangplank and got a numbered tag to wear, and unless you understood English, had to take it on faith they weren't herding you to some gulag."

They strolled up a pavilion-like covered incline and entered a hall that couldn't have resembled what Mary had seen: a clean floor, freshly painted walls and pillars, and people milling about in shorts and Hawaiian shirts or summer dresses. The signs and plaques were modern; only the sepia photographs on display gave a sense of the past.

"The famous Baggage Room," Sam said. "You checked your stuff if you didn't want to haul it upstairs." They must've been on the same wavelength, because he added, "It didn't look like a tourist stop: hundreds of people crammed like sardines, in clothes they'd been wearing for weeks, weighed down with suitcases, bags, baskets, screaming babies. But my relatives swore it wasn't bedlam—people were too scared of the men in uniforms. In Europe, a single government official could haul you to jail or in front of a magistrate for total BS. Or conscript you, right off the street, no goodbyes to family or anyone. Government officials were *dangerous.*"

Nathan, who was often critical of the government's treatment of Native Americans and Black people, tried to impress upon Addy and her brothers how radically better the US political system was compared to other countries'. The idea that government officials were public *servants*, that the public was *their* boss, was "the great American experiment."

Sam pointed to a room the other tourists were inspecting. "That's the dormitory. Could sleep thousands if it had to."

She followed him to the bottom of a staircase that spiraled at sharp right angles. Starting up, he said, "As the immigrants came this way, doctors watched like hawks—down here and up there, this army of white coats. The point was to find anybody who was sick physically or mentally—the official terms were having a 'loathsome disease' or being 'insane' or an 'idiot.' TB and VD, cholera, small pox, trachoma, favus—some kind of scalp disease—were what they were on the lookout for. Trachoma's an eye infection—they'd peel back your lids with one of those buttonhook things. You wonder if they knew to sterilize the instrument between people or else spread the disease themselves."

She stayed close behind him on the stairs. "How could they diagnose things on the spot, without tests?"

"It wasn't the *complete* Dark Ages: they had stethoscopes, thermometers—knew what trachoma and favus looked like and probably measles and chicken pox. If they weren't sure, they sent you to the hospital. You saw the size of it. Had whatever medical expertise existed at the time: docs, nurses, lab techs, different wards, a contagious-diseases wing, even a morgue. So most sick people got better and weren't sent back to Europe."

"Some *were?*" Her naivete made her blush. Still, it shocked Addy that after all the trouble and expense of packing up your belongings and leaving home and traveling to a coastal town maybe in a different country, then paying for a ticket and crossing the ocean to another continent, some official could make you go back.

"You know what they called this place," Sam said, "Island of Hope, Island of Tears. At least the return trip was at the ship's expense. Which is why the company did its own exams before the ship left port. Fumigated for lice—parasites and infections could spread like wildfire, given they packed six, eight hundred people into steerage. Don't blow it out of proportion, though: the immigrants were told ahead of time that getting past the docs wasn't a cakewalk."

"What if it was just the *crossing* that made you sick?"

"If you had a cough, diarrhea, something like that, you got labeled 'medically certified' and, like I said, sent to the hospital till you recovered."

They'd reached the top of the staircase and now entered the Registry Room, what Addy overheard someone call the Great Hall. It *was* a great hall, a grand atrium with a broad polished floor and enormous half-moon windows both at ground level and up high, and a row of high, concave white-stone ceilings. The elegant brass chandelier seemed superfluous in all the daylight.

"This also looked different back then," Sam said. "For one thing, most of the space was taken up with rows of benches. Metal rails separated people into lines—you could have to wait hours. Over there, along the sides, they had desks and areas partitioned off for special inspections. Most people got the 'six-seconds physical'—scalp, face, hands, neck—but if you didn't pass that, you got sent into a private room for the full monty. Say they thought you weren't all okay in the head—the doc would put an X here in chalk." He tapped her at the top of her right shoulder. "If over here, that meant you had some disease, but the doc wasn't sure what. You got an H if they thought your heart wasn't so hot and a Pg if you were pregnant."

"Would pregnancy keep you out?"

"Not if your husband was with you or waiting for you. They weren't too happy about single mothers or mothers-to-be in general."

"What if a pregnant woman was a widow? And had a situation lined up—a family to stay with and work for?"

"One of my great-aunts or great-great-aunts started to go into labor when the ship was entering the harbor, and they bribed ship's officers to get her moved into first class and skip the whole Ellis shtick."

"Say a woman had her baby before the ship arrived, and the child looked a little premature, and they didn't know if it was going to—"

"I'm guessing it would be sent to the hospital."

"Would they let her stay with him, to nurse him?"

"I assume so. Generally, families stayed in the dormitory while waiting for their sick relatives to recover. The reason it's so big is because if a ship docked late or a storm kicked up, and the ferry couldn't leave, *everybody* had to stay overnight. The kitchen could cook for thousands—I'm serious—and a dining room, and obviously they needed beds. Staff came in to wash the sheets, serve the food, do cleanup—it was like a small town, a heavily policed small town."

"And when the baby was better, they could leave?"

"There's a story—I don't know if it's apocryphal—that a baby with a clubfoot was born in the hospital, and a sympathetic nurse told the mother it would be sent back to the old country, but if the mother wanted, the nurse would smuggle the kid into Jersey—in a satchel or something—after work. So the mother went through the whole processing bit alone, and when she took the ferry to Jersey, the nurse or somebody met her with the kid. It was all for a fee, naturally. Like I said, the story might be apocryphal. In any case, I'd bet working here was a pretty lucrative deal."

"What a choice—give your child to a stranger or risk being sent back to Europe!"

"That one's pretty easy—who's going to steal a child with a clubfoot? But the translators were in the best position to take bribes. Most American officials didn't understand Norwegian or Polish or Bulgarian, so the translator could make arrangements for a payoff in the mother tongue."

"Did that go on a lot? I mean, if everyone is being watched all the time—"

"Money talks. They might not let you bribe your way in with smallpox or TB, but say your kid was deaf—I'd bet some doctor would find he wasn't, for the right price."

"Just being *deaf* was enough to keep you out?"

Sam laughed. "It was 'immigration of the fittest.' Kids older than *two* had to be able to say their names and walk without any help—if they were deaf or mute, forget it. Don't look so sad—most made it."

Addy only half listened as he described other procedures—she was stuck on the problem facing a family with a deaf or Down syndrome child, say—a condition the child would never shed. The parents had the choice of either leaving him or her behind or not emigrating. What if no one in the old country was willing to care for your child? Even if there was, you'd be separated. How did a person decide between giving a much better life for some of their children and not leaving a disabled child without family? Maybe it was a *good* thing that people could bribe their way in.

"Immigrants were prepped on how to game the system," Sam was saying as they walked around the Great Hall, "how to hide deformed hands or feet or anything that might get you labeled 'insane' or 'feebleminded.' The authorities knew it and had their own tricks."

He paused to take pictures of the high ceiling. "They didn't want anybody who couldn't earn a living, might end up a ward of the state or turn to a life of crime. Do me a favor—I'd like to make Grandma happy by including a shot of her one and only grandson." He handed Addy the camera and posed by a Registry Room desk, one hand in his pants pocket, tilting his head a little to the side and starting a smile.

"Things changed when the industrialists started screaming for more muscle. Who cares if a strapping Swede isn't quick on the uptake, he'll be hauling lumber. The steel mills and factories actually demanded more immigrants, and the government kept you out only if you had something blatantly infectious."

Sam pointed to the bottom of another staircase. "Once you passed the legal and financial bit, you were in and got to ferry to the mainland. Down there's the currency exchange. Folks were coming from all over: France, Germany, the UK, Scandinavia, Italy, the Ottoman Empire. Constantinople was a *big* jumping-off point because the Turks persecuted everybody: Armenians, Jews, Slovaks, Croats."

After they descended and Addy saw where the immigrants could purchase food and railway tickets, Sam took a few more photos and checked his watch. "Jeez, better run if I want to catch the next boat. How about you?"

"I'm going to wander around a little longer." She knew the south side of the island with the hospital buildings was off-limits but wanted to explore the northside grounds more.

Sam seemed to notice her briefcase for the first time. "F.W.? Fats Waller?"

She laughed. "Francis Wallace—it was my grandfather's."

"Anyway, gotta run—" He stopped and turned. "Not *the* Francis Wallace, the Henry James guru?"

"You know him?"

"I've *heard* of him—every James aficionado has. He's your *grandfather*? No shit! And you weren't an English lit major?"

She pointed at the clock.

"Christ!" Throwing her a wave, he ran toward the exit.

THE WATER WAS A NICE teal blue, and the breeze mild. She didn't want to leave the lawns, the picturesque views of the bay, the sunshine and outdoors. Joe knew the odds were small she'd learn why Mary had been sent to Ellis Island or whether she'd given birth before arriving in Clopes—Addy wasn't really worried about a chewing out. "I just don't want them whining I should've sent someone," he'd said. "If you come up with anything, we'll bill your time, otherwise write it off."

She watched the ferry pull away and for some minutes just stared out at the water. Carson used to marvel at the amazing mix of currents, the different colors the waves took on depending on the light. She wanted to keep track of things to write about if he ever wrote to her, things that would be kind without giving false hope. And Francis's comment when they ate dinner in the kitchen Saturday night: "It is strange to be without our usual soirée." Was he aware he sounded disappointed?

In the full sunlight, the massive lady gleamed blue-green. Supposedly America was the land of opportunity, and the statue represented liberty and justice for all, and the nation was a harmonious melting pot of nationalities: these stories from her father and teachers had happy endings. But reality included the Island of Tears: people dreaming of a new life being turned away, parents faced with splitting up their families, maybe seeing some of their children for the very last time. Did the children *themselves* feel torn? Was returning to their old country with their parents and siblings more important than a life in America? Francis would say the child's age would have made a difference.

JOE DID SHRUG OFF HER not finding out anything. "We'll stick with the assumption we've had all along: she gave birth to Brian in Clopes. The Scots had the chutzpah to complain we're three-quarters through the budget—*they* convinced the court to extend the deadline. If they can't find an heir before next summer, they have to go with what they've got. Anyway, dictate up your notes and leave them for Michelle."

Addy started toward the door, but Joe kept talking.

"Sure, the publicity's great for business—new clients coming in the door—I should be grateful. But those damn penny-pinchers pore over invoices like they're panning for gold. *You* don't pad your hours—I'll say that. And your research and writing skills are fine—Stan loved the *in limine* motions—it's amazing how lousy most law students write—lawyers too. But let's see you get more aggressive in interviews. Brad, Simon, they're not afraid to fly by the seat of the pants. Brittany—you heard how she got a hunch during the Pittsburgh interview and ran with it? Planning only gets you so far, sometimes you've got to take chances. Now don't get down in the mouth—I've given this lecture to plenty of other female—jeez, now don't go suing me up the wazoo."

CHAPTER 35

OLIVIA'S VOICE PEALED THROUGH THE receiver. "Congratulations: you're a great-grandfather again. Alex and Mindy have a baby girl, Madison Claire. Seven pounds, nine ounces; mother and daughter doing fine. Marcia's thrilled, even if she won't admit it."

"She says she's *not?*"

"Says being a grandmother makes her feel old."

"In her fifties! My goodness—I am not sure I remember being that *young*. Well, that certainly is good news. And I have some news as well, although not nearly as important. You recall my mentioning on Sunday that Adelaide was going to Ellis Island? She had an encounter there that was gratifying, quite gratifying."

"What happened?"

"As you know, among my former colleagues, a few might allow that I had a somewhat distinguished career—"

"Not just a *few*."

"I would characterize my standing as that of a big fish in a small pond. I do not speak of the university as a whole. I think it is fair to say that *any* English department is a small pond—we do not grace the front pages of the news. Not that the front pages are a pond I care to swim in. In any event, imagine my surprise when Adelaide told me that a young man she met on the ferry inquired about the initials on my old briefcase—which I gave her—and hearing my name is Francis Wallace asked if she meant '*the* Francis Wallace—the Henry James guru.'"

Olivia, I knew, was impressed. "Will Addy be seeing him again?"

"I have no idea."

"Still, that's very flattering."

"Yes, it was. Well, I had better finish my preparations for our expedition. She has gone to pick up the rental automobile tonight so we can leave for Maine first thing tomorrow."

"I hope the trip does her good."

ONCE WE HAD NAVIGATED PAST the Bronx, the parkway quickly became scenic. Trees of so many types whisked by, I had scant time to identify them. The tall ones with spreading boughs were surely oaks, and the slender white-barked were birch, but otherwise all I could distinguish was evergreen from leafy.

Woods were not the sole delight, for bright-purple flowers infiltrated the long grass beside the highway shoulder, not unlike wild grasses in Indiana, and what looked like prairie dropseed. Coral-colored vines could have been Virginia creeper, and white clusters reminded me of my mother's dogwood. The tree leaves, although still green, had in some instances shed their dark intensity in augury of autumn.

The parkway cleaved residential neighborhoods, exposing charming homes and pleasant gardens, manicured lawns, the occasional pool or tennis court, outdoor furniture of one sort or another, small ponds, and weeping willows. Stone overpasses dating back to the 1800s, if not earlier, and a variety of architectural styles—brick and Tudor and Hansel-and-Gretel cottages—rendered the landscape anything but monotonous. And moments after a sign welcomed us to Connecticut, we were deep in forests and hill and dale, sending my thoughts along a path of reminiscences.

"My father used to hunt deer and wild turkeys in the woods near our farm. Once he brought home an opossum, which my mother was reluctant to cook. I don't recall the taste—I suppose she disguised it in a stew. I learned to handle a rifle, but my eyesight lost its sharpness—hence my efforts were not worth the cost of ammunition. I suppose a good snow in these parts makes travel difficult. My mother certainly welcomed the warmer seasons, not being so housebound, going to church potlucks and ice cream socials. And yet farm life seemed to agree with her; if she had yearnings for a different type of existence, she never expressed them. And without minimizing the efforts involved, physically strenuous labor offers rewards. The ache in one's shoulders after an hour of cutting up wood or hoeing or storing the hay—even *exhaustion* can evoke a sense of satisfaction, of accomplishment. You are nodding?"

"It might seem trivial in comparison, but after soccer practice, being exhausted was a good feeling."

"Imagine that sensation when the products of one's efforts are *tangible*, my dear: when one has brought in buckets of berries and rhubarb and apples about to become pie filling or preserves. The changing of the seasons, as well, is experienced more keenly on a farm. The break of winter's long siege infused us with an indescribable buoyancy. The cold trudge through snow and slush to school, the face assailed by the wind, the sky a shroud, in spring's sunshine became a Marco Polo adventure, an exploration of wildflowers and new territories and a host of young creatures: chipmunks, squirrels, fox kits, beavers, tadpoles. What I have heard my students refer to as 'spring fever' is but a weak tea compared to what we felt when the scents of hyacinth and lilac and rose wafted by. Does my paean to Nature surprise you?"

"No. It's why people go camping."

"I suppose." Yes, there was a piquancy in the inception of *each* new season: summer, fall, even winter. The first snowfall, *the farm, like a wanderer white.*

"When did you last go back to Indiana?"

"Go back to Indiana? Not since my father's funeral. I did not remain in contact with the neighbors or childhood friends, and Miss Perry, she passed away before the war."

"Do you miss it sometimes, the farm?"

When did remembering rise to the level of missing?

"On the whole, I would have to say no. Spring, while a joy in many ways, was also the most demanding season. In winter, I had little to do besides caring for the animals and chopping wood; we were forced indoors for much of the day, and I could read. My father, of course, was busy mapping out where the crops would be planted and which fields would lie fallow. Once the ground thawed, however, we had to burn and cut the corn stalks and fertilize and plow and seed. The lion's share of these tasks fell to the hired men; I was occupied with the newborns, the calves and foals. They required feeding, special bedding, various ministrations."

"Did you ever consider teaching somewhere rural? Like a college town?"

"There was a time, yes; as the war wound down, I did consider it. Universities all across the country presented possible employment opportunities, and I applied for assistant professorships any number of places, including a few in small towns that were distinctively rural in character. Intellectual endeavors do not require an urban environment. Or an academic one! Look at Thoreau: he found intellectual stimulation, for a time, in nature. Jane Austen, the Brontës, Thomas Hardy—they spent most of their lives far from a major metropolis. But when the university offered me the opportunity to return to my old position, your grandmother and I, we did not hem and haw.

"Perhaps having three children dampened our enthusiasm for a change in scene. Claudia used to claim the war had *humbled* everyone— those at home as well as those sent overseas—but I recall my ambitions being rekindled to no less a flame than before, eager as ever to spread the gospel of great literature to young minds. How did we get on *this* subject?"

"I was just wondering if you ever missed things about living on a farm."

"I retain happy memories, but Thomas Wolfe's wistful yearning 'homeward' was never a yearning of mine, perhaps because I know the irrefutable truth of the saying 'You *can't* go home again.' Physically returning does not resuscitate the feelings one had there long ago. Even if the place hasn't changed, *we* have. I presume your trip back to Seattle demonstrated this. Indeed, Proust's masterly exploration of the past begins not with the narrator traveling to the *geographical* locale of his childhood but with him tasting something he had often eaten as a child, which triggers 'going home again' in *memory*. It is memory, not locale, we must visit to reclaim the past."

Adelaide made no further comment on the subject, merely pointing out that my seat could "go back" if I wanted to nap. I expressed doubt that I could sleep in a moving automobile but did press the button that allowed me to recline.

Closing my eyes, I floated in that strange dimension between wakefulness and sleep. Images from childhood summers, of bicycle riding and swimming, of fishing for bluegills and smallmouth bass, of reading in the hammock before dinner and then well into the evening by lantern light, these by and by yielded to the recollection of my final summer home. A time of restless anxiety following on the heels of my return from England. And nurturing a single hope: to attend college.

Even the death of one of my beloved dogs affected me less than it would have the year previous. Every day the stride to the mailbox was followed by a desultory slog back to the house. But one blessed afternoon, the hand reaching into the old tin tunnel withdrew an envelope with an embossed, ornate uppercase *U*. In an instant I ran a thumb under the flap and read the answer to my unceasing prayers.

How still the house was—preternaturally still. The shutters had been thrown wide open, and sunlight slanted onto the brown braided rug and rocking chair with its green cushions and quilted blanket. I went back out and spotted Tom and Vern in the west field where the grade dropped toward the creek. My mother had gone to fetch flour and sugar from town; perhaps my father was in the barn.

On impulse I ran almost the entire mile to school. Miss Perry, in the midst of English lessons to the Dutch families new to our community, took a few moments aside to read my letter. Yes, room and board and tuition would be paid for, she confirmed. What other expenses would I have, I anxiously asked. Primarily transportation, books, and clothes, but as the letter indicated, the college had available a number of jobs that could help defray such costs.

I hurried home and quickly completed my remaining chores, all the while watching for my mother's return. The moment she stepped inside and I relieved her of the packages, I showed her the letter, in vain trying to conceal my joy.

Righting the car seat, I explained to Adelaide, "Neither the year in Cambridge nor my four years in college—*nor* my postgraduate studies—imposed a financial burden on my parents. Tuition, room, board—all were paid for. I found part-time employment for what might be termed incidental expenses, and I distinctly recall paying for my train tickets home. Nor was my presence on the farm in any way essential: our family finances were solid, despite the Depression. A girl from town came out to do the laundry. It is true that when the stock market crashed, no one knew what the future would bring, but farmers are used to uncertainty. And my parents never abandoned their view that we would survive whatever economic turmoil lay ahead because we could always fall back on subsistence farming. If 'push came to shove' and my presence on the farm *had* been required, I would have done my duty, I truly believe. But they suffered no diminution in creature comforts—as I have recounted many times, they acquired electricity and indoor plumbing."

I reclined the seat again, and before I knew it, I was awakening from a nap! Feeling a bit like Rip Van Winkle, I inquired as to our progress. We were in northeastern Massachusetts, Adelaide said, and I should be on the lookout for a restaurant for dinner.

Reminding myself of the purpose of this mission, I awaited a quiet stretch of highway to broach the delicate subject preoccupying me these past few weeks. In my tone I vied for a certain solicitude. "I cannot help wondering, my dear, if this expedition fills you with any trepidation. Do you harbor fears of a reopening of wounds?"

Her response was remarkably matter-of-fact. "Actually, I'm looking forward to it. To feel I'm not the only one who remembers him—really remembers him."

"I had hoped that would be your perspective."

Her mouth formed a frown. "I'm a *little* nervous—what to say, exactly. Obviously, some things are off-limits, but since I've driven all this distance, it seems weird to just say we were in the same group of friends."

"Perhaps initially they would enjoy hearing about things you did together—attending plays, concerts. Were there museums near your school?"

"We went to movies. Went camping a few times. And bowling twice. We were awful."

"Perhaps you could mention some films he particularly enjoyed."

"I don't think they would've seen them."

"When was the last—and feel no compulsion to answer my questions if you judge them intrusive—when was the last time the wound *was* reopened? I don't mean to suggest it is completely closed—mental scar tissue is far more porous than physical—but when was the last you had what your grandmother used to call 'a good cry'?"

Adelaide squinted at the windshield. "Maybe junior year? What about you—when did you last cry over Grandma?"

"Me? I am not a person prone to *lacrimation*; I believe that is the technical term. My sorrow manifests itself in other ways. But I did have one long bout. Not immediately—I wasn't at the hospital during the night, and when I came the next morning and they told me she had passed, at that point I was simply stunned. Although the nurses had been very candid about the possibility—pneumonia can cause death in a person *without* weakened lungs. Still, I was too dazed then to cry. You could say I was in a daze from the moment Dr. Conti sent her by ambulance to the hospital, from that time through her days in the intensive care unit and the funeral. And after the funeral, with everyone crowded in the apartment—were you there? You must have been— I'm sorry, I remember so little. But you did not stay over?"

"A high school friend of Mom's put us up. She was afraid it'd be too hard on you if we were at the apartment."

Yes, Olivia had been a godsend. "Your mother remained after all the guests had gone. She sat with me in the bedroom until I fell asleep. I wonder if she got much sleep herself. No, it wasn't until the following morning, Adelaide, after the funeral, that my bout of weeping occurred. I had awoken to an empty bed the few mornings previous, after Marjorie had died, but I suppose the commotion of people coming over—family, friends, colleagues from my department—to be honest, friends I had forgotten, people we no longer socialized with, all sorts of people came by. And with Olivia and Richard and Marcia and their spouses and your generation, and being questioned about the arrangements—I had to speak to the minister—all these goings-on conspired to keep me in a state of befuddlement. But the morning following the day she was buried, I sat up in the empty bed and looked around the room. On the top of her dresser sat her hairbrush and the blue ceramic vase one of the children had made in school and a small pink enamel box, another art project. The curtains had not been drawn all the way and daylight showed me these everyday articles on her dresser. That was when I fully realized she was gone."

The small pink box had weighed down a shop receipt—what was it she needed to return? The toes of her leather walking shoes poking out from under the chair. The "old house sweater," she laughingly called it, an orange woolen cardigan with deep pockets that was her favorite garb on lazy Sunday mornings. The beribboned pot with a cactus she kept on the window sill. The calendar in the kitchen where she scribbled her appointments. The postcard taped to the refrigerator of God's arm reaching toward Adam that Richard had sent from Rome. Every inch of the apartment contained furniture and art and photographs and little objects of day-to-day life that were as much aspects of her as her hair and eyes and wide, wide smile.

Again recalling the errand we were on, I recovered my poise and added only, "Marjorie was in her early seventies, however, not her youth. There is a special pain when people die young."

Briefly turned toward me, Adelaide's face registered surprise. "I would've thought the opposite: that because you and Grandma went through so much together, you'd miss her more."

Out of the mouth of babes and sucklings. "There *is* a special hurt," I conceded, "in losing a person one has long taken for granted. 'Grown accustomed to' is the better phrase. 'Taken for granted' connotes a lack of feeling, and that was never the case. In any event, that morning was when I cried—bawled, if you will. The absurd thing, Adelaide, was that it was *loud*. Not my crying, although it may have been. Her *absence* was loud."

DARKNESS OVERTOOK US ON THE two-lane road. The headlights showed woods and more woods, a very occasional road sign, and an occasional house. Few vehicles approached, and none showed up behind; only once did we espy the remote red glows of a fellow automobile. I was determined to banish all thoughts of a vehicle mishap and the horror-movie possibilities that could flow therefrom and considered myself quite successful on that score, although the motel's red-and-yellow neon sign was a most welcome sight.

Eager to stretch my legs, I accompanied Adelaide into the office, and we were given the keys to our adjacent rooms. Adelaide confirmed with the clerk the route we would take into Bickville on the morrow. Yes, we would accept the offer of a morning pastry, but could we have tea instead of coffee?

My room exuded an appealing snugness promising comfort. The bathroom was immaculate, the pillows plump. The sheets felt crisp to the touch as I climbed into bed. This being my first night away from the apartment since Marjorie's passing, it brought me no small satisfaction to realize I was not too old for adventure, even if a trip such as this would be considered tame by most people. Yes, the pleasures of novelty, of uncharted waters, could still beguile. And the morning promised a visit to Zach's family and hearing about the boy Adelaide had loved and who had loved her.

CHAPTER 36

BICKVILLE WAS A VERITABLE GROVER'S Corners. The simple, gleaming white church and its bold white spire oversaw the town green, the spire's shadow pointing toward a row of small well-tended shops. The homes on the adjacent streets—modest clapboards with picket fences—evoked an earlier period in history, when summer days stretched lazily and mischievous boys whitewashed fences, or finagled other boys into doing it for them. The pedestrians on the sidewalks seemed to know one another, to pause in passing, perhaps to exchange mild gossip. We passed a girl skipping rope and a gent on a bicycle.

Adelaide drove slowly, our windows open to the scent of new-mown grass. I peered briefly inside the bank, and into the law offices of Nichols Taney, and the line at the register in Anderson's Pharmacy. The Bickville Bakery—advertising blueberry pies—came next, then a coffeehouse, a laundromat, and Munson's hardware store, tidy enterprises all. Nora's Emporium appeared to be a general store in the oldest tradition, but we encountered modern shops as well, including a florist with large pots of zinnias along the sidewalk. But who could not take pleasure in quaint touches like the red-and-white-striped pole beside the hand-painted *Bob the Barber* sign and the old lettering on the marquee advertising *Gwen's Antiques*? I pointed out these bits of small-town Americana while Adelaide concentrated on the directions Zach's parents had sent. In the nick of time, I stopped myself from murmuring Yarborough Lumber, possibly the site of the tragedy.

"They lived in town until he was fourteen," she said. "The year before, his sister died, and right after, his father got injured at the sawmill. Not horribly, but bad enough to get workers' comp. That's when they moved to where they are now. Out in the middle of nowhere, Zach said, but near their new church and other families in the congregation. So all through high school, he had to walk half a mile just to catch the school bus, and during the winters here, it's a big deal."

I assured Adelaide I could readily empathize, for my trek had been close to a full mile—not to a bus stop but to the school itself. "There were no buses back then, not where we lived. Or snow plows. We had a blizzard one year that obscured *fences*. Fences and trees are the markers one relies upon to locate the road."

Departing the town, I navigated while Adelaide steered. We passed woods on the left and meadows of larkspur and wildflowers on the right, interspersed with the occasional farmhouse, tilled acreage, and grazing cows and horses. After the turnoff, dense forest crowded in on both sides, an almost-ghoulish route to a bus, it occurred to me, particularly in the dark of winter. The woods ended abruptly, however, depositing us happily in sunshine.

I gestured at the house on the left. "This is it." The structure was modest, not in pristine condition yet not in obvious disrepair. On the roof, dwarfing the chimney, an enormous satellite dish reigned supreme. Adelaide parked the car in the dirt driveway beside a gray pickup truck, also in decent condition.

We exited the rental vehicle and stood for a moment surveying our surroundings. The spot commanded quite a view of meadows and hills. The pastures closer in were fenced off with wooden boards, yet for all my neck craning, I detected no signs of a working farm: the barn roof in the distance had fallen in, and I could discern no coops, sties, troughs, or silos. And no dog on hand to growl at us.

Adelaide helped me up the two porch steps and pressed the bell. The woman who opened the door looked older than Olivia, older than I had expected, her hair gone quite gray. Neither short nor thin, she nonetheless conveyed a frailness. My granddaughter extended her hand and introduced the two of us, but the woman receded, bidding us to enter, much in the manner of a deferential servant.

To our right was a living room furnished somewhat spartanly: a brown sofa, a few nondescript upholstered chairs, and small nondescript tables, one of which held a television. The mantelpiece contained only a wooden cross, a black-covered book I presumed was a Bible, and a small American flag on a small wooden pole. The windows were raised and shaded by some kind of awning; the temperature was not uncomfortable.

A bearded man looking to be in his sixties rose ponderously from a chair and came toward us, creaking the floorboards. I extended my arm. "Francis Wallace, Adelaide's grandfather. Pleased to meet you."

"Mr. H."

We shook hands; Adelaide and Mrs. Henley nodded all around. Urged to have a seat in the living room, Adelaide and I selected the sofa. Our hosts made no offer of tea or coffee or even a glass of water, a lapse that my own mother would never have committed—one did not need to be versed in etiquette to treat guests with a certain civility, especially when they were travelers. On the other hand, I have always been a little leery of using other people's facilities, so abstaining from a beverage had its advantages.

"Thank you for letting us visit," Adelaide began. "Zach and I met during orientation week and had two classes together. He meant a lot to all of us." She turned from one to the other with a look I would describe as supplicating. "Everyone liked him. He was really nice and friendly."

Mr. and Mrs. Henley did not return her smile; in fact, they avoided eye contact—with her, with me, with each other. The father seemed to examine the small drab rug in front of him; his wife looked off toward the kitchen as if expecting a kettle to whistle. Were they preparing tea? Perhaps I *would* welcome a cup.

"People gravitated toward him," my granddaughter continued. "He was always willing to help, like if you needed to move your furniture or carry heavy cartons."

I could tell she was nervous. At least Mr. Henley punctuated their immobility by reaching for his pipe and tobacco pouch. My father had had just such a pouch, and lighting his pipe had been the signal that he was not to be disturbed; it was the abbreviated part of the day when he could be carefree. Mrs. Henley's gaze remained off toward the kitchen.

"I remember he loved seafood," Adelaide said. "When the guys in his dorm were ordering pizza, they would groan when he wanted anchovies or clams. But at a fancy restaurant—I think it was someone's birthday, and we all chipped in—he wouldn't order lobster because he said it wouldn't be fresh. As fresh as the ones here."

Her expression suggested she thought this tidbit would hold special significance for them, would crack the hard veneer they thus far presented, but it did not. She began to talk about some of his friends and how he had helped one repair a bicycle; another, his bed frame. When one acquaintance had purchased a desk too large to fit through the dormitory door, and everyone told him to "give up" and just return it to the previous owner, Zach contrived a set of pulleys, enlisting others to help, and successfully hoisted the cumbersome object through a wide second-story window. The feat disclosed quite an impressive combination of ingenuity, resolve, and team leadership in the young man—indeed, I was sorry Adelaide had not shared the story with me earlier. Yet even this encomium to their son's laudable qualities failed to dent the implacable parental facade.

She switched tacks. "He told me about this house, what it was like when you bought it. How the attic had a hole, and bats got in, and you had to call some agency, and they trapped them and tested for rabies. And about the year the snow plows didn't turn up this road? You went door to door taking grocery orders from the neighbors." She spoke of Zach's fondness for his mother's apple pie, caroling at Christmas, riding bikes with friends.

The Henleys' persistent refusal to even look at Adelaide convinced me that they had guessed at the relationship, even if not realizing its full carnal extent. Were they surprised their son had had a girlfriend? Offended that he had made no mention of it? Or did Adelaide appear a peculiar choice? Did they surmise she was Jewish and took affront at that, even in this day and age? I saw nothing objectionable in her outfit—slacks falling almost to the ankle, a loose-fitting summer blouse. Her facial expressions and manner denoted an eagerness to please, and she was appreciably more gregarious and affable than I could recall her being with Carson or Olivia. Perhaps I was being allowed a glimpse of the Adelaide *Zach* had known.

Whatever the reason, our hosts' stoic aspects never altered. Was I mistaken in ascribing to them *coldness*—could the stony silence conceal deep emotional turbulence? Perhaps she was Zach's first girlfriend and presented their first experience, their first *confrontation*, with a rival for their son's affections.

"He liked to hike and always had his camera. The hiking club chartered a bus; we went to the Allegheny National Forest. And the Monongahela, in West Virginia, over Memorial Day weekend. His roommate sprained his ankle the first day, and Zach bandaged it and broke off a tree limb and made him a crutch." She turned to me. "He was just two badges short of Eagle Scout."

I nodded, and she looked again at the parents. They showed as much animation as the couple in *American Gothic*, a painting whose appeal I never understood.

"He liked movies, the old ones they showed on campus. Billy Wilder was his favorite director. And old comedies—Buster Keaton and Charlie Chaplin . . ." Adelaide's nervousness on full display, she rattled off the names of countless films and directors. I wanted to shake these people, to shout, *Do you have any sense of how difficult this is for her, talking to complete strangers about a person she still mourns? Meet her halfway! Christ was the spirit of mercy and compassion!*

"He organized a group for the Cancer Society walk."

Eventually, she, too, recognized that her efforts were doomed to failure. The Zach she was describing—a friendly, convivial, altruistic helpmeet—was likely a complete stranger to them. He was certainly not the boy *they* knew, the serious and dutiful son. I suppose Adelaide's stories implied she was privy to a part of him walled off from his parents, the very people who had birthed and raised him. Viewed in this light, her visit was repugnant, an affront. And any suggestion of deep grief on her part constituted a rude presumption of equivalence.

The recitation ceased, and for a long moment, no one spoke. The breeze coming through the window now carried the smell of manure—there *were* working farms nearby!

"I was wondering if you still have any of his things, you know—leftover from his childhood? That I could see?"

This was the first comment that struck me as intrusive, but Mrs. Henley promptly nodded and proceeded to the staircase. Adelaide quickly followed. I could hear the elder woman's clunk, clunk, clunk on the wooden steps. Clunk, clunk, clunk.

Left to our own devices, Mr. Henley and I each groped for a topic of conversation, or so I thought, and I was on the verge of asking about farming in the area when, pipe in hand, he asked if I minded if he smoked. I answered in the negative, and he proceeded to hold a match above the chamber while inhaling. Silence being a comfortable state of affairs in *his* book, I decided to do as the Romans did and maintain silence as well, conviviality be damned. So for several minutes, "Mr. H." and I let our eyes roam everywhere but at each other. The situation was not without its comic aspects. I imagined Marjorie observing the scene from above, astonished at the complete absence of those social graces which lubricate stressful human interactions. Optimism grew in me that Mrs. Henley had shown amiability outside her husband's presence and was regaling my granddaughter with stories about Zach's childhood, although a momentary panic disturbed such thoughts: Would the woman ask Adelaide to kneel and pray with her? I could not imagine Adelaide refusing. Was it incumbent upon me to attempt to climb the stairs and put an end to such a mild form of torture?

Fortunately, the two ladies descended forthwith, Adelaide holding a slip of paper. Mr. Henley and I rose, and Adelaide offered him her right hand. "I'm glad to have met you." He shook it glumly, and she repeated the gesture with Mrs. Henley, who likewise proffered a limp appendage. Their faces revealed nothing.

THE AUTOMOBILE BOUNCED ALONG THE dirt road. We entered the dark grove of trees and emerged back in sunlight. Did I mind a stop at the cemetery, Adelaide inquired. My reply was that I had assumed all along such a stop would be on our itinerary. She gestured at the slip of paper on the dashboard and said it had the directions. Again I played navigator through the rural countryside, and we skirted pine forests and fields and the occasional house.

"I don't know what I expected," she said. "That they'd share stories? Show me photos? Laugh about his quirks? Cry together? I guess I thought we'd share *some*thing."

"A fellowship in grief, my expectation as well."

She carefully turned onto River Road. "Was I rude?"

"Not at all; you were a model of respectful decorum. Eager, as you say, to find things in common. I don't see what you could have said or done differently."

"He had his mother's eyes. His dad's jawline. I tried to say things that would trigger happy memories, if you know what I mean."

"I *do* know what you mean, and you would have succeeded with most people. The deck was stacked against you for a reason I cannot fathom. Perhaps they are still shell-shocked. Your mother has said that incomprehensible misfortune causes people to behave incomprehensibly."

Did poor Sue Bridehead act reasonably, forcing herself into an unhappy marriage and abandoning the man she loved—and who loved her? I had wished to shake Sue, to shout, *What are you doing, in your grief? What are you doing not only to yourself but to poor Jude?*

"Is this where I turn?"

I consulted the slip of paper. "Yes, left."

"At least now I know why he wasn't gung-ho about me meeting them."

"But if things had progressed between you—what I mean is: Do you think they would have reacted the same if he hadn't died? Surely his death was what launched them into—I don't know what to call it."

"When his sister died, they didn't cry—at least not in front of him. They just kept saying it was God's will. It got so weird, he felt like he lost *them* too. They hadn't been like that before. That's when the cousin at the fire-and-brimstone church got them to join. They had rules, like you had to pray before this or that. No dating without a chaperone, so he never bothered. In high school he thought of running away but couldn't, not after what they'd been through—his father's injury too. He felt really guilty going away to college, but he couldn't stand being at home."

"Quite understandable. From what you described, he was an energetic and resourceful young man."

"Easygoing was more like it. And sociable; he could stay up all night talking with people." She gave a light laugh, slowing the vehicle at the cemetery entrance. "I sure couldn't."

Easygoing. Yet he fell in love with a sensible, serious young woman, not a silly frivolous one. Someone whom, *temperamentally*, his parents could not possibly have objected to.

THE CEMETERY WAS AS CHARMING as the town, a two- or three-acre patch encircled by an old stone wall. The small monuments and gravestones varied in shape and size, age and composition, some dating back to the 1700s. These appeared more slate-like; the newer were thick and a shiny light marble or light gray. I reassured Adelaide I could manage alone on the uneven ground and she should feel free to go on without me, and camera in hand, she hastened up and down the rows, scanning the epitaphs.

Dearest Gladys, Your Soul Now in Heaven read one stone with the dates 1817–1857. *The Lord has taken our Alfred too soon.* The saddest, perhaps, were the coupling of mother and child dying within days of each other. How common such fates were—and probably still are in other corners of the world. My own mother had suffered three stillbirths and three children dying in infancy. Yet despite being their sole issue to see a first birthday, I was not spoiled. Of course, on a farm, needs are too great.

Adelaide had ceased her meanderings and stood by a single gravestone. I shrunk back and turned at an angle to allow her to feel unobserved, in the event she desired privacy. After a few moments and careful of my ankle, I made my way over. She stood to one side, and I read, below a cross, *Zachary Christopher Henley*, along with the dates of his birth and too-recent death. Nothing was added.

"That's his sister."

Margaret Jane Henley was etched into the adjacent gravestone, also beneath a cross, and the dates of her birth and death. I paused long enough to signify a paying of respects and retraced my steps to the parking lot.

ON THE ROAD ADELAIDE BECAME quite talkative. Perhaps she felt— as I did—a certain relief that the day's grimmer tasks were behind us; all that lay ahead was the drive home, to be broken up by meals and a motel stop in central Massachusetts or possibly Connecticut. What she spoke of, initially, was about their dating: the disastrous evening bowling, the fancy restaurant where they tried caviar.

Eventually she wound around to Zach's parents, wondering aloud if they had realized the two were romantically involved.

"They didn't treat me as anyone other than a casual friend. No curiosity about me at all."

"My own opinion is that they did not want to imagine their son as having changed in any respect—which would include having fallen in love."

Our conversation darted to other topics—the countryside,

climates, cemetery visits portrayed in literature, and so forth. My granddaughter made only one additional comment about the Henleys, the following morning after we crossed the Connecticut border into New York.

"Like you said, nothing's worse than losing a child, and you have to forgive people if they act weird."

"I can forgive their conduct toward *you*," I responded. "After all, you're a stranger to them. But how they behaved toward Zach after the death of his sister—to ask him, in essence, to stifle his nature, his youth, his *soul*, if you will—in my mind that is somewhat less forgivable."

She graced me with the kind of smile that enables us to forgive everyone everything.

CHAPTER 37

"YOU'RE FINALLY HOME." CARSON PLOPPED down onto the futon sofa the second Lucy answered. "I tried you the last couple of weekends."

"Saturday, he had some speech in Baltimore, and we made a holiday of it. The humidity was *awful*—we barely left our room."

"Spare me the details."

"The weekend before I went on a three-day shindig with my salon girls. Leanne's parents have a cabin near the Finger Lakes with a Jacuzzi. But we kept hearing noises all night, and nobody could sleep."

"Did you think a bear would break in?"

"It's in the Bermuda Triangle. Not the *real* one. I told you: they find empty cars by the side of the road and no sign of the people."

"I pity any extraterrestrial trying to take on you and your girlfriends."

"So I fell asleep on the deck in the morning and almost got sunburned—now *that* would've ruined the trip to Baltimore. How's the job? Do you like the city?"

He leaned against the futon back and stretched his legs. "Doesn't feel like a city, or not like an East Coast city. It's open—the skyscraper area is pretty much limited to this one section, and everywhere else, the apartments are only two or three stories, so you can see distances, at least when the fog lifts. And when you go up hills, you get views of the water: the ocean, the bays. I think it affects people—there's not that grimness. And they don't race wherever they're going."

"How's the job?"

"Okay." Carson stood abruptly and walked to the living room window. Across the street a group of old ladies emerged from the Korean grocery store. The laundromat looked packed. "I'm not sure computer transactions are my thing—cross-licensing deals involving technology. The other associates catch on quicker. But it's a big place, and I haven't a clue what half the partners do."

"Are there other specialties you can try?"

"When it gets to that point. Right now I'm just a grunt shoveling whatever they dump. The past few weeks it's been research for some trial. The case is eating up half the litigation associates. No, nothing juicy like the MacDonalde—software copyrights and antitrust. Sound fun? I heard there's a partner who once in a while gets an admiralty case."

"Your colleagues decent?"

"So far."

"No special friends?"

"I got a cat—does he count? I named him Sidney. Wasn't that the Hendersons' dog?"

"I mean at the firm. Yes, what a lovely Irish setter."

The time they couldn't take the boat out—some problem with the rudder—the Hendersons brought Sidney and picnicked in the park. Carson had been scared at first, but by the end of the afternoon, he was hugging the boisterous animal.

"Two other first-year associates are into regattas—they have them all year round here."

"Will they let you crew?"

"I go on the water to get *away* from the rat race."

"Any nice *female* associates?"

"Tsk, tsk, Luce. These days, mixing business and pleasure is a no-no. The firm could get sued from here to Hackensack."

"What about outside of work? Have you found places to—"

"Who's got time? Anyway, that's low on my agenda."

"Don't tell me you've decided you're gay! Is that why you moved there?"

"It sure would make life easier. No, unfortunately I'm drawn to the fair sex."

Carson moved to the kitchen window. One nice thing about a small apartment—the phone cord reached everywhere. The water was a deep blue.

"Still in touch with Addy?"

"We write. Her last letter was really long, said all kinds of stuff. It can feel like she's pulling closer, talking about things that really matter—not that *I'm* on the list. But really personal stuff. Pull, push, pull, push."

"Just because she's rejecting you as a boyfriend, that doesn't mean she doesn't want to be friends. *Close* friends. You can care a lot even if you're not in love."

"Ouch. My own lines coming back to bite me."

"I hate seeing you hold out hope when it's hopeless. Isn't she staying in New York after graduation?"

"I guess."

"She thinks she's being nice by not breaking up, but it's the opposite. Letting you hang on is not doing you any favors. People need to shit or get off—"

"I know, I know. Well, time and distance should do the trick. I've done the distance part, but I can't move time."

"What's that old song you used to tease me—"

"'Love the One You're With.' Ouch again."

"Don't write back to her—or *you* make the clean break. But before you do, pump her for everything about the MacDonaldes."

THE FOLLOWING WEEK HE GOT another letter.

I found out Sheena got an offer last week. She's been working on tax cases mostly, and I know they need more tax people, but it still makes me think I won't get one. Maybe I'm just delaying the inevitable, but the thought of writing a new résumé and figuring out where to send it is depressing.

Try the Bay Area! He skimmed the paragraphs about school and work—classes, reviewing documents, preparing for some witness interview.

Joe said I stuck to my outline too much, have to learn to think on my feet. He was right, I get nervous.

"You have plenty of other strengths," Carson said out loud, "plenty of other qualities to bring to the firm. Nobody's going to mistake you for a brown-noser, a pathological networker, or some two-faced toady. There are plenty of *us* but few of you." He was getting an erection.

Two weeks ago Francis and I went up to Maine to visit Zach's parents. I didn't know whether to tell them about us—Why would they want to know about us?

Zach never told them we were a couple. They belong to a very strict fundamentalist church. . . . His mother showed me his bedroom, and it was weird. I'd seen a picture, and his guitar had been hanging from a hook on the wall, plus there were posters of Bono and some bands and a picture of the Grand Canyon. Now the only thing on the wall is a cross.

So much for that. Carson leaned down and petted the cat.

His grave was next to his sister's. I kept waiting to feel something. About an hour later, driving home, I suddenly felt a lot of anger. Outrage, kind of. How could the universe confine him to a box! I know that sounds stupid. It's just that he was lighthearted and whimsical. After his sister died he felt like he was living in a straitjacket, and then at college he got one short year to be himself. Ever after he's confined again. I wish he'd been cremated and his ashes tossed from a mountain.

The remaining page dealt with Francis's and Robert's doctor visits. Francis needed orthotic shoes. Robert had heart scans. *Millie is afraid he'll need surgery. It's risky, but so is doing nothing. He still plays with the man-of-war*

"Not one word about missing me, Sidney. Not one! Yet she did pick *me* to write to. A long letter, and about things that are important. Doesn't that count for *some*thing? Jeez—I should've gotten a pet rock, for all the sympathy *you* give."

CHAPTER 38

JOE HOLLERED THE SECOND SHE reached his doorway. "What do they put in the Edinburgh drinking water, LSD?" As always, his shirtsleeves were rolled up to the elbow, the shirt unbuttoned at the top, his tie dangling from the desk-chair back. "They whine about claimants coming out of the woodwork, but do they keep their mouths shut and the story out of the news? Nuts are calling from Yakima. Brittany and Simon are busy as hell—West Coast, Denver—any day now somebody's gonna send us a picture of a carving on a sequoia."

Addy moved a stack of files from the chair to the desk corner and sat. She took a pen and notepad from her briefcase and waited for Joe to continue.

"You think I'd be happy—more billables. But these Scots have excuses for getting out of everything. Don't want to pay for word-processing—it's 'secretarial,' 'overhead.' Half my day is trying to run this case so we break even, never mind make two cents' profit."

He splashed among the papers on his desk as if looking for something. "The old lady Brittany spoke to last month—Julia somebody—she gabbed to somebody about the interview, who gabbed to somebody, who gabbed to somebody, and the next thing you know, there's some article in a Spokane paper." He pronounced the city with a long *a*. "So, fine—that doesn't mean people on the East Coast and everywhere else will hear about it. But the Scots figure: public is public. So they tell the reporters in the UK the *dates* Mary was there, on the 'fruit ranch,' they call it. And do they tell us they spilled the beans? No! We find out about it during an interview Brad did up in Boston. The claimant knew the whole story, practically. Just you wait: some nut from Alabama whose grandfather lived in Podunk, Washington, in 1910 will decide he's a relation. Like I said, I wouldn't care—it'd be a goddamn gravy train—but these misers—" He finally seized a piece of paper from the mess on his desk. "We got the Mamaroneck scheduled, for next week. Mr. Hoity-Toity Bruce Grey-Davison."

"Next week—when?"

"Connie wrote it down. He's in the 'fine-antiques' business."

"How is he related?"

"Mary's *grandson*. Mary to Helen to Brucy."

Addy wrote on her pad *Mary>Helen>Bruce G-D*. "Helen—Mary had a daughter? Did he send any documents?"

"Hundreds. What's-her-face pored over them—pile of crap. All they prove is he's the son of some Helen Hill Grey-Davison and her husband, James Grey-Davison Jr. And practically every last document is about Daddy—James Grey-Davison *Junior*—who we don't care squat about. No documents for his mother, Helen, who's supposedly Mary's daughter. Sure, and I own the Brooklyn Bridge."

"Did he say if Mary's still alive?"

"No. Didn't send a copy of her death certificate either. Sent one for each of his parents. Helen croaked in '76, I forget where—Raleigh—somewhere down south. James croaked I don't remember when. Same place."

"What about Helen's birth certificate?"

"Are you kidding?" He handed Addy a loose-leaf notebook. "We've got Helen and James's *marriage* license—1936—and baby *Brucy's* birth certificate—1955. Big surprise for Helen and husband, huh? How'd you like getting pregnant almost twenty years after the wedding, long after you'd stopped trying and actually started *enjoying* your freedom?"

"He didn't say anything about an uncle—Helen having a brother?"

"No. You'll have to grill him on that."

Addy opened to the first notebook tab, *BWGD*, and the first page after the tab, a copy of a birth certificate for Bruce Windsor Grey-Davison, born in 1955 in Richmond, Virginia. He'd be what now—thirty-nine?

"So far they look kosher," Joe said. "We're still checking against public records. But the only thing saying he's Mary's grandson is a self-serving cover letter. Says he'll provide a photo and some letters at the interview. Tried copying the photo, he claims, but came out blurry. And the letters—he's damn secretive. This fellow's slick, I tell you. His lawyer—somebody named Pierce from Atlanta—I'd like to pierce his high-falutin' ego—wants a liquidated-damages clause: if we leak Grey-

Davison's name, we have to fork over a hundred thou. I told him to go to hell. In so many words. If he wants to play the game, he goes by *our* rules. I didn't even bother asking the Scots."

Addy looked behind the tab labeled *HHGD*. The first page was a copy of a Virginia marriage license between Helen Hill and James Grey-Davison Jr., dated June 1936. "So Mary married someone named Hill? Are there documents about him?"

"Not diddly."

"And he didn't say if Helen had any brothers or sisters?"

"No. What happened to Brian? Good question. I tell you, this Brucy's got a sense of entitlement thicker than the Harvard and Yale Clubs combined. He's already heir-apparent, in his mind. His goon, Pierce, he writes that the letters Brucy's holding on to, they'll explain everything. But we only get to see copies—the originals are socked away in some safe-deposit box." Joe changed his voice to sound snooty. "'They will only be made available to a trained document examiner and only if their authenticity is questioned.'" He threw his hands in the air. "And we need to ask permission to do chemical analysis! He actually said 'carbon dating'! It might 'threaten the integrity of the paper.' These rascals got to be kidding. Talk to Connie about time and place. And about the brother-sister jokers in Jersey I sent you the memo about: you're doing them next week, right?"

ADDY CHECKED THE PARALEGALS' WHITEBOARD and saw she currently was assigned the Hoboken siblings, Mr. Grey-Davison, and Ms. Bettles; the three or four other names that had been added had been erased. "Here's the Jersey," Connie said, handing her a notebook. "They only sent a couple of documents. I haven't made copies of the Grey-Davison until I know which you want—he sent *hundreds*. There are a few in the notebook—the ones that came with the letter—but mostly it's the questionnaire responses."

THE AIR-CONDITIONING WAS BROKEN, AND the subway was a sauna. Addy got a seat after the first stop and sat with Francis's briefcase on her lap. Like zombies, the other passengers stared straight ahead while their bodies swayed in unison to the motion of the car. Early on, the impassivity had appealed to her. There was an *economy* in it—zoning out conserved energy. Even the rattling and banging and screeching brakes had made her feel cocooned. But now she remembered there was also something nice about the quiet, lumbering bus rides in Seattle.

At her station, she shuffled with the herd onto the old, dingy subway platform with its dark tunnel walls and rust-brown iron columns and along the shabby cement and up the steps to the street. As a pleasant surprise, the air was sharply sweet. The pale pea-green leaves on the saplings here and there along the pavement were beginning to show hints of yellow. Yet barely a week past the equinox, most of the block was in shadow.

AFTER SIFTING THROUGH THE MAIL, Addy went into the living room. Francis immediately rested his magazine on the end table.

"Joe has given me two interviews."

"Two? A good sign, is it not? That he trusts your abilities?"

"I guess. Anyway, the first is Tuesday, in Hoboken."

"Leave me the name and address."

Addy perched on the arm of the sofa. "I can't really do that. I already tell you too much confidential information about Mary. I can't tell you the names of the claimants—we have nondisclosure agreements with them."

"So you will travel to a secret location to meet with an anonymous person? No, no, that is unacceptable."

"People at work know where I'm going."

"Yes, but if you do not return by six o'clock, how will *I* know you have come to no harm? If I telephone your firm, will someone answer? And if so, will he or she assist me in locating you, in reassuring me you are safe? And who is to say that the person or persons at Engel Klein who haven't gone home for the day are in possession of the information as to your whereabouts? *I* will be the one watching the clock and worrying." Francis shook his head over and over. "Many of these claimants are shady characters, to put it mildly—you have said so yourself."

"I'm not *allowed* to tell you."

"To whom will I disclose these facts? Most days *you* are the sole person I converse with. I don't go down the hall to discuss it with Millie and John. Or the super, if we chance to meet. I have never discussed the *public* aspects of the case even with your mother, to whom I speak every Sunday."

Addy could imagine him pestering people at Engel if she was a minute late. "You promise not to tell anybody?"

Francis smiled and held up his hand. "'Scout's honor,' as I have heard people say—I will not breathe a syllable of what you tell me to anyone. And I will delete all references to the MacDonalde case in my opus."

"How about: I'll leave the name and address of the person I'm interviewing on my desk."

"If it is someplace obvious where I can find it should the need arise—I don't want to go burrowing among your papers."

"I'll leave it right on top."

"And would you be willing to telephone if you are later than, say, an hour after your estimated time of return?"

"I can do that too."

THE HOBOKEN QUESTIONNAIRE ANSWERS WERE useless. Some were left blank; others were either vague or incoherent. *Mary MacDonalde give Sean McConnell a silver ring not from Scotland but same. She had sky terrier.* The handful of documents were equally useless: copies of phone and electric bills. Nothing tied the brother and sister to Mary except the bare allegations that she was their grandmother on their mother's side. The claimants didn't say where and when they had been born—much less where their mother had been born—or where Mary or their parents had lived, what schools their mother had attended, nothing other than a regurgitation of details that had been in the papers. Was Joe sending her because it was going to be a bust and she was cheapest? Or because she needed the practice? Well, she did need the practice.

The Grey-Davison responses were the opposite: lengthy and detailed. Mary gave birth to Bruce's mother, Helen, on December 2, 1913. Helen married James Grey-Davison Jr. on June 7, 1936, in Richmond, Virginia, at such and such a church. The dates and places of Bruce Grey-Davison's birth, the schools he attended, and his parents' deaths were all specified.

Still, the answers were vague on certain things, like Mary's marriage to Mr. Hill. It had occurred *between 1910 and March 1913*. And the location of Helen's birth was *likely in the north Midwest*. Didn't Helen know where she was born? Hadn't she ever told her son? What did her birth certificate say? Would they have to comb through dozens of states' records for a listing for Helen Hill?

And the answers were evasive on other key points. Certain records and information would *be made available at the interview*. At least there was *something* to start with: Mary MacDonalde had married a Mr. Hill, and on December 2, 1913, she had given birth to a daughter named Helen.

The details about Bruce's father's side of the family weren't relevant, but Addy read them anyway, in case something useful showed up. *The Grey-Davisons came originally from Savannah, Georgia, and later were of Charleston, S. Carolina before settling in Richmond, Virginia.* She smiled, remembering Carson saying his grandmother had once boasted the family "was originally from the Cotswolds." Laughing, he'd added, "No one's 'originally' from anywhere. There's just some point when family history is forgotten or people *want* it forgotten. Besides, if you go back far enough, everyone was either a farmer or barbarian who raided farms." She realized then he didn't take the social-classes stuff seriously.

Mr. Grey-Davison's lawyer had enclosed newspaper articles with his letter, several printed in an old-fashioned font. Addy had to squint to read the date on one, *August 17, 1946*. Someone had highlighted the sentence *Mrs. James Grey-Davison Sr. supervised the preparations for the Veterans Benefit Luncheon*. Another contained a photograph of well-dressed women standing on a stage. The caption read *Sarah Grey-Davison was honored for her work in the Ladies' Symphony Guild*. Why send these—what did Helen's mother-in-law or this Sarah have to do with anything? Okay, here was an article mentioning Helen, at least. *Helen Grey-Davison was seen at the Talbot Arms having dinner with the Vanderberg sisters*. Someone had handwritten *1948*. But again: Who cared? It would've been nice if the clipping had included a picture of Helen—if she bore a striking resemblance to Mary, it would say something.

The notebook also contained a summary of Grey-Davison Imports, Inc., a *privately held corporation* that dealt in *antique furniture, books, letters, and art.* Attached to the summary were additional documents from the Atlanta attorney. Addy paged through them but, again, couldn't see any relevance. Why had he produced a Sotheby's catalogue containing a small ad for Grey-Davison Imports?

By the time Addy'd made it through the entire notebook, all she could say for sure—assuming the documents were authentic—was that Helen Hill Grey-Davison was Bruce's mother and James Grey-Davison Jr. was his father, and the two had married in 1936 in Virginia. But where was the marriage license for Mary and Mr. Hill and Helen's birth certificate?

Wait a sec—Addy grabbed the MacDonalde notebook and quickly flipped to the last letters. She checked the photocopies of the envelopes. If Mary had married Mr. Hill sometime between 1910 and *March* 1913, why did her letters to Violet in September and October of 1913 put *MacDonalde* in the return address? Was this something Addy could use to trip up Bruce Grey-Davison? Why hadn't Joe or Brittany noticed that? A sense of self-confidence pulsed through her. Maybe, finally, she was beginning to think like a lawyer.

CHAPTER 39

AN HOUR HAD ELAPSED SINCE Adelaide left for Hoboken. How much more sensible it would have been for these interviews to have been conducted at Engel Klein's offices instead of sending young people hither and yon. But the directive in Violet's will that *claimants shall not be compelled to travel* was to be enforced without exception, despite the claimants asking for a windfall of twenty-five million dollars!

The bedroom was in its usual tidy state. Aside from Richard's collection of atlases, the only books here were Adelaide's law tomes and the short stack on the dresser: the Ogden Nash and Wizard of Oz volumes we were giving Robert for his birthday. A yellow pad in the center of the desk contained names and an address in Hoboken.

Two letters sat in the side drawer, the first dated almost a month ago.

With 3 full weeks under my belt I can say with confidence that life as a lowly associate is a mixed bag. The paralegals and messengers (and others doing the unglamorous work) treat you like royalty. So do the younger secretaries. But some of the older act like you're an obnoxious upstart, even before they get to find out you're an obnoxious upstart. Most of my day is spent in the library. I shouldn't complain. That's what you sign on for when you pick a larger firm, not the excitement of tracking down lost heirs.

The weather's been nice. Golden Gate Park has palm trees, so I'm not surprised your Palo Alto brother has one.

The letter described this view and that, a promontory here and a promontory there, minutiae that only one's mother would find absorbing. Carson's apartment apparently was *walking distance* from the beach—which to my mind could mean a block or a mile—so when specificity was actually warranted, he avoided it.

Your environmental class sounds interesting. I considered taking it, but dealing with any kind of admin law makes my eyes glaze over. Let me know if

Engel gives you e-mail. Our network is going to connect to clients' networks and some other firms and maybe some larger networks.

He signed the dull and verbose epistle simply *C.*
The second letter was dated a mere five days ago.

You're obviously trying to tackle rough memories, which is damn brave. Rehashing painful stuff can be just as painful as the original events, but with any luck you'll get some kind of catharsis.

What had Adelaide discussed in her letter—the trip to Maine? Carson's glib use of the word 'catharsis'—from the Greek *katharos*, meaning 'pure'—annoyed me; the term was bandied about for every little venting of emotion. I suppose my quarrel was more properly with Tony's profession; psychologists were the first to vulgarize the term's usage. While aptly descriptive of the emotional change occurring in a reader or audience member experiencing a work of art, the appropriation of 'catharsis' to describe general psychological changes was pure balderdash.

I'm drowning in work but that's a plus because otherwise missing you takes over. My feelings haven't changed. And you're always welcome here, just for a visit or longer—my treat! I think you'd like SF. It has NY's anonymity but is way more manageable. You'd get a kick out of the ocean, bay, hills, weird trees, cliffs. And we're a hop, skip and jump from Yosemite and the Redwoods.

His cajoling was insufferable. I returned the letters to the drawer. Of course, I possessed a natural curiosity as to whether her letters mentioned me, but that curiosity remained unslaked. At least nothing in his suggested that she was unhappy he had moved away.

DESPITE VALIANT EFFORTS TO RESUME work, my concentration flagged, and determined nonetheless to be productive, I placed a telephone call to Olivia on the off chance she would be home. Luck was with me, and although she had only a few minutes to talk, expressed interest in hearing my latest hypothesis.

"I have been focusing on Hardy's heroes and heroines. Naturally every generalization has its exceptions, but I think one can aver that, whatever their flaws, Hardy's heroes and heroines—the ones who are brought to sad endings—suffer primarily because of sad *circumstances*: poverty, social taboos, lack of education, or lack of awareness of a broader range of choices than their provincial upbringing allowed. Now, I know my viewpoint conflicts with your tragic-flaw theory—"

"Didn't we debate this years ago? You said Eustacia wasn't flawed, and I disagreed. I waffle on Tess, but what about Henchard—you can't deny his tragic flaw precipitated his misery."

"*The Mayor of Casterbridge*, I confess, is the sole major novel of Hardy's that I have not focused on either in my publications or in my courses. I read it during the war, at a time of grave preoccupations. I do intend to reread it—indeed, it is at the very top of the pile. But, as I recollect, the work was about aging and loss."

"Yes, but also Henchard's angry, impulsive temperament."

ADELAIDE RETURNED EARLY; A PARALEGAL from Engel had telephoned her at the claimants' house to say that records just arriving from Drecker disproved the siblings' connection to Mary. I commiserated over the expedition having been made in vain.

"That's okay—it was good practice, and I have more time to prepare for my next one, up in Mamaroneck. Joe wants me to ask whether the guy has a family Bible. He says people used to record births, marriages, and deaths in them, so it could provide evidence."

I lifted myself from the chair and went to a shelf by the window. "That is absolutely correct. Here is my parents'—my *grand*parents'—Bible." I brought the black-cloth-covered volume back and carefully lowered myself onto the sofa beside her. "See, it shows everything from their wedding date forward. It must have been a gift to the newlyweds."

Together we perused the entries, beginning with my paternal grandparents' marriage in 1880. "Yes, here is my father's birth and baptism and my aunts'. And their marriages. Those are my father's siblings who died in infancy. And there, my own siblings who died in infancy. Alas, such tragedies were all too common. And my birth, November 1914, and baptism."

"Someone else wrote this."

"Yes, my grandfather's death was probably written by my grandmother—her handwriting had that unusual slant. And this entry, *her* death, is clearly in my father's hand. The Bible passed to him. This, too, is his handwriting, recording my marriage and then your mother's birth and Richard's and Marcia's. Your generation, so little exposed to materials written by hand, does not appreciate the idiosyncratic aspects of script."

Adelaide leaned closer for a better view of the entries. "How come you didn't name Richard 'Francis III'?"

"We probably did not want to saddle the boy with such a long moniker. Besides, the tradition of naming the eldest son after his father was beginning to wane."

"It doesn't have Mom's getting married or anything after."

Now I was the one to lean over. "You are right; the last entry is Marcia's birth. The next event would have been my mother's death, in 1945, a few weeks shy of VE Day. They suspected ptomaine poisoning, which nowadays is easily treatable with antibiotics. My father may have been too grief-stricken to record her passing. And he died within a year, presumably from a heart attack—he was discovered in bed by the hired man. There was only one then, most of our land being rented out. I would conjecture that a broken heart was closer to the mark. That is one of the hazards of rural isolation—the loneliness that can attend loss of a loved one. Not that those of us in urban environments don't suffer from loneliness, too, in widowerhood. Or widowhood. But we have neighbors and others to populate our day."

"Why didn't he move?"

"To where?"

"To be closer to you and his grandchildren."

I flexed and relaxed my lower leg to rid it of pins and needles. "Myriad reasons come to mind. For one, it wasn't clear how long we would remain in New York; I did not at that time have tenure, and there was no guarantee I would attain it. So the possibility that my family would have to relocate was a distinct possibility."

Details long buried in oblivion now came back quite startlingly.

Being summoned from a faculty meeting to receive a message from Marjorie and telephoning her to learn of the hospital call. Hastily arranging for someone to teach my classes. The train to Cincinnati and then the bus. A simple service: a few neighbors, the hired man—a young fellow with a cowlick. Meetings with a lawyer, the real estate agent, the bank.

"I'm going to reheat leftovers for dinner, okay?"

"Fine, fine."

And the long hours at the farm deciding which possessions to ship back to New York and which to have the hired man keep or dispose of. The Bible must have been among the handful of books I had selected to ship—there couldn't have been more than a dozen volumes in all. Not the Dickens abridgments, which had belonged to my mother, although it had pleased me, during visits, to see the stack by her bedside. She had liked *Little Dorrit* and *Nicholas Nickleby*, neither one a favorite of mine, yet I was nothing but encouraging. Nor my father's collection of farming manuals and catalogues and the volume on fly-fishing.

How long had I stood by the cast-iron stove surveying the main room, trying to pinpoint the changes since my mother's death? The walls and mantel looked different. Had the room been painted? I wondered. Only later did it become clear, much too clear.

"I am sorry, my dear; I did not catch what you said."

"Dinner's ready." She gestured at the Bible. "It's kind of nice to have all major family events written down in one book."

"Your grandmother had her own way of recording." I pointed to the array of photographs and birth announcements on the shelves by the piano.

When we were both seated in the kitchen, I said, "I am one of those people who puts less stock in—shall I make a pun?—less stock in what stock I hail from. Henry James would say that this trait makes me more American than European; we are less in the thrall of the past. But many Americans are keen to know their genealogy, to learn which relatives migrated from where and when. Perhaps my indifference to my 'roots,' if you will, arises from the fact that all four of my grandparents were born here—and possibly both sets of great-grandparents. In any event, I have never felt a curiosity about their

European origins. On the other hand, I feel a strong kinship with persons with whom I share *no* blood relationship: Thomas Hardy, Henry James, George Eliot, to name a few."

Adelaide eating in silence, I returned the subject to her case, asking if the claims were starting to 'dry up,' so to speak.

"*More* claims are coming in, now that it's public she moved to eastern Washington. The papers there are carrying the story."

"Yet her last letter stated that she was *leaving* Washington."

"Yes, and that she was thinking of going back to Clopes, but there's no proof she ever did. And the reason she gave was that it was 'familiar.' Seems more like the path of least resistance than a goal."

"For a woman uprooted at an early age, familiarity could count for quite a bit."

"I'm not blaming her, just saying she might've changed her mind."

"True, true." I wanted to remind Adelaide of the Small Agency report, which suggested that Mary and her son reappeared near Clopes, but I was not certain Adelaide had ever mentioned the report in my presence. And the Anne MacDonalde of the birth certificate was no more than a mirage.

"Will you be assigned to interview any of the Washington State claimants?" I inquired. "Your mother would be delighted."

She shrugged. "I'm guessing it'll depend on how I do on the Mamaroneck."

"Why is this claimant only now coming forward? Didn't you say notices were placed in the Westchester—"

"He's been in Europe on business. The Continent, not the UK. He buys and sells fine antiques."

A chuckle escaped me. "The fine-antiques dealers I have met in my lifetime—through your grandmother, they all were—what a fuddy-duddy set! One even wore a pince-nez, which places him before *my* time. Come to think of it: I even recall a gentleman with a lorgnette. The fellow who sold us the so-called vanity, however, was thoroughly modern, thoroughly misinformed. Marjorie was no expert—she would have been the first to admit—but she could tell an Edwardian from a Victorian from a Georgian. Leave me this antiques dealer's address just the same, although the odds of his being a ne'er-do-well are slight."

CHAPTER 40

THE HOUSES ON THE BLOCK weren't huge, but they all looked well maintained; some windows were so crystal clear that Addy could see the furnishings inside. The taxi inched along the clean-swept street, past one manicured lawn after another. Mr. Grey-Davison's yard had a marble birdbath, and all his pruned shrubs were evenly spaced.

The bell made a pleasant three-note chime. The man opening the door was handsome, maybe athletic, his face and neck tanned. He wore one of those white V-neck sweaters with the red-and-blue-striped border that you saw on tennis players.

"Ms. Cohn, I presume?" He held out his hand energetically. "Bruce Grey-Davison, but please, call me Bruce. Come on in."

He stepped aside to make ample room for her and her briefcase. He was wearing the same kind of rubber-soled shoes Carson wore when they looked at the schooner near City Island. The way Mr. Grey-Davison helped her off with her coat also reminded her of Carson, although Mr. Grey-Davison's movements seemed more natural.

"My directions didn't send you too far afield, I hope?"

"I took a taxi, and he seemed to know the neighborhood."

"I hope you mean from the Mamaroneck train station and not from New York City—the taxi ride. Or I would be well within my rights to complain at your squandering my estate, which must pay your expenses." Mr. Grey-Davison's smile left no doubt he was teasing.

The friendliness was nice—the claimants' guardedness at previous interviews had been exhausting. Her role was to expose lies, and the Nagy guy and Hoboken people had planned to deceive her, so it made sense they had to play cat-and-mouse games, but the idea that an interview could be businesslike but genial—a straightforward question-and-answer conversation with neither side braced for antagonism—was a welcome change. What buoyed her even more was the implication that Mr. Grey-Davison had nothing to hide. Wouldn't it be great if she was interviewing Mary's actual grandson!

While he hung her coat in the closet, Addy scanned the huge living room, which was more like a suite of rooms. There were several sofas and love seats upholstered in fancy fabrics you'd be afraid to sit on, plus leather chairs and straight-backed chairs, rockers and hassocks, and an amazing assortment of end tables, coffee tables, lamps, and small statues. Nothing looked modern, though—the only glass she could see was on the doors to the bookcases. A small bronze statue of a boy holding a satchel was actually an umbrella holder. She counted three Tiffany lamps and two old brass standing lamps, the kind with the fringed shade. The sheer size of the space took away any sense of overcrowding or clutter, and despite the fragility of some of the furniture and vases and the paintings of flowers, the room somehow still felt masculine.

"I hope I have selected a comfortable spot." Mr. Grey-Davison motioned toward two dark-red leather armchairs and a long, low, polished wooden table with several folders.

"I have a tape recorder," she said. "Is it okay for me to reco—"

"Absolutely. You can place your apparatus there. It won't be a deposition under oath, will it? I don't object to being deposed—it's just that my attorney—he can be a pain in the rear sometimes—he insists on being present for any deposition. There's an outlet down there; if you'll hand me the cord, I'll plug it in."

From the spot he had selected, Addy had an oblique view of sliding glass doors out to a patio and back lawn. The tall fence and shrubs made it look private.

After arranging the tape recorder and her own folders and pen and notebook, she sat in one of the leather armchairs.

Mr. Grey-Davison was still standing and pointed to Francis's briefcase. "I thought your name was Adelaide Cohn. Did you swipe that from some unsuspecting commuter?"

"They're my grandfather's initials."

"I should've guessed. You don't see such fine leather much anymore, not on this side of the pond. In *his* day, it was probably considered run-of-the-mill. It's beautiful."

"Thank you."

"Most people your age wouldn't appreciate the workmanship going into an article like this. And for it to have a family history—that makes it doubly special. Before I forget, would you like something to drink? Coffee, tea, iced water? I'm guessing alcohol is frowned on at these things, and this is a little early even for me. I have a client—in France, naturally—who has what he calls a 'breakfast wine'—*un vin de petit-dejeuner*—and I admit it *does* go well with cheese and shrimp croissants. But I'm a fan of the English breakfast—all that sausage and bacon and potatoes. It primes you for the hunt. The French can be a little too civilized, if you know what I mean?" His disarming smile made her turn away. She smoothed her skirt.

Mr. Grey-Davison sat in the other dark-red leather chair. "I have some papers here for you to look at—three letters, a photo, and a fair amount of background materials my mother and grandmother collected. And papers I have collected over the years. They're copies, so I don't mind your taking a look at them, but I'm uneasy about letting you take them *with* you—the letters, I mean. I know how law firms operate, running the Xerox machine like it's making popcorn. Who knows how many people would get their hands on them. Do you know offhand how many copies you'd make? And would they be made at your office or taken to some Kinko's?"

"We'd make them at our offices, just for people on the case. And we'd send a copy to the lawyers in Scotland. I don't know if they'd make more. We can ask them not to make any more than necessary." She could hear Joe: 'Those penny-pinchers are the last to use an extra sheet of paper.'

He asked if she wanted to look at the papers first or when they became relevant to her questions, and she said she would wait. She was eager to delve into the routine recitals and questions and restore some of the formality moments ago she'd been glad was missing.

"You probably find my secrecy a bit over the top, but you'll hear why." Mr. Grey-Davison rested his left ankle on his right knee. His socks matched the gray of his pants, and his calves and thighs looked muscular. He pointed to the recorder.

"I'm ready. Shoot."

She did the introduction and stressed the need to use proper names instead of terms like *mother* and *father* and *grandmother*. Mr. Grey-Davison answered the routine background questions with ease. He was born in 1955 in Richmond, Virginia, although his family traced itself back to Savannah, Georgia. After attending prep school in Richmond and graduating from Emory, he had "dabbled in finance" before going into his second cousin's fine-antiques business. The cousin, Phillippe Clemenceau, had retired in 1988 and sold Mr. Grey-Davison his share of the company. Mr. Clemenceau died in 1993 in Phoenix. He was related to Mr. Grey-Davison on his paternal grandmother's side.

"Are you married?"

Mr. Grey-Davison laughed. "Not currently. I have two ex-wives, who, I'm happy to say, have remarried, sparing me more alimony payments. I have no intention of making another mistake, though they say 'Third time's the charm.' My current girlfriend knows my state of mind, so you don't have to worry I'm stringing her along."

"Do you have any children?"

"Whatever bug impels men to give up their freedom and procreate hasn't infected me, at least not yet. I could be immune. Being the only son of an only son, the Grey-Davison line stops unless I take action. Will I relent? Who knows. As of now, there are no little Grey-Davisons populating the earth." Again, the smile. Mr. Grey-Davison repeated his questionnaire answers: Mary Agnes MacDonalde Hill gave birth to his mother, Helen, in December of 1913; Mary died in the early '40s, but he didn't know where; and Helen died in 1976 in Richmond.

"Quite a shock. I was barely twenty-one, still in college. She was only sixty-two. To you, that probably seems old. To me—well, in any case, she was my mother. And we had a special bond—widowed mother and only son. After years and years of wanting children, I believe my parents had given up all hope, and then, at forty-one, boom: she becomes pregnant. You're not surprised to hear I was spoiled?"

Addy shook her head. "What was your mother's full name?"

"Helen Hill Grey-Davison."

"What was your father's full name?"

"James Avery Grey-Davison Jr."

"When did your father die?"

"Back in '58. I was only three. From rheumatic fever—he'd had scarlet fever as a child. My memories of him are dim. My mother died from a heart attack. The heart seems to be the weak organ in our family. My ex-wives think it's defective."

"Was there an obituary for your mother, for Helen Hill Grey-Davison?"

"I *assume* there was a notice in the papers. I thought I sent you people copies of that stuff. I was too overwhelmed to compose an obituary myself—imagine getting a call at your fraternity. I'd hardly known my father, and now I was an orphan. I wasn't what you'd call a serious student, not then, but I grew up fast." Mr. Grey-Davison clasped a knee with both hands and looked at the ceiling. "My great-aunt Sarah might've composed an obituary. Do you think the Richmond papers archive that sort of thing?"

"Who is your great-aunt Sarah?"

"Sarah Mabel Grey-Davison, my grandfather's—James Grey-Davison Sr.'s—sister."

"You say your father, James Grey-Davison Jr., he died when you were three. Where was he living at the time?"

"Richmond. I could've sworn I sent you a copy of his death notice."

"You may have."

"I did send your firm a ream of documents—you can be excused for not remembering everything. The Grey-Davisons have a long and distinguished history, first in Savannah, then in Charleston. A state senator, two judges, a cavalry officer in the Confederacy—I know, I know: for some, 'the Confederacy' and 'distinguished' are contradictory. Anyway, James Sr. married a French woman named Sylvie, Sylvie Clemenceau—a *very* distant relative of the prime minister. They had a son—my father, James Jr. My father, James Jr., met my mother, met Helen, while he was on vacation—she was waiting tables at a resort. They fell in love, decided to get married. My grandfather, James Sr., might've objected to the class difference, but he had no moral leg to stand on."

While Mr. Grey-Davison was speaking, Addy scribbled follow-up questions. Was Helen living with her mother when she was waitressing at the resort? If not, where was Mary living? Where was Helen's father?

"And you said you're an only child?"

"Yes."

"Was it your mother Helen's first marriage?"

"I *presume* it was—no one ever said anything to the contrary. She was around twenty when she met my father. If there was a previous marriage, I'd have to believe it had no 'issue'—isn't that the legal term?"

"So you're not aware of any half brothers or sisters?"

Amused by the question, Mr. Grey-Davison shook his head. "I suppose this is as good a time as any to air the family dirty laundry. You'll understand *one* of the reasons I've been such a pest about the nondisclosure agreement. So here it is." He took a deep breath and exhaled. "My grandfather James Sr. was a philanderer, back when they lived in Savannah. He contracted syphilis and gave it to Sylvie, my unsuspecting grandmother. The only silver lining is the infection happened *after* my father—James Jr.—was born, so he wasn't directly affected. Not physically. He was *emotionally* affected, as you might imagine. His father's sins visited on his mother? It's like a Greek tragedy. To make matters worse, my grandmother—Sylvie—was the first to develop the mental problems of untreated syphilis. This was before antibiotics."

Mr. Gray-Davison leaned forward, resting his elbows on his muscular thighs and clasping his hands together, his gaze going to the left and right but not to Addy. "So my father hardly had the happiest of childhoods, despite considerable wealth and the long, proud Grey-Davison name. His mother was mentally unstable, and his father either showed signs of it too, or was cantankerous from guilt and shame. This was the scandal that made the family leave Savannah when my father—James Jr.—was a child. Tail between the legs. Fortunately, the gossip did not follow them to Charleston—as far as we know."

"How old was your father—James Jr.—when they moved to Charleston?"

"I'm not sure—nine, ten, eleven? Maybe younger, maybe older. This wasn't a topic my mother dwelled on when passing down the family lore. But you're not here to hear about my father's family."

"Where were they married, Helen and James Jr.—what city?"

"I'm not sure exactly. Near Norfolk, Virginia, it's safe to say, because a Norfolk newspaper carried a small item on it. My father—sorry: James Jr.—was working or living near there at the time—I was actually under the impression he'd been living in North Carolina, but possibly near the Virginia border—his old hunting hat had a Kitty Hawk decal. I can't imagine what people hunted in Kitty Hawk—ducks, I suppose. Hawks? He did used to tell my mother about hunting escapades in the Great Dismal Swamp, which spans the border, is in

Virginia *and* North Carolina. A colorful name, wouldn't you say? Not exactly a tourist-industry slogan. Anyway, the stories my mother told are jumbled in my mind. Here's the photo from the wedding—the only one I have of Grandmother Mary."

He opened a folder and handed Addy a copy of a newspaper photo.

"This is a picture of Mary MacDonalde?" She turned off the tape recorder to examine it. What a find!

A young couple stood outside what appeared to be a small church. The bride's veil was pulled back so her full face was in the sun, and her hair fell in a wave that reminded Addy of Bette Davis in some old movie. The groom bore an obvious resemblance to Mr. Grey-Davison. An older couple stood at the groom's side, the woman's face partly obscured by a veil on the front of her hat. On the bride's side a slightly plump middle-aged woman held herself erect. She, too, wore a hat with a veil, the veil descending to the bridge of her nose.

The caption below read,

On Sunday, Helen Hill was wedded to James Avery Grey-Davison Jr. The bride's mother, Mary Hill, and the groom's parents, Sylvie and James Avery Grey-Davison Sr., were among those in attendance.

"But this says—the caption under the photo—it says Mary *Hill,* not Mary MacDonalde?"

"They didn't include her maiden name. When we get to these"— Mr. Grey-Davison rapped his knuckles on another folder—"you'll see that Mary Hill and Mary MacDonalde were one and the same. Mary Hill, née MacDonalde."

Addy examined the photo again. Was it Carson or Francis who'd hypothesized that Mary had married and changed her name? The veil didn't let you see much more than that her face was roundish. Why hadn't she told Violet she'd married and given birth to a daughter? Addy tried to imagine this face as the older version of the one in the photo of Mary as a teenager. Could an expert compare the photos and declare them the same person? Rule it out?

Turning the recorder back on, Addy had Mr. Grey-Davison identify the newspaper, describe the photo, and identify the people pictured.

"Was Helen's father at the wedding?"

"No, he died decades earlier, in 1915."

"He was married to Mary MacDonalde?"

"Yes."

"And when was that—when did they get married?"

"I'm not sure—1911, 1912—by early spring of 1913 at the latest."

He stuck with the story that didn't jibe. If Mary had become Mrs. Hill before the summer of 1913, why did her letters to Violet after that, like the final October letter, use MacDonalde in the return address?

"Did Mary divorce Mr. Hill?" Addy asked, to rule out that possibility.

Mr. Grey-Davison's reply came easily, complacently. "No."

"Did she ever remarry after Mr. Hill died?"

"No, she never remarried."

"Or have additional children?"

"Like I said, I'm sure my mother—excuse me: Helen—would have told me if she'd had half brothers or sisters, so, no, I don't think Mary had more children, even with a different husband."

It was a physical sensation, the burst of self-confidence Addy felt, catching Mr. Grey-Davison in an admission that didn't fit the facts, even though she didn't dislike him. "So by summer of 1913 at the latest," she said, "when Mary MacDonalde married Mr. Hill, her name became Mary Hill?"

"Yes and no."

"What do you mean 'yes and no'?"

"I mean that Grandmother Mary continued to use MacDonalde for a number of years. I don't know how many or exactly when she started using Hill for herself and Helen—although I do know it was after her husband died, which was in 1915." Mr. Grey-Davison again cradled his knee with both hands. A small lock of hair fell across his forehead.

"Why didn't she start using Hill when she got married? Let me back up. What was Mr. Hill's—your grandfather's—full name?"

"This is where it gets interesting. And where the nondisclosure agreement becomes even more important. You see, Adel—Ms. Cohn—my life has had a certain *simplicity*, despite the two ex-wives. Which will go by the wayside if the reasons behind my grandmother's use of her maiden name comes out. She did it because of who my grandfather was. And there's no need for that, is there? I can't believe that my great-aunt Violet would've wanted her heir to suffer unwanted publicity. From the little I've read in the papers, she was a very private person."

He looked at Addy so unflinchingly her cheeks warmed. "The nondisclosure agreement," she stammered, "we've signed it—the firms have signed it."

"Yes, I'm just trying to emphasize its importance. You want to know who Mary MacDonalde's husband—Helen's father—was. His full *legal* name was Joel Emmanuel Hagglund. He also used the name Joseph Hillstrom. You probably know him as Joe Hill."

"How is Hagglund spelled?"

"You don't recognize it?" Mr. Grey-Davison blurted out. "My *God*, you make me feel old!"

Rising, he paced back and forth. "Here I reveal what I expect will shock you—the name of a man of singular fame and notoriety, *unfair* notoriety—and you deliver the more shocking news that he's faded into obscurity!"

Addy felt stupid—she *had* heard the name before, she was pretty sure, but couldn't remember when.

By the time Mr. Grey-Davison had stopped pacing, his astonishment seemed to have become bemusement. "My poor grandfather, martyred for a great cause and in less than a century consigned to oblivion. Maybe it's for the best. After all, labor unions are the rule nowadays, not the exception. And they've become powerful institutions—as powerful as management in some industries. You really don't know who Joe Hill was?" Addy shook her head.

He sat again. "I'm afraid I'm going to have to give you a history lesson. I'll make it as short as possible, but I can't brush this under the rug. You do know about the Haymarket Riot and the Pullman Strike—the violent beginnings of the labor movement? You have a general idea. Organized labor was not greeted with open arms at the end of the nineteenth century and beginning of the twentieth. The major industrialists at the time felt their existence threatened if the workers banded together to demand decent wages and working conditions. Strikes were outlawed, demonstrations broken up.

"Joe Hill, my grandfather, became part of the labor movement. He'd been born in Sweden in 1879. His parents were poor, and he'd had to work in a factory as a mere child. It might have been how he contracted TB. Life was tough. Still, his parents taught him to play the violin and guitar and other instruments—it was a very musical family.

"He emigrated to the States with one of his brothers—that was in 1902. Traveled around looking for work—Chicago, California, you name it. No surprise he joined the labor movement and the Wobblies. You've heard of the Wobblies? Possibly? The nickname of the International Workers of the World. I don't know if they're still around. They were the more radical of the organizations and believed in international communism—no national boundaries, just one big workers' paradise. OBU, they used to say—One Big Union. People called them anarchists—I'm not sure that's fair.

"Obviously I'm not a gung-ho labor advocate—the Grey-Davison genes won out in my psychological makeup. But if you understood the wages and conditions back then, before laws limited the workday to eight hours and required basic safety precautions on the factory floor, it's hard to think the labor movement was a bad thing. Did you learn about company towns in school?" Addy shook her head, embarrassed.

"What *did* they teach? The coal company didn't just own the coal mine—it owned the stores where the workers had to buy their groceries, it owned the housing where they had to pay rent, it owned *everything*. You ended up forking over your entire paycheck to the boss, who gouged you and forced your family to survive at subsistence level.

"Please tell me you've heard of the Pinkertons? Just the detective agency, probably. The government and hugely wealthy families like the Carnegies and Rockefellers and Morgans, they hired the Pinkertons for 'protection.' Usually, it was the organizers and strikers who needed protection. I'm talking about industries like steel, coal, mining, the railroads, docks. Notorious thugs, the Pinkertons, happy to beat up men, women—the old, the poor, the infirm. Sure, the strikers were violent too, but we're talking ragtag groups up against private armies. And not always private! The police and National Guard took their orders from government officials in the pockets of the big corporations."

Mr. Grey-Davison pulled a linen handkerchief from his pants pocket and wiped his brow. Addy could see it was monogrammed.

"As an aside, does the name Elizabeth Gurley Flynn mean anything to you? A high school girl, younger than you, a Joan of Arc—she ran around all over the country giving speeches to organize workers. Got herself arrested—chained herself to a lamppost during the Spokane free-speech rallies." He pronounced Spokane correctly. "She wanted to organize servants, domestic cooks, cleaners. One of Grandfather Joe's songs, 'Rebel Girl,' was to her."

Mr. Grey-Davison laughed. "Listen to me! I'm beginning to sound like him. Anyway, he wrote lots of protest songs. The early ones, he just added new lyrics to popular songs, but later he wrote his own melodies—his musical training as a child paid off. Here, read yourself to sleep." Opening another folder, Mr. Grey-Davison lifted out a bundle of clipped pages and set them on the table. "And take a look at these articles. He was a hot topic, especially after being convicted of murder on trumped-up charges and executed."

Addy turned off the recorder and thumbed through the packet. How could Violet's investigators have missed this connection? Clippings from the *New York Times*, the *International Herald Tribune*, *Salt Lake Tribune*, *Manchester Guardian*, *Boston Herald*, *San Francisco Chronicle*, *Minneapolis Tribune*. "HILL GUILTY OF PHARMACIST MURDERS."

She turned on the recorder and asked if Joe Hill's marriage to Mary MacDonalde was mentioned in the articles he had handed her.

"No, it's in these letters. But you won't understand the letters unless you understand who Joe Hill was and what happened to him. I'll try not to take all day. Let me get you a glass of water. I could use one."

Addy checked her watch. She'd have to call Francis from the station—the interview would go late.

Returning with two tall glasses of ice water, Mr. Grey-Davison said genially, "I shouldn't tease you about the gaps in your history education—I have enormous ones in mine. And learning when I did that Joe Hill was my grandfather, a fact my mother didn't entrust to me until high school—I believe the family had an agreement to keep it under wraps, the Grey-Davisons being so publicity-shy—naturally I read up all I could on him. Each generation has its blind spots. Mine was ignorant of the lynchings and other tragedies committed against Black people practically under our noses. We assumed whatever stories we heard were isolated events perpetrated by a few bad apples. Did you see the movie *Mississippi Burning*? My second wife couldn't believe all that corruption was news to me. The police we knew in Charleston weren't like that. But I have to say our schools did little to expose us to the wider culture. So with that admission of guilt, you'll have to allow me a little teasing about my grandfather's descent into oblivion."

"I'm going to turn this on again?"

"The recorder? Shoot."

"You were saying that Mary MacDonalde married Joe Hill, a labor organizer—"

"Not just *a* labor organizer—one of the most famous. Although he liked to describe himself as just another 'wharf rat.' Spent most of his time trying to organize in towns along the West Coast—down in the San Pedro part of LA and clear up to Vancouver, in Canada. Dock workers—"

"When did Mary MacDonalde meet Joe Hill?"

"Sometime between 1910 and early 1913, I suspect."

"Do you know where they met?"

"No. Portland, Seattle, some town near there? Down in California? It's fun to speculate on the circumstances. A workers' rally? A tavern or maybe at church? A chance encounter? What I *do* know is their courtship was kept under wraps. But think about it: two immigrants from northern Europe, far from family—not hard to imagine a friendship starting."

"When did they get married?"

"By March of 1913, at the latest, as I said, but I don't know exactly when—it could have been 1911, 1912. Before Mary became pregnant with my mother, I assume, given the customs of the time."

"Do you know who married them—a minister or priest or justice of the peace?"

"No idea."

"Do you know *where* they were married—what city and state?"

"All my mother—all Helen ever said about it—maybe all Mary ever told *her*—was that they had a secret ceremony in someone's house. California, Oregon, Washington—maybe up in Canada? The protests took him lots of places. I doubt she was an organizer, given what Great-Aunt Sarah said—more likely they met on the sly. When I used to think about them getting married—which, to be honest, wasn't often—I imagined a minister looking like Karl Malden. Maybe I'm remembering *On the Waterfront*. Did you ever see that, with Marlon Brando and that blond—"

"So you don't have a copy of their marriage license?"

"No."

"Are you sure they weren't married in a church?"

"I'm not sure of anything! All I know is what my mother was told: it was a private ceremony in someone's house. Keep in mind he was a marked man—being his wife wasn't something to advertise. That wasn't the only reason they would've wanted to keep the courtship and marriage secret: Mary's employers would have fired her. But retaliation had to be the bigger fear. Politicians, government officials, law enforcement, industrialists were out to get him any way they could. If arresting his wife was an option, they would've jumped at it. They already had been beating strikers, even committed murder. You think I'm exaggerating? Read about it." He gestured at the folder of clippings. "My grandfather's protest songs could gin up a crowd. And he was a savvy tactician. Like I said, he knew he was a marked man."

Abruptly Mr. Grey-Davison laughed. "I want to say he was down to earth, not pie in the sky. You don't get the joke—'Pie in the Sky' was one of his most famous songs." In a nice clear voice, he sang,

Long-haired preachers come out every night,
Try to tell you what's wrong and what's right;
But when asked 'bout something to eat
They will answer with voices so sweet:

You will eat, by and by,
In that glorious land above the sky;
Work and pray, live on hay,
You'll get pie in the sky when you die.

Mr. Grey-Davison handed Addy the thickest folder on the table. "Here are his songs. You're free to take them."

She turned off the recorder and carefully paged through the photocopies. Several of the originals might have been on scrap paper or napkins. She turned the recorder back on.

"Do any of these songs you handed me say anything about Mary MacDonalde?"

"'Ballad to my Secret Wife,' something like that? No, I don't think there are any lyrics that would give away her identity, not after the pains they went to keep the marriage secret. If the secrecy strikes you as far-fetched, go look up the number of labor organizers thrown in jail on trumped-up charges. Debs went to prison, Big Bill Haywood had to flee the country. And look at the transcript of my grandfather's trial. Convicted in Utah of shooting and killing a druggist after the eyewitnesses described someone completely different."

Mr. Grey-Davison frowned. "My grandfather was in a fight at the time over some woman, but he refused to divulge her name, though the alibi would have saved his life. People speculated he didn't want to get her in trouble. It's also possible he didn't want Mary to know he was seeing someone on the sly. On the other hand, maybe it *was* a lie— about seeing a woman. He might've thought that rumors of a lady friend would throw people off the scent, off any suspicion he'd gotten married. Anyway, the miscarriage of justice was blatant. Look it up." Again he gestured at the folder of clippings. "*Try* reading the details of the prosecution and appeals without thinking he was railroaded."

Mr. Grey-Davison sat back in his chair, cupping his hands so the fingertips touched, and looked directly at Addy. "If there *was* a mystery woman, she wasn't my grandmother—Mary wasn't in Utah, not then. She'd gone east, like he wanted. I'm skeptical about the fight-over-a-woman story—like I said, I prefer to think he encouraged that kind of speculation to throw people off. Maybe that's what I *want* to think— who chooses to imagine his grandfather an adulterer? I already have one forbear who went that route. So here I follow the straight and narrow, and where does it get me? Eleven years of paying alimony."

CHAPTER 41

THEY TOOK A SHORT BREAK, and when they resumed the interview, Addy began with, "You said Mary MacDonalde and Joe Hill got married by March of 1913 at the latest?"

"Yes."

"And you know this because your mother, Helen, told you?"

"She told me they were married, and I always assumed it was before Mary got pregnant. Once she began to show, that was when she had to leave—she couldn't tell her employers who the father was."

"Did Mary have a child before she met Joe Hill?"

"According to the newspapers. That part of the story never got passed down to me. Maybe my mother—Helen—knew but didn't see the point in mentioning it. I'm assuming the child died—either before Helen was born or when she was a baby."

Mr. Grey-Davison looked toward the glass door to the patio. "And I have to accept this possibility: that he'd gotten Mary pregnant and just wanted to do the honorable thing. He had strict morals—a strict Swedish upbringing. So maybe the actual wedding was in the summer of 1913. All I really know is Mary didn't see him again, after she headed east in 1913, when she was pregnant with my mother. Mary had escorts along the way—perhaps Wobblies—but it was difficult, or that's how my mother—Helen—heard it described. Partly by train and partly by car, different people—workers' movement people—met Mary and took her home, fed her, and put her up till she was ready for the next leg. Either in one of the Dakotas, Minnesota, or maybe Wisconsin, the weather forced her to stop at an Indian reservation."

"Do you know which one?"

"All I remember being told was they were hit by a blizzard, and Mary was stuck there for some time, and that's when my mother, Helen, was born. December 2, 1913." Mr. Grey-Davison looked at Addy. "Does that mean, under some technicality, Helen—my mother—wasn't an American citizen?"

Addy jotted a note to herself to find out whether an almanac could pin down which reservations were hit by a blizzard that winter.

"That must've been heart-wrenching," Mr. Grey-Davison went on, "being marooned among strangers in a harsh climate. However bleak Scotland is cannot compare with the icy gales of the prairie states. And as I say, among strangers with strange customs. Isn't there a book *Stranger in a Strange Land?* Seems to me I read something like that when I was younger. Sorry—that's off topic. Okay, so Mary suffers through a harsh winter, but she and her baby—Helen—eventually make it back east."

"When you say 'back east,' where exactly?"

"I wish I knew. New York was one place, so was Vermont, I think. Wherever they landed, they didn't stay put for too many years. My mother said she went to half a dozen schools by the time she was ten."

"Do you have a copy of Helen's birth certificate?"

"Birth certificate? Did the reservations issue them? I have no idea."

"How did Helen get a driver's license or social security card when she was older?"

"I don't know. But I said on your questionnaire that she had a driver's license when I was a child, so if the motor vehicle people keep old records, you should be able to get a copy."

"Where in New York did Mary and Helen live?"

"I was never told, or if I was, I don't remember."

"Do you remember *any* of the specific towns Helen lived in as a child?"

"Besides her saying she lived in New York, Vermont, and Massachusetts, I have no idea. I can't swear to it, but they may have traveled up to Montreal. Wherever my grandmother—wherever Mary MacDonalde Hill could find work."

"What kind of work did she do?"

"Early on she worked for families, in some tutor or servant capacity, because Helen remembers Mary being happy at finally landing 'a proper job,' which was something secretarial, I believe. That's when they moved into their own place. I had the impression it was a cottage, a small house. It would have been a rental property."

"How do you know it was a rental property?"

Mr. Grey-Davison looked surprised. "They never had much money—Helen remembered having to pinch pennies. Even if

Grandfather Joe had been able to send money when he was alive, he was executed in 1915."

"Can you tie *any* particular place to a date, like 'Helen lived in Vermont when she was in kindergarten'—something like that?"

His glance returned to the patio doors. "I don't think so. No, wait: I *do* remember a time and place. Whatever year Rudolph Valentino died, my mother—Helen—was attending school near New York City. She told me the school year had just begun, but none of the teachers showed up. They had gone to watch his funeral procession, maybe on Fifth Avenue. It was as big a deal as the Lindbergh parade. Don't tell me I have to explain who Valentino and Lindbergh were?"

"So Helen went to school in New York City the same year that Rudolph Valentino died?"

"It could have been in one of the suburbs. Yonkers, Mount Vernon, somewhere on Long Island, possibly Jersey. The locations didn't stick in my mind. For many of us, an interest in family history doesn't surface until we begin to look mortality in the eye. Coming up on forty does that."

"Do you have any documents at all that could show Mary MacDonalde married Joe Hill?"

"Other than my great-aunt Sarah's letters, I can't think of anything, not offhand. Excuse me for being amused—I'm trying to imagine teachers calling in sick today to go to some movie star's funeral. Seems absurd, doesn't it? But nowadays we can see the pictures on TV—in those days, all you had was a newspaper."

Addy asked when Helen learned that her father was Joe Hill and when she and Mary changed their last names, but Mr. Grey-Davison didn't know. And he didn't know what state they were living in when they changed their names.

"Where was Mary living at the time Helen and James Jr. got married?"

"I don't know."

"Do you know where Mary was living at any time *after* Helen's marriage?"

"No."

"So you don't know when or where Mary was living at the time of her death?"

"Is that a trick question: Where was she living when she died? I'm only teasing. No, I don't know those details—it was before I was even a gleam in my parents' eyes."

Addy said she wanted to take a break to look at the letters from his great-aunt Sarah and asked if any of them specifically mentioned Mary MacDonalde. He said all three did.

The first was dated July 16, 1939.

Dearest Helen,

I received yours just before the 4th, and what a lovely treat it was. How very busy you are kept with your groups and functions. I have often thought of moving near you, but Charleston has a claim on me.

I well understand your curiosity, but you cannot be surprised your parents fell in love, two souls adrift, facing Poverty and Hardship. And sharing the vision of a Better World. Yet their Destinies were fated to divide like the branches of a river, hers to the tending of a child, and his to championing the Cause. I am certain it was to protect her that he married in secret. And a heavy weight I know it must have been for him, for his own mother had been branded as illegitimate, and he would not have wanted that for you. Yet the dangers he would expose you to by declaring the marriage would have been far worse.

The remainder of the letter was about fashion and the latest hats. It was signed *Your Aunt Sarah.*

Dated February 11, 1940, the second letter contained only a postscript Addy could tie to the case.

I worry those fanatic Nazis are drawing the rest of Europe into another War. I am particularly concerned for your relations. Your mother still had not heard from them at the time of her death.

So Mary had died between 1936, when the wedding photograph was taken, and early 1940. With those dates as bookends, maybe Joe would want a wider geographic search of death-certificate records.

The third letter, dated October 23, 1947, spent the first two pages on changes in Charleston since the war had ended. The final page read,

As to your question, your dear mother only spoke of it once, during the visit not long after your wedding. No, your parents did not stop loving one another. His sole aim was shielding wife and child from the public glare and the unsavory elements of the Cause who would use you to gain sympathy. The most protective thing he could do for his family was to hide the connection. Condemn him not for that.

Nor condemn her for delaying to give you his name. It took time to ease her worry of you becoming a pawn in the Fight, and when she judged you old enough to understand, she bestowed his name on you and took it for herself. Wear it with pride. He adhered to his Cause with an Apostle's devotion.

Addy turned the recorder back on and had Mr. Grey-Davison identify the letters by date, author, and recipient. She allowed him to explain the relevant passages, and he ended by saying that to hear that praise of his grandfather from "an unrepentant aristocrat like Great-Aunt Sarah" moved him more than he liked to admit.

Was there anything else he could think of, Addy asked, that would corroborate what was in the letters—other documents or witnesses?

He smiled disarmingly. "I was hoping *you* could corroborate it— you've got so much more information at your disposal. *If* it needs further corroboration. You have my memories, and the letters corroborate what my mother, what Helen told me."

"Are there other family members who know your grandfather was Joe Hill?"

He leaned forward, his elbows on his knees. "The part about wearing it with pride—his name—why do you think my great-aunt Sarah had to write that? Because my mother—Helen—was *not* proud of her origins. She meets and falls for this young man from a distinguished family, a family that looks *down* on the working class, and you expect her to own up to having a father considered an anarchist and murderer? Who was killed by firing squad? Either she adopted the Grey-Davison trait of craving privacy—Helen, my mother did—or she had it on her own. To be pursued by reporters was worse than by robbers."

"Who were Helen's close friends?"

"I don't remember. You're wondering whom else she might have confided in about grandfather—about Joe Hill? Possibly no one. Keep the laundry, dirty or otherwise, within the family: that was the Grey-Davison policy and her own inclination."

Addy nailed down dates and locations relating to Sarah Grey-Davison, for whatever it was worth, and continued with her outline. In an effort to fly by the seat of her pants she mixed in some questions she'd already asked with new ones, just in case Mr. Grey-Davison's answers changed or he became flustered, but he continued to answer without reserve.

"Just to clarify: you have no children?"

He laughed. "Which is *another* reason I would like to keep my name out of the news. I have no doubt that if my inheritance were to become public, women whom I casually dated will swarm out of the woodwork and claim their child is mine, and I will have to endure endless rounds of paternity tests. But no, as the only son of an only son and an only daughter—I'm assuming that Mary's first child died—I don't have siblings or aunts, uncles, first cousins. My only second cousin—Phillippe Clemenceau—he was a confirmed bachelor. His relatives, the ones I met at his funeral—let me just say we never hit it off. To get back to your earlier question, unless I enter into a third marriage and produce some offspring, the old and venerated Grey-Davison name will die out. What is *your* advice? After two failed marriages, should I take on a third? With someone who could produce heirs? It would be a crying shame if all Great-Aunt Violet's efforts to keep the family fortune in the family ended because the family ended."

"So, none of your estate would go to your former wives or their families?"

"None. Those alimony agreements are sealed tighter than a submarine. I do thank my pain-in-the-rear lawyer for that."

"How did you hear about Violet MacDonalde's will?"

"By accident! I had hardly been back from the Continent a full week when I was riding the train and noticed the magazine someone had left on the seat beside me. Not the type I usually read, but the name MacDonalde in the headline caught my eye—the unorthodox spelling. Then the first names, Mary and Violet. The early history was news to me."

"When did you first learn of the spelling of MacDonalde with an *e* on the end?"

"Aha—something I *do* remember! I have a vivid memory of correcting my teacher, Mrs. Templeton. We'd been handed music books containing "Old MacDonald Had a Farm," and I pointed out they'd misspelled the name by leaving off the *e*. It was quite embarrassing to be told I was wrong, especially because I was so proud of my ability to spell before my peers could."

"How did you learn your grandmother's maiden name at such an early age?"

"Why, from the song—but I didn't know it was her maiden name. I came home from school singing it, and my mother—Helen—said that it was Grandmother Mary's last name before she married my grandfather. Wait a minute!" Mr. Grey-Davison slapped his thigh. "My mother showed me a picture of my grandmother—taken at the Statue of Liberty—I can't believe now I am remembering this. And it had her name printed or typed—I don't remember which—at the bottom. *Mary MacDonalde from Glynnis, Scotland*, it said. My mother taught me to spell both—MacDonalde and Glynnis. After all these years to have this memory pop up! I wonder if the picture still exists."

"Where would it be, if it still existed?"

"In some family album, I assume. I thought I had rummaged through them all when you sent the questionnaire. I would have noticed the picture if I'd come across it. I wonder if there's another album."

"Where would it be, this other album?"

"In Richmond. When my mother died, I had a house full of furniture and belongings to dispose of, so I rented a storage locker—an enormous locker. And I've hardly done anything to get rid of things. I'll have to find time to go down and look."

He brushed back hair from his forehead. "I don't know when. I'm leaving for Japan next week and then off to Singapore and won't be back in the States until after the New Year, and then I have to hit the deck running, for Kids Camp. You've heard of it? We're a nonprofit raising money for summer camps for sick children. Kids with diabetes, kids with special challenges—what used to be called mental retardation. We're starting one up for kids with cancer—there's a property along the Hudson we're dancing around, trying to get the owner to come down in price. When I say 'we,' I'm on the board.

Anyway, God knows when I'll find time to go to Richmond and fight through that mess."

"What did you know of Mary MacDonalde's family—her parents and sister—before you read the magazine article?"

"Not much—that my grandmother came from Scotland, like my paternal grandmother came from France. That Mary had a sister named Violet—I had a classmate named Rose, and being named after a flower for some reason tickled my childish imagination."

"Even during World War II, Helen never tried to contact Violet, that you heard?"

"She never said anything."

Addy continued to the end of her outline, and it was almost four when she recited the date and time the interview was ending. Mr. Grey-Davison shifted in his seat but not uncomfortably—more like an athlete restless from prolonged sitting.

"Tell me, what's the next step?" he asked. "Does my attorney file a formal claim in the Scottish courts? I believe he's already been in touch with the estate solicitors."

"I'm not sure. Can I take copies of the letters from Sarah to your mother?"

"Will you agree to take precautions that they are not copied willy-nilly? And kept in some sort of secure location at your offices?" He stood when she did.

"I'll say those were the conditions under which you agreed to give them to me."

"Terrific. I should ask you to state that on tape, but a handshake is good enough for me." He smiled engagingly and held out his hand. She shook it, relieved that he was businesslike. Then she began gathering her materials and putting them in the briefcase. Mr. Grey-Davison took care of unplugging the recorder and rolling up the cord.

"When the estate's finally probated," he said, "I guess I'll have to deal with all the disappointed people who say they're related. That will be *my* headache, not yours. I hope I don't have to pay them to go away. Or will the court rule that I'm the only surviving relation? It will be interesting, when I fly there for the final folderol—in Edinburgh, I presume? It will be interesting to visit my grandmother's village, her ancestral home. I may find some cousins. Is there a family plot, do you know? Where Violet and the great-grandparents are buried?"

"I don't know."

"It's ironic, isn't it: one of the most famous martyrs of the workers' revolution had a grandson who inherited a fortune." Mr. Grey-Davison's eyes twinkled.

"Do you mind if I use your phone? I'll pay for the call—it's long distance."

"Long distance? To where?"

"Manhattan."

Mr. Grey-Davison laughed. "That's pocket change. I thought you were going to say Paris or Prague—I have clients there I talk to regularly. Tomorrow I'm calling one in Istanbul."

She'd be home by seven, she told Francis. Was he okay with leftover lasagna?

ON THE TRAIN, ADDY PAGED through the copies of old newspaper articles. The first few were from November 1915, right after Joe Hill's execution by firing squad, and were either obituaries or condemnations of the Utah government for framing him, although one column implied he might have been guilty but should have been granted leniency. She couldn't translate anything from the articles in *Le Figaro*, *Corriere della Sera*, and the German paper.

How would Mary have dealt with the conviction and death sentence of the man she loved, the father of her second child? Was she ever tempted to write to her family—Violet, at least—about her emotional turmoil? If Hill himself didn't dare write to her, did their friends—those who knew of the secret marriage? Did Mary get letters she destroyed after reading?

Mr. Grey-Davison had also provided copies of IWW pamphlets and letters Joe Hill had written to various people, although none were addressed to Mary. Addy put the clippings and letters back in the briefcase and took out a few sheets from the songs file.

The first said it was to be sung to the tune of "My Old Kentucky Home."

Hill's version began:

299

We will sing one song of the meek and humble slave,
The horn-handed son of the soil,
He's toiling hard from the cradle to the grave,
But his master reaps the profits from his toil.

It was too late to drop the documents off at Engel; she would bring them by tomorrow with the recap. Although she'd thought the Nagys and Hoboken people were lying, she'd written what Joe had said for the subjective part: *The claimant's manner gave no indication of dishonesty.* With Mr. Grey-Davison, for once she'd mean it.

While re-sorting the papers in her briefcase, she noticed one with an IWW heading. The article below was titled "Joe Hill's Obituary" and said it contained the words he'd written the night before his execution. She read it carefully, hoping for mention of Mary or a wife and child, but there was none. Still, the middle stanza got to her.

My body? Oh, if I could choose
I would to ashes it reduce
And let the merry breezes blow
My dust to where some flowers grow

The train clanked noisily crossing the Harlem River, and the brakes seemed to squeal unusually loud as they pulled into 125th Street. Addy packed everything up.

CHAPTER 42

WITH ADELAIDE GONE FOR A good part of the day in Mamaroneck, curiosity eventually drew me into her bedroom. My ardent hope that her correspondence with Carson would diminish in frequency had been again dashed by the arrival of yet another letter—did the fellow not have a job to do? At least he was not telephoning; no doubt she had made clear she preferred the more arm's-distance mode of communication.

Two single-spaced pages was a treat. And I apologize my reply is short. Have to research Ga. law before a client meeting Monday. Forum shopping is a big deal here—California juries strike fear in the hearts of corporate defendants.

But I'm learning about franchise agreements. If I stink as an attorney, maybe I can open a MacDonald's (without an e).

His attempts at humor always missed the mark.

I get your insecurities at EK, have same and more. Partly my own fault for unrealistic expectations. Corny and old-fashioned, but I believe lawyers should act courteously and respectfully. The whole point of the legal system is resolving disputes in a civilized way, not jousting and eye-for-an-eye. If that's true, what's wrong with courtesy and respect?

The negotiations they let me sit in on aren't jousting, not physical anyway, and no yelling or throwing things. Everyone's polite on the surface. Both sides want an agreement. But the mood is like high-stakes poker. You get the sense there can only be one winner, and each party thinks they haven't done their job unless after the contract is signed, the other guy regrets the whole thing.

If things get you too down, remember you're always welcome here. My feelings haven't changed one whit.

The postscript said *Regards to Francis and Robert.*

I returned the letter to the drawer, turned off the lamp, and went back to the kitchen to zap my tea, my annoyance at Carson's refusal to end his suit only abating when I reminded myself of his function as rebound boyfriend. What better situation could one contrive than for his unrequited attentions to be foisted from the safe distance of three thousand miles? Especially in light of the criticisms Adelaide had been receiving at work, Carson's supplications may have been providing a much-needed morale boost.

"MY GOODNESS, WHAT A LONG interview. Was it productive?"

"I won't know until we check up on some things. But he could actually be legit." My granddaughter stepped out of her work shoes and, with a stockinged foot, pushed the shoes against the wall.

"He provided helpful documents?"

"A newspaper photo of his parents' wedding. Says Mary is in it." She riffled through the mail on the vanity.

"In the photograph? My, my—imagine, a *photograph* of the ever-elusive Mary MacDonalde!"

"The problem is, it's not a close-up and she's wearing one of those hats with a lace veil hanging in front."

"I remember the style. Was it Marlene Dietrich who used to wear them to great effect? That is his *only* photograph of Mary?"

"Yes. And the caption identifies her as Mary *Hill*."

We trooped into the kitchen. Adelaide opened the refrigerator and removed the leftover lasagna and set it on the counter, and I sat in my usual seat and watched as she deftly employed the spatula to separate off two portions. Her movements were neither brisk nor lackadaisical—simply economical. Olivia often gave the refrigerator door an emphatic push with her hip, suggestive of a gremlin inside poised to resist. Marjorie's movements in the kitchen had been a magical combination of both the efficient and casual, as though her mind were on something else entirely, not the wonderful meal she was in the process of concocting.

Adelaide leaned with the small of her back against the counter. "You have to swear to keep this confidential—not tell *anybody*."

"Haven't I numerous times promised—"

"Have you ever heard of Joe Hill?"

"Joe Hill the labor protester?"

"Yes. Mr. Grey-Davison claims that Mary married him, and he—Mr. Grey-Davison—is their grandson."

You could have "knocked me over with a feather," as my secretary used to say. "Seriously? Joe Hill's grandson? My goodness—Joe Hill. Of all the people for Mary to have married—it's astonishing. But shouldn't that be simple to verify? Joe Hill was in the public eye—articles, *books* have been written about him. Quite a legend. Before my time but quite a legend."

"He said the marriage was kept a secret because Joe Hill had many enemies. He was afraid of retaliation against Mary."

"Hardly a far-fetched fear," I had to concede. "Not only in the early days of the labor movement, back in the eighteen hundreds, but well into the 1920s and perhaps after, strikes and protests *often* turned quite violent. Some elements of the labor movement resorted to brutal acts against not only property but against those crossing picket lines, people denominated 'scabs.' I am not defending the men who ignored strikers and took their jobs; I am only saying that the consequences could be harsh. Dreiser's description in *Sis*—"

"He said the government framed Wobblies for crimes they didn't commit. And that sometimes the police started the violence, or it was done by private security hired by the companies. Articles he gave me say the same thing."

"I seem to recall in Joe Hill's case—it was talked about when I was a child—I believe there *was* a murder. And a trial."

"Apparently he had an alibi—he was already injured from a gunshot wound in a fight over some woman."

"And the woman was Mary MacDonalde?"

Adelaide disappointed me on that score—but what a story it would have made!

While we ate, she relayed details of Joe Hill's life and death I was unfamiliar with as well as facts about Mr. Grey-Davison. I opined I was inclined to believe him, because fabricating such a sensational story and selecting a person in the limelight the way Joe Hill had been, about whom so much had been written, was risky. "There could still be people alive—quite advanced in age, to be sure—who knew Joe Hill personally. And, as you say, he and Mary had a very good reason to conceal the relationship."

"He was on the West Coast the same time Mary was."

"While we are on the subject of the West Coast and before I forget, let me bring you up to date on my conversation with your mother. She wishes to visit—with Tony in tow—in early November for my birthday. They would make the cross-country flight as the first leg of a trip to London for a short vacation—there are some plays they are keen to see."

"That would be a great way to celebrate your eightieth."

I demurred, noting that no celebration was necessary but that I was glad to furnish the excuse for Olivia and Tony to visit.

AFTER DINNER, ADELAIDE BROUGHT MY old briefcase into the living room and showed me letters from Mr. Grey-Davison's great-aunt to his mother. The penmanship was easier to decipher than Mary MacDonalde's and lacked all those annoying curlicues on the maternity form for Anne MacDonalde's mother. While I perused the missives, Adelaide went to the window.

Only two living room lamps were lit, and the one near the piano reflected a nice warm brown off the polished surface. *It is a beauteous evening, calm and free*, that seamless border between twilight and night bespeaking pensiveness, the hour the last of the animals is shepherded into its nighttime quarters, the last bundles of hay distributed among the horses and ruminants, the last replenishment of troughs and water bowls. And a memory returned of a vespers service in Cambridge, an evensong, where the music and chanting seemed to emerge from the lofty reaches, the colors of the stained-glass windows softening in harmony.

The wistful timbre of my granddaughter's voice was of a piece of this meditative mood. "Did you ever love anybody besides Grandma?"

How the mind meanders in moments of tranquility. "I suppose you could say that before I met her, I had what might be termed infatuations. In those days, we did not engage in the kind of premarital liaisons subsequent generations have. An intimacy would progress only so far, and if marriage was not in the cards, we would tactfully distance—"

"Was there anybody else you *wanted to marry*, before Grandma?"

How long ago—*lifetimes* ago—those days seemed. "Put that way, I would have to say no. Marriage had not been in the forefront of my mind—I was not financially in a *position* to marry. You see, it was expected that the husband would provide for his wife. At what juncture I would have begun to entertain the notion of proposing, I cannot be certain. The issue was thrust upon me, one might say, by a second suitor. I may have mentioned him—a stockbroker named Edward?"

"I think so."

"He, too, was 'calling on her,' as we were wont to say. Or perhaps that was Cecil and Claudia's phrase, a vestige from their generation. In any event, what transpired was this: Marjorie and I were at a small coffeehouse near my department, and she mentioned a 'tiff' with her parents—you don't hear that word much anymore either. Upon my pressing for the cause, she revealed that Edward had formally proposed some weeks previous, and her parents, who were fond of the young man, worried that she was—what is the idiom?—'stringing him along.' She was refusing to say yes or no, and her indecision was unfair to him. Somehow in the course of our back-and-forth, I found myself—perhaps in a sort of panic—I found myself asking her to marry me instead."

Adelaide had begun turning my direction but pivoted again to watch the river.

"Your grandmother was not so quickly won over. She said she would have to think about it and deferred our getting together until the subsequent week, when we had a date to see *The Merchant of Venice*—a campus production. I returned home a bit shaken by my actions but without a single pang of buyer's remorse. Indeed, I was glad I had conveyed to her during that brief conversation that I had no debts to pay off and that my stipend would be increased by ten percent the following year when I assumed more teaching duties. Although Marjorie's family was in the upper reaches of the middle class, I fully expected to be her breadwinner and was determined to provide a certain level of comfort as my career advanced.

"The next we saw each other was at *The Merchant of Venice*. As I walked her home, I repeated my proposal, stating it far more gallantly than I had the first time. She quickly accepted. I never had regrets—never. I try to believe she felt the same."

Adelaide remained with face averted, her profile at the window undefined against the darkening sky. Finally, I inquired what had prompted the question.

"I was just wondering if falling in love a second time is very different from the first."

"I would hazard a guess that it *is* different, yet not necessarily better or worse."

Examples of first and second loves in literature came to mind—*David Copperfield*, first silly Dora and then serious Agnes; a not dissimilar pairing in *Adam Bede*; Bathsheba's journey in affection from soldier to shepherd; and Marianne's, from Willoughby to Colonel Brandon.

"Your grandmother often said to your mother and aunt Marcia when they were unsure of how they felt about a young man: 'If you can imagine a happy life without him, then it's not true love.' In other words, the person must be essential to your equanimity."

Now Adelaide turned full-face. "Equanimity? Isn't love the *opposite* of equanimity?"

Ah, youth, youth! Yes, there was a time when one welcomed, one *exulted in*, upheavals of the heart. "Weren't you asking about a deep-rooted love," I queried, "a love worthy of marriage? I believe there must be some measure of equanimity in the bond. It was Edward Rochester, I believe, who told Jane Eyre he imagined a cord tied to a rib below his heart and connected somehow to a corresponding rib below hers. If the cord were severed, he would bleed to death. Contrast that with poor Swann, whose passion was ignited by jealousy. Such a passion once fulfilled burns out—a momentary escalation in intensity does not transform a temporary infatuation into a permanent one. In any event, when your mother visits in another month, you might consider putting this question to *her*. She was in her twenties when she married your father. To use a cliché, life stretched before her. Would she have fallen in love with Tony if she had dated him in those days? I am doubtful. Yet even if it is a question she cannot answer with any certainty, her thoughts may provide some insight."

Yes, Olivia would be quite pleased to hear that Adelaide

concerned herself with such a question. For this very reason I swore to myself I would not raise the matter in our Sunday conversation, as my daughter surely would magnify the incident's significance.

CHAPTER 43

JOE SHOUTED, "YOU SHITTING ME? Joe Hill?" He was seated behind his desk and tossed a marked-up brief into his out-box. "This Grey-Davison meshuggeneh?"

"I don't think so. I mean he didn't come across as crazy. He has reasonable explanations."

Joe grabbed the receiver and punched some buttons on the phone base. "Ready for final." Dropping the receiver onto the cradle, he looked at her intently.

"You couldn't trip him up? What about the documents—isn't he the one with the carbon-dating crap?"

She explained what was in Sarah Grey-Davison's letters and told him about the photo of Mary Hill. "I left them for Kimberly to make copies."

Kimberly came in at that moment, and Addy looked up and smiled politely, but the secretary made no eye contact with her or Joe, snatching the brief from the out-box and leaving. That usually meant Joe had been hollering nonstop since he got in.

"But Sarah's dead," Joe said, "and you want to bet there's no copies of her handwriting except for what this clown has?"

"She lived in Charleston and was very active in the community—charity boards, that kind of thing. So there could be samples of her handwriting."

"Have the paralegals ask the investigators. No, not yet—let me talk to the Scots. The only actual piece of evidence is some photograph of his mother's wedding with the caption Mary *Hill*? You know how many Mary Hills there must be? And Helen Hills? Tell Michelle I want the transcript ASAP. You've been putting in extra hours—take a week or two off. Brush up on your school work." Was he pissed at her or just on a hair trigger over getting a brief filed?

THE WEATHER HAD GOTTEN COLDER, and the days it rained, Addy was able to hole up in her room and concentrate on her courses. Even on the few sunny days, the view from Richard's desk was mostly shadow and the gray stone of the adjacent building. Once in a while a pigeon perched on a window ledge, pick, pick, picking at the cement. Honking sounded from below—a delivery van blocked the alley, maybe, and some car wanted through. All the windows opposite kept their shades down.

It was raining heavily now, the water splattering on the ledge. She remembered playing soccer in pelting rain and sleet; the refs and coaches wouldn't call the game except for a thunderstorm. Wearing sweatshirts under the team jerseys did nothing to stop them from getting soaked. Her mother made them remove their shoes and shin guards by the door—Addy was better about it than Michael.

How old was Noah, six months? Aunt Addy had a nice ring to it. It wasn't even November, yet the rain was endless.

JOE HAD HER COME IN the following week and was on the phone when she arrived, so she took her usual seat. In the center of his desk sat a transcript with dozens of yellow tags sticking to the margins.

"You want first crack at the arbitrators or us?" he barked into the receiver.

"Fine. The sixteenth." He slammed the phone down.

Luckily, he didn't chew her out as badly as he had over the previous interviews, but he did complain that she should've asked Mr. Grey-Davison the names and addresses of his exes. She pointed out he didn't have any children, but Joe shot back, "Sure, he *said* that. Your job is to find out if it's true. Ex-wives are great witnesses—they'll know his family history. Even girlfriends and ex-girlfriends—it'd be nice to know if he's paying child support."

He paged through the transcript. "Our job isn't tracking down *one* heir—it's *all* of them. Legitimate and i*l*legitimate—this is about beneficiaries. Don't forget what started this whole thing: a ten-minute toss in the hay and hushed-up baby. Just a lousy phone call to one ex might unravel the whole damn story."

"Shouldn't their divorce decrees be public records?"

He glowered at her. "You didn't ask where they were filed. The Scots aren't going to want to pay to track that down."

Addy sat in awkward silence as Joe continued reading his notes. After a few minutes, he said, "I'll see what those misers are willing to fork over in follow-up. They're in a good mood this week: Simon and Brad both pulled the rug out under a couple of frauds. The Graveyard drawer is filling up, and Limbo thinning."

Taking the hint, she rose and put on her coat and grabbed Francis's briefcase. The second she stepped into the hall, though, he called out, "You'll be getting a letter in the next few days. Offer for full-time after you graduate."

It rained heavily as she hurried to the subway. Descending into the dank corridors, Addy told herself that if nothing else, Engel's offer meant she wouldn't have to draft a new résumé right away and figure out where to send it. After she passed the bar exam and had some experience under her belt, she could look elsewhere. And the news would cheer Francis. His cold was in its second week, the coughing keeping her awake half the night. She had sat with Robert down at Millie and John's so the boy wouldn't catch it.

FRANCIS'S ROOM WAS TOO DARK for her to make out the bed, but the rhythm of his breathing said he was asleep. The cough medicine seemed to be working. The smart thing to do would be to catch up on sleep herself. It had been a rough week: classes and homework and the minute she got home having to practically forcefeed him soup and juice so he wouldn't get dehydrated.

She ate dinner in her room with only the desk lamp on. Afterward, she opened the side drawer and removed Carson's letters. His experiences as a new associate resonated, described her feelings at Engel, especially that sense of hidden minefields. Civil Procedure didn't teach things firms expected you to know, like which forms to use in the different state and federal courts, what a bailiff did versus what a law clerk did, what questions you could ask a witness and what ones you couldn't. And that was just in litigation—Carson also had to deal with corporate minefields.

She wrote him back on the weekend and described the developments in the MacDonalde case that had become public, mainly Mary's moving to Washington in 1908 and then leaving in 1913. She also wrote about her Environmental Law class—ever since he'd read about pollution and other damage to the oceans, Carson had seemed interested. The remaining paragraphs were chatty: her mother and Tony would be visiting for Francis's eightieth birthday; Robert went through a rough period but was doing better. *Unfortunately, he has to have an operation next summer. Every visit he wants me to show him the vessels book.* The one piece of good news Addy included wouldn't strike Carson as good, but she had to tell him. *Engel made me an offer. I'll start in August, after the bar exam.*

CHAPTER 44

A PLEASANT SIGHT IT WAS, the dining room table set and a bottle of wine awaiting on the sideboard. Although the 'official' birthday dinner would be on the weekend, when Marcia and her family came down from Connecticut, the more intimate dinner at home where I would meet Tony as part of our foursome appealed more. And odd as it may seem, memories of the Saturday-night dinners with Carson seemed cast in a felicitous glow. How the mind plays tricks, turning tedious trials into pleasant soirées. Yet, if nothing else, Carson's presence offered a break from the usual routine. All work and no play makes Jack a dull boy, and Francis, as well.

Tony's appearance was not a complete surprise—the full head of hair, the modern-style glasses—although in person he conveyed more energy than photographs could suggest. By the standards of middle-aged women, he may have been considered attractive, but something in his manner reminded me of assistant professors eager to be popular among the students—assistant professors who often won teaching awards but rarely made tenure. This impression of Tony—as an intellectual lightweight—*did* surprise me, for notwithstanding his being a psychologist, I had assumed Olivia would marry an intellectual equal. Nathan, a self-proclaimed "nebbish," was every bit her peer and, on a number of topics, her superior. In any event, to Tony's credit, his manner toward me was respectful without being obsequious. Adelaide may have been correct in her assessment that he was someone who could hold his own against her mother.

The dinner conversation lacked neither in liveliness nor intellectual stimulation. Tony proved an able raconteur, regaling us with stories of the safari, which included a zebra stampede, a stray baby giraffe, and a brief confrontation with hyenas. Olivia recounted several amusing incidents at the university, one involving the mislabeling of a container of milk one of the graduate students—a new mother—had "pumped."

And I was on my best behavior, allowing only one very minor cavil directed at the psychology profession. We were concocting impromptu lists of twentieth-century thinkers most likely to leave a lasting impact on civilization, and Tony numbered Freud among his nominees. "We talk about people wanting or feeling something *un*consciously or *sub*consciously—it's part of our everyday view; we don't give it a second thought," he said. "But Freud's theory of the unconscious mind was a new model at the time."

"Like gravity," Adelaide said. "Everyone knew things fell down, but Newton gave it a framework that was useful to science."

Her need to flatter Tony was of the same impulse that had caused her to laugh at Carson's jokes—no doubt Marjorie's solicitude toward guests had been passed down. I made the simple observation that Freud was not the *first* to posit the existence of an unconscious mind. Many early classical writers had made equivalent observations, and, in any event, Pascal articulated the idea several centuries previous. "*Le coeur a ses raisons que la raison ne connaît point,*" I said. "The heart has its reasons that reason knows nothing of. What is this, if not a statement about our unconscious mind?"

Olivia opined that the works of twentieth-century *painters* might not prove enduringly popular, but she believed that certain pioneers of the film industry would leave a lasting mark. The group—myself excepted—became engrossed in a comparison of directors, actors, and actresses, a discussion that I enjoyed but was unable to join, my knowledge of films being limited.

The gaiety waned only when the conversation wound round to Adelaide's plans after graduation. I could not refrain from vicariously boasting that her firm had recently made her an offer for full-time employment come next summer. "That is no small accomplishment," I emphasized, "impressing a group of partners to such a degree that they are eager to hire her even before seeing her third-year grades."

But Olivia wanted to know if Engel Klein had offices elsewhere or just in New York, and she was unable to mask her disappointment at the answer. To rekindle the lightheartedness of moments earlier, I brought up that the firm was handling a matter generating a fair amount of publicity in the press, and, Olivia and Tony responding with enthused curiosity, Adelaide enumerated the salient details of the MacDonalde case. To both her and my surprise, the case had *not* been discussed in the Seattle papers. Human nature being what it was, our guests were drawn into the saga.

"Can't they just give the claimants lie-detector tests?" her mother wanted to know.

"They're not reliable."

"Employers use them. I can't believe human resources departments would rely on a tool that's—"

"There's a *reason* they're unreliable," Tony interrupted. "The machines depend on a physiological response to guilt: changes in respiration, pulse, blood pressure. Con artists can be guilt-free."

My mind leapt to both Harold Skimpole and George Wickham, and I half expected Olivia to refer to them herself when she began to speak.

"You're right. They're shameless. A poster in the coffee shop I go to advertises tarot readings for twenty dollars. People pay real money for utter nonsense."

"One man's nonsense," Tony said, "may be another man's religion."

"But ministers, priests, and rabbis *believe* in what they preach," Olivia rejoined. "Madame Voodoo or whatever she calls herself doesn't believe it. She knows she's running a scam. Why can't people see that?"

"She peddles hope," her husband said.

"Buying lottery tickets is hope. Ripping off the ignorant and vulnerable?"

Tony removed his glasses, breathed on the lenses, and used his napkin to massage them between thumb and forefinger. "The customers aren't ripped off. They *choose* to believe her. She charges a lot less than I do." He smiled at Adelaide and me as he put his glasses back on. "And may give more comfort."

"Don't let him kid you," Olivia told her daughter. "He thinks he helps his clients enormously."

"*Most* of them," Tony said.

I was pleased to see he did not endow his profession with transcendent powers. I ventured to offer my own opinion. "I doubt these so-called prognosticators are consistently accurate in their predictions, so their customers cannot credit them with reliability, and in that sense, the customers *are choosing*—they are choosing to be deceived. And to being duped out of their money."

"Money that could be spent on food and clothing for their children," Olivia said.

"But would it go to that," Tony asked, "or to alcohol and drugs?" He had more on the ball than I had realized.

Outnumbered, Olivia pointedly inquired of Adelaide her opinion: Were these prognosticators—"clairvoyants" was Olivia's term—were they con artists or just benign pseudo therapists?

Adelaide reflected a bit before responding. "It's kind of two issues. What's the morality of the people doing the lying, and what's the morality of the people who seem willing to be lied to?"

Olivia glowed with parental pride. "You sound like your father, answering a question with a question."

As if thinking aloud, Adelaide continued, "I guess it's immoral to lie to people, especially when you're asking for money, and when they're poor and uneducated and desperate to believe something."

"The way you put it, I have to agree," Tony said with a laugh. "But when the customer's rich and silly, and the *clairvoyant* has mouths to feed—"

Olivia turned to me. "None of which settles the larger question: Where do you want to go to dinner for your birthday celebration?"

"Your coming to visit is celebration enough—there is no need for further commemoration. It has never been my practice to—"

"Don't be silly—we're taking you to dinner. Marcia and Ted have already said they will come down for it. I hope Alex and Mindy can come too."

I gestured feebly. "Why don't you all decide. As long as it is not too difficult to travel to."

"We'll take a cab," Olivia said. "What if we let Marcia pick? She doesn't get into the city often, and that way she won't complain about our choice."

"I have a meeting tomorrow morning," Adelaide told us, "but I shouldn't be back late."

I RETIRED IN GOOD SPIRITS, not from the prospect of a dinner celebration but from the pleasant evening that had just transpired. Except for briefly playing the inquisitor in regard to Adelaide's job plans, Olivia, by and large, avoided the kinds of personal campaigns that had marred visits past. And if Tony's efforts at self-deprecation were not as convincing as Nathan's, he nonetheless did not try to 'wear his erudition on his sleeve,' a fault for which I myself was once or twice chastised, although in my defense I would only say that literary classics are a more deserving field for erudition than psychology folderol.

In the morning, Adelaide departed for Engel Klein, and I settled in the living room with several journals that had arrived in the mail. Olivia and Tony, no doubt suffering from jet lag, 'slept in,' as Marjorie would have put it.

The titles in the table of contents of the first journal did not entice me into further perusal, for I had read enough Shakespearean criticism to last five lifetimes, and the virtues of *The Great Gatsby* eluded me completely. The more modern writers—Salinger, Cheever, Updike—were well beyond my ken. The article about *Ulysses* could not snare my attention even if adorned with pictures of scantily clad women, not that such pictures meant much to me anymore.

The second journal contained an article piquing my curiosity, and I thumbed to the beginning page, but Olivia emerged from the hallway to join me, so I set the publication aside. She was still in her robe.

"I was about to embark on an article comparing Victor Hugo and William Faulkner, a matchup I have not encountered before."

"Both like melodrama. Has Addy left for her meeting?"

"Yes. There's coffee, you know, but I'm afraid you will have to make it yourself as I am not conversant in its preparation."

"I'll wait for Tony."

"Is he still asleep?"

"No, in the shower." Olivia sat on the sofa, adjusting the robe to cover her knees. Both of my daughters remained attractive women even into middle age.

And I was fortunate that Marjorie had never lost her seductive lively warmth.

"I'm curious, Dad. Has Addy talked about moving into an apartment with people her own age after graduation?"

316

"What people?'"

"I'm not saying she *is* going to—I'm asking if she's ever brought up the possibility."

So much for the absence of personal campaigns! With a small effort, I kept my tone even. "Why should she? The rent here is free. She can come and go as she pleases. Her obligations are few—grocery shopping and chores she would do for herself anyway. Plus, helping with Robert a few hours every other week, but that has become a pleasure for us both, not a chore."

Olivia plucked a piece of lint off her robe. "It's the isolation from her peers that bothers me."

"She sees them every day in class. And at her firm."

"From what she says, she hasn't made friends."

"Friends are not easy to come by—true friends."

"I don't mean lifelong—just casual friends, people to do things with. She shouldn't be socially isolated."

"Isolation is not always a bad thing. Writers, scholars, certain artists and artisans *require* solitude. Surely you recall my diatribes about what I would have given for an office on a desert island?"

"I remember." Her smile quickly inverted to a frown. "Your life had *balance*. You wanted a little more solitude, but you did have *some*. You went to sherry hour with your colleagues and that 'pub,' you used to call it, over on—"

"She has her classes and ten hours a week at the law firm. That is considerable mixing with colleagues."

"It's not *socializing*."

I took a deep breath and allowed some seconds to tick by. "You grew up in Manhattan, my dear, and went to college in a city and moved to a city, a small city. You have never lived somewhere rural. In this one respect, at least, you have led a sheltered life. In rural communities, socializing with one's peers outside of school and church is far from an everyday occurrence. Farmers do not regard their existence as deprived; they find companionship in nature, in work, in the changing seasons. *Have sight of Proteus rising from the sea; or hear old Triton blow his wreathèd horn.* Besides, Adelaide shows no signs of missing such interactions. You cannot imagine I *prevent* her from fraternizing with people her own age?"

"Not intentionally. All I mean is: social interactions would happen naturally if she lived with other young people."

"If she ever expresses such a desire, I will not discourage her—you have my solemn promise."

The smile Olivia bestowed was one I have always associated with the imminent delivery of a blow. I was not wrong. "Your dependence on her is an implicit discouragement."

What an effort I expended to maintain my casual lightheartedness! "You seem to forget, my dear, that I had been living by myself before she moved in here. And except for the brief period when I injured my ankle, I am no less capable of taking care of myself *now* than I was *then*."

My daughter rose and tightened the belt of her robe. "This is about her, not you." That smile again. "And you have to admit you're not on the lookout for signs of loneliness. I'm not complaining—Mom handled that, and marriages develop their own distribution of labor. You did plenty of other things."

Any qualms I may have had about sounding irritated vanished. "You cannot mean to tell me you suffered from loneliness! This house was a *riot* of children; *hordes* traipsed through these rooms; I was never able to learn their names! Richard had friends, Marcia had veritable *armies*—"

"But Addy doesn't. And this isolation is not typical of her. She was on a soccer team in middle and high school. She had girlfriends she studied and went to movies with. She had this big romance in college, this Zach, and after that, no romance, no friends, nothing. It's pretty obvious she's still grieving over that poor boy. But *five years* have passed. We're not programmed to grieve forever. People are constituted to begin anew."

"A convenient theory, coming from you."

The look Olivia threw me was both wounded and reprimanding. "That was uncalled for. I loved Nathan, and he'll always be a part of me. But what's the point of remaining mired in the past?"

"What's the point of anything, one might well ask."

She walked to the credenza, picked up the small bronze horse, and put it down. She did the same with the mosaic dish, turned the glass wren around and deposited it, held the scrimshaw a moment. Although lacking a firm sense that I was decidedly in the right in this discussion, I did feel justifiably resentful that the issue of Adelaide and my living arrangement was perpetually revisited.

Our stony silence was broken by Tony's entrance. Were his ruddy cheeks due to the shower, or had he and Olivia recently been connubially engaged? He exuded a self-confidence that made me suspect the latter.

"Hope I'm not interrupting," he said.

"Dad and I are arguing about whether Addy should get an apartment with people her own age after she graduates."

Tony raised his eyebrows as if to suggest the topic was altogether new to him.

I said, "Feel free to ask Adelaide if I pressure her to do anything other than what she pleases. Except, on rare occasion, as pertains to her physical safety."

"Dad, calm down."

"I am calm. You suggested that I am sabotaging her efforts to move out, which is so far from the truth as to be laughable. Tony, you have walked into the middle of a long-standing disagreement not about where Adelaide should live—that is and has always been *her* choice—but Olivia's notion that Adelaide's lesser gregariousness, compared to Olivia's and her sister Marcia's—that this lesser gregariousness is a problem to be corrected. My view is that human nature permits of great variety, and those of us less inclined to socializing are as emotionally fit as those for whom frequent social interaction is as necessary as breathing. To consider solitariness a fault! History is replete with examples of individuals who shied away from society. I am not talking simply about the likes of Thoreau, who developed a *creed* of solitude, one might argue, but untold numbers of writers, artists, philosophers, scientists—"

"People often called introverts," Tony said.

"Exactly! Yes, Adelaide may be an introvert, which is not to say she lives like a hermit. She attends classes, meets with people at—"

"Even *you* said," Olivia cried out, an accusing look hurled husband-ward, "*you* said she had a flat aspect. It's worse than last year, when I visited at Christmas. When she's talking to me and Dad, or with Marcia and Alex and—"

Truly, I was unable to restrain myself. "Not everyone expresses feelings through their countenance! Certainly not to the same extent. You should have met my father; he always displayed a solemn mien. It was his natural expression. Olivia's mother, Tony, she was the opposite; emotions were writ large—in her eyes, her cheeks, her mouth. One was never at a loss to discern her feelings."

"That's where *you* get it, Ollie."

Olivia inhaled deeply, her breasts rising. "This is beside the point. Introvert or extrovert, don't you agree a person who shuns social activities with her peers is likely depressed?"

Tony stroked his chin. "I haven't spoken with her enough to attempt to diagnose something like depression. But she seems to be coping with life's daily difficulties. She doesn't avoid classes or work, right? She held down a summer job?"

I had to concede: the man was not a complete lightweight. "She even gets good grades," I volunteered, hoping they would not repeat the remark to Adelaide, as she did not know I had surreptitiously peeked at her reports.

Olivia again picked up the glass bird and rotated it in her hands, directing a question to Tony—or perhaps herself. "But is she happy? I don't think so. She must miss the pleasures of friendship, of romantic—"

"If she misses them," I said, "she would seek them."

"Not necessarily."

"Francis is right," Tony told her. "Some people are happy with a small number of close friends. A person passionate about his work might *prefer* being single."

Now Olivia positively glowered; any post-connubial bliss turned to dust.

"Just because we can't always *find* love and friendship doesn't mean—"

"Look at Mother Teresa," I said. "Do you honestly believe that at the end of a full day's work she is eager to join friends for a round of bridge? Or seek out a romantic liaison? Did Rembrandt put away his paints and go off to play doubles tennis?"

Tony took up the baton. "Or Van Cliburn, after performing Rachmaninoff, hitting the neighborhood bar to toss one back with the locals?"

After a few more such quips tossed onto the fire, Olivia hissed, "You can talk all you want in the abstract, but Addy's *not* Mother Teresa or some driven artist. She wants and *needs* human companionship."

I should have better controlled the sarcasm in my voice. "The implication being that she is devoid of it? Am I a subhuman? A Neanderthal perhaps, or Java man?"

In exasperation, Olivia threw her hands in the air, a gesture I realized, with some embarrassment, echoed not Marjorie's movements but my own. A moment later, she murmured, "Well, if she does make noises about moving out, I hope you won't discourage her. And you might then consider taking us up on our offer for you to move in with us. As I've told you before, space and privacy are not an issue."

At long last, Tony rallied for his wife. "And between the two of us, Francis, you'll find a partner for whatever amuses you. I follow the Seahawks and Mariners. We have subscriptions to two theaters; I have a jazz bar I like; and Ollie is always getting tickets to the symphony and opera."

His wife drily added, "Where you can get good seats without taking out a mortgage."

"That is very kind of you both. And in your own minds, you cannot see how I could object. But you have to understand: this old, dilapidated furniture is not old and dilapidated to me. These objects, these walls with their paintings and prints and even their cracks and peeling—these are my old friends. As we age, we cling more and more to the familiar. We *prefer* the routine. Trying out a new locale offers none of the sparkle that adventure does in youth. We become—"

"Dad, that's depression. Tony and I went to Kenya in March and had a wonderful time. I haven't been to London for twenty years, and I can't wait to go."

"My dear, the difference between fifty and eighty—"

"I'm fifty-seven, and Tony's fifty-six."

"And when you are eighty, you will look back at fifty-seven as scarcely a step past adolescence. Admittedly, I exaggerate, but by our seventies, if not earlier, we become creatures of habit. We want the foods we are familiar with; the music we are familiar with; and, especially, we want the *surroundings* we are familiar with."

Olivia sat on the sofa close to my chair and spoke softly. "We understand that. We know the transition will not be easy in every way. But you can have your furniture shipped out. Not the entire apartment's worth, but favorite pieces. You can bring the sheets and blankets, the towels, some dishes. We don't want the move to be more disruptive than it has to be."

"My dear, just to *select* among these furnishings would take a lifetime—a lifetime longer than I have remaining."

"What's the plan for this evening?" Tony asked.

Olivia studied his face a moment. "Marcia and everyone are due at six. The reservation's for seven-thirty."

"Why so late?" I inquired, surprised. "Will we have something to feed them beforehand?"

"Alex works Saturdays and needs to get home and change. Addy and I plan to go shopping when she gets back from her meeting. We'll pick up drinks and hors d'oeuvres."

I nodded at Tony. "It sounds as if the ladies have things well in hand."

CHAPTER 45

TONY AND FRANCIS WORE SPORTS coats and ties, and Olivia wore slacks—stylish ones but still slacks—so Addy didn't feel too casual in her dark pants, gray sweater, and the silk scarf her mother'd given her. They sipped wine while waiting for Marcia's family to arrive, Francis anxiously checking his watch.

"Voilà," Tony said, the buzzer sounding.

Marcia marched in and immediately handed Olivia a Brooks Brothers shopping bag and removed her coat, which she gave to Addy. She was wearing an elegant black dress and heels that had to be more than two inches—*Olivia's* heels looked impossible to walk in and were lower.

While the two sisters exchanged compliments on their outfits, the buzzer sounded again. Addy pressed the intercom; it was Alex.

"Is Ted trying to find street parking?" Olivia asked.

"He couldn't come and sends his apologies. Another patient emergency."

"Oh, really? I'm sorry Tony won't get to meet him."

They remained by the vanity until Alex and Mindy arrived. Mindy reminded Addy of the temp at Engel who'd called her Ms. Crane for an entire week. Kimberly had complained the temp combed her hair more than she typed.

After they'd all moved into the living room and made introductions and Tony took drink orders, Mindy asked if there was anything to eat. Her voice was the kind that carried across a room, but she probably wasn't aware of it.

"I thought you were going to eat a sandwich before coming," Marcia said.

"There's cheese and crackers." Addy pointed to the platter of appetizers, plates, and napkins on the coffee table by Francis. Mindy sat on the sofa and reached over and loaded her plate.

"You can't be *that* hungry," Marcia said. "It's not even the size of a fingernail."

"It keeps me from getting nauseous."

"Are you pregnant?" Olivia asked.

A cracker in her mouth, Mindy nodded.

"Barely," Marcia muttered. "She found out yesterday."

"Congratulations," Olivia said cheerfully. Addy echoed her mother.

"You can't be *barely* pregnant, Ma," Alex said. "Either you are or you aren't."

"At seven weeks, she has no business having an appetite like that."

"How old is Madison?" Olivia asked.

"Four months."

"Was your trip into the city without incident?" Francis asked Alex.

"We live on Staten Island."

"I told you last spring they moved," Marcia said. She sipped her drink and seemed to listen for its taste.

"It still takes Alex an hour to get to work," Mindy said, "but it's a *lot* cheaper. The subway instead of the train all the way from Bridgeport."

"Where do you work?" Olivia asked him.

"Off Amsterdam, mid-nineties."

"It wouldn't take long from here," Mindy said.

Marcia turned to Tony. "So you two are off to London."

"Yes, for two weeks."

"His niece is getting married," Olivia said. "There are some plays we'd like to see, and we were coming this far for Dad's birthday anyway, so we decided—"

"To go for broke," Tony said. "And will be by the time we get home."

"I'm teaching only one class this quarter," Olivia went on, "and the TA can handle it."

"Why don't you retire?" Marcia asked, crossing her legs. "Can't you afford to? Or are you one of those people who has to milk the last drop out of social security?"

"I like working. So does Tony."

Marcia squinted like she thought Olivia was trying to fool her. Addy started to ask if they thought it was a good time for Francis to open his presents, but Mindy stood abruptly. "Can I get a tour?"

"I'll play guide." Tony gestured toward the hall leading to the bedrooms.

Alex followed Tony and Mindy, bringing his bottle of beer.

"So how's the birthday boy?" Marcia asked Francis.

"Sometimes I *feel* like a boy. And not in a good sense, not in the sense of having energy. In the sense of not always catching the drift of the conversations around me."

"You haven't missed anything. Mindy's pregnant, and Madison isn't even teething."

"That used to be the rule, not the exception, when I was a child. People did not let several years elapse before having additional children, the way they do nowadays. Of course, reliable contraception was not widely available."

Olivia laughed. "What contraception?"

"There were reliable forms," Francis said, "but not available in all communities. And farming communities often considered large families a blessing."

"Let me tell you," Marcia said drily, "not all reliable methods are reliable."

Addy tapped Olivia on the shoulder and whispered, "Shouldn't he open the presents before we leave?"

"A good idea. Marcia, why don't we have Dad open the gifts before we go to eat."

"Okay, let me track them down—speaking of the devils."

"This place is so *big*." Mindy came in with her arms stretched out and her jaw gaping. "I can't believe all the rooms. Just for *two* of you."

"The guest rooms get plenty of use," Olivia said. "It's nice that Tony and I don't have to camp out on the living room sofa. Dad, we want you to open your gifts."

"Gifts? I don't need gifts. Is there time?"

"Yes—the restaurant's only seven blocks away."

"Are there more crackers?" Mindy asked.

"You'll ruin your appetite," Marcia warned.

"No, she won't, Ma."

"In the kitchen cupboard by the refrigerator," Olivia said.

Addy brought the pile of presents to the coffee table. Francis looked embarrassed as he tried to unwrap Alex and Mindy's, so Marcia took the box and quickly tore the paper off.

"A necktie," he said. "Very, very nice. I'm not sure where I will wear it, but I thank you just the same."

"The point is to go somewhere that you will have an occasion to wear it," Olivia told him.

"This one's from us," Marcia said.

"Also very nice!" Francis held up a pale-blue cardigan.

"Is that cashmere?" Olivia whispered.

"Yes, it's cashmere," Marcia snapped.

Francis opened an envelope from Olivia and looked puzzled.

"It's a gift certificate to the theater," she said. "You can redeem it for tickets. Find something you want to see, and call the box office about what seats are available."

"Then you can wear the tie," Tony said.

"Adelaide, perhaps you and a—"

"We'll go to something," Addy told Olivia and Tony.

Marcia asked Olivia, "Any word from our wandering brother?"

Addy's gifts were lighthearted: a series of hand-drawn coupons entitling *the bearer* to various things, like a pastrami with the works and an hour of her time devoted to obtaining requested articles from the library. He read each coupon out loud, clearly most pleased with the last.

"This coupon entitles me to assign Adelaide required reading in the form of one novel of my choosing, the reading to be accomplished after she graduates from law school and takes the bar examination. The novel may be by Henry James, Thomas Hardy, or any other writer."

"You may regret it," her mother said. "What if he picks *Remembrance of Things Past*? Or worse: *Finnegans Wake*."

"Joyce is not at the top of my list," Francis said, "and *Finnegans Wake* is not on the list at all."

"No literary talk," Marcia said. "And someone's at the door."

Addy went to check and brought Millie and John into the living room. Millie handed Francis an envelope.

"So sorry to interrupt—I didn't realize you had company. We came to drop this off for your birthday. Can't stay—dinner's on the stove."

"My goodness. This is far too much acknowledgment, but thank you, thank you very much."

"I remember speaking with you at my mother's funeral," Olivia told Millie.

"Aren't you going to open the card?" Mindy asked.

Francis removed it from the envelope. "*Happy Birthday*," he read.

"Robert did the drawing," Millie said.

Francis turned the card so people could see.

"It's you," Addy pointed out. "The brown sweater."

"So it is, so it is. And what is this—a gift certificate?"

"The deli Addy says you like."

"You shouldn't have—you and John should not have so much as *recognized* the day!"

"Oh, it's little enough, considering all you've done for Robert." Millie turned toward Mindy and Alex. "Every other Thursday, I bring my grandson over for a few hours, and Francis and Adelaide keep an eye on him. He has many medical issues. They are so patient with him."

Marcia whispered to Olivia, loud enough for at least Addy to hear, "I guess I should've been a special-needs child."

TONY, ALEX, AND ADDY WALKED to the restaurant while the others took a cab. Tony kept Alex and Addy laughing most of the way with stories about Olivia's and his efforts to get rid of moles under the front lawn, raccoons on the roof, and mice in the attic. Addy wondered if her mother had been disappointed in Nathan for being so quiet, though he'd had a wry sense of humor. She caught only the tail end of something Tony was saying about Rhoda.

"Yes, Pat, her partner, will be discharged in January."

"One of my coworkers is gay," Alex said, "and it's lucky she doesn't live on Staten Island, at least in our neighborhood."

"Portland's pretty mellow—most of the West Coast is," Tony said. "And even Staten Island is way ahead of Nairobi."

THE OTHERS WERE ALREADY SEATED at the circular table. The dining room wasn't too dark or too large and the tables spaced far enough apart that Francis would be able to hear everyone at their own.

After the waiter brought the wine and they ordered, Tony stood and held up his glass. "To Francis: happy eightieth birthday."

"To Francis" and "Happy birthday" they echoed.

"As we all know," Tony continued, still standing, "Francis has passed the eighty-year mark with all his faculties intact—and I say that as someone who is beginning to lose a few of my own. Our modern technological society is pretty demanding and requires a steep learning curve. Francis grew up on a farm without running water, without central heat, without TVs and stereos and refrigerators and microwaves—*several* technology revolutions have happened in his lifetime. Yet he hasn't run away from these modern conveniences— he's learned how to use a computer and knows word-processing commands better than people decades younger." Tony paused and, looking directly at Francis, let out a fake moan, "So why, oh why, won't you spring for a thirty-dollar answering machine?" Even Francis laughed along.

"The size of Francis's book collection is immense," Tony went on. "He owns fiction and nonfiction—I saw history books and philosophy and art and music and the *Oxford English Dictionary*. But why, oh why, when Ollie and I get into an argument about the '59 World Series, don't you have one lousy almanac!" Again, people laughed.

"The Dodgers won," Alex said.

"The *LA* Dodgers."

Tony kept going, alternately praising and teasing Francis, and at the final toast, everyone joined in with abundant cheer—even Marcia, who was on her second glass. Embarrassed in a good way, Francis thanked them and said it was gratifying to be surrounded by so much family.

Before Tony sat back down, Mindy said to Addy, "Wasn't he *funny*? When Alex said he was a psychologist, I thought he'd be old and boring."

The appetizers arrived, and the group broke into smaller conversations. Addy listened a little to Tony and Mindy comparing impressions of the city, then to Alex and Marcia talk about Westport friends and neighbors. The wine bottles quickly emptied, and Marcia told the waiter to bring a Bordeaux and Australian chardonnay the same time as their entrées. Francis was pink-cheeked.

"Did you really read all those books in your apartment?" Mindy asked him.

"My dear, I have had many, many decades in which to do so. My profession required me to read a fair number, even if my natural proclivities had not propelled me in the identical direction."

"I bet some were your wife's," Tony said. "Ollie's books outnumber mine by two to one."

"Yes, some were Marjorie's. And I believe we still have a shelf of Cecil's books. He was a big fan of Tocqueville."

"Was Cecil your father?" Mindy asked.

"No," Olivia answered for Francis, "Cecil was Marjorie's father."

"Maybe there's another shelf of *your* father's books," Alex said to Francis, "and when you subtract out the books belonging to your father and father-in-law and Grandma Marjorie and Mom's and Aunt Olivia's and Uncle Richard's, only twenty belong to you."

He was only trying to be funny, Addy could see. Francis turned to Mindy.

"My father was not a big reader. He was a farmer, like his father and grandfather."

"Why didn't *you* become a farmer?" she asked.

"My nature impelled me in a different direction. I responded strongly to stories, to literature. And in time to the *craft* of story writing, of literature. Which is not to say I wasn't helped along—"

"It's nice when parents are supportive," Marcia said to no one in particular.

Francis continued to address Mindy. "In their own way, I suppose they were supportive. They did not *forbid* me to go to college. Yet my choice of careers was, for them, bittersweet. You see, I was their only child to survive infancy. There were miscarriages, stillbirths, and two siblings who succumbed to infection at less than a year, so—"

"Dad," Olivia whispered, "Mindy's pregnant, so this isn't the best—"

"It was only natural for my parents to hope that I would continue to maintain the family traditions. Literature was not one of those traditions. They had never experienced the astonishment of immersion in a new existence that could be on a distant or imaginary continent, or at a different time, or among different people. To be so enthralled as to forget one's surroundings, to believe that one is aboard a submarine or in the jungles of Malaysia or on a forlorn heath in England."

"How's your steak?" Marcia asked Alex.

"Okay."

Olivia called across the table to Tony, "The Carl Jung books were my mother's. She liked the idea of the collective unconscious."

He smiled. "It's not a big topic among therapists."

"What *is*?" Marcia wanted to know. "Drugs? A friend of mine, whatever they put her on, it's like talking to a zombie."

"Jake's mom?" Alex asked.

"No, the garden club—the one from Darien. I don't know how she can drive."

"Usually medications are a last resort," Tony said, "if talk therapy isn't enough."

"Well, she's paying a lot less than my friend Carol. On the couch for twenty years! And just as depressed as ever. Her therapist—*he's* doing great. Three kids in private school."

"Is she going to a psychoanalyst or a clinical psychologist?" Olivia asked.

"What's the difference? How much they charge?"

"The therapies," Tony said. "Psychoanalysts often use Freudian—"

"She pores over her dreams," Marcia said, "my *God*, does she. He tells her this means that and that means something else. All of it sexual. Hocus-pocus, if you ask me."

Tony loosened his tie. "Clinical psychology has come a long way since Freud's theories of dream interpretation. It's like comparing a Mercedes to a Model T."

"Explain how you treat depression nowadays," Olivia said.

"It varies," Tony explained to the table generally, although Francis was still talking to Mindy. "It depends on the patient and how severe the symptoms are."

"Hocus-pocus," Marcia repeated. Olivia looked a little offended.

"Don't psychologists have to know some neurology too?" Addy asked Tony. "Things that weren't known in Freud's day?"

"Absolutely! We have to stay current on medication options."

Marcia laughed. "*Medication options*—you mean *pill popping*. Carol's shrink won't give her any—he makes oodles listening to her. Though how he can *stand* it, I don't know. I'm sorry, but I don't think he's done a thing for her except soak her for twenty grand a year."

"Does anyone else want the last dinner roll?" Mindy asked.

"A friend of mine," Addy said, "his sister went to a therapist for some trauma she'd been through as a child—I don't know what—and after a couple of years just talking to him, without medication, she was able to get past anxieties that had been making her miserable. Not past all of them, probably, but—"

"Talk therapy isn't hocus-pocus," Tony said. "It can help a person undo responses learned in childhood that aren't constructive anymore. And offer practical steps for recovery. Sometimes as basic as: Get regular exercise and eat a healthy diet. Maintain friendships and a level of social interaction. Go see a play, for instance!"

Again, Marcia laughed. "You sound straight out of an assisted-living brochure! My in-laws—"

Addy was sorry to see Tony losing his easygoing expression. He looked about to say something before Francis broke in. "Mrs. Procrustes, the woman who helped me when Adelaide went to Seattle last winter, inundated me with brochures just like you say. And because I was virtually immobilized with a sprained ankle, I could not escape her lectures—I was the proverbial captive audience." He dabbed at his mouth with a napkin. "My fundamental quarrel with those who would 'cure' us, and the psychology profession, is that they do not take into account the myriad variations among human temperaments and natures. If you want insight into the complexities of human thoughts and feelings—if you *truly* want to study the human mind and heart—put down your textbook and pick up Thomas Hardy or George Eliot. Skip William James and read his brother Henry."

Olivia called over to Tony, "You're under attack from all sides tonight."

"William James's ideas are pretty dated," Tony said, "but at least he didn't buy into anti-Semitism, like Henry did. Very nasty stuff Henry James wrote."

"Adelaide, my dear, Henry James was not a saint, and sainthood is an unfairly high bar to set for artists—it is not unusual for them to subscribe to the racial and ethnic prejudices of their time. And to judge them as harshly as we would judge those of later generations who are exposed to more education and greater enlightenment would be to discard the wheat with the chaff."

"If we throw out all literature that treats *women* in a demeaning way," Olivia said, "our libraries would be almost empty."

"Getting back to the point," Tony said, "while writers might make reasonable observations about human nature in *general*, it's the trained therapist who leads an *individual* to understanding him- or herself. And guides them through some form of recovery."

"Recovery?" asked Francis. "Recovery from what? Sorrow and loss and death are the human condition—what does it mean to *recover* from them? Do you mean to dull one's heart? If there is to be any salvation—and I don't mean in the religious sense—if there is any salvation, it is in the experience of art."

"Art's just a temporary escape," Tony said. "Sorrow and grief are unavoidable emotions, sure, but the goal of therapy isn't to prevent them—it's to help manage them day to day."

Francis almost knocked over his wineglass. "*Manage?* Like one manages a baseball team? A sales force?"

"Manage depression and anxiety so they're not paralyzing or so intense that a person can't function."

Olivia tried to say something but Francis drowned her out.

"Is there a *schedule* for when grief is to cease? How many days and how many months? Where does this wisdom come from—is it given to you like Moses was given the Ten Commandments?"

"Patients bring us their own goals, Francis—we don't impose them. People *want* to change—people who aren't afraid to ask for help—"

"So those of us who do not bring our sorrows to the therapist are *afraid*—is that your contention?"

"Dad, calm down."

"I am calm. Tony is a grown man, Olivia, he can defend his profession. And if he cannot—"

"I don't need to *defend* clinical psychology," Tony said. "It's been a part of mainstream medicine for decades."

Marcia said to no one in particular, "Alex was complaining about missing a wrestling match tonight, but this is way more fun."

"I wasn't *complaining*, Mom."

Addy leaned forward to catch what her mother was telling Francis.

"Your only exposure to psychology is from literary critics who use Freud as a way to read fiction. Those aren't real psychologists."

"Do we get to order dessert?" Mindy asked.

"When everyone's done eating," Olivia snapped.

Mindy peered around the table. "Everyone's done."

"Francis isn't."

"Are you finished?" Marcia asked him.

"I would only add, Tony, that I have had exposure to psychological theories through Olivia. And they presuppose a worldview that we should all be smiling, sociable creatures, with no allowance for loss, not to mention differences in temperament, ambition, and a host of other qualities."

"Are you finished with your *meal?*" Marcia asked. "Do you want them to wrap it up?"

"It was very good, yes."

Olivia motioned to the waiter and pantomimed wrapping up the uneaten portions on Francis's plate. When the waiter got within earshot, Mindy asked for dessert menus.

Not knowing how else to defuse the situation, Addy began to tell Marcia, Alex, and Mindy about the MacDonalde case. It did grab their interest, and Addy answered the questions that didn't call for confidential information. Mindy said she didn't know lawyers did "fun stuff," and Marcia asked if it was contingency—did Addy's firm get to keep a percentage of the estate. Addy shook her head.

"Some crackpot sued your father because her kid's teeth only got straighter, not smaller," Marcia told Alex. "It was one of these contingency things. They wanted millions because they said the kid lost a modeling contract. The judge tossed it. And her eyes were crossed!"

Luckily, they broke up into separate conversations again, Olivia talking to Francis, and Marcia switching seats with Tony so he and Alex could talk football and she could talk to Mindy. Addy was just fine letting her thoughts wander.

She also was glad no one wanted to come back to the apartment with her and Francis afterward. Olivia and Tony decided to escort Marcia to Grand Central and then stroll around Midtown, and Alex and Mindy headed for the ferry. Francis didn't talk in the cab, and Addy wondered if he was out of sorts or just tired and maybe a little drunk. He was unsteady on his feet in the elevator but walked down the hall without any trouble.

When Addy took his coat to hang in the closet, he abruptly asked, "Did people have a good time?"

"I think so."

"Well, that's what's important." He headed toward the bathroom.

CHAPTER 46

A FEW WEEKS BACK, DURING his wanderings on Thanksgiving, Carson had noticed the bistro. It wasn't the first time he hadn't celebrated the holiday, not by a long shot—way back in sophomore year, he and Lucy had called it quits on going out. Hardly any restaurants were open, and besides, their attempts to imitate a normal family just seemed to highlight how theirs wasn't.

"*Every unhappy family is unhappy in its own way,*" Francis used to quote somebody or other, but in Carson's opinion, some were so unhappy, they didn't qualify as families. He had volunteered at a soup kitchen serving turkey dinners till the year a crazy guy mouthed off at him, which put the kibosh on that. The times he'd had the option of going home with a girlfriend, he'd always declined, pretending to be visiting his sister—showing up at a large family gathering implied more than he'd wanted to imply. Eventually he'd decided: pretend Thanksgiving is a Sunday, get some work done, and go for a stroll and explore somewhere you haven't been.

He and Lucy did have a long conversation the previous weekend. She was going to a potluck kind of thing with friends—her *National Enquirer* reading group, he called it.

Now it was almost mid-December, and the bistro window was decorated with a glittery Christmas tree on the pane and red and green lights hanging around the rim. Carson went inside.

The room was fairly dark except at the bar, maybe because of the light from the TV screen showing a football game, the sound off. The young men and women at the counter casually glanced his direction—enough simply dressed women to convince him the place wasn't gay.

He ordered a draft at the bar and brought it to a small table. Music came on from some speaker, a song he didn't recognize. That was usually the case; after Gloria, he rarely listened to the radio. She'd learned to play the piano as a kid and listened to every type of music imaginable—classical, jazz, show tunes. Jennifer had preferred rock. Was that his problem: he had no real tastes of his own and just adopted those of his current girlfriend? What did Addy like? The radio was never on when he went to dinner.

The song ended, and a voice nearby said, "You're lost in thought."

He turned. Two young women sat at an adjacent table. The blond was someone Lucy would call 'striking.' The brunette was pretty attractive too.

"Lost, yes, but don't credit me with thought."

"We're trying to guess what you are," the brunette said. "I think you're a trader. She says banking."

"Both wrong—just a lowly associate at a law firm."

After sipping from a highball glass, the blond said, "'Lowly' and 'lawyer' don't go together."

The brunette asked what firm he worked for, and he told them, and they nodded as though recognizing the name.

"So what do you two sirens do besides lure lawyers?"

"You sound quaint, like my voice teacher," the brunette said. "*Old* voice teacher. I don't mean I have a new one—I gave it up. But he was old. Ancient."

"We're in interior design," the blond said.

"And *please* don't ask if that's the same as interior decorating."

He was relieved to be spared a faux pas. "My name's Carson, but please don't ask if that's my last name too."

"I'm Signe," the blond said, "and that's Chelsea."

"Sidney? Is that with an *i* or two *y*'s?"

"*S-i-g-n-e*. It's Swedish."

"Can't you tell she's Swedish?" Chelsea asked.

"Swedish *descent*, Chel. I'm as American as you are."

"Hello, Signe and Chelsea."

"Please don't ask if I was named after the London neighborhood. Or the New York hotel."

"Can I ask if you'd each like another drink?"

"Only if you join us."

They were lively company. Chelsea was on the way to becoming drunk, but Signe acted normal. They compared San Francisco to their hometowns. Chelsea was from Idaho, "where there's nothing, nothing, nothing, unless your idea of fun is tractor pulls." Signe grew up in San Diego and could see moving back in the distant future, maybe when she retired. But both thought San Francisco had "more going for it," in Chelsea's words. "Just not enough straight men."

"How many do you need?" Carson asked.

"One apiece," Chelsea answered solemnly.

"We're picky shoppers," Signe said.

"I'm not," Chelsea said.

"I don't think Larry would like to hear that."

"Oh, Larry—he's a joke." Chelsea finished her drink in one long gulp.

"I guess she decided to break up with him tonight after all," Signe told Carson.

"I've broken up with better guys than Larry," Chelsea said. She signaled someone, who came over and took her empty glass. "One more of the same. You want another, Sig?"

"Not yet, thanks."

"Put it on my tab," Carson told the waiter.

"Signe turned down royalty," Chelsea said.

"He wasn't royalty."

"An earl is too royalty. And he was young—only thirty. Not much to look at, but rich as bejesus."

"He had a nice face. Not movie-star nice, but nice."

"So why did you reject the poor earl?" Carson asked.

Chelsea hiccupped. "He wasn't poor! She has her standards. He kept saying her biological clock is ticking. Like she doesn't know?"

Carson squinted at Signe. "You're not even twenty-five."

Signe pushed her hair back gracefully. "Smooth, nicely done. Twenty-seven, which I put at ten o'clock. Still time to party before the clock strikes midnight."

"Did you always want to be a lawyer?" Chelsea asked. "Like ever since you saw *Kill a Mockingbird*? Or were you a lit or soche major and went to law school because there was nothing else to do?"

"I thought of being a teacher until I realized they're paid near-starvation wages."

"Tenured professors do okay," Signe said. "What were you going to teach?"

"Not sure. Maybe junior high or even—"

Chelsea shook her head emphatically and hiccupped. "They don't do okay. Unless fancy private school. Like Signe went to."

"I didn't go to private school," Signe said.

"Like the earl went to," Chelsea said. "Duke of earl, duke, duke."

"I wanted to be a travel writer once," Signe told Carson. "Wouldn't that be nice: being paid to travel?"

"A restaurant critic," Chelsea said, "is better. No, a *wine* critic."

"You have to write articles. It's not just drinking."

Again, Chelsea shook her head. "Write five reviews, one for each star. Then all you do is fill in the name of the place and what you drank."

Signe smiled indulgently. "I don't think you'd get away with that."

"With what?" Chelsea asked.

"It's a difficult business to break into," Carson said.

He bantered with them for another half hour, a comforting, familiar game. When the women returned from the restroom, Chelsea picked her coat off the back of her chair, saying she had to meet someone, "but not Larry." Carson asked Signe if she'd like another drink, she said yes, and he went to the bar, getting himself a club soda.

They bantered less with Chelsea gone, but Carson had no trouble keeping up his end of the conversation, especially after Signe said her father had a twenty-eight foot that slept six. He was thinking of giving it to her when he bought a new one, provided she could find an affordable moorage.

"The slips are crazy expensive—I'll look farther south. My dad's berth costs half as much." She'd been sailing since she was seven.

"I'm a rank amateur," Carson said. "I've nosed around here a little about classes. Maybe next summer it'll work out."

By the time he returned from giving the bartender his card, Carson wasn't pretending when he told Signe they should go out sometime.

"Can you memorize my number?"

"Why take chances?" Carson pulled a pen from his pocket and wrote on a napkin.

"How can you live without taking chances?"

"*Unnecessary* chances."

BACK IN HIS APARTMENT, HANGING up his pants and jacket, Carson thought how for all her poise and clever repartee, Signe was a decent sort. Chelsea might be a bit of a flake, but people fell into friendships for a lot of reasons. And maybe Chelsea had more on the ball when she was sober. In any case, something about Signe's personality appealed to him. He'd call tomorrow. Would she want to go see the whaler that was docking next weekend? No, he would just suggest a movie and dinner for their first date. The partner on the cross-licensing contract told him about a place with a great view of the bay. It did feel good, Signe's seeming to like him, giving him her phone number. It had been a long time since his ego had gotten stroked.

He went to the kitchen and poured a glass of milk, a nighttime habit he'd picked up after the bastard had croaked—they'd rarely had milk in the house before then. He drank half the glass, threw some food in the cat's dish, and grabbed the remote to see if anything was on. Even if he didn't pay attention, the background noise was soothing.

Could he move on: Was it possible? He'd moved on from Gloria and Jennifer, and those relationships were the whole shebang. Just recently—the last phone call, in fact—Lucy had asked what he saw in Addy, and he had been at a loss for words. He could have described her face, her eyes, her body—all those things aroused him—but they were just incidentals. If she'd become disfigured in an accident, he'd still feel the same. What *was* the draw?

He picked up the last letter. Her mother and the new husband had visited for Francis's eightieth birthday, and that went *pretty much okay*. Her last MacDonalde interview was *really interesting*, but she couldn't say more—not yet, at least. The implication that she might have interviewed a real heir made him smile.

The Secured Transactions class is really hard; I'm only taking it for the bar. It's amazing you passed without a review course. I'm not going to risk it.

Carson had torn open the envelope with the bar association insignia, glimpsed the *Congratulations*, and then tried calling her while unfolding the letter. But there was no answer by the third ring, so he'd hung up to avoid getting Francis. He would've called his sister, but she was on another one of her getaways with His Honor.

Some variety show was on the TV, and a group of children were singing. Their faces looked so sweet and earnest.

On the side of a hill in the deep forest green.

The cat rubbed against Carson's leg, and he reached down to pet him.

CHAPTER 47

"FRANCIS WALLACE'S GRANDDAUGHTER!" SAM WAVED from the far cashier's line. There were easily fifty people between them, the crowd of holiday shoppers holding stacks of books, board games, journals, calendars. That Addy heard him was amazing, given the commotion and "Winter Wonderland" playing in the background.

She waved back. After paying, she took the bag of books to a spot by the door and waited.

"Abby, right?"

"Addy."

Together they went outside. The snow had stopped, a light powder trimming the street signs and building ledges. The pavement looked slick and shiny, like after a rain.

"Looks like you just bought out the place. What does Francis Wallace's granddaughter read?" Sam peered into the bag. "*Treasure Island*, *Kidnapped*. Don't tell me you're married with kids?"

"No. I babysit for the neighbors."

"Look, I've got to get down to the village in half an hour but have time for a quick cup of coffee. Would you? My treat?"

"You don't have to treat."

"My pleasure. I wanted to call you, but you said your number was unlisted."

"It's not unlisted, just in Francis's name."

"Damn, so all this time—"

The light changed, and they hurried across the intersection.

THE FIRST WORDS OUT OF Francis's mouth when she came into the living room were "I was worried I would be entertaining Robert by myself."

"Sorry. I ran into Sam—the guy at Ellis Island, the one who's heard of you? We had coffee, and I invited him to dinner next Friday. Is that okay? He can't Saturday—has to go up to New Haven."

"I have no plans." The worry left his face.

She saw that the porcelain dishes and other fragile things had been put on the upper shelves. She moved back the chairs and ottoman to make space for Robert's blanket.

"WE'RE GOING TO START *TREASURE Island* today," she told Robert. "It's by the same author who wrote the shadow poem. It might be confusing at first—people's names and places—but you'll catch on."

Francis began, "*Treasure Island, Part One: The Old Buccaneer. The Old Sea-dog at the Admiral Benbow.*" After a few pages, he handed the book to Addy.

She first explained words like 'capstan' and 'sailing before the mast' and a few idioms, and, hoping it would help Robert's comprehension, used different voices for the different characters. His gaze never wavered, even when the vocabulary was difficult. At the Black Dog part, though, he was ready for a nap. She gave him the pillow and helped arrange the blanket over his shoulders.

JOE ASKED HER TO COME in the week after Christmas to help out on some clerical stuff for the two tax attorneys, and Addy was happy to— the paycheck would be nice. He also said the Scottish court had ruled to the effect that the estate attorneys—and hence Engel—had satisfied their obligation to publish notice of Violet's will, so presumably no more claims would be coming in. Brittany and Brad were "dropping claimants like bird shot," and Simon detected a forgery "with his own two eyes, no five-hundred-dollar-an-hour document examiner." It was on a change-of-name form in Illinois, and "the idiot didn't realize the date he forged for the clerk was a Sunday. Should've consulted a calendar before he went to all that trouble."

The Drecker firm meanwhile had retrieved a slew of society pages from Charleston newspapers mentioning Sarah Grey-Davison—she had attended this benefit or concert or that theater or function. A few of the articles also mentioned Helen Grey-Davison or Helen Hill Grey-Davison, and one long list of guests at some horse-club banquet in 1937 mentioned Mary Hill, *guest of the GreyDavisons*. There were no photos, unfortunately. Bruce Grey-Davison had shipped a carton from his storage locker along with a letter apologizing that he hadn't had time to sort through the papers himself, but the only item even remotely relevant was board-meeting minutes at the Hollis Textiles Company saying James Grey-Davison Jr. was among the directors voting against hiring scab labor during a strike. Joe was furious that "Mr. Hoity-Toity thinks we have nothing better to do than pore through his garbage."

ADDY GOT A HOLIDAY CARD from Carson saying he was *drowning in grunt work for the M & A crowd* and couldn't write more.

CHAPTER 48

FOR THE BETTER PART OF the morning, I sat at my computer struggling with what should have been a relatively simple problem: When is renunciation an act of *atonement* and when is renunciation simply an act of *obedience to duty*? Of course, renunciation also can be an act of *love and heroism*, as it was for Sydney Carton, and of *impulse*, as it was, ultimately, for Eustacia. But I was trying to tease out the difference between Sue Bridehead and Isabel Archer, two young women returning to unhappy marriages. The *impressions* their renunciations created, and the characters themselves, were far from identical, but I was having difficulty pinpointing how and why. So it was with no small amount of relief that I heard the telephone ring and interrupt my unprofitable cogitations.

"I assumed it was you, my dear. Unfortunately, Adelaide has gone into Engel Klein's offices, so you are stuck speaking to me only. But tell me: How was your trip to Portland?"

"A lot of fun. Rhoda and Pat took us to a jazz club." Olivia sounded quite chipper.

"I have doings to report as well. Not quite on a par with all your trips hither and yon, but excitement in our own homebound way. You will recall my mentioning last summer how a young man Adelaide met on the ferry had heard of me?"

"The English-literature student?"

"Yes. She ran into him recently at Barnes & Noble and invited him to dinner. What a delightful evening we passed! He graduated with a bachelor of arts from Yale and currently is assisting in the making of a documentary film about Lithuanians fleeing the Soviet Union in the forties. Next year he plans to apply to graduate schools to pursue his PhD in literature. And he is Adelaide's own age—almost to the month!"

"What's his name?"

"Sam Rosen—possibly shortened from Samuel. Imagine my pleasure at a dinner table conversation about Henry James and George Eliot, with a dash of Hardy. A delight, Olivia, a delight. Do you know, he had planned to write his senior paper on Henry James! He had planned to contrast James's views of European and American families."

"So close to your own dissertation!"

"His ideas were quite insightful—I could hardly disagree with any point he made—not without repudiating my own publications. Oh, we had quite a discussion—James, George Eliot, Jane Austen, Dickens, the Brontës. I talked about my own trajectory in literature. As you will recall, it began with the adventure stories, and then in my high school years—"

"Your Jude phase."

"Yes, my Jude phase—although not exclusively Jude: Copperfield, Lord Jim, and later Robert Jordan, Proust, even Stephen Dedalus played a role in my self-discovery journeys. But James ushered in my love affair with language. The young man, Sam, he asked what phase ensued: what literature did I come to love in *recent* years. Such a perceptive question—it caught me quite off guard, and I had to ponder a bit. I find myself drawn to the novels I enjoyed as a young adult, I told him, those where stories and character take precedence over style. Perhaps it is part of the aging process, the regression, and soon I will be paging through *Tom Brown's School Days*."

"You said he *planned* to write on James—what did he end up writing on?"

"Quite an interesting topic: violence in eighteenth- and nineteenth-century novels. His thesis was that certain writers, Jane Austen and Henry James among them, eschewed violent crime in much of their work because they wanted to focus on certain aspects of refined society and people among whom violence was a rarity. For this 'aesthetic'—the word he used—violence smacked of sensationalism. Dickens, of course, never shunned the sensational or the violent; nor did Conrad or Melville. But they were very different kinds of writers. Sam's point was that for most of us who are not soldiers or living in slums, violence is an aberrant event, perhaps a news item—"

"What was Addy's reaction—did she—"

"My dear, the poor girl understood she was trapped between two literature aficionados and would have trouble getting a word in edgewise."

"I just meant—"

"You would have loved it, Olivia, participating in our discussion. He had nothing good to say about those two deconstructionists—the Harvard fellow and the other—remember, the pair I used to call Tweedledum and Tweedledee?"

"I remember Mom saying your editor told you to tone it down."

"He was quite right, my editor, and the version that ultimately went to the printers was a little lamb compared to my earlier leonine drafts."

"Dad, did Addy have a good time?"

"Certainly. She is not the kind of person to resent being the quiet listener on occasion. When the young man comes again, I will make a point of introducing topics on which she is comfortable opining."

"Isn't she going to see him on her own?"

"I would expect so. But he lives in New Haven and only comes to the city on occasion."

Olivia's cheerful tone returned. "Well, speaking of publications, they accepted my paper on father-figure antagonists. I thanked you for reviewing the manuscript, so you'll get to see your name in print again, although in a footnote."

"I do not need to see my name in print. Congratulations. Do let me know which issue, and I will send away for a copy. I have cancelled all but three of my old subscriptions as I do not seem to have as much time for reading."

The remainder of the conversation with my elder daughter was pleasant even after we moved on to more routine subjects. Mindy was carrying twins; Elliot's new girlfriend was covered in tattoos. Olivia was visiting Taos in two weeks to see Michael and Patty and little Noah, who was crawling everywhere.

After hanging up, I attempted to return to the renunciation conundrum but found myself hearkening back to some of my earlier published articles and the withering sarcasm I had been fond of employing in the drafts. Certainly those clever put-downs flavored the writing process, but how many bridges I would have burned had I not benefited from the careful oversight and excisions of journal editors, as well as Marjorie's admonitions!

Of course, Olivia had every right to be proud—the journal

publishing her father-figures essay was a scholarly one. Truth be told, however, the piece was not among her most insightful. She had carefully avoided much of the jargon of psychology but not the concepts. Rochester and Osmond as father figures in the minds of the women who loved them, for example: pure balderdash! Knightly was the only plausible example fitting her hypothesis, and even then, such psychological theorizing was a silly diversion from the literary issues that mattered.

Yes, it had been a delightful dinner. That the young man was head-and-shoulders above Carson could not be gainsaid. And Adelaide put more attention into her appearance, it seemed to me—although she wore dungarees, not the nicer slacks she typically wore to Engel Klein. At least the dungarees looked brand-new. And the young man wore dungarees—the uniform of youth, I supposed—along with an olive-green corduroy jacket that took me back, took me back, indeed, tweed and corduroy having been the uniforms of academia in *my* day. Yet the casual informality of Sam and Adelaide had an appeal I was beginning to appreciate. In the 1960s, the adoption of dungarees as standard college attire had come as something of a shock to those of us who had been happy to leave behind the garb of the farm.

ALAS, BY THE END OF February, Sam had been able to come to dinner on only one additional occasion; his documentary film work kept him tethered to New Haven.

But at the second dinner he again was impressive, his knowledge wide-ranging. And in a short foray into literature, he was able to meet me at my level, so to speak, able to converse about certain sophisticated literary ideas so esoteric that few people were aware of them outside a small set of professors with whom I had sparred in literary journals. Yet mindful of Olivia's concerns, I steered the discussion to other issues so as not to leave my granddaughter a mere spectator.

The young man did escort Adelaide to a production of *Lear.* I was asleep when he brought her home, but he was kind enough to come upstairs and leave a short note reassuring me I would not have liked the directorial choices. Imagine: the fool played in blackface and Gloucester wearing a miter!

The remainder of winter did not live up to its early promise. Dreary weather and long nights, faltering progress on my opus, Adelaide's law classes lacking the novelty of her early ones—it was a winter of discontent. Joe was "breathing down everyone's necks" about completing the MacDonalde case, and although most claims had been relegated to the Graveyard, Grey-Davison and others dangled in Limbo, frustrating the Scottish solicitors.

And every few weeks, another envelope bearing Carson's return address arrived in the mail. Either Adelaide disposed of the letters or stowed them somewhere not easily accessible—I preferred to think the former. Only one did she leave in the drawer, and it contained a photograph of him in front of an old sailing ship. The caption, in his clear hand, read *The Ferdinand Aloysius docking in SF 02-22-95*. A short note was enclosed.

Three-mast square rigger from late 1800s. 6 sails to a mast, look at the size of them! Cannery ship, in spring took workers to Alaska and brought them (and cans of salmon) back to SF before cold weather. I guess your Seattle wasn't ready yet to compete in intn'l seafood trade. You would've loved guide's stories, squalls, cyclones, broken masts.

Wishful thinking, I suspected: they were stories *he* loved. Not once had I heard Adelaide express an interest in what might be termed 'adventure tales.' *Cultural* adventures—something along the lines of E. M. Forster—would be more to her liking.

I returned to the living room windows and gazed into the night. The river was a panoply of colored incandescence: glowing neon signs in yellow, blue, green, purple. The sky, an admixture of reflections and refractions, forged a distinctly different palette from that of southern Indiana—there, a pallor after dark presaged snow, presaged the stasis and hibernation of long winter months. Here, night played through all seasons in a major key, not a minor. Yet even bright lights could not wholly banish something forlorn.

CHAPTER 49

PLOP! THE MAGAZINE LANDED LOUDLY on the glass table. The man continued reading.

He wouldn't complain, Lucy knew, if she picked up the briefs he was done with—they were 'public records'—but they were boring, even the ones in murder cases. Was the concealment of exculpatory evidence harmless error? Did the admission of lay opinion violate Rule blah-blah-blah? Defendant's Motion for a New Trial, State's Countermotion blah-blah-blah.

He cared way too much, in her opinion, about the appeals court reversing him. "They can't fire you," she'd once reminded him. "And every judge gets reversed sometimes—you said so yourself."

She sat with her legs stretched out on the sofa—if she pointed her toes, she could poke him in the thigh with the red fuzzy socks Carson had sent for her birthday. Instead, she asked, "When do you have to be back?"

"The hearing is at two. What's on your calendar?"

"Just my salon appointment. But the weekend you'll be having fun at your son's wedding, I'm taking Carson's ex to lunch."

"You didn't tell me she lives here." His eyes remained on the brief.

"She doesn't—New York. She agreed to meet me in Norwalk."

"You stayed friends?"

"We never met."

Now he turned to look at her. "Then why—you said ex, right?"

"Yes, ex. Carson's still hung up on her, but he's not—what did you call your sister? A glutton for punishment. He's the opposite—hates rejection." She lowered her feet to the floor and scooted over and nestled against his shoulder. "So if he's still into her, it means she's holding on to him. Is she saying 'maybe' instead of 'no'? Or 'just wait a little longer'? I want her to either shit or get off the pot."

"So he asked you—"

"He didn't ask me to do anything. I'll tell him afterward."

She'd snuggled so close, he had to crane his neck back to look at her. "You think that's wise: interfering?"

"We look out for each other."

After some moments, he leaned over and kissed her hair. "How will you accomplish this, my beautiful schemer?"

"I have to find out why she's holding on. Does she think he's rich and can't bring herself to say no to all that moolah? I'll set her straight."

"He's a lawyer in a large firm—he can become rich. The starting salaries these days—my God, it took me years to pull in that much—years after making partner!"

"I'm not sure it's the money. Maybe she just likes the attention of a good-looking guy but thinks he's not up to the standards of her snooty family."

"And how will you convince her he is?"

She ran her hand along the inside of the man's thigh. "That's not my goal. If she's stuck-up, the hell with her."

He arrested her hand. "So you plan to get her off the pot—how?"

"By letting her know his lovely family tree."

"That could make her like him more. For some people, pity is an aphrodisiac."

"If it is, it is—I just want her to decide either way."

Again, the man leaned over and kissed her hair, his hand still gripping hers. "Carson's lucky to have such a caring sister."

"Like I said, we have each other's backs." She was silent a moment. "We see brothers and sisters fight and think they're stupid. The one good thing our miserable childhood taught us."

His hand loosened its grip, and his fingers stroked hers.

"And if nothing else, I'll pump her for details on the MacDonalde case."

"The what?"

"I told you—the Scottish lady who croaked and left behind fifty mil. Carson's ex works for the firm trying to find the heirs."

The man laughed. "*That's* why you want to meet her."

Instantly, Lucy's fingers became mobile. "You're entitled to your opinion."

"Hey—I've got to go soon. And I'm not as young as you. We can't all—"

"Not the impression I'm getting."

CHAPTER 50

"I'M SENDING YOU TO NEW Mexico. Brad's up to his neck in documents from some clown in British *Columbia*, for Chrissake. Simon's following up a lead on that Grey-Davison—he's one of yours, right? His attorney wrote directly to the Scots, some mishegoss. Brittany's with the Idaho clan, and Dan's sifting crap from Malcolm MacDonald, smuggled out of Paris when the Nazis invaded. I'm not making this up!"

"When do you want me to go?" Addy wondered if she'd have to postpone the Norwalk trip.

Joe waved a batch of papers. "Takes me half the day to go through the time sheets, write off charges that would send the Scots through the roof. You think I can bill *my* time for that? Ha! But they want the Canadian clown vetted, *and* the Idaho yokels, *and* the refugee from Hitler—sure they do, but not pay for it. Did I ever *say* pro bono? Now I'm supposed to go ahead with the Lincoln—no, she's in Taos—Mary Agnes something. Where's the sheet? Here, Mary Agnes Bettles. Says she's Mary's granddaughter. A real estate agent. A real estate agent, but can she produce a deed or title search with the original spelling?"

"One of my brothers lives in Taos. When's she available?"

"Terrific—have him put you up. Saving those misers some dough might keep them from taking it out on us when the trip's a total bust. Here's the genealogy."

The page contained a horizontal line at the top connecting Mary Agnes MacDonalde to a Calvin Twist. Three children were listed beneath them: Abraham B., Enoch I., and Josephine C. Twist. Josephine was the only one who married; she and a Walter Bettles had one child, Mary Agnes.

"Did she send any documents?"

"Not yet. Gave some song and dance about them being up in Nebraska—she's just down in Taos temporarily, 'opening the office.' The date's written there somewhere."

BEFORE LEAVING ENGEL, ADDY SKIMMED the Bettles questionnaire responses. Mary MacDonalde supposedly had lived somewhere in rural Texas and then moved to Houston with her daughter, Josephine Twist. Where did Mary's sons Abraham and Enoch go? What happened to Brian?

The thought of visiting Michael and Patty cheered Addy—she'd finally get to see her nephew. With any luck, Francis wouldn't be too stressed out. After her mother's visit in November, he'd joked that Addy should go away for a few days so he could prove he was fine on his own. "It will be Exhibit A against your mother's next campaign." But lately, anything out of the ordinary rattled him. She'd been procrastinating telling him about lunch with Lucy.

"GREAT—PERFECT TIMING FOR NOAH'S first birthday party," Michael said. "I'm driving a cab, so it's no big deal to get you at the airport and take you around. Without running the meter."

"The client will pay for it."

"I'll run the meter."

Francis came into the kitchen just as Addy hung up. He stood behind his chair, leaning on the back, one of the ways he tried to spend less time sitting. She took their cups from the dish rack.

"Joe wants me to do an interview in Taos. I just called Michael. I'll stay an extra day so I can spend some time with them."

"When is this to occur? How long will you be gone?"

"I'll leave a week from Sunday and come back that Tuesday night. Do you want me to hire someone?"

"No, no. My ankle is fine." He shuddered. "They might send Procrustes again. But will you be gone on a Thursday?"

"No, like I said: from a Sunday to Tuesday night."

"And who is the claimant?"

"A real estate agent—says she's Mary's granddaughter." The kettle whistled, and Addy turned off the burner and poured the water, telling Francis the line of descent.

He continued standing, his palms resting on the top of the chair back. Despite age and ailments, his arms and hands still retained a lot of muscle. Was it from genetics or all the hard labor in childhood?

Carson was in good shape from swimming. The time the subway jerked her into him, she could smell the chlorine.

"By the way: I'm going up to Connecticut Saturday, just for the day—actually, just for lunch."

His smile surprised her. "A long way to travel for a meal, my dear! You can't find anything in the city to suit your palate? Or even Westchester? You have become quite the fussy gourmet. Where will you be trundling off to?"

"Norwalk. Carson's sister, Lucy, she asked if I'd meet her there."

Slowly Francis came around the chair and sat. "Carson's sister? Did he mention she would be calling?"

"No, I haven't heard from him in a while." Addy brought Francis's cup to the table.

A moment passed before he said, "I wonder if he plans to move back east."

"His last letter was really positive about San Francisco."

"Perhaps the job is not up to his expectations?"

Addy gently dunked her own tea bag. "I was wondering if he's sick."

"Has he mentioned anything to warrant such a concern?"

"No, but it's been a while, and Lucy seems eager to do this."

Neither spoke again until Addy sat too. Watching her face, Francis said, "You do understand that the invitation is *his* idea?"

"No—she said she wasn't telling him she'd invited me."

Francis cupped his hands around the mug. "Perhaps he asked her to say that. At the very least, she must know he would be *pleased* at the two of you getting together."

Addy silently watched the steam rise.

"Norwalk is quite an expedition," Francis continued. "Over an hour by train, if I am not mistaken—even on an express. How long did it take us, the time we went up to Marcia's? You would be well within your rights, so to speak, to decline the invitation because of the imposition on your time. After a few demurrals of that nature, she may 'get the hint,' as your grandmother used to say. Or at the very least, she could travel down here."

"She lives in Hartford, so it's kind of a compromise."

"She gave no reason at all for the meeting?"

"She just asked to take me to lunch in Norwalk, and I said yes."

"And you have no *urge* to decline? Well, I suppose you must feel some curiosity as to her motive. But with all your schoolwork and—"

"I'll get some done on the train each way."

He looked off at the wall calendar. This month's picture was a Hopper farmhouse. "The sister's invitation puts me in mind of stratagems employed by various characters—literary characters—to effectuate a liaison that was not in one of the parties' best interests. I am thinking primarily of *Portrait of a Lady*, in which the plotting was conducted by a suitor and his confederate—not the suitor's sister in that case but a close female friend. The heroine, Isabel, despite great intelligence and admirable inclinations, was no match for their intrigues." Addy drank her tea.

"Hardy's characters scheme but in more rudimentary fashion. Arabella certainly entraps Jude, and Eustacia—it must be admitted—keeps Wildeve on a short leash while having no serious interest in him as a lover. Yet James's characters more fittingly fit the paradigm of the puppeteer, the carefully manipulative and—yes, even Dr. Sloper would fit the mold."

"I probably should get some studying done." Addy rose and picked up her cup.

"My point, again, is that most of the matrimonial scheming in literature did not involve an accomplice. Even Becky Sharp—perhaps the *personification* of matrimonial scheming, although a far more sympathetic character than the Edith Wharton—"

"I'll probably order takeout later, if that's okay."

"And before you bring out your feminist artillery, I fully concede that the majority of instances of cruel seduction were perpetrated by men. The terms 'Lothario' and 'Don Juan' and 'Casanova' attest to this. Although it is difficult to assign *all* blame to Wickham and *none* to Lydia. Yes, yes, takeout is fine."

CHAPTER 51

CLOUDS HUNG LOW AND BROODING, and fog clung to the water's surface. The opaque gray barrier seemed impenetrable, composed of something denser than vapor—a ship would have to use its horn and lights and cut the engines. A dog ran past, chasing something invisible. Just ahead in the sand lay a hypodermic. Carson picked it up by the plunger, scanning the paths for a garbage bin. Not seeing one, he found a makeshift barbecue pit and pressed the syringe into the ground needledown, his best guess for a spot barefooted children wouldn't go. It was a shame you had to worry about things like that.

He stood where the sand changed color and stared at the grayness. The summer mists in Hammonasset were different—the creamy film hovering above the yacht masts could burn off in a minute. He and Lucy had liked to sit on the edge of the pier, legs dangling, waiting for the sun to blaze and make their goose bumps vanish. The water twinkled and farther out became a beautiful deep blue. White mainsails and jibs would glide by like the sunlight was nothing special.

Here, though, the long slate waves moved like dull planks. The wind picked up in fits and starts, and a page of newspaper rose and descended, billowing and collapsing. A jogger knelt and tied her shoe. Two homeless types sat on the rocks smoking. Dog walkers huddled together. An elderly woman trekking against the wind held on to her kerchief with both hands.

The scene mirrored his own mood, a gray weight, a smothering, a loss of air. He began to walk slowly, so he could concentrate. Guilt—it was always guilt. But about what? What had he done? Dr. Kim had taught him the technique of conjuring up images, and Carson ran a mental tape of the people he might feel guilty about, waiting for that indescribable click of recognition.

It didn't take long. Lucy—it was Lucy. He hadn't called for weeks. She'd even left a message with his secretary—*Nothing important, just want to say hi*—something she wouldn't have done if she hadn't tried reaching him multiple times. He did leave a return message at her apartment, at an hour he assumed she'd be out. "Drowning at work."

Which was true. But that wasn't the reason. The reason needed no Dr. Kim techniques: he was keeping Signe a secret.

Why? Their pact, made under the covers twenty years ago, was kind of silly today. And they'd never compulsively told each other everything anyway—when he went to college and Lucy got her own place, weeks might go by without their talking. She didn't mention every guy she dated; he didn't mention every girl. His sessions with Dr. Kim rarely came up, even though she was the one who'd pushed him to go.

So why was he reluctant to mention Signe? The conversation was easy to predict. 'Practically every weekend at her place? You got serious fast.' Signe loved to sail, he'd say, and try new restaurants, nightclubs, travel—she had carpe diem to the hilt. A sense of humor. "Sounds like all the specs," Lucy had said about Jennifer. And Gloria. But look how those had turned out. Still, his sister would be glad to hear about Signe.

And that was the problem. He didn't *want* her to be glad. Sure, it would be for his sake, but that didn't make it go down easier. *Dr. Kim: help me figure this out.*

Signe definitely wanted kids. Getting back from the party at her friend's gallery—it must've been three in the morning—and sitting on the sofa with their brandy snifters, they'd talked till dawn. He'd told her some things about his rotten childhood, and she'd joked she was "*spoiled* rotten." A car at sixteen—though she'd had to earn her own gas money. Sailing lessons, piano, ballet—"I was a total *oaf* in a tutu." Her parents never punished her for the high school high jinks, and as for the pranks they pulled at Chi Omega—"we should've been prosecuted." She'd even smuggled a climbing harness and suction-cup lifters into a sixty-story building so her friend could scale it.

"But I did eventually grow up." And then came the earl. Visiting his family at their ski lodge in Switzerland and the Mediterranean villa "taught me what to hope for." A small cottage in Austria or Switzerland, and maybe another somewhere tropical or on the Mediterranean—houses that didn't have to be luxurious but where you could vacation without scrambling to make reservations. Places that would give the kids great memories. And they'd be multilingual—the earl's family spoke fluent English, French, and German.

Carson had reminisced about the summer of outings with the

Hendersons, the couple's graciousness and generosity, the freedom of being on the water. He couldn't remember how, but the conversation wound around to Lucy.

"I dated a married man," Signe'd said. "She'll snap out of it. Judging from the picture, she's got plenty of bees buzzing around, and they can't *all* be taken."

The judge was actually a huge step up from the Cadillac dealer Lucy had dumped because he was "getting too friendly with slick leather jackets."

Signe wasn't pressuring Carson to move in—she, too, believed that paying separate rents was the price of avoiding messy breakups. But San Francisco wasn't cheap, and her father was nearing retirement. "I *want* to cut the umbilical cord. I'm not as spoiled as you think."

Her hips did that emphatic back-and-forth to the kitchen. "I don't think you're spoiled," he'd called after her. What he really thought was that everyone should be spoiled.

A sailboat burst through the gray, easily a forty-footer, the guy at the tiller probably surprised to be so close to shore. The evening of their first sail with the Hendersons, after they'd returned and Mr. H. taught him how to make a clove hitch and bowline knot, Carson and Lucy had sat on a low wall in the parking lot waiting for their parents. Twilight had settled in, and the sky was a deep dark blue, a beautiful fairy-tale color. Moths fluttered around the streetlight above. The long day had left him feeling tired but happy—they'd eaten fried clams at a dockside restaurant and sandwiches on the boat and had had ice cream from the little freezer.

How come the Henderson kids got those parents, he'd asked Lucy, and they got Louise and *him*? Was God punishing them?

"No, His plan is to give us good stuff when we're older. Maybe we'll be millionaires."

His young imagination had immediately filled with images of illustrations—probably from books like "Cinderella" and "Sleeping Beauty"—palaces and white coaches drawn by horses, kind servants in livery and powdered wigs, sumptuous feasts. A universe away from the darkening parking lot where the engines were starting up and headlights coming on and the sounds of tires crackling on bits of gravel as the cars drove off. Carson never knew if he was more afraid of being left there all night or of his parents returning to fetch them.

Sometime after their father died, Lucy had let on she didn't believe in God. Who you got for your family was luck, she had said, good or lousy. But that was just your family. 'Carpe diem' meant that you could make your own future if you worked hard. But you had to want it badly enough. He did, he really did.

A decade and a half later, here he was, in a lovely city on the water, in a decent-paying job, contemplating proposing to a woman "with all the specs." He'd pulled himself out of dungeons, out of terror and pain and hopelessness. This one should be a piece of cake. He climbed to the high, dry sand and headed home.

THE CAT JUMPED DOWN FROM the ledge and went to its dish. Carson spent several minutes staring out at the ocean. *You have only yourself to blame. She never gave you one shred of encouragement.*

An hour at the computer, and he had little more than a paragraph to show for it.

Addy, you know I've treasured knowing you, and that's an understatement. But our correspondence has to end. The thing is, I've started seeing someone. What choice do I have? I won't say I'm over you. But stopping all communication is the only way I can see to get there. I'm not thinking of myself only. It's to be fair to her, to give her a fighting chance. I guess that old Norwalk high-society upbringing is hard to shake. Take care of yourself.

He addressed the envelope carefully. Francis had once complimented his penmanship—maybe the only nice thing the strange old coot had ever said to him. Still, Carson had loved those evenings at the dining room table—the three of them spinning Mary MacDonalde scenarios, Francis going into long digressions about Jude or Eustacia or growing up on a farm. If nothing else, the guy was predictable.

Carson placed the envelope on the small blue bookcase, which he'd found by a fire hydrant, lugged home, cleaned, and painted, hoping nobody from his office had seen him take it. He wouldn't mail the letter just yet. Maybe in a week or two, when his resolve had had a chance to gel. Carpe diem wasn't the only thing Lucy had taught him. No, she was a mine of survival tactics—she should write a book. Another was patience. Contradictory principles, patience and carpe diem. A third one was handy right now: losing yourself in work. It didn't hurt that the partners were dumping it on like the day had thirty hours.

CHAPTER 52

LUCY RECOGNIZED ADDY THE SECOND she stepped off the train. They wouldn't go anywhere fancy for lunch, not with Ms. Cohn dressed in jeans and some sort of hiking boots and lugging a backpack. Maybe the place out on Route 7. The photo definitely showed her to advantage. She wasn't ugly, just nothing to boast about. Were the jeans a statement she was above them? Or, as Carson liked to say, just "the insouciance of the true upper class"? The judge had looked surprised when Lucy'd used the phrase. At least the girl was respectful enough not to wear jeans with holes.

"Addy? Thought so. Carson sent me this."

"Hi. That was taken in Greenport."

"You haven't aged much." Lucy slipped the photo back in her purse. "The car's there. I know a restaurant with a varied menu. On the way, I'll show you where Carson and I grew up." In the car, she turned the key sharply in the ignition and glanced in the rearview mirror. "Have you heard from him lately?"

"No."

"I haven't for about a *month*. Said he'd been pulled into some big trial and is up to his ears in motions. The last we talked—for two minutes, max—he was about to go to work on a *Sunday morning*. They run their associates ragged—the new ones anyway. Of course, he's used to working seven days a week. Macy's made him come in four hours on Saturday and four on Sunday. Instead of letting him work a full eight one or the other. That was in Luggage—his supervisor was a jerk. Men's Casual treated him better."

Cruising slowly, one hand on the wheel, Lucy pointed out the drugstore where their mother used to shoplift, the bus stop where a friend's older sister was raped, the junior high, the shoe repair that was a front for something, though they never figured out what. The high school walls were covered in graffiti. "Did he tell you about elementary school?"

"He mentioned a Miss Andrews' class."

"I don't remember all the teachers' names. We were only two

years apart, but they rarely lasted that long, not in *our* school. Except Mr. Eigler. Yes, Mr. Eigler stuck around. Then stuck around FCI Danbury for five years—the state pen. Couldn't paw any twelve-year-olds there—*any* girls, for that matter—it used to be all men. Lucky for me I had Miss Wheeler for sixth. Her only sin was gin. Not the card game."

Lucy turned off the commercial two-lane and up a narrow street of old brick apartment buildings. Along the curb, garbage overflowed the cans and plastic bags. A red five-pointed star was spray-painted on the side of a car; the back windshield of another was covered in duct tape. Pulling into a space by an alley, she pointed to the building ahead. "That was home sweet home. We had the back basement apartment. Only the kitchen got daylight." The street-level windows were covered by metal grilles. Shards of brown and green glass speckled the sidewalk.

"Has the neighborhood changed much?"

"Blacks moved in and made it worse." The judge would have raked her over the coals if he'd heard her say that, though she'd once explained her statements never meant *all* Black people. Dannie was one of her best friends, and Lucy had tried setting her and Carson up. "It was pretty bad when it was poor whites—Irish, Italians, a couple of German families, and mongrels like us. Then came the Puerto Ricans and Jamaicans. That was the wino stoop, rain or shine. There's where the big dumpster used to be—Carson would climb in and get the returnable bottles. And the liquor store our father kept in the black. See that gutter? Carson and another kid used to trap rats there. Our version of soccer."

Lucy peeled out from the curb and drove to the intersection, then turned and followed the road through better neighborhoods.

At a red light, Addy asked, "Your mother's in Florida?"

"Near Tallahassee."

"Do you go down there often?"

"Carson never told you about Louise and our father?"

"Not really. Just that he died when Carson was ten, I think?"

"I'll tell you during lunch. And I brought along a class photo."

CHAPTER 53

FOR PERHAPS THE TENTH TIME, I peered at my watch. In another hour or so I should have the answer. Of course the question was not merely whether Carson would be returning to New York but, more importantly, how Adelaide would react to such an event. Could she not see that Sam was far superior, perhaps in terms of intellect, undoubtedly in terms of character? What a shame his documentary work kept him in New Haven.

But the day had proved productive. I concluded my rereading of *The Mayor of Casterbridge*, impressed with Hardy's ability to have me care deeply about a character quite different from myself. Henchard was impetuous, and his ambitions were directed to the public sphere: he rose to a mayoralty, acquired riches far exceeding those of his neighbors, and kept a comely mistress. *I*, in contrast, was a dutiful scholar and faithful husband who lived comfortably but simply. Yet I came to care more deeply about him than for the enterprising young Scotsman he befriended. The most I would say on behalf of Farfrae, often heralded as the hero of the work, was that he was Mary MacDonalde–like in enthusiasm for *his* adopted home.

Finally hearing a key in the lock, I picked up a journal to hold as if I were reading. "How did the trip go?" I called out.

"Okay, I guess." Adelaide came into the room and went to the windows. "Lucy drove me around the neighborhood where they grew up."

"Did she offer any explanation for the invitation? *Was* it at Carson's behest, do you suspect?"

"No. No, it wasn't. She told me things I doubt he'd want me to know."

"Really?" My imagination seized on a host of possibilities. Did Carson have a girlfriend—a romantic interest other than Adelaide? Several? Was he married—had he been married all the time they were dating? My curiosity could not be tamped. "What, for instance?"

She kept her back to me. "They were very poor growing up—on food stamps, school lunches. Their father had trouble holding a job."

Easily a full twenty seconds elapsed before I could formulate a response. "This *is* a surprise. You mean that all his talk about high society was nonsense and lies?"

She nodded.

"But why—why do such a thing?"

"He left out other things too."

With almost superhuman effort, I held off on further questioning and said merely, "This must affect your friendship, and not in a positive way." I watched Adelaide's head for a nod or some sign of assent—even a reluctant one. "I *feared* he might be a fortune-hunter."

"He knows I'm not rich." Now she turned partly toward me and picked up the scrimshaw from the side table, rotating it in her hand as though it were unfamiliar.

"Nothing to suggest he is ill—as you feared? Or planning for some reason to return to New York?"

"No. She hasn't heard from him for a while either. He's helping out on some big trial."

Adelaide disappeared in the direction of her room. The thought occurred to me that Lucy's motive may have been to undo whatever damage her brother had caused. To 'clean up after him,' one might say. Such an odd pairing, the sister and brother—a Good Samaritan and a scoundrel, a truth-sayer and falsifier. If there was poetry in his lies, I did not see it.

THE FOLLOWING WEEK A HORRIFIC event transpired that occluded all other concerns: madmen had set off a bomb in Oklahoma City, killing over a hundred people, including a number of children. Olivia telephoned that evening, expressing to me not only her sorrow at the tragedy but her worry that the senselessness of the deaths might prove especially painful for her daughter. I was able to reassure her that Adelaide, while saddened, showed no signs of excessive distress. And her travel plans to Taos remained unchanged.

The eve of her departure, another envelope arrived from Carson, quite thin, the typing confined to half a page, from what I could discern. Presumably Lucy had 'spilled the beans,' yet all he could muster in his own defense was a paragraph?

Moments after arriving home from Engel Klein, where she had spent the afternoon reviewing documents, Adelaide took the envelope into her bedroom. She did not emerge to discuss dinner, so I knocked gently, assuming she was at her desk and using the gooseneck lamp, with its circumscribed penumbra. When she opened the door, however, I could see the room was dark.

"I hope I did not wake you—were you napping?"

"It's okay; I've got stuff to do. I didn't sleep that well last night."

"There is only one portion of the pot roast left."

"I'm not hungry—you can have it." She went to the desk and turned on the lamp.

"It is more of a lunch portion than a supper."

"Do you want takeout?" She leafed quickly through a notebook.

"No, no—not if I would be the only one eating."

"I'll order something for myself—maybe I'll be hungry later. What do you want?"

"You don't mind going out?"

"If it's somewhere close. Chinese?"

"I am amenable to any suggestion. Millie gave us the menu for the new—"

"Let's just get Chinese—it's closest."

"Are you sure? You are not fending off a cold?"

"No, I was just catching up on sleep."

I swallowed to reassure myself that my own throat felt fine.

CHAPTER 54

MICHAEL PULLED INTO THE DRIVEWAY by the sign advertising *Elegant Extended Stay Apartments* and pointed to the pay phone. "Just give a call when you're done."

Addy peered back at her nephew, fast asleep in his car seat. He'd watched, fascinated, when she dangled the tiny silver soccer ball attached to her key chain, a present from her father. "Will he be awake for the party?"

"Six p.m., sure. Eight is meltdown."

Addy got out and closed the car door as quietly as she could. The sun was bright and the temperature in the low sixties, not the kind of day to spend in a conference room conducting an interview. Taos Mountain and the peaks of the Sangre de Cristo Range stood out clear and beautiful, grayish-green, patches of white in their upper shadows. But in just a minute's lingering, she felt too warm in her navy-blue wool suit—she should've brought the cotton one. The new shoes were stiff as boards.

At least the lobby was air-conditioned. She pressed the buzzer for 3-C. When the door opposite finally opened, a Black woman came through. Her hair was cut stylishly short, and everything she wore matched: the coppery-gold pants and jacket, the earrings, heels. "Ms. Cohn? I'm Mary Agnes Bettles. We can use this." She gestured at a door; her right hand held a manila envelope. Her buoyant walk and bright, polished appearance made Addy feel drab.

The room contained a table and six chairs plus a cart holding a pitcher of water, several urns, and glasses and coffee cups. "I reserved this for two hours," Ms. Bettles said. "Hope that's long enough. I'm not sure how much I can tell you." While Addy unpacked her folders, the camera, and tape recorder, Ms. Bettles sat and set the manila envelope to the side. "You're here at the right time. In summer, the heat's bad."

"But it doesn't get humid, does it? Do you mind if I tape the interview?"

"Fine by me. Humidity's a killer. Spent seventeen years in Baton

Rouge, so I know what I'm talking about. That's one of the downsides to my white genes—can't take the humidity."

Addy turned on the recorder and gave her standard introduction. Ms. Bettles gave her full name as Mary Agnes Bettles; she was born in 1947 in Baton Rouge, Louisiana, to Josephine and Walter Bettles. She lived in Lincoln, Nebraska, and was currently employed by a Lincoln-based real estate agency. "I'm just in Taos to supervise opening our first New Mexico branch. They picked me because I lived in Albuquerque a few years ago and got my New Mexico license."

"How did you hear about the MacDonalde estate?"

"A coworker told me. He says, 'Too bad you're Mary Agnes Bettles and not Mary Agnes MacDonalde.' I'm about to say she was my grandmother, and he shows me the newspaper. The second I see the spelling, I know it's got to be her."

"You brought some documents with you. Do any contain that spelling—MacDonalde with an *e* at the end?"

"No, these aren't my grandmother's. They're things the lady I spoke to at your office—Brittany somebody?—she asked for them."

Ms. Bettles's answers to other background questions were straightforward and direct, and her tone barely changed when the subject turned to Mary MacDonalde. Ms. Bettles had "no idea" how her grandparents had met. Calvin Twist, Ms. Bettles's grandfather, was descended from slaves in Alabama who moved west during Reconstruction. Mary and Calvin had lived in Texas and raised three children: Abraham, Enoch, and Josephine. Josephine had married Walter Bettles, and they had only one child, Mary Agnes. Mary Agnes Bettles had never married or had children.

"Is Mary MacDonalde Twist alive?"

"Good Lord, no. She died before I was born."

"Do you know when?"

"Not exactly, but would've been around '43, '44—1944."

"Is your grandfather, Calvin Twist, still alive?"

"He died in 1930. I never knew any of my grandparents—even on the Bettles side."

"Is your mother, Josephine Twist Bettles, still alive?"

"She died in '74. My father—Walter Bettles—died in '60, 1960. Pancreatic cancer. That's not the way to go. Though there's worse. Believe me, there's worse."

"Now after Calvin Twist died, did Mary MacDonalde Twist marry again?"

"No."

"She had no children after the three with Calvin Twist?"

"Lord, no."

"Did Mary MacDonalde Twist have children *before* she married Calvin Twist?"

"According to the newspapers."

"I mean to your knowledge—based on anything you heard from anybody in your family or growing up."

"No."

In response to Addy's questions about what she knew of Mary's history before meeting Calvin Twist—aside from news accounts—all Ms. Bettles said was that Mary came from Scotland and did some traveling around the country. Calvin had gone north to look for work, and when he returned to Texas, Mary was with him.

Ms. Bettles had no records of Mary's and nothing containing the name Mary MacDonalde. The only things her mother, Josephine Twist Bettles, had saved from her childhood were her brothers' water cups.

"Do you know when and where Mary Agnes MacDonalde and Calvin Twist got married?"

"You mean when did they start living together?"

"No, when did they officially get married."

"Never did."

"They were never officially married?"

Ms. Bettles leaned back in her chair and bobbed a copper-colored shoe up and down. "You know Blacks couldn't marry whites in those days—it was illegal. Miscegenation laws. You could only marry your own race. My grandparents were common-law married."

Addy turned the recorder off and jotted down some follow-up questions to ask. She could hear Joe yelling, 'Just what the Scots want to hear—Mary shacking up with a Black man and not bothering to move somewhere they could legally marry!'

367

Addy turned the recorder back on. "When did Mary MacDonalde and Calvin Twist begin their common-law marriage?"

"I don't know. She took his name, though. She was Mary Agnes MacDonalde Twist."

"Where were they living at the time?"

"Not sure. The only place I know about is in southeast Texas, not all that far from the Louisiana border. A farm. Not big but enough for raising hogs, chickens."

"Do you know the name of the nearest town?"

"Was towards Marshall is all I know. When someone at church asked my mother—sorry: I'm supposed to say Josephine Twist Bettles—where she'd come from, she'd say 'Near Marshall, Texas.' I'm talking about when we lived in Baton Rouge and they'd ask her."

"So you don't know the years Mary MacDonalde Twist and Calvin Twist were common-law husband and wife?"

"All I know is they would've been common-law married when their kids were born."

"Okay, let's start with the eldest child. I believe you said—"

"Abraham."

"When was Abraham Twist born?"

"I don't know exactly, but he was fourteen when he died, so I'm guessing he was born in 1916."

"He died when?"

"August 23, 1930."

Addy jotted down a note to follow up on why Ms. Bettles knew the exact date her uncle Abraham had died. Joe might be pleased if she pursued it—if nothing else, it could narrow the search for documents. "So after Abraham Twist came Enoch Twist?"

"He was born in 1917."

"Is Enoch still alive?"

"No, he died August 23, 1930."

"The same day you said Abraham—were they in an accident?" Addy perked up—an accident could mean hospital records or a newspaper story.

"It was no accident."

The Spanish flu, Addy wondered—didn't Francis say it had spread everywhere?

"How did they—how did Abraham and Enoch Twist die?"

"They were lynched with their father, Calvin Twist."

Reflexively Addy's hand pressed the recorder's off button. It took a moment for her to regain her composure—she hoped Ms. Bettles didn't notice. Murmuring she was sorry, Addy stood and went to the cart and poured a glass of water. Returning to her seat, she spent several moments paging through her outline.

"I'm sorry to have to ask—"

"You've got to do what you've got to do. I'll answer whatever I can."

Addy turned the recorder back on and, unprompted, Ms. Bettles said, "Some white lady claimed Calvin whistled at her, but he wasn't dumb. This was southeast Texas. People said it was to get back at him for marrying a white woman."

"Where exactly did this happen—the lynchings?"

"Near the farm, near Marshall."

"Do you know anything more specific, location-wise?"

"No. My mother, she never liked to talk about it. She told me the fact of it when I was young—I grew up knowing my grandfather and uncles were lynched. My father—sorry, you want names—Walter Bettles, he was careful mentioning something on the news, something he thought might hit her close to home." Ms. Bettles abruptly sat erect. "Only once, once she talked about it, *really* talked about it. A month before she died, my mother—Josephine—maybe all those painkillers loosened her nerves up. I was visiting Baton Rouge, and she said, 'Mary Agnes, there's things you need to know that shouldn't be buried and forgotten.' I figured—not then, but after—she knew she was going to die, and this might be her only chance.

"She was nine when it happened. In the middle of the night. They were sleeping downstairs because of the heat. Usually they slept in the loft, the kids did." Turning toward the wall, Ms. Bettles spoke softly, and the space between words lengthened. "What she heard first was rumbling. Low rumbling, like thunder, like a storm coming. A lot of it—it didn't stop. With thunderstorms, even bad ones, the sound comes and goes. It might clap again, and you might hear rain, but the rumbling stops. Not this. She could see everybody sitting up—"

"They were—"

"Everybody was sitting up: my mother—Josephine—and her parents, Mary and Calvin, and Abraham and Enoch. When the rumbling got closer, somebody said it was a car. Then they could hear more than one. Most people didn't have cars in those days, so my mother, Josephine, even though she was only nine, she knew something . . . important . . . was happening. Her parents stood up but didn't light the lantern. Then her brothers stood, so Josephine went and held her mother's—Mary's—nightdress. 'I held my mama's nightdress,' she kept telling me. 'I held her nightdress.'

"The headlights came right at them through the window, and they could hear the cars up close. They didn't open the door. Nobody moved. Somebody knocked. Knocked loud. The door opened, but my mother—Josephine—she couldn't see much. The headlights were too bright. Mary made her let go of the nightdress, and she—Mary—went outside and closed the door. Their father, he said for them all to hide. Abraham or Enoch, one of them put my mother, Josephine, in the cupboard and said to be very, very quiet. Next thing, the door *burst* open. Mary was screaming, and there was all sorts of noise. My mother, Josephine, she couldn't tell who was shouting—some voices sounded strange—and the floor vibrated like a whole herd of deer had gotten in and panicked. Then the noises went outside, and all she could hear besides the motors again was Mary screaming. My mother waited in the cupboard till Mary came and got her out. No one else was there."

Again, Addy turned off the tape recorder. She remembered the photo of Mary MacDonalde as a teenager and now tried to imagine her twenty years older, down on hands and knees, crying, pleading. At what point did Calvin, Abraham, and Enoch know what was going to happen? And when Mary ran outside, was she pleading to the white men for her husband and sons' lives or was she calling out to those she loved—urging them to have faith, trying to reassure them God was watching? What would you tell your husband and children at a time like that?

Addy couldn't help that she, too, was talking softer when she resumed the interview—at least Joe would see only the transcript and not hear the tape. "Was it reported—to the police?"

Ms. Bettles cocked her head. "You kidding? Probably was the police who did it."

"So nobody was arrested?"

Ms. Bettles glared right at her.

Addy asked, "Do you know if any newspaper articles mentioned the lynchings?"

"I have no idea. This is all I have." Ms. Bettles reached into the manila envelope and withdrew a thick booklet.

Addy read the title aloud. "'Distribution of Lynchings in Texas and Oklahoma, 1910 to 1940.' What is this?"

"Some kind of report from somebody at UT. It says on the second page."

"And does it mention Calvin and Abraham and Enoch Twist?"

"Page forty-eight."

Addy quickly leafed to page forty-eight. The left-hand column listed years; other columns were for names, dates, and locations. Across from 1930 she read:

Calvin R. Twist, Harrison County, 08/23. Abraham B. Twist, Harrison County, 08/23. Enoch I. Twist, Harrison County, 08/23.

"Are Calvin, Abraham, and Enoch Twist mentioned elsewhere in this report?"

"No."

"I was wondering what the authors used as the source of their information." Addy paged to the back—there seemed to be a bibliography. "How did you come across this report?"

"A cousin sent it. He was a student at UT. Maybe knew folks working on it."

"Your cousin's name?"

"Bernard Twist."

"Do you have contact information for Bernard?"

"I have it at home—up in Lincoln. He lives in Galveston—might be in the phone book there."

"And you don't know if there was ever a newspaper article about the lynchings?"

"Never saw any." Ms. Bettles gestured at the report. "Lynching Black men and boys wasn't news."

Ms. Bettles didn't know where Mary or Calvin, Abraham, and

Enoch were buried; Josephine was buried in East Baton Rouge Parish. Mary and Josephine moved to Houston right after the lynchings to stay with relatives on the Twist side. To Ms. Bettles's knowledge, Mary never went back to the farm.

"Too much heartache, I'm thinking. My mother, Josephine, never talked much about her childhood, only stories about later. When the Second World War broke out, she got a job in Biloxi and met somebody, and they got engaged, but he was killed in a factory accident. I remember her saying she wished her mother—Mary MacDonalde Twist—had still been alive because her fiancé, he had Scottish blood in him too."

"What was Josephine Twist's fiancé's name?"

"I don't know. She just mentioned it once—that she'd been engaged and wished my grandmother had known him."

"And that's why you concluded Mary MacDonalde died before the Second World War ended?"

"That's not the only reason. I remember Josephine saying Mary was worried the Germans might invade Scotland, and she—Josephine—was sorry her mother didn't live till the end of the war to find out we won."

Ms. Bettles didn't have any more information about Mary—where she had lived and when and where she had died. "She could've stayed in Houston or gone to Biloxi or gone with some Twists elsewhere. The war had people moving—jobs opened up different places, especially in factory cities. Look, if you're thinking: why didn't Mary go north, take her little girl, take Josephine, to Chicago or Detroit instead of Houston—that Mary would've had an easier time among white people—you don't understand. White folks would look down on Josephine. And Blacks up North, they aren't as tight as Blacks in the South. A young *man*, okay, he might want more opportunities and go. But a woman, especially one breaking the rules, Mary was better off in Houston, with Twists. Their community would look out special for Josephine. They'd treat her good."

Ms. Bettles did produce what appeared to be a marriage license issued to Walter Allen Bettles and Josephine Charity Twist in Baton Rouge in January 1943. It didn't include the names of their parents. And she gave Addy a church newsletter which said:

Josephine Charity Twist Bettles, 53, died Tuesday after a short illness. She was born in 1921 to Calvin and Mary Agnes Twist, who preceded her in death, as did brothers Abraham and Enoch Twist. Josephine married Walter Bettles in 1943, and he preceded her in death. She is survived by their daughter Mary Agnes Bettles of Lincoln, Nebraska. In lieu of flowers, please donate to the Bethel AME or Southern Poverty Law Center.

Addy leafed back through her outline. "The farm Mary MacDonalde Twist lived on near Marshall: Do you know who owned it?"

"No. Could've been Mary and Calvin. Or they could've been sharecroppers. I actually tried to find out, a long time ago—being in the real estate business, it was a chance to see what title searches looked like. Found a property with a mortgage to a *Herbert* Twist—maybe my great-grandfather or a cousin or no relation at all. It was never paid off—the bank foreclosed in '31. I'm sorry I can't give you more information. Like I said, my mother—Josephine—didn't talk much about her childhood. Can you blame her? 'The future is what matters,' she always told me. 'Don't be afraid of what *might* happen, because if the worst is going to happen, it's going to happen anyway, without your fretting over it.' I've done my best to follow that philosophy."

Ms. Bettles showed Addy a small photo of her mother. Josephine couldn't have been more than seventeen or eighteen when the picture was taken—possibly for her high school yearbook. Her skin was lighter than Ms. Bettles's, and her hair had been straightened in that stiff style of decades ago. Was this actually Mary MacDonalde's daughter? As she had with the photo Mr. Grey-Davison had shown her, Addy wondered if there were any telltale traits—the shape of the earlobes or widow's peak—that would disprove the claim. Joe had some expert on hand "if the Scots ever want to fork over the money for him."

When she restarted the recorder, Addy asked about a family Bible. Ms. Bettles laughed a little harshly. "Want to know what happened to the family Bible? My grandmother—sorry: Mary Agnes MacDonalde Twist—she left it on the table at the farmhouse near Marshall. Told my mother, told Josephine, just before they left for Houston, 'Maybe it will do more good for those who come next.' Made an impression on my mother. She thought that was the end of Mary's faith."

After going through most of her remaining questions, Addy asked if Ms. Bettles wanted to take a short break.

"Let's just get it over with."

"I appreciate your willingness to revisit these painful events."

"I know you have a job to do. Let me tell you, times have changed, and they haven't. Taos is supposed to be some little liberal sanctuary down here, but everyone I meet says, 'You're new in these parts.' Not too many Blacks—they can memorize our faces, I guess. Still, I moved two properties this week. Shocked the shit out of my boss." She laughed and pointed to the tape recorder. "Glad that wasn't on."

Addy paused before punching the on button. She took a deep breath. "As you know, part of the purpose of this interview is to find out if anybody is still alive who's related to the Mary Agnes MacDonalde mentioned in Violet MacDonalde's will. You state that Mary MacDonalde Twist is—*was*—the same Mary MacDonalde, and so I need to explore all possibilities, in terms of . . . where her heirs are, which ones are still alive." Unfazed, Ms. Bettles nodded.

"So as part of that, part of that exploring, I need to consider that while Abraham and Enoch were alive, they were potential heirs to Mary MacDonalde Twist's estate, just as your mother, Josephine, was." She waited until Ms. Bettles nodded. "Josephine gave birth to you, but you say no other children."

"That's right."

"I need to find out if Abraham or Enoch might have had children. Because if they did, their children would also be heirs."

Ms. Bettles's forehead wrinkled; she looked like she was trying to add numbers. "Let me get this straight. You're asking if a fourteen-year-old boy and his younger brother had *children*?"

"It's just a formality, for the record."

"You think they raped some white woman? You think—"

"No, no—I'm asking if they had *consen*—"

Ms. Bettles stood so suddenly her knees knocked the table, spilling some of Addy's water over the side of the glass. "Where did you even *get* such an idea? I know where: from this racist culture that says Black men are wild, uncontrollable sex animals. They were children *themselves*, for heaven's sake." She stared at Addy a moment, her mouth open, her expression some mix of hurt, indignation, and disgust. She hurled the manila envelope onto the table. "You can have those. If you have any more questions, put them in writing, and I'll get a lawyer to look at them. I'm not putting up with your racist crap." The heels made a click-click-click-click staccato marching out of the room.

For some minutes Addy remained in her chair watching the sunlight slant through the windows. The sky was a dour blue. The clock seemed to tick louder, a click, click, click, click. Rousing herself, she packed everything in Francis's briefcase. She matted the spilled water with a napkin.

IT WASN'T UNTIL AFTER PHONING Michael that she allowed herself to wonder if she'd crossed some ethical line. Would even Joe say she had gone too far? What would the Scottish lawyers think when they read the transcript? But wasn't it her responsibility to find out if one of the boys *had*, in fact, fathered a child? Why shouldn't the offspring of a lynched boy gain some recompense, no matter how meager? So why did she feel uncomfortable?

Francis would defend her, agreeing she had to ask the question. What would Carson say? She pictured him sprawled in his chair at the dining room table after the dishes had been cleared, when Francis had turned his own chair to stretch his legs. It was always a pleasant moment, everyone full and relaxed from the wine. Elbow resting on the tablecloth, Carson would posit strange scenarios: Mary had joined a traveling circus, married a politician who wanted to hide her history, joined a religious order and sailed to some Pacific island as a missionary.

He might pay lip service to the professional ethics of Addy asking the question, but his main point would be that Abraham and Enoch would have been *flattered*, not offended. His own horniness during adolescence, which he often joked about, must have been among the few pleasant early memories. What was the girlfriend like—did she want to visit old vessels?

MICHAEL PULLED TO THE CURB, and Addy hurried over.

"Thought you wouldn't be done this early."

"Where's Noah?"

"Patty took off early to get the place ready for the party. Want to go for a short hike? We'd stay out of her way then."

"Yes, that'd be great." *The perfect antidote*, to use a Francis phrase.

As they drove off, Michael said, "Mom asked me to spy on you. She thinks you don't tell her anything. Don't worry, I didn't agree to— she wasn't willing to pay me."

"She knows my cases are confidential."

"Social life, friends—probably whether you're dating anyone with *potential*."

"Not right now."

"She told me about Zach. Was she not supposed to?"

"I don't care."

"She's freaking out you'll never date again."

As they drove up the hill, the valley—more a shallow basin— looked yellow and golden and in parts clay-red under the bright sun. Across in the distance, the low, soft shapes of the Sangre de Cristo reminded Addy of sleeping dogs. She liked the open, uncluttered vastness painted in broad strokes, muted browns and greens, and the way the mountains ringed the city protectively so it wouldn't seem so exposed.

The house was near the end of a bumpy unpaved road cutting through cactus and sagebrush. It was the same ranch-style as the handful of other stone or stucco homes they passed. Several front yards had strange objects: one, a pole with large hoops dangling from cords; another, a copper tangle. Michael and Patty's yard had metal-and-wire shapes and a wooden sign carved with the words *Take only what you need and leave the land as you found it.*

"An Arapaho saying," her brother said.

"Are they still in the area?"

"Never were—Wyoming, Colorado, Canada. This is Navajo, Apache, Pueblo."

"What about Hopi?"

"To the west."

NOAH SAT IN THE HIGH CHAIR, his chin covered in something purple. Patty turned off the kitchen tap. "A guy named Joe called. I wrote down the number. Use our bedroom phone if you want some privacy."

Had Ms. Bettles complained already? Joe couldn't be too happy that she'd deeply offended someone who might be Mary's granddaughter, someone with a very painful family history. Plus, Addy hadn't gotten any hard evidence connecting Ms. Bettles to Mary. The whole trip was a disaster.

"WHAT DO YOU MEAN," HE hollered into the phone. "She *left in the middle*? What the hell did you say? The Scots won't be happy paying someone else to finish it."

As briefly as she could, Addy explained about Mary and Calvin, the three children, and the lynchings. Twice Joe had to ask her to speak up.

When she finished, instead of yelling, he said in a completely normal voice, "Well, that's a first. Hold on a minute." His voice was muffled, and she couldn't make out who else was with him. When he didn't get back on right away, she watched the second hand on the wall clock go through a complete rotation.

"You still there, Cohn? Plans have changed—Bettles on the back burner, unless you tell me she has damn convincing documents."

"There might be property records from outside Marshall, Texas, but not with Mary's name, just her husband—"

"No marriage license? Birth or death certificate?"

"No. She said—"

"Then forget her for now. You're going to Wichita. Kimberly will switch the tickets and set the interview for Wednesday morning—you'll fly there tomorrow. Hold on." His voice was muffled again. Then it came loud. "Guess who turned up? Give you one guess, and it's not Mary Agnes MacDonalde. Anne! The Anne MacDonalde on the birth certificate application."

"In Wichita?"

"Yep. Finally, a person with a verified record. I better say, somebody named Anne sent us a copy of the birth certificate—could be an impostor."

"With the same date as the one on Dr. Lomond's application form?"

"Same date."

"Then it must be her."

"All we know is the Wichita lady is *in possession* of the birth certificate. Maybe she works for the New York health people and stole it. Or got somebody to forge it."

"But if she lives in Wichita—"

"So she has a *co-conspirator* in the health department. She's Jane Doe *posing* as Anne MacDonalde."

"Shouldn't that be easy to prove? She should have other ID—a driver's license—"

"That's why you're going to Wichita. You need to see it—her driver's license, tax filings—she can redact the social if she wants, at least for now—and a marriage license if she's got one. And anything to prove who her kids are. Take her picture if she can't pass for thirty-three. Keep in mind, though, that even if she's a real Anne MacDonalde, it'd be nice to show some connection to Mary. Her father's birth certificate would work. Not that the Scots will necessarily be picky—they're so damn sick of these claims, they might run with any MacDonalde with an *e*, especially from New York, not the territory of Guam. But you'll have to rake this Anne over the coals—she's as closemouthed as the rest. Hold on."

A few moments later: "Wouldn't say diddly-squat till we sign the confidentiality. Overnighted it to her—she'll call if we need to change anything before you get there. Maybe she'll try putting in some liquidated-damages clause like that Mamaroneck clown. But *nothing* to the press, Cohn—not even that she's alive. We sent the questionnaire and records requests overnight too, so she'll know what info to make available, but obviously you'll be there before we get her written responses. You'll need a car—Wichita's a sprawling cow town. The Scots should be happy you're killing two birds with one stone, even if one bird walked out on you."

When Addy hung up, she told Michael about the change in plans. He said it was all the more reason to get a short hike in right away.

CHAPTER 55

MUCH TO MY SURPRISE, THE envelope was on top of the other papers in the desk drawer. Perhaps Adelaide had taken a page from Poe's "The Purloined Letter" and left the missive in plain sight on the assumption that a curious person would ignore an item its possessor had taken no pains to conceal. The address was written in Carson's careful penmanship, but the letter itself was typed.

Tiptoeing out, I found myself subject to a medley of emotions. Yes, I was relieved the affair, such as it was, had concluded. Although not the spoiled young man I had earlier supposed, Carson was sufficiently dishonest to constitute a poor choice in a mate. Some disappointment entered into the mix as well: I would fain have had *Adelaide* be the one to prompt the fissure. The feelings that accompany rejection—even from a suitor one does not take seriously—may shake a fragile self-esteem. Still, I comforted myself with the knowledge that she would eventually reap the benefit of the cessation of that tension his unwelcome advances engendered. And as the bond was destined for dissolution, why not have the act over and done with?

Of course, this development rendered the sister's invitation all the *more* puzzling. Was she not up to date on her brother's affairs? Another possibility presented itself: perhaps the sister was not fond of the new woman. Yet nothing Adelaide had recounted of the visit to Norwalk suggested this.

One thought leading to another, I found myself wondering why Sam hadn't telephoned these past few weeks. Surely the long-distance rates from New Haven were not prohibitively expensive. Did Adelaide inform him of her travel to New Mexico and, being forgetful of the exact dates, he awaited her call once she returned? No, Francis, you cannot expect him to call to talk to *you*, no matter how many interests you and he share!

A few more minutes of contemplation assuaged my minor twinges of anxiety over Adelaide suffering from Carson's rejection. After all, how large could his attentions have still loomed after seven or eight months on the opposite coast? Besides, she had weathered other slings and arrows since his departure: the frosty reception at Zach's parents, frustrations at Engel Klein, the long winter. Far from being the straw that broke the camel's back, Carson's disappearance from her life was likely to be the palm leaf resuscitating it!

"I'M SORRY I COULDN'T CALL yesterday, Dad; Tony and I were up in Vancouver."

"Yes, you had said you might not telephone; I assumed we would talk again next Sunday. I am doing just fine on my own."

"How's the 'nettlesome issue' you mentioned last week—something to do with Tess?"

"A minor point, I've concluded. I want to answer those critics who fault Tess for her relationship with Alec—the initial one—for becoming his mistress, as it were. Although Tess blames *herself*—which to my mind is all the more reason to forgive her. Let me read to you, it is right here, one moment, I have marked the page. Yes, here it is. Hardy writes, *She had dreaded him*—Alec—*and winced before him*. I am leaving some out to get to the gist. Hardy has her consider that she was *temporarily blinded by his ardent manners*. That was it, her great sin: being temporarily blinded by ardent manners! My goodness, if such were a serious character flaw, who among humanity would be fit to cast the first stone? And here, I am quoting again, she *had been stirred to confused surrender awhile*."

"In other words," Olivia said, "she allowed herself to be seduced by someone who lifted her out of poverty for the first time in her life."

"Yes, but she quickly comes to her senses and rues it all."

"Like many women in real life."

"That is my point exactly, my dear: there is no deep character flaw here, simply a brief suspension of better judgment in the face of a benefactor's blandishments. The idea these critics propound, that Tess coveted a life of luxury, is *preposterous*. Consider whom she loved and married: no wealthy aristocrat, far from it! Poor Tess; she was simply saddled with a timid soul, hardly a mortal sin, especially for a penniless young woman contending against a wealthy young man. That she remained with him for a period of weeks is no great surprise or cause for condemnation."

"And don't downplay the initial trauma, Dad. You can throw in a footnote about Stockholm syndrome."

"Stockholm syndrome?" I tried to recall if I had heard the term before. My memory of Strindberg plays was dim.

"It's well known that kidnap victims and prisoners can come to identify with their captors and want to *please* them, not escape. It's named after a group of people held hostage during a bank robbery in Stockholm who refused to testify against the robbers because they grew to care about them. And then Patty Hearst."

Fortunately, Olivia could not witness my roll of the eyes. Despite being equipped with a razor-sharp mind, she swam around in silly psychological theories, no doubt the consequence of being besotted by love. Yet we had a very pleasant conversation overall, and some of the ideas she proffered were certain to make their way into my opus.

THE NEXT TIME THE TELEPHONE rang, Adelaide was on the other end, informing me she would not be coming home until Wednesday night.

"You will be back in time for Thursday with Robert?"

"Yes, Wednesday night. Francis, you can't breathe a *word* about what I'm going to tell you."

"Of course not."

"Anne has surfaced—Anne MacDonalde! I'm going to interview her in Wichita."

"My goodness—in Wichita, of all places."

After she filled me in on the particulars, I said that Joe must trust her abilities to assign her such an important interview. To which she responded, "It's just cheaper if I stop off on my way back." *My* pleasure was not diluted. The mystery of Mary MacDonalde's descendants had teased for well over a year, and all Engel Klein's labors would be in vain if the firm never succeeded in their mission, so the news of a strong candidate for heiress having been located was delightful. Adelaide playing a pivotal role in that outcome would be— to use one of my mother's expressions—the bee's knees.

CHAPTER 56

THE TOP OF THE RIDGE lay a quarter of a mile from the trailhead. The incline wasn't steep, and wild grasses grew abundant on both sides, laced with red and yellow wildflowers. The mountains all around were covered in conifers, but here the land was open. They passed a small lake that Michael said was just snowmelt. Coming over a rise, they descended into sagebrush, the trail wide enough for them to walk side by side.

"Have you talked to Elliot since Christmas? He said Mom and Tony took down the blankets, mask, headdress—all the Native American art Dad's clients gave him. And put up old French and Van Gogh repros."

Addy tried to imagine their home looking different. "Maybe it's because they decided to live in *her* house," she said, "and Tony wanted it to feel like his place too."

"Another *Starry Night*—give me a break."

Birds flew overhead to the north, a flock with bright-white stripes on their wings. "It's so different from Seattle here—I mean weather-wise. You like it?"

"Sunlight all year round? Ya, sure, ya betcha. We're in high desert, so the summers aren't humid."

Where the path narrowed, they went single file. To either side the mountains showed patchworks of rock in the forest.

How did people cope with lynchings, with people they loved not just dying but being tortured? Nathan's uncle had lost his wife and daughters in the camps. He emigrated to the States after the war and settled in Cleveland, got married, and raised five kids. Was he able to love them fully, or did part of him always hold back?

Michael was waiting for her where the trail forked. "This one loops back to the parking lot."

"What's that?"

"The gorge? Rio Grande. Next visit." He continued on, and she followed.

It was weird to think that Mary, growing up in cold, damp

Scotland, might have ended up in hot, dry Texas. But adjusting to a new climate had to have been the least of her worries. Was that an eagle circling above the trees? The wingspan was broad, but Addy couldn't make out the color of its head.

Again Michael was waiting for her. Here the path flattened out as it widened. He grabbed a tall grass shoot and pulled it until it broke, then twirled it idly as they walked. She thought she could smell cedar.

"Did Francis flip when you told him you weren't coming back until Wednesday?"

"No."

"Why do you have to report to him anyway?"

"It's natural he'd worry if I didn't show up when I said I would."

She flashed on a visit to New York back when she was ten or eleven and Michael wanted to know why Francis never went with them to museums. Olivia explained that he worked very hard. "Besides, he's not the dandle-on-the-knee type." The three kids had exchanged knowing looks—their mother wanted an opportunity to explain what 'dandle' meant. None of them gave her the satisfaction by asking.

Michael used the shoot to whack at the low bushes. "Mom still wants him to move to Seattle."

"She'll never give up on that. What are those?"

"Junipers. Wouldn't you rather live with people your own age? Instead of being an old man's nursemaid? Move to the burbs—at least you'd be around nature. The Lakotas have a saying: *When a man moves away from nature, his heart becomes hard.*"

"I didn't expect so much greenery."

"Come for a long visit, and I'll take you to Carson." Michael tossed the shoot into a patch of wildflowers. "The national forest. Not that different from the Cascades."

Why *had* his sister invited her to lunch? Did he tell her they'd like each other? Lucy hadn't seemed comfortable either. Francis would have seen the letter by now—Addy'd toss it when she got home.

MOST OF THE GUESTS WERE in their twenties or thirties, and some brought kids. Except for Patty's colleagues, who had come straight from work, everyone was dressed casual, and it was obvious that

Noah's birthday was just an excuse for the adults to party. Wrapped gifts were placed on the hall chair, but the potluck dishes got what Olivia used to wryly call "the oohs and aahs."

Michael introduced Addy to his artist friends and neighbors by describing what they made or the materials they worked with: "pure metal," "wood and copper," "jewelry—beads and glass." "You'll have to see Greg's obelisk."

"Don't bother," someone said in passing. "It's just a giant rectal thermometer."

"Marielle does woven sculpture—silk and cotton."

"Hemp too, Michael! I have to keep them indoors—the sun ruins the colors. Come by and see."

Several of the guests painted. A thin guy with a braid said, "Oil only—wouldn't do watercolor if they paid me."

"Sure you would," Michael shot back.

Addy got herself a beer and bowl of chili and sat on a patio bench. The conversations seemed to be about local galleries, whether they were "creative" or just showed "tourist trash." Patty walked around with Noah on her hip, the boy's expression some mix of worry and boredom.

Adapting the Bettles outline to the Anne MacDonalde interview shouldn't be too hard. Addy would add specific questions about the birth certificate and really focus on other forms of ID. Fortunately Michael had a stock of tapes he could give her for the recorder—he'd bought his own recorder when Patty was pregnant so they could tape Noah learning to speak.

After bringing her empty beer bottle to the kitchen and dumping her paper bowl in the compost barrel, Addy volunteered to carry her nephew. He liked it when she took him outside and pointed to the setting sun. Instead of the colors gradually changing, the horizon was an orange band under a strange bright teal. A few lights flickered in the foothills. From the east, a long, low howl echoed indistinctly enough that it might have come from a wolf, coyote, or even an owl.

The air cooled quickly, so the guests lingering went indoors and sat in a circle on the large woven rug in the living room. Michael built a fire in the hearth. The children curled up on large cushions scattered around the room, and a woman with rings on every finger strummed a mandolin quietly in the corner. Sitting cross-legged, Addy looked past the others in the circle and watched the embers glow. The stress of the interview finally receded. Voices were kept low, maybe so the children would drift off to sleep. Only when Michael spoke was her attention snagged.

"If you're not Anglo, you get labeled a primitive regardless."

"If Grandma Moses had been indigenous, no one would've heard of her."

"Did you see those bead sculptures at the waterfall—the tall green rows?"

"He had to pay big-time for the space."

"He's from Barcelona. If he'd been Mexican or what's-his-name—"

"That guy from Honduras? His stuff is ten times better."

"I thought the beads were good."

Would Ms. Bettles feel comfortable here even though everyone was white? Had Mary MacDonalde felt comfortable in a Black community? Addy thought back to high school and middle school and how the cliques were all one race or another.

"At a party like this, my parents would've sent us down to the rec room so we wouldn't 'bother the grown-ups.' In Nicaragua, you never saw that."

"Latino cultures are about family."

"Which tribe is it that's big on the council of elders?"

"The Mohawks believe that children don't belong to their parents—they're loaned out by the Creator."

The discussion stopped for a moment while everyone looked at the kids.

Twin girls about five or six were playing cat's cradle; a boy lying on his stomach watched the fire; and Noah and a little girl not much older slept draped by an earthtoned blanket. In its own way, the room seemed a kind of *Peaceable Kingdom.*

CHAPTER 57

CARSON LEANED CLOSER TO THE phone to block out the flight announcements. "You're impossible to reach, Luce."

"What are you doing up? It's not even five out there."

"I'm in Tallahassee—I took—"

"Of all the places for your firm to send you. We just got back from DC. He wanted to do some schmoozing, in case—"

"Well, don't unpack. I'm not here on business. Got a call from the hospital last night. Louise died."

"What?"

"Car accident."

"What was she doing behind the wheel of a car? Or was she a passenger?"

"Neither. Walked across a driveway while a truck backed up."

"Wasn't his beeper working? She's not deaf."

"That's all they told me. Can you come down? I booked us rooms at a motel not too far from her house. I'm going to the hospital now—see about, you know, arrangements. Leave me a message with your flight number—I'll meet you at the airport."

FORTUNATELY, THE RENTAL'S AIR-CONDITIONING GOT cold in seconds—outside was worse than a sauna. He was no dummy, picking the dry, temperate West Coast—not that he would've picked anywhere within a thousand miles of Louise. Had she died at the scene? Despite everything, he had never wished her pain.

The hospital, a small old brick structure, was in the outskirts or maybe even outside city limits—the tallest thing in the neighboring blocks of stores, diners, and bars was a four-story office building. Carson stepped into a lobby Signe might call 'classic fifties,' the walls white plaster and the floor tiles dark green. The lady behind the information desk directed him to an office where a short, large-breasted young woman with bright-red nail polish asked for ID and had him fill out forms.

The placard on her desk said *Cindy*. She hit five buttons on the phone, said, "Hi, Harry" and gave Louise's full name, then hung up.

When Carson was done with the forms, she skimmed them over, murmured consolations, and gestured toward the door. He followed her out and along the white-walled corridor and into a stairwell to the basement. How could she walk in stiletto heels without falling forward?

She rapped loudly on a metal door. A man in a white lab coat opened it, and Cindy stepped back for Carson to enter.

"Come by my office when you're done," she said before leaving.

He was relieved that Louise wasn't in one of the large metal drawers against the wall. The man directed him to a gurney with a sheet draped over the body. He also was relieved the eyes were closed.

"Yes, that's Louise. How come her face isn't messed up?"

"Possibly because she got knocked onto her back. The medical examiner may authorize an autopsy to find out whether an artery was crushed causing hemorrhaging or a concussive brain injury was the cause of death. In either case, she may have lost consciousness instantly."

Carson nodded to acknowledge the courtesy. "I'm not from this area. I'll have to find a funeral home."

"Cindy can help you." He handed Carson a large turquoise plastic bag. "The deceased's belongings. The shoes and clothing are in the smaller bag inside. There's a lot of blood on them."

In the stairwell Carson peered inside the turquoise bag. Besides the smaller bag it contained a black vinyl purse.

Cindy had left her door ajar. "I have some materials you might find useful." She pushed a packet across the desk, and he sat and leafed through it. Some were forms with references to *Medical Examiner's Report* and *Notification of Death* and *Disposition of Body*; others were colored brochures. "If they want an autopsy," she said, "we have a backlog, so it could take a week."

"Do you know where this happened—was it near her house or somewhere downtown?"

Cindy made her sad face. "Just two blocks from here. Call them for the police report. You may want to meet with a lawyer about whether to ask for an autopsy if the medical examiner doesn't want one."

She rattled off more information that he tried to scribble in the margins of the *In Your Time of Grief* pamphlet: how long the hospital would hold on to the body after it was approved for release, the range of prices for burial in the area, and the approximate cost of transporting the body by plane if buried elsewhere—around the price of a passenger ticket. An insert listed funeral homes and cemeteries in the county. Carson had no idea where his father was buried—there'd been no funeral that he could remember. He doubted Lucy would want to pay to transport Louise up to Connecticut. He'd ask, though.

BACK IN THE MOTEL ROOM he opened the purse, wondering—with amusement—what he was afraid of finding. A joint? Uppers? The hospital must've gone through it, to find ID if nothing else, and probably confiscated anything illegal. It didn't have much now. A hideous pink wallet containing twenty-three dollars, what looked like a Medicaid card, and, behind the clear plastic where people usually put their license, a small card preprinted *If you find this, please return to*, which Louise had filled out with her name, address, and telephone number. A key chain with a plastic four-leaf clover, dangling a single key. A pack of cigarettes with two remaining.

He flipped the book of matches over. *The Lilac Lounge*. In the change purse he found six lottery tickets. He put them in his wallet and pocketed the key.

The phone light was blinking. Carson listened to the message and jotted down Lucy's flight number. After stopping at the front desk to ask directions, he went out and started up the rental, turning the air-conditioning fan to high.

THE FOUR-LANE ROAD SEEMED TO go into a nowhere of nondescript shrubs, low grass, pockets of nondescript trees—a far cry from the lush gardens pictured in travel ads. Everyone drove eighty. Carson was amazed at the number of dead animals in the road and on the shoulder.

The turnoff was onto a shunt that ran alongside the four-lane. He passed a bus stop and had to veer to the right, into a wooded area and past a sign saying *Children at Play*. He didn't see any children—he didn't see anyone—but you wouldn't want to drive fast, snaking around among the tall trees. The one-story bungalows were far enough apart for a sense of privacy, and the shade was nice—plenty of deciduous mixed in with the pines. A short asphalt patch beyond the post with the reflective *15* led to a carport covered in dry leaves. Underneath was an old refrigerator without a door. He remembered there was no car key on Louise's key chain.

The patch of woods was so quiet, the car door shutting sounded like it had been slammed. Even the traffic noise along the main road barely penetrated. The path to the front door was strewn with twigs, long-dead leaves, pine needles, bits of log. No grass grew, just some mosslike growths, ivy, ferns. For a moment Carson stood completely still, sensing the tranquility. A chirrup-chirrup came from above, and a chipmunk rustled among the leaves on a log. The grove was peaceful. Had Louise found any peace?

The key worked easily, and Carson stepped over the threshold. There was no overhead, but the curtains weren't drawn, so despite all the shade outside, he could find his way to the table lamp. Louise hadn't improved as a housekeeper: the ashtrays were full, a vodka bottle sat on the floor, and a few cans of cola—he didn't recognize the brand—lay on their sides. *Good thing they're diet, or the place would be crawling with ants.*

Her leaving the curtains open was probably a smart move: anyone peering in would see there was nothing to steal. A cheap yellow futon sofa, a green vinyl coffee table, a thirteen- or fourteen-inch TV resting on an orange crate, a pile of blankets on a rickety-looking chair—hauling it away would have been more trouble than it was worth. And the thief would have to wade through trash, bottles, receipts, empty cigarette packs, dirty glasses, bags of potato chips, and magazines.

He recognized the *Star* and *Enquirer*. Should he check for articles on the MacDonalde case?

The small set of particle-board bookshelves contained more magazines, scattered bobby pins, and matchbooks. The remote worked, the TV tuned to a channel showing lions in the savanna devouring some kind of carcass. He turned it off.

The kitchen was pretty much an extension of the living room. The refrigerator contained a six-pack of wine coolers, pizza box, loaf of raisin bread, and jar of raspberry jam. Wasn't there some poem that went *a loaf of bread, a jug of wine*? Francis would know.

Carson stepped into the bedroom slowly. Here, the curtains were drawn, so he had to locate the lamp. He also felt a strange shyness, like he was snooping. The mattress was a double, but the two pillows were stacked one on top of the other. The sheets on the unmade bed had little pink flowers. Besides the ashtray and jar of ibuprofen, the only thing on the end table was a magazine called *Terriers*. Did Louise have a dog? Had she been walking it when she was hit? No one had said anything about a dog or leash.

He opened the dresser drawers just enough to see if they contained papers—the idea of pawing through her clothes repulsed him. He eventually found the papers in a metal toolbox, which he put by the front door. There was no dog dish or water bowl, even outside.

The bathroom wasn't as bad as expected—she was doing some basic hygiene. The medicine cabinet was empty except for a package of disposable plastic razors.

He remembered to check the mailbox, finding only advertising circulars. He put the hospital bag with the clothes in the garbage. Scanning the living room, he realized how little of Louise's history could be constructed from her possessions. For the first time, really, he allowed himself to conceive of her as scared—as having once been young and scared. At what age had she morphed into master manipulator? Now it was a question he could mull over without any urgency for answers.

LUCY MARCHED ALONGSIDE HIM THROUGH the terminal. Her suitcase was light enough he didn't bother with the wheels.

"How did the hospital know to call you?" she asked.

"Tracked down the landlord."

Without slowing her brisk pace, she looked up at him. "You okay?"

"I'm fine except outdoors. The humidity's a killer."

"I mean about Louise."

He nodded. "Can't say I feel grief. But never expected to."

"Relief is more like it."

"It's weird, Luce—I actually feel a little *guilty*."

She stopped in her tracks. "Why on earth?"

He stopped too. "It doesn't make sense, I know . . . do you think maybe children of *nice* parents feel guilty?"

"There would be gratitude mixed in." She began walking again, and he stayed alongside.

"Her face wasn't banged up. I went to the house. It's a pit—dishes in the sink, bottles everywhere, clothes on the bedroom floor. But the TV works."

"Not all soda."

"Wine coolers and vodka. Yuck. Luckily, she has a supply of garbage bags, but I didn't get around to cleaning. I was worried I'd have to wade through a swamp of papers to see if she wrote a will, but all she had was a toolbox with the lease, SSI kind of stuff, a debit card, and thirty dollars. No checkbook. Anyway, one of my colleagues gave me the name of an attorney here who does estates work, so we can give him a call, see what hoops we need to jump through."

"For what? To inherit a bunch of empty vodka bottles? I don't need another TV."

"We can donate the TV to Goodwill—furniture too. I just want to know that it's legal for us to proceed with the funeral arrangements since she didn't specify any."

"Funeral? Who'd show up?"

"Maybe she made friends among the neighbors. She probably bummed rides from some, don't you think? There's no car or car key."

"She couldn't get a license. Don't you remember: that was part of the disability application that fraud in Bridgeport cooked up?"

"Did she just take cabs everywhere? I guess she could walk to the bus stop."

"She could walk *fine*," Lucy said. "That was all bullshit. Let's just cancel the utilities, notify the landlord, and cremate her the cheapest way. I sure hope we're not stuck with debts. I was very careful about what I co-signed—I hope you were too."

"Went over it with a magnifying glass."

"Where should we toss the ashes? Or do you want to keep them?"
He shook his head. "Then let's just tell the cremating people to keep
them. Save us the cost of a dumb little box."

ON THE HIGHWAY, LUCY SAID, "I know I sound bitter, but I don't like
having to drop everything to deal with crap for somebody who
sacrificed nothing for us."

"No good memories?"

"Nope. Do you?"

"I could count on her to leave us alone. Did you ever wonder—
wonder what her childhood was like? Do you think her parents really
died when she was twelve?"

"Don't you remember him yelling he shouldn't have married 'a
goddamn orphan'?"

"Why did she marry *him*?"

"Drunks of a feather."

Carson glanced at Lucy briefly. "She was that way before?"

"Nobody sober would have married him."

His sister was probably right. "The matches in her purse were
from a place called The Lilac Lounge. I could stop by—you wouldn't
have to come—and see if anyone knew her. Just to let them know."

"She probably ran up a tab they'll want us to pay." Lucy shifted in
her seat. "Let's talk about something else. How's the job going?"

"Okay, it's going okay. The big trial is over, and I'm mostly
working on licensing contracts."

"Who won?"

"The trial? Judge split the baby."

"They do that. Dating anyone?"

"Actually, yes."

"Really? Since when?"

"December."

"*December*? You never said anything."

"I wasn't sure it would gain traction."

"That was a day wasted. Never mind. What's she like?"

"Name's Signe—*S-i-g-n-e*. She's an interior designer, not to be
confused with interior decorator. She works for this upscale firm that

sends her to people's homes to help them design changes. She's really good at it—has an eye for furnishings, décor, space."

"Unusual name."

"Swedish."

"I hope you brought a photo."

At the red light, he reached into his wallet.

Lucy studied the picture. "Now *that's* someone worth moping over."

"We'll see."

THE PINE NEEDLES LOOKED BLUE in the late-afternoon light. Carson noticed a car at number 3, some ancient gas-guzzler, but otherwise the grove was the same as before. And as quiet. A gentle breeze rustled the leaves on the ground. Addy could identify lots of trees just by their leaves. In Central Park, she'd tried teaching him the differences between sugar maples and red maples, horse chestnuts and elms, this oak and that. "It's all above me," he'd said. But she had bothered to learn the names of vessel parts, even the rigging.

He and Lucy got to work separating the bottles, cans, papers, and garbage into separate bags—it was weirdly reminiscent of their childhood.

"Did they make us clean," Carson asked, "or did we do it on our own?"

"*I* made us do it. I wasn't going to live in a sty." She moved over to the particle-board shelves and began dumping ashtrays.

"Hard to believe she was a cleaning lady. Maybe she'd had enough of—"

"I once wrote 'cleaning lady' on some school form, and she yelled bloody murder—I was supposed to put 'custodian.'"

Carson finished stacking the magazines. "It's amazing there are no ants and roaches."

"*That's* the smell," Lucy said. "Pesticide."

"I thought it was air freshener."

They worked in silence until Lucy stood from a squat by the window. "A visitor." She pointed at a nice white sedan behind Carson's rental and a large baldheaded man in a light-colored suit getting out.

He lumbered up the path with such difficulty, Lucy said, "He better not have a heart attack." She went outside to meet him, and Carson followed.

"Are you the family of Louise R. Smith?" The man was panting.

"Yes, I'm her daughter."

He pulled a business card from his jacket pocket. "When you're ready," he said, handing it to her, "we'd like to talk to you. At your convenience, at your convenience. Condolences." He nodded at them both before lumbering back to his car.

She held the card so Carson could read it. He whispered, "The company whose truck hit her." Lucy arched an eyebrow.

As soon as they were back inside, she said, "Let's call before the phone's disconnected."

"Now? It's almost five."

"Why not?" She put the business card on the plastic table, grabbed the receiver, and jabbed at the buttons. Carson decided to clean the stove top, which had brown streaks encrusted down the front.

"Yes, tomorrow morning at nine will work. Could you provide directions?" He watched her scribble in the margins of the *Enquirer*. She hung up and smiled. "Leave the talking to me."

THE MODERN GLASS BUILDING WAS in a small downtown area of Tallahassee proper. The lobby was spacious but not imposing. They took the elevator to five, and a young woman ushered them into a conference room. Carson wasn't sure where to sit—the long rectangular table seated at least twenty. Lucy immediately sat in a black leather chair in the middle. Carson went and stood nearby.

Only a minute later the door opened. Three people entered: a short man in his forties, a spruced-up guy about Carson's age, and a woman in her late fifties or older. The woman carried a steno pad, and the older man carried a manila folder. Everyone introduced themselves and shook hands. The older man, giving his name as "Fred, Fred Nickels," urged Carson to sit, so he took the chair next to Lucy. The three company people sat facing them and handed out business cards. Carson had a few of his own in his wallet, but Lucy didn't seem to expect him to reciprocate. Besides, he was not likely to drum up business here.

"Let me say, first, on behalf of myself and the company, we feel terrible," Mr. Nickels said. "This was a tragic, tragic event, and our deepest sympathies go out to you. Our driver, too, is very, very upset. In fourteen years with us, he hasn't injured a single person. But may I start by asking your names and relationship to Ms. Louise R. Smith? I believe you said—"

"I'm Lucy Smith, Louise's daughter, and this is my brother, Carson Smith, her son."

"Are you her only immediate family? We need to be certain we are talking with—"

"Yes. She was a widow and had only the two of us. Her parents are long since deceased. She didn't have a will."

"And you live where?"

"Hartford, Connecticut, and Carson lives in San Francisco. Would you like our addresses?"

"Yes. And some other information."

The older man looked at the woman, who was taking notes, and she proceeded to ask things like where they worked, if they were married and had children, even the name of the motel where they were staying. The younger guy took their driver's licenses to make copies in another room. The woman then asked a bunch of questions about Louise—her social security number and date and place of birth and whether she had been employed. Lucy rattled off most of the information, ending with, "Mommy was between jobs." Carson kept a straight face.

When the young guy returned with their licenses and the woman finished her list of questions, Lucy asked if there was a police report. Mr. Nickels opened the folder and removed the top sheets, which were stapled together, and pushed them across the table. He repeated how very, very sorry they were.

Carson and Lucy spent a few minutes reading the report. The accident had happened at 19:14. Two witnesses, a couple with the last name Fuller, had just exited a pharmacy across the street from the alley. They said the truck had its backup lights and beeper on *but deceased kept walking. Truck speed estimated 5 mph.* Three additional witnesses, on the same side of the street as Louise, said she appeared distracted, and they disagreed among themselves only on whether she stepped toward the curb or was busy fishing for something in her purse and not watching where she was going. They agreed with the Fullers that the truck had its backup lights and beeper going.

"We recognize that no amount of money can compensate for the loss of a loved one. Our company would like to do what it can, what is fair."

Frowning, Lucy raised her chin. "What do you mean by 'fair'?"

Eyeing her anxiously, Mr. Nickels pushed the entire manila folder toward her. "We believe this is fair, what we've set out in this agreement. I am authorized to make this offer available for seventy-two hours. This will give you time to consult an attorney. If no agreement is reached within seventy-two hours, the offer is automatically withdrawn, although naturally we remain committed to pursuing a settlement satisfactory to all."

The younger guy threw in, "We'll need to verify that you represent the estate and are the only—"

"That's fine," Carson said.

Lucy opened the folder and glanced at the top of a thick set of stapled pages. She closed the folder, rose, and offered Mr. Nickels—who had also risen—her right hand. "Thank you. We'll be in touch."

Carson stood too and leaned across and shook the man's hand. "If we retain an attorney, he or she will call you." He nodded at the other two people before following his sister out.

When they were alone in the elevator, Lucy flipped through the sheets of paper. Her eyes widened, and she broke into a smile. "The driver must've been stoned off his ass." She pointed to a line with a dollar sign. Carson whistled.

THEY FOUND AN ESPRESSO SHOP and took their drinks—an Americano for him, a tall skinny almond latté for her—to counter stools by a window. For a minute they just watched the pedestrians going past. Lucy was the first to speak.

"This is their *opening*!"

"You really want to counter? I realize I'm a novice at this, but they obviously haven't done their homework."

"I'm sure they'll go up ten percent *minimum*. They want this off the books. Trust me, they *really* want us to go away."

"What if they *do* do their homework? Now that they have her social, they can find out she's getting disability. They could demand an autopsy—find a dozen drugs in her system. They took a liability off our hands, Luce. Let's accept pronto and seal the deal."

His sister cocked her head and made the partial smile that deepened her dimple. "We should ask for their internal investigation report."

"Look, the last thing we want is for them to get pissed."

She squinted out the window. "The actuaries are giving her twelve more work years. Why didn't they check?" She turned to him and smiled gleefully. "He was stoned, *and* it wasn't the first time."

"I still say a bird in the hand is worth two in the bush."

She laughed. "A big fat bird." They sipped their drinks and watched the cars go by. "The girls were talking up this vacation package—Aruba. We all chip in and get a cute little cottage. I've been holding out, but now I don't have to."

"Nope."

"We'll fly through the *real* Bermuda Triangle."

CARSON PHONED THE ATTORNEY HIS firm recommended, and after the guy made some calls, he told Carson the good news: that if they settled and the police weren't filing charges, the medical examiner probably wouldn't bother with an autopsy. He suggested only minor changes to the agreement, nothing likely to scotch the deal, and by late afternoon the following day, the parties had exchanged signed copies. The check, made out to Louise's estate, would be delivered to the attorney's office the following morning.

After Lucy left, Carson would stay four more days in Florida to wind things up—the voicemails he got from the partners assured him he could take whatever time was necessary. The medical examiner released the body, and a funeral home cremated Louise relatively inexpensively. Signe asked about making some gesture in his mother's memory, so Carson suggested a donation to a charity like the Humane Society. *His* preference would have been to an organization helping abused children, but he gave Louise's wish preference, or at least his best guess of her wish. And he would scatter the ashes at a pond near her bungalow.

LUCY'S LAST EVENING IN FLORIDA, they went to a quiet, elegant seafood place. Once the waiter brought the bottle, did the label-and-cork bit, and left with their orders, Carson asked his sister if she thought Louise's death would change them.

"Not as much as his did. I finally learned to sleep through noise."

"I wonder if *she* learned to sleep through noise."

"She learned that when he was alive. No, some things won't change, not for either of us. We'll still be doers, not mopers and piners."

The bastard croaking *had* changed things. Carson eventually learned to walk through the apartment without scouting it out. The shadows on the hallway plaster didn't send his heart racing; a half-open door didn't make him retreat. The gruff cough outside was just a passerby.

For some reason, though, he'd totally blanked on his mother's reaction. Had she grieved—had she even cried? They'd lived disconnected lives. Louise worked a three-to-eleven at the hospital, so after school and later in his teens, after his two hours bagging, Lucy would make dinner from whatever he'd bought on the ten-percent employee discount. They'd hidden leftovers in creative ways, like in washed milk cartons—Louise hated milk. She also hated turkey, so that's what he bought for school lunches. And any kind of vegetable. Bread was the main thing they had to hide. "Louise can use her own damn earnings to feed herself," Lucy used to say. And her habits.

"How are the scallops?" His sister smiled merrily, her fork in the air. "The flounder isn't up to Greenport standards, but it's still good. Isn't it fun to order something on the menu that says *Market Price*?"

"They broiled them just right." He refilled her wineglass.

Carson remembered the time he'd talked Francis into retrieving a photo album with pictures of Addy as a child. Even in the blurry shot of her on a seesaw, you could see the ear-to-ear grin. Still, she was wrong in thinking she had died on the inside and was just going through the motions of living. *Louise* had done that. Addy's eyes were never opaque.

He leaned back against the seat cushion. "Being debt-free will be nice."

"You can pay off your student loans! But you might be better off investing."

"No, I'll pay them off—I'm more risk averse than you think." He sat forward again. "I don't feel giddy, like I might blow a wad on a yacht or something. I'll never be that carefree. But this is nothing to sneeze at, and once it hits me that I have more freedom about—"

Lucy shot him a stern look. "You won't quit your job!"

"No, not right away, at least—not before I have something else lined up. I'm not planning to *retire*, Luce. But now I *can* look around."

"What I'll change is little things. Have the cleaning lady come in *every* week." She laughed in a full-throated way. "I'll get a new teddy I've had my eye on. He wears a monocle and top hat. Wouldn't that be fitting? I'll tell you what will change for you: you'll see how nice it is having a financial cushion, savings to fall back on if something goes wrong. You never had that."

"Yes, a kind of freedom."

"Not just freedom—security! Pretty funny: Louise giving us financial security."

"It *is* ironic. Maybe I'll join the gym near the office—it's supposed to have a nice pool. But you're right: certain things won't change for us."

She slapped both hands on the tablecloth. "Remember when you were little and asked why God gave us him and Louise?"

"And you said He'd even things out—someday we'd be rich."

"It's come true!"

They weren't Bill Gates rich or rich enough for grand palaces and servants in wigs and livery. He and Lucy weren't close even to Violet MacDonalde rich. But he was rich enough to be brave, to take some risks. The first would be to ask to switch practice groups. After more experience under his belt, he might apply to a firm specializing in admiralty. Or even, in a few years—who could tell?

No, they weren't piners, he and Lucy. But wasn't the *capacity* to pine something good? How to explain it? Pining required a reserve, a pool of strength that let you look sorrow head on. It took *courage* to stare into pain. To miss someone and not try to forget.

LUCY HATED LONG, DRAWN-OUT GOODBYES and insisted on getting dropped off at Departures. Her face was animated with joy and affection when she leaned over to kiss his cheek, and that pleased him more than the money. As he watched her confident march into the terminal, it struck him that Louise's death meant they had survived some difficult journey. Sure, they carried scars from the old country, but they had landed on terra firma. Why waste that triumph with regrets? He wouldn't; he would seize the present.

Back at the motel, he called Signe and gave her the details of the settlement. She encouraged him to ask about switching practice groups at his annual review.

In the lobby, he fished in his wallet for a single for the soda machine and came across the strip of lottery tickets. He'd forgotten all about them. He bought a newspaper at the front desk and looked up the winning numbers. Louise's tickets were a total bust. That would've been *too* ironic.

CHAPTER 58

THE FIELDS GAVE OFF A vibrant green shine. This was plains country, flat and open, and in the sunshine, the vastness was scenic, not intimidating. A small plane buzzed overhead.

The sign at the development entrance said *One, Two, and Three Bedrooms Still Available!* The asphalt looked new, and the cinder-block houses were separated only by driveways, not shrubbery. The handful of trees were barely four feet high, too young to give shade. A few yards were strewn with bikes or toys—what Francis liked to call "the flotsam and jetsam of children"—and one had a large gray plastic castle with turrets. Anne MacDonalde's yard was empty, a battered blue pickup parked in the driveway.

The bell chimed loudly, and the door opened just enough for Addy to make out a face a few inches above hers.

"I'm Addy Cohn from Engel Klein?"

The door swung open, and after she'd entered and her eyes adjusted to the dark hallway, Addy could see that the woman letting her in was white and probably in her early thirties. Once they reached the sun-filled living room—the windows had no curtains or drapes—Addy noticed the woman's leopard-skin design top and black form-fitting pants. Her hair was dyed reddish and eyes heavily penciled both above and below. For some reason, Addy was reminded of a cabaret singer or what she imagined a cabaret singer looked like.

"Are you Anne MacDonalde?" The woman nodded.

There was hardly any furniture, just an olive-green couch, a chair upholstered in a dark-red paisley fabric, an unfinished wood coffee table, and two new-looking chrome-framed chairs with plastic cushions. The bare walls gave off the smell of paint.

Anne sat in the paisley-patterned chair, reached into a black purse on the floor, and took out a pack of cigarettes. Addy put her folders on the coffee table and plugged the tape recorder into an outlet. As she sat on the couch, she heard a toilet flush. Moments later, a white man maybe in his late thirties came in. He had short hair and wore jeans, dark sneakers, and a black V-neck sweater with no shirt underneath. His left wrist dangled an ID chain.

"She wants to tape it," Anne said.

The man looked a little annoyed, so Addy said, "It's just easier for me to record than take a ton of notes."

He held out his right hand; she shook it. His fingers were callused. "Reggie."

Addy went through the introductory speech and instructions and started with the basic questions. Anne spelled her name the way it was spelled on Dr. Lomond's documents and gave her parents' names as John Patrick and Lynne Lowe MacDonalde, also spelling them the same as on the documents. The only unusual answer she gave to the initial questions was that she didn't have a social security number.

"Why don't you have a social security number?"

"She doesn't earn enough to pay taxes," Reggie said. "Barely scrapes by. I help her out. That's not a crime." He shook a pack of cigarettes and grabbed one that popped up and lit it with a flat silver-colored lighter. After exhaling, he said, "Look, you said this would be private, right? What she says? She signed the form—the—you know—no-disclosing thing."

"We won't disclose the information except to the Scottish firm representing Violet MacDonalde's estate," Addy said, "but we can't guarantee that the firm or Scottish courts won't someday make it public. And they might have an obligation to report payments to the IRS or an equivalent British agency. I don't really—"

"Why do *they* need to get involved?" Reggie asked.

"I don't know the legalities—just that people generally have to report income. But—"

"Okay, okay." He gestured impatiently. "Let's say she writes a contract giving all her income to me. Then it's okay if *I* report it to the IRS?"

"I don't know, and I'm not your lawyer, or yours, Anne, so I'm not allowed to give you legal advice. I'm just saying that the nondisclosure agreement doesn't necessarily keep the law firms involved from reporting certain things to certain government agencies." Addy hoped they wouldn't seize on what she said to postpone the interview, which would piss Joe off.

"Just to make sure taxes get paid, is what you're saying?"

"I don't know, and again, I can't give you or Anne legal advice. I'm not your lawyer."

"But other than that, everything she says is kept secret, right?"

"We'll abide by the nondisclosure agreement."

Reggie told Anne, "You can always apply for a social security. Better late than never."

Addy asked Anne if she was married to Reggie, and she said yes, so Addy asked him some basic questions. His last name was Timm, and 'Reggie' wasn't short for anything. He reluctantly told her when and where he was born, his parents' names, and the dates they died, but when she asked about his meeting Anne, he said, "I've been told you can't ask her and me about each other, that we have a privilege and don't have to answer."

Should she tell him the privilege only covered private communications between the two of them, not things they said in front of other people or things they each observed? Brittany had stressed it wasn't the interviewer's place to argue with claimants, "just to suck information out of them." Addy told Anne and Reggie that the more information they provided her, the easier it would be to process Anne's claim.

When she asked the date they got married, the couple exchanged surprised looks. "Why do you want to know?" Reggie asked.

"It's relevant to ownership interests in the estate."

He looked doubting but said, "Couple of weeks ago."

"Do you have a copy of the marriage license?" He nodded and left the room.

"Are you employed?" Addy asked Anne.

Anne peered after Reggie. She inhaled on her cigarette and exhaled before answering, "Not right now."

"You don't have a job?"

"Not this minute."

"But in the past, have you worked?"

"On and off, here and there."

Reggie returned with a sheet of paper, a State of Kansas marriage license issued for Anne MacDonalde and Reggie Timm dated about two weeks earlier.

Addy placed it on the coffee table and photographed it.

"What kind of work do you do?" she asked Anne.

"Waiting tables, mostly."

"Do you have any pay stubs from the restaurants you worked in?"

"They weren't restaurants—they were bars."

"Do you have any pay stubs from the bars you worked in?"

"No."

"What's this got to do with anything?" Reggie asked. "The will doesn't say she's got to have pay stubs, does it?"

"The more documentation you provide, the stronger your claim," Addy told Anne.

"She sent you her birth certificate," Reggie said. "And there's the marriage license."

Addy kept her attention on Anne. "Didn't your employers require a social security number?"

"No. I was paid under the table."

"Always?"

"Look, she's gonna plead the Fifth if you keep asking questions like that. This stuff is none of your business. She should get a lawyer if you're—"

"I'm just trying to collect evidence—"

"Like she says, she got paid under the table. They did it to save on withholding. But it's not her choice—she goes along or can't work there."

"Do you have a driver's license?" Addy asked Anne.

Anne reached into the handbag, pulled out a thin black wallet, and removed a glossy card. Addy stopped the tape and examined the card—it appeared to be a Kansas driver's license. The name on the card was Anne MacDonalde, and the picture was definitely the woman Addy was interviewing. Addy asked if she could see the original birth certificate, and again Reggie left the room. The paper he brought looked official, having an embossed seal, and had the MacDonalde spelling and February 1962 date. Addy took a photo of the certificate and driver's license.

"What was John Patrick and Lynne Lowe MacDonalde's address at the time of your birth?"

"I don't know."

"But they were living in Treurig, New York?"

"No, traveling through on their way to some gig in New Jersey or Pennsylvania or somewhere. My dad was a street musician."

Anne gave vague answers about her parents: they both had died, but she didn't know when or where, having lost touch with them and having found out about their deaths only through chance encounters with friends. She had never tried to track down any inheritance because they were always "flat broke" from always being "on the move." She didn't even know where they were born or grew up or lived as adults or were buried. "Maybe they were cremated."

Anne's entire childhood had been rootless; they had lived out of a van, and Anne was "home schooled." She didn't know of any uncles or aunts; the only family history she'd ever learned was that her great-grandmother Mary MacDonalde had come from Scotland and had had a son named John who wound up in an orphanage "maybe or else was adopted." John married "maybe somebody named Susan" and had Anne's father, John Patrick MacDonalde. John Patrick MacDonalde married Lynne Lowe, and they had "just" Anne.

When Addy tried to pin Anne down on anything specific about her childhood, such as any city or state she lived in during a given year, Reggie would interrupt that Anne would be "speculating," and she wasn't supposed to speculate.

"Do *you* have a social security number?" Addy asked Reggie.

"Yeah, I got one. But a lawyer friend told us not to be giving it out."

Addy pressed for additional documents with Anne's name on them, like a lease or title to a house, utility bills, or a passport. Reggie came up with a lease for the address where they were, signed April 17. In the space for lessees was typed *Anne MacDonalde and Reggie Timm*. The second document turned out to be an April 21 letter from the telephone company to *Anne MacDonalde* announcing the starting date of service. Addy made sure she took at least two photos of everything. "The lease says it was entered into April 17 of this year. Where did you live before?"

"All over," Anne said, yawning. "We've been crashing with friends in different places. Never had our own place."

"But we got tired of living like that," Reggie said. "We decided to get married and settle down. Sure took us long enough, but now we're ready."

"What do you do for income, Reggie?"

He looked surprised. "I guess I'm gonna plead the Fifth. It's not like we're armed robbers or anything. Could you turn that thing off?" He motioned at the tape recorder.

Were they drug dealers? Addy turned off the recorder.

"Look, I don't want to get in trouble. Truth is—and I'm banking on that non-disclosing thing—truth is: I play cards. I do the ponies too and sometimes even the puppies, but mostly it's cards. And no, I don't tell the IRS, so if you tell them, I'm gonna deny everything. The point is that we decided to settle down, like I said. So we got married, rented this place instead of crashing with buddies, and we're serious about making a go of it. Anne here likes animals and might be a veterinarian. I've got this magazine on starting an alpaca farm. But nobody's pretending we've been living on the straight and narrow."

Had Anne been in prison? A conviction could mean lots of useful documents—court records, especially. But the Bettles interview had made Addy skittish. She turned the recorder back on and asked Anne the name of the last place she worked.

"It's been a while." Anne pushed the leopard-skin sleeves up over her elbows.

"Where was it?"

Anne looked at Reggie. "Denver?"

"That's right. That tavern."

"What was the name?" Addy asked.

"I don't know," Anne said. "We called it Jim's—he was the owner."

"What's Jim's last name?"

"Never really knew."

Addy quietly asked, "Have you ever been convicted of a crime?"

"No."

"What's that got to do with anything?" Reggie said angrily. "Anyway, the answer's no—you can check every state in the country—she's clean as a whip." Addy asked how Anne learned about the search for an heir to Violet MacDonalde's estate, and Anne answered without hesitation, "In the newspaper at some mini-mart off 70. Forget where exactly."

"She noticed the spelling right away," Reggie said.

"Tell me what you remember hearing about Mary MacDonalde before you heard about Violet MacDonalde's death and will."

"Hearing about her?"

"From your parents or anyone else."

"That she was from Scotland," Reggie said.

"Yeah," Anne said. "I knew she was from Scotland—that I was part Scottish."

"Is that all?"

Sounding annoyed, Reggie asked, "How many people know much about their great-grandparents?"

"I'm just trying to gather more evidence to support your claim," Addy told Anne.

"All I remember is my mother saying her grandmother—grandmother Mary MacDonalde—came from Scotland when she was a teenager because her parents kicked her out for getting knocked up."

None of Addy's additional questions or rewordings of earlier questions yielded any useful answers. In the back of her mind she could hear Joe yelling, 'Anne just sprang up two weeks ago when she got married and signed a lease? Between that and her birth certificate, you found out nothing she ever did, no place she ever went?'

Reggie did let Addy photograph his driver's license. When she was packing up her briefcase, he said, "According to the paper, twenty-five million of the estate goes to these other guys—some caretakers and church. Does she"—he gestured at Anne—"does she have to agree that she's only entitled to the other twenty-five?"

"I don't know."

"Because we talked to some lawyer, and she might be entitled to more."

"I don't know," Addy repeated.

KIMBERLY TOLD JOE THAT ADDY was calling from the airport, so he had her put through right away.

"Don't tell me she walked out on you," he barked.

"It sort of went well and sort of didn't. She has a few documents proving she's Anne MacDonalde but nothing at *all* tying her to Mary." Addy gave a brief summary of the interview, including Reggie Timm's date of birth.

"You found a MacDonalde with an *e*—the Scots will be jumping up and down."

ADDY LUCKED ONTO A WINDOW seat, and as the plane gained altitude, she watched the land spread farther. Long, narrow roads bisected fields of crops differentiated by shades of color, vast tracts that a century ago must have lacked these geometric shapes. How stalwart the pioneers must have been, crossing expanses unprotected not just from hostile Native Americans but from bandits and disease, from winds and storms, from the uncertainty of finding additional food and water beyond the stores packed in their wagons. "Adapt or die out," her biology professor had liked to say. Probably a lot had died.

Francis claimed that huge swaths of Indiana used to be forests, swaths so great that when the settlers cleared the woods for farmland, they made Indiana the nation's top lumber producer. Addy and Zach had driven across the northern part of the state, one large flat plot after another. Was it more intimidating as a pioneer to venture across endless prairie or to enter an unfamiliar forest? Where did a family decide to stop and lay down roots? What did you need to believe in if you wanted to break with the past and make a new life practically from scratch? What did Mary MacDonalde believe in? Or did she just do as Carson said, put one foot in front of the other, and only by looking back realize how far forward she'd gone?

CHAPTER 59

ADDY DROPPED OFF THE FILM at the camera store on her way into Engel. Before going to see Joe, she stopped by Michelle's cubicle and gave her the tapes.

"He wants me to transcribe Anne first, then Bettles," Michelle said. "I won't get to all of it today, and I don't have backup—the temp's dealing with the fax machine puking. This file's taking over the whole office."

"The faxes are for MacDonalde?"

"Drecker's people are sending stuff from Little Rock, Memphis, Miami."

The second Addy stepped into Joe's office, he shouted, "Your Reggie Timm has a rap sheet a mile long. Small stuff—rolling back odometers, forgery, fencing. Down in Florida adding an extra zero on a paycheck earned him a vacation in the pen for second-degree larceny."

Joe did his usual swimming in papers on his desk until grabbing one and tossing it in his out-box. Addy filled him in on more details, like Anne and Reggie not having had a prior address, supposedly just moving around the country and "staying with friends." Yes, she got the names and addresses of the friends. "The most recent ones they lived with had a camper in western Kansas—their last name was Jones."

"Why does the one person with a legitimate document sound the fishiest?"

"Anne probably could use the money." Addy wanted to find a silver lining.

"If this Timm fellow doesn't gamble it all away."

"He said one weird thing at the end. He wanted to know if Anne got the inheritance, would she have to agree to not go after the other twenty-five million—the part left to the caretakers and church and nonprofits."

"Just what the Scots want to hear!"

"How could she challenge that?"

"Argue Mary was entitled to half the estate when her mother died—the parents *couldn't* disown her, not legally. Something in the Scottish system—they're not paying me to understand it, so I don't. There *is* the contract, but who knows if it'll hold up."

"Contract?"

"The contract Mary signed. Agreed to take her entire inheritance in the form of a fixed payment when she emigrated. It paid for her ship fare with a bunch left over. It was no twenty-five million—that came from investments later on—but Mary's heirs could argue—"

"Her parents actually drew up a contract and made her sign—"

"And if Anne can prove the sum was an undervaluation of what Mary'd been entitled to—who knows how their accountants could work the numbers."

ROBERT NAPPED THE ENTIRE VISIT, so Addy used the time to tell Francis about the Bettles interview. How plausible was it that Mary would have shed the prejudices of her upbringing, Francis wanted to know.

"Her last few letters to Violet were pretty critical of racial prejudice," Addy said.

"Theory and practice are separate things, my dear. On the other hand, an interracial marriage *is* a plausible explanation for Mary's decision to stop writing to her sister. She may have anticipated reprobation from Violet on both accounts: living with a Black man *and* living outside the bonds of matrimony."

"Assuming Ms. Bettles's story is true, I wonder what happened to Brian."

"He may have died. Childhood mortality was not the rare event it has become today in industrialized societies. Recall: the 1920s pre-dated antibiotics, and many children died from routine—perhaps I should say 'common'—infections. As for the report on lynchings Ms. Bettles provided, allow me to give you a short story to read called 'Dry September.' A heartbreaking masterpiece by William Faulkner—in ten or fifteen pages, he draws a starker portrait of the barbarism and cruelties inflicted upon Black people in the South than one can get

410

from a *hundred* pages in a history book. Of course, many writers have tackled prejudice, from Mark Twain to . . ."

While he was talking, Addy debated bringing up Ms. Bettles's outburst, ultimately deciding not to—it would make Francis defensive. In her own mind, she'd come to believe that her questions weren't wrong—she *did* have a duty to try to locate any of the boys' offspring—but maybe she could have phrased the question better or apologized in advance for having had to ask it. Her discomfort at the memory of Ms. Bettles's hurt and indignation was not going away anytime soon. Still, her discomfort must be nothing compared to Ms. Bettles's pain. Nathan's face had always changed when he spoke of the Holocaust.

"But what about your second interview—you haven't said a word about Anne. Is she the real McCoy—the real MacDonalde?"

Once she started telling Francis about Anne, Addy found herself eager to describe all the strange details, ending her description by paraphrasing Joe. "It's as if she had no life before a month ago, except for the birth certificate."

Francis didn't seem surprised; he pointed out that Anne's secrecy could have been the consequence of criminal activities. "Consider the facts that seem incontrovertible: a doctor delivered a baby named Anne MacDonalde—with the *e*—for parents with the *e*, and they requested a birth certificate, and this young woman is in possession of it. And she was born less than a hundred miles from the spot Mary once lived and to which she was intending to return. *And* there are no other persons with that spelling to be found in a thousand-mile radius. Surely those are strong reasons to believe Anne, despite her perhaps living only a step or two ahead of the law."

Addy bent down and adjusted the blanket on Robert's shoulders. His face was pale. Sometimes when he napped, his cheeks turned pink.

"So is the Limbo drawer almost depleted," Francis asked, "except for Anne and Ms. Bettles?"

"And Grey-Davison."

"The fine-antiques dealer—I had forgotten he was still in the running. What has your document examiner concluded about the letters from his great-aunt?"

"Joe hasn't sent them for analysis yet. I think he's hoping the investigators turn up something that disproves the claim. And now we'll probably put *everything* on hold to vet Anne's."

"Let me pose this, for you seem dissatisfied: Has Joe found fault with the job you did, either in Taos or Wichita?"

"He hasn't read the transcripts yet, so I don't know. But I feel like Anne and Reggie were hiding something, so I feel stupid not figuring out what."

"If you are correct that they are concealing something, keep in mind that they have had *experience* in deception. It is an unreasonable expectation that you would be equipped to expose it. Especially because you had no time to prepare for the interview. Certainly Joe and the Scottish firm will understand that?"

The telephone rang, and still Robert did not stir. It was Sam, saying he only had a minute to talk. After hanging up, Addy told Francis, "Sam got back his GREs and did great."

"That is wonderful! Do tell him next time you speak that if there is any assistance I can provide, I hope he will not hesitate to ask. I feel as if I know him as well as any student I have recommended."

WHEN ADDY WENT INTO ENGEL the following week, after Joe was done listing the topics she should have pursued in the interviews, she asked if the Scots thought Anne was telling the truth about having no social security number and no documents from before March or April.

"She's no Girl Scout, but their duty is to find Mary's heirs, not upright citizens. Until we can prove she's lying, the spelling is the strongest evidence anybody's got. Drecker's following up on some stuff, so are the paralegals. We're holding off on the interracial for now."

OVER DINNER, FRANCIS LAUNCHED INTO his pep talk about her being "in an apprenticeship," saying she shouldn't react too strongly to "falling short" of other people's expectations. "I am no stranger to feeling one is a disappointment—no, indeed. I lack sufficient digits on my hands to count the times. It smarts more, perhaps, when one is young, before *the heart grows older* and comes *to such sights colder.* Although the sting was still strong that last trip to Indiana."

Addy looked up from her plate—this wasn't a story she knew.

"Returning home after my father's death, nothing seemed out of the ordinary, not initially. The fireplace and rocking chairs, the cast-iron stove, the pine table—I knew them all. The same pots and skillets hung from the lower beams. The lamps and shelves were not new. Yet *something* was different, *something* had been altered.

"It was only when sifting through the items in my mother's trunk—what had been her hope chest—did I realize. I found the journals with my articles, my high school diploma, and Cambridge certificate and copies of the later diplomas and letters announcing my teaching awards. All of it, Adelaide, was buried under the camphor-laden blankets. My father must have removed them from the shelves and mantelpiece after her funeral. All my accomplishments, born of hard work and diligence, of scrimping and saving and acts of self-denial—could not redeem me."

"But maybe he—"

"Why dwell on old wounds? The acorn *did* fall far from the oak, and that is that."

CHAPTER 60

BY MAY, PERSEPHONE EMERGED IN all her glory. Cherry blossoms surprised us from trees we had mistaken for skeletons. Tulips and daffodils crowded the florist stands; daisy petals showed colors new to their repertoire. The windows were opened, and sweet breezes chased off the staleness of darker months. The season of optimism bloomed around us.

"Is spring fever subverting your efforts to study?" I queried, noticing Adelaide's aimless wandering about the apartment.

"The only claimants left whose relationship to Mary hasn't been disproved are mine," she said. "Anne, Grey-Davison, and Bettles. Yet every proposal I make to nail things down gets rejected as too expensive."

"There are *no* other claims in the Limbo drawer? Then perhaps you have been assigned the most nettlesome."

My effort to make a silk purse out of a sow's ear unsuccessful, Adelaide meandered to the vanity and began sorting the mail.

"You may have noticed," I called over, "that I have cancelled a number of magazine subscriptions, which should make sorting a tad easier."

"I did notice. And Carson's not writing anymore."

"Oh?"

"He's seeing someone."

I kept my tone breezy and nonchalant. "Did his sister tell you that?"

"No, he wrote me."

Relieved that the breach was in the open, I remarked that although no one wanted to be bereft of an admirer, a dissembler with high-society pretensions was the proverbial 'bad rubbish' to which one bade good riddance.

FOR THE THIRD VISIT IN a row, Robert was out of sorts, evincing no appetite for drawing, being read to, or playing. Within minutes of his arrival, it seemed, he reclined against one of Millie's pillows, his gaze languidly roving from object to object before his lids closed and he fell fast asleep. I made mention of the boy's listlessness, and his grandmother said simply, "It's his heart. They're going to operate again."

At least work on my opus was proceeding. I modified some paragraphs on the *The Mayor of Casterbridge*, allowing that Henchard's impetuosity precipitated a number of the calamities befalling him, yet contending that this self-same tragic flaw also underlay the *good* passions that reigned in him. I would take this up with Olivia when next we spoke.

"ENGEL DOESN'T NEED ME TO come in until after finals, and then only part-time so I can study for the bar. The review course begins in July."

"But didn't you say that the Drecker firm procured more documents?"

"The paralegals are going through them. The Scottish lawyers—barristers—they're filing something in a few weeks, and the court will decide how the money gets divided. Joe might go over in case they want to ask any last-minute questions."

"Which claimant is the Scottish firm proposing be deemed Mary's descendant?"

"I don't know. I don't know how their system works—whether they make a recommendation or the court sorts through Anne's and Bettles's and Grey-Davison's briefs. The organizations—the ones helping single mothers—may argue that none of the evidence is strong enough to prove a connection and that *they* should get it."

"In other words, the situation is ripe for another Jarndyce versus Jarndyce."

SAM WAS ABLE TO ESCAPE New Haven several weekends in a row, and although his schedule precluded a presence at dinner, he was able to cajole Adelaide into attending an exhibit on Silk Road artifacts and a documentary on the Boxer Rebellion. The young man's range of interests was admirable. And after each date, he stopped by the apartment to discuss literature for upwards of ten or fifteen minutes, projecting a most heartening enthusiasm for the powers of language. Indeed, so much so that I shared with him the concluding sentence of my opus introduction—a paean, in essence, to Austen, George Eliot, Hardy, and Henry James.

Where is it writ that the gritty improves upon the melodious, that in literature, the Brecht ditty surpasses the Beethoven symphony?

"Nowhere," the young man succinctly answered.

HOW WOULD I FEEL, ADELAIDE inquired one afternoon, about joining her on a short excursion upstate once her final examinations were over. "I'd like to get away somewhere," she said, "before the bar review course starts."

"Did you have any particular locale in mind? Are you considering a resort, perhaps in the Catskills or Adirondacks?"

"Actually, I was thinking of snooping around where Clopes used to be. I'm curious if maybe some older person remembers Mary or hearing about her."

"Has no one done that?"

"Drecker just looked at newspapers and official records. The only time people were questioned was back in the twenties. Joe said the estate wouldn't pay someone to go now, but I could do it on my own."

"But won't the case be concluded?"

"Maybe. I don't really expect to find anything. I guess it's kind of an excuse to go for a drive in the country."

I readily acceded to her invitation but suggested we first consult with her mother, as she and Tony might want to visit for commencement.

Adelaide appeared surprised. "I guess I didn't tell you: I'm skipping it."

"You are what?"

"I'm not going to graduation."

To say I was taken aback would most assuredly have been an understatement. "But why? Surely we can still arrange a drive up—"

"I didn't go to my college one either. I don't like fanfare."

Fanfare! Fanfare! "My dear," I exclaimed, "a graduation ceremony isn't fanfare—or *mere* fanfare. It is a well-deserved recognition of academic achievement."

"Studying is a lot easier than working in a factory, say, or a refugee camp. Or being in the military. There are a million things much tougher—"

"That is not the point! No one is dismissive of the difficulties in other forms of toil. But academic achievement has its own demands, requiring a special blend of self-discipline, attention to detail, *considerable* intellectual—"

"Like I said, I was planning to skip it anyway. Sorry if you were looking forward to it." As if to exasperate me still further, she gave her trademark shrug.

"You needn't be sorry on *my* account," I rejoined. "Heaven knows I have attended enough commencements in the course of my career—I have even handed out diplomas. But I fear you may come to regret such a decision."

"By the way, Millie stopped by while you were napping. Robert's not coming for a few weeks. His parents are taking off work."

"How nice for him," I said, perhaps snappishly.

"No, it's because of the surgery."

I RETIRED TO MY OFFICE and applied myself to a task procrastinated for far too long: sorting and shelving the books sitting in cartons in the far corner of the room, cartons that had gone straight to the basement storage locker from my office at the university. Most of the volumes were novels and short story collections in the original French or German—a *Madame Bovary, Contes de Guy de Maupassant*, plus several Hugo and Balzac tomes. I had both hardcover and paperback copies of *Faust* and *Die Leiden des jungen Werther*, each with fairly typical Romantic era illustrations. And Thomas Mann, heavy both in weight and meaning. Alas, my fluency surely had diminished; I would need to resort to a bilingual dictionary to plumb these masterpieces now.

The bending and lifting proved an exhausting enterprise, and I sat in the desk chair to recover my stamina before embarking on folding up the emptied cartons. Loath to rise immediately, for some moments I did nothing save survey my domain. This *palpable* evidence of the quantity of literature I had read—literature I had experienced, studied, and in some cases taught—this *array* of fictional narratives and dramas lightened my mood considerably. It was akin to being surrounded by old friends. Certain spines I could recognize from a distance, the volumes of *À la recherche du temps perdu* the most obvious, of course, but also *Le rouge et le noir* and *Buddenbrooks*.

I turned to the shelves of English-language works and translations. My glance crab-walked past *Tess* and Hawthorne's stories to Hemingway's oeuvre. The well-worn, tattered copy of *For Whom the Bell Tolls* I could never bear to part with; I had used a later edition for my classes. In the spring of 1941, almost a year after the fall of France and the Low Countries, after Britain had survived the Luftwaffe onslaught yet knew not whether a Nazi invasion still threatened, how that novel engulfed me! Robert Jordan's emotions became *my* emotions; his worries—eluding the fascist forces, holding together the band of compatriots and protecting them, setting the detonators— became *my* worries. Spain's rugged countryside was as vivid as the Bethesda bedroom where Marjorie lay asleep beside me. *My* heart pounded against the pine forest floor.

My mood improved, and I was able to spend profitable time at the computer.

"YOU WERE IN MY THOUGHTS not ten minutes ago," I said, telephone receiver in hand. "I have been writing about how both Hardy and James endowed female characters with complex emotions, emotions beyond romantic love and maternal urges."

"I'd be happy to talk at length, Dad, but another time. Tony and I are leaving for Ashland soon, with a stop in Portland to see Rhoda and Pat."

"That's right. What plays are on your agenda?"

"A lot—we're going for almost a week. Then down to Crescent City to visit old friends of his. By the way, Pat—Rhoda's partner— she's decided to go back for her master's, after eight years in the army. Guess what in—comparative literature!"

"I'm confused—Rhoda or Pat? He was the one in the army, not she, was my understanding."

"Both are shes, Dad. Rhoda and Pat are lesbians."

I stammered something to demonstrate I was not prejudiced, urgently preoccupied with trying to recall if I had inadvertently said anything in Tony's presence during last November's visit that could have been deemed offensive. Fortunately, Olivia changed the subject, saying she had mailed me the addresses and telephone numbers where they would be staying.

"I trust that with all this gallivanting around," I responded, "you are not disappointed that New York cannot be included in your itinerary? You do know that Adelaide has decided not to attend her law school commencement ceremony?"

"Yes. We'll probably visit in the fall again. Marcia won't have her hands quite so full."

"What is she busy with?"

"Mindy is due soon. Twins, remember? And Madison's a handful at not even a year. Alex is very busy at work, so Marcia's helping out."

"How can Mindy be having more children with the oldest not even a year? Methods exist nowadays—"

Olivia laughed. "I told Tony: it's a good thing she's young. Just turned twenty-one!"

Omitting any mention of the connection to Adelaide's job, I said that we would be taking a short excursion as well, upstate, to enjoy the countryside before Adelaide applied herself to the exacting task of studying for the bar examination. Olivia seemed pleased with the news, closing the conversation by voicing the expectation we would speak again in a few weeks' time with travel stories to share.

Carrying a cup of tea back to my office, I recalled a discussion with my daughter long ago about women in literature generally and Shakespeare's characters in particular. We were of one mind: the great playwright eluded pigeonholing. For every Katherine there was a Portia; for every Lady Macbeth, a Desdemona; for every Ophelia, an… Olivia.

THE SATURDAY BEFORE HER FIRST examination, I overheard Adelaide talking and entered the kitchen just as she was hanging up the telephone.

"A wrong number?"

"It was Sam. He wanted to know if I'd go see *My Dinner with André* tonight."

"I have heard of it—it impressed many of my colleagues."

"I told him I can't—I have finals through Thursday."

"But you have been studying 'around the clock,' as they say. Surely you could take off a *few* hours? Sometimes a break helps clear—"

"He understood—he apologized for it being so last minute."

"Such a shame."

What was truly a shame, to my way of thinking, was Adelaide's calm manner on the telephone. My mind involuntarily hearkened back to *Pride and Prejudice* and Jane Bennet's placid demeanor toward Mr. Bingley, concealing the ardor of her affection—with grave consequences. A young man who is sensitive or diffident requires a clear, unambiguous sign of having earned a young woman's favor in order to summon the courage to continue in pursuit. I feared Adelaide might have committed Jane Bennet's blunder by failing to show enough pleasure in her suitor's company for him to risk further wooing. In contrast, the conquest-seeking types—and it was difficult to banish Carson from my thoughts in this regard—such types are not dissuaded by the absence of encouragement. But the finer souls—the Bingleys—often are.

"Perhaps, my dear, you could find time for a brief get-together Thursday night? I can do most of the packing myself, and there is no need for us to leave for Syracuse at the crack of dawn Friday."

"He's going back to New Haven Tuesday."

I consoled myself with the thought that our trip to the erstwhile town of Clopes would provide ample opportunity for me to discuss the perils of a Jane Bennet–like manner and the importance of displaying one's affections forthrightly.

CHAPTER 61

THE SUITCASES, COOLER, CAMERA, MAPS, AND a manila envelope were positioned by the front door when Adelaide left to pick up the rental automobile. She had moved with a singular alacrity, conveying an unalloyed eagerness to 'hit the road,' as modern parlance would have it. For the most part, I stayed out of her way, and although I was tempted to address her as 'esquire' to honor her recent change in status from student to attorney, I restrained myself, fearful of alluding even indirectly to our quarrel about commencement.

Despite the limitations occasioned by my weakened ankle, I was not entirely useless, making the journey down the corridor to leave our mailbox and apartment keys with Millie. She answered the door absent the usual smile; indeed, she looked haggard. When I proffered the piece of paper with our travel dates and motel information, she appeared befuddled.

"Oh yes, your trip. I'm sorry—I'm a little distracted. Robert passed away yesterday."

"He—"

"We knew it was risky—oh, what does it matter what we knew."

"No, no, it doesn't matter."

Jolted, I murmured condolences. Millie nodded, her eyes becoming watery.

My sorrow was real, and yet I worried that Adelaide might be on her way up in the elevator to fetch the suitcases. If she had parked right out front in the no-parking zone or had double-parked, I would need to descend immediately and sit in the vehicle to forestall our getting a ticket. How could I avoid appearing brusque or rude to my grieving neighbor?

Millie took the paper and keys from my hand. "You'll be back Sunday evening?"

"Yes. So sorry, Millie, so sorry. Perhaps we should shorten our trip and return in time for the funeral?" I glanced again toward the elevator.

"Oh no, Francis, please. It will be a private service. You and Adelaide go enjoy your vacation."

I returned to our apartment, and Adelaide arrived some minutes later, saying she had lucked onto a spot nearby. The need to rush with the luggage obviated, I broke the news about Robert, repeating Millie's insistence that we not alter our vacation plans. Adelaide immediately went down the hall and upon returning said that Robert's parents preferred only family at the service. Hence, we began the process of ferrying our suitcases and such downstairs.

IT WAS A LOVELY JUNE morning—sunshine and blue skies. The Palisades blended gold and brown near the top and silver and bluish hues below. Ledges and crevices emerged in sharp detail in such clear air, even slender shadows discernible. And the river flowed majestically, sunlight dancing off its surface.

The only bit of conversation we could muster prior to crossing the Hudson was Adelaide's suggestion that when we stopped somewhere, we telephone a florist to send flowers. And when we returned, make a donation to a research organization in his name, she added. I, of course, was in full agreement.

Yes, the beauties of nature were now lost to Robert. And when had he known the ordinary joys of childhood: games with friends, bicycle rides, or merely gamboling about a playground? The joys of budding sexuality and love? The bone-deep satisfaction of hard work and accomplishment? And if such joys were to have been kept from him directly, could he not have savored them vicariously, through the miracle of literature?

That his sufferings had ended was meager consolation. And, ironically, the realization that I would never be called upon to read to him afforded no solace. The gods have a mischievous way of casting an activity as a chore, a burden, until the moment we are relieved of it.

Adelaide concentrated on the traffic, which had not thinned appreciably as we left behind the city and suburbs. No doubt, with school being out, families were heading to the Catskills and other resort areas. But in due time, the highway cleared sufficiently for me to broach a sensitive subject.

"Have you by any chance read *Pride and Prejudice*?" I inquired.

"I think so. My sophomore year I had to take—I took Comparative Lit. Remind me what it's about."

"The Bennet sisters—Elizabeth especially—and a Mr. Darcy? The eldest Bennet sister, Jane, is enamored of a Mr. Bingley, yet she fails to make her emotions manifest. There are, of course, sensible reasons for not 'wearing one's heart on one's sleeve,' as they say, but in this instance, her modesty deceived him into believing her indifferent to his attentions. With the consequence that he abandoned his suit for her hand."

Adelaide said nothing, appearing to take pleasure in brief glimpses at the surrounding mountains and hills.

"Perhaps you wonder why I bring this up? I have some concern that you will make a similar mistake with Sam, that you will leave him with an impression of indifference."

She peered quickly at the rearview mirror. "I like him, but not romantically. I mean, he's nice and all—"

"Oftentimes romance develops over time, ensues from friendship."

"I guess. You once mentioned 'chemistry' with Grandma. It's not really there with him."

Not there *yet*, I longed to say. Perhaps chronicling *Elizabeth* Bennet's trajectory would have been more instructive. But I contented myself with exchanging remarks on the beautiful scenery of the Hudson River environs and, subsequently, the jaunt west toward Syracuse.

When we checked in at the motel, the obliging front-desk clerk drew a map illustrating the best route to the county road intersection Adelaide had specified, a spot she was able to piece together as the center of erstwhile Clopes. The fellow had never heard of the town, which did not surprise us, in light of his youth. The Great Depression—the period when Clopes ceased to be—was as remote in time to him, I suspected, as the Civil War.

SATURDAY MORNING, WE BEGAN OUR sleuthing in earnest. The scenery was, in spots, quite lovely: hills and glens and meadows, an abundance of verdant nature. But the county road intersection was merely a series of forlorn shops. I was barely able to decipher the faded lettering on an abandoned, boarded-up building: *Gartmann's Department Store*. The few functioning businesses, judging from our inching along the main street, were a laundromat, a barbershop, and the U & I Luncheonette. Adelaide suggested we patronize the luncheonette as it would afford her the opportunity to ask questions of the staff and other customers.

We were the sole customers. Adelaide told the waitress, a middle-aged woman sporting a pin that read *Kathy*, we were looking for a local entity that kept records of births, deaths, and marriages—a municipal or county office, for example, or even a newspaper. Embellishing the truth a tad, my granddaughter added that our relatives had once lived in the region, and we were curious about family history.

"Nothing's left—not Gartmann's, the bus stop, old Arthur's," Kathy replied, explaining she had grown up in the area. All that remained were the gas station, grocery, and hardware store "up on Hamilton."

To Adelaide's inquiry about the area once comprising the town of Clopes, Kathy boasted that she was one of the few residents who knew the neighborhood had once been so named, owing to the fact that her husband's family had run the Clopes drugstore. But when the factories "all shuttered," the downtown stores had had to close too, and the town's population had dwindled. The few unabandoned farms were owned by "city retirees" looking to make "chemicals-free crops just for themselves." Was there a local newspaper? People usually read the *Gazette*, a county weekly, or got the *Post-Standard* or *Herald-Journal* if they worked up in Syracuse. No, Kathy knew no one in the area named MacDonald.

But as to her inquiries about the local churches, Adelaide got an earful.

"The Catholics go to Saint John's, and the Lutherans go to Saint Mark's, and the Meths"—Kathy laughed midsentence. "I need to start calling them Meth*odists*. I'll draw you a map. There's a couple of others—I don't remember the names—newer ones."

After paying the bill and, at Adelaide's insistence, leaving a generous tip, I followed her to the car. We drove to the Lutheran church first. It was closed and locked, but Adelaide suggested we walk through the cemetery behind the building, and it being a short distance, I assented. We wandered among the gravestones for ten minutes or so, finding no MacDonaldes; there were a handful of plain McDonalds.

At the Methodist church, a relatively young man identifying himself as the pastor said there were several MacDonalds in the congregation. He directed us to a bulletin board with a newsletter tacked up listing congregants who had volunteered for this or that. Again, the spellings of MacDonald were the conventional ones. Adelaide hesitantly inquired whether any of the MacDonalds attending the church spelled their last name "different" than the ones on the bulletin board, and he said no—but he had been in the area only twelve years.

THE CATHOLIC CHURCH CONTAINED THREE living people—a priest and two parishioners—all of them eager to speak with us. The only MacDonalds they recalled were a group of families in the Christmas tree business who had moved away in the early eighties. Did they spell their name the same as the fast-food restaurants, Adelaide asked? No one could recall if they spelled it *M-a-c* or *M-c*.

The Presbyterian church windows were boarded up. The abutting cemetery contained perhaps two hundred graves, and Adelaide and I strolled up and down the rows. We discovered quite a few MacDonalds employing the *M-a-c* spelling and some, the plain *M-c*, but none used a final *e*.

A man approached, a rough-looking fellow unlike any minister or deacon or, indeed, any parishioner dressed for services. My misgivings were quickly allayed by his introducing himself as the groundskeeper and readily engaging in conversation. He worked for several cemeteries, but no, he was unaware of anyone named MacDonald with any unusual spelling. The question did not seem to intrigue him— possibly the story of Violet's fortune had not penetrated these backwoods. The sole question *I* posed was whether he was aware of any paupers' cemeteries. He answered in the negative but, as an afterthought, mentioned a triangular patch of land near the road leading to the interstate, which had "a monument and bunch of graves from the old boardinghouse fire."

Back in the car, Adelaide asked if I minded stopping at the triangular patch of land. In truth, I was weary and would have liked to go directly back to our rooms; whatever small optimism I had incubated at the beginning of our quest had hatched and flown the coop. But I was reluctant to confess my fatigue. Nor was I insensible to the fact that for Adelaide, the prime motivator for this trip was the detective work, despite her contention of simply wanting to get out of the city. So I rallied and gave an enthusiastic endorsement, quipping that she was "leaving no gravestone unturned."

As we continued along the winding roads amid meadows, woods, and the occasional farm, clouds developed, yet they remained too thin to harbinger rain. The sign for the conduit road to the interstate came into view, and I pointed to a grassy clump to the right. "That must be it."

Adelaide pulled the automobile onto the shoulder. "I will rest here," I said. "Let me put down the window before you turn off the engine." I watched her stride purposefully in the direction of the row of stones peeking out above the tall grass.

Bit by bit, the air around me became 'close,' an adjective that invariably puzzled students my last few years of teaching. As I explained, "'Close' is a synonym for warm and humid, not unlike muggy, but performs the additional function of expressing one's sense of being hemmed in, of the air impinging on one's ability to breathe freely." Perhaps we were adjacent to a lake or reservoir. The sky was a pale gray now, and I was put in mind of an afternoon fishing at the creek—

"Francis, come here!" Adelaide waved excitedly.

I exited the vehicle carefully so as not to jeopardize my ankle's recovery and wended my way through the Timothy weeds and long grass, blades clasping at my pants legs. Off to my right, gnats swarmed in their silly circles.

The first stone I encountered was a small granite obelisk, and I paused to read the inscription.

In memory of the twelve souls who perished in the Rourke fire, January 12, 1914. Only two could be saved.

Several yards away, Adelaide stood by a row of dark-gray slabs. She pointed to one that slanted into the ground at quite an oblique angle. I gingerly made my way over and bent to read the inscription: *Mary Agnes MacDonalde.*

Neither of us spoke. Silence reigned. A breeze rustled the leaves on the trees nearby, and a yellow butterfly flitted past. Time elongated.

An elusive ghost we had pursued for a year and a half found substantiation in an undeniable, physical, tangible block of stone. It was a wonder to behold. Was this not akin to stumbling upon the burning bush or some other miracle whose validity could not be questioned? No flimsy piece of paper that might or might not prove fraudulent, no object that might refer to some other Mary MacDonalde, this was Truth. Unimpeachable like the Great Pyramid. I read and reread the name, as if it refused to etch itself in my conscious mind, before murmuring, "It's her."

My voice must have acted as a spur rousing Adelaide from similar contemplations, for she peered down at the adjacent gravestone, set at a different angle, and I followed her gaze. *Iain Brian MacDonalde.*

No longer contemplative, Adelaide hurried to the grove of trees and returned holding a short, thick stick. She squatted and began to dig away the grass and earth obscuring the bottom of Iain's stone. I fancied myself a lookout, although what crime my granddaughter may have been committing I would have been hardpressed to say. Were we trespassing? In any event, the occasional cars and trucks that whizzed by did not slow.

When Adelaide ceased digging and rose from her squat, I could read the bottom of Iain's stone:

February 5, 1904–January 12, 1914.

Not yet ten years old!

I watched Adelaide perform a similar excavation in front of Mary's stone. Here the grass was knottier, harder to dislodge, but eventually Adelaide dropped the stick, stood up, brushed off her hands, and moved back so I could read the epitaph too.

May 3, 1888–January 12, 1914.

"I'm going to get the camera."

While she hastened to the automobile, I remained by the mournful graves. A more lonesome locale was difficult to imagine, oblivion rendered by an unmown pasture partially hidden by an unremarkable stretch of road on the outskirts of a town that no longer existed. What obscurity! And Mary could not have foreseen who eventually would bear witness to the site of her interment: strangers with only the slimmest and most tangential of connections to both her and her sister.

More clouds drifted by, and the long grass seemed to perspire, to seep its moisture. The ferns drooped their heavy fronds, the lugubrious atmosphere at one with Mary's and her son's premature demises.

Adelaide took quite a number of photographs of the obelisk and Mary's and Iain's gravestones. Some were from a distance; some up close.

"It is a shame," I said, "that no one notified Violet of Mary's passing. Presumably a letter addressed to the MacDonaldes of Glynnis-on-Tay would have made its way to her."

"Maybe she never mentioned her family."

"I wonder why her heart was set on returning to Clopes. Perhaps, as the letter indicated, she yearned for the familiar. Her first journey, from Scotland, was not a journey of choice. That may make all the difference."

Adelaide slung the camera strap around her neck. "I'll be back in a sec—I want to check the other headstones just in case." My granddaughter reported back that there were no additional MacDonaldes. The two of us repaired to the car.

Determined to shake off my despondency at Mary's and her son's fates, I congratulated Adelaide on solving the mystery. "A mystery that has bedeviled your law firm for almost two years, my dear. But alas, I am a little too worn out to think clearly. What light does this discovery shed on your claimants?"

Adelaide treated me to a wry smile, Mona Lisa–like in its

suppressed merriment. "Ms. Bettles had Mary alive all the way into the 1940s, so she's out. Mr. Grey-Davison had Mary giving birth to a daughter, Helen, in 1913, which *could* have been true, if the child was rescued from the fire and then adopted. But he produced a newspaper picture of his parents' wedding in 1936 and said the Mrs. Hill listed in the caption was Mary. *Anne's* claim is still possible. Her grandfather might have been a second son of Mary's and either rescued from the fire or put up for adoption before then. At least now we have something specific to research. There could be archived news articles."

"But is there still time before the Scottish court makes its decision?"

"I don't know. I'm going to leave Joe a message at work."

"Will the firm reimburse? Calling from a motel can be more expensive than one might expect."

"They didn't ask me to make this trip," was her inadequate reply.

ON THE WAY TO DINNER, Adelaide told me the substance of her telephone message to Joe: that we had discovered the graves of both mother and son, the date they had died, and that Adelaide had taken photographs of the gravestones. She also mentioned the Rourke fire, suggesting someone look into the names of the survivors.

The small Italian restaurant a few miles from the motel could hold its own against fancier establishments in the city. Holmes and Watson, as I had dubbed us, elected to enjoy a carafe of wine, and the meal was marked by a levity my granddaughter and I had not shared for many, many moons.

"One has to positively marvel at the lengths to which the claimants went to contrive their fabrications," I said. "The *absurdity* of so many claims—a judgment I have been holding in abeyance for so long because, for all we knew, the stories might have proved true—the absurdity now blazes comically. Tell me: Do you consider the tree stump the most outlandish? Or the trapeze artist one of your colleagues investigated?"

"The World War II double agent—Malcolm MacDonalde—was pretty wild."

"What accolade befits our Mr. Grey-Davison and his tale weaving in the legendary Joe Hill? 'Most daring,' for picking a character so much in the public eye? And slain with his own sword, furnishing the photograph. Wasn't that going out on a limb and establishing Mary's existence—and appearance—when facts could surface to prove him a fraud as they now have?"

"Maybe he thought he had no choice—that we'd find articles in the Richmond papers mentioning her. Which we did—*lots* of society-page columns from the mid-1930s mentioned Helen and her mother."

"I suppose the newspapers do retain archives. But if he were denominated Violet's heir—her great-nephew, in effect—wouldn't historians as well as newspapers and others find the Joe Hill story too important to ignore?"

"I'm guessing he's researched enough to know there's nothing to disprove it. And if he convinced the Scottish court to seal the record, nothing would come out other than he was Violet's heir."

"In any event, Grey-Davison's identifying Mary in the photograph did lend a patina of authenticity to his claim. Although I prefer to think that he was simply taken with his own imaginative prowess. As Tony says: Deciphering the mind of a fraud is not simple. In *that* I will allow him—Tony—some credence. On the other hand, perhaps he was telling the truth about descending from Joe Hill. If so, I don't doubt he can parlay that fact into a golden goose of its own, by writing a book or selling his Aunt Sarah's letters to collectors."

"Even if the letters are genuine, there could have been some local activist in the Carolinas or Virginia with the last name Hill. He didn't have to be a labor activist—maybe part of a breakaway church sect. Or someone against racial segregation."

"Speaking of that: What do you think of Ms. Bettles using the illegality of interracial marriage to account for the absence of documents? That took some careful planning as well. I suppose she may have felt Violet's fortune becoming hers effected a kind of cosmic justice. In *Tess*, Thomas Hardy says—although no doubt ironically— that Tess's rape may have been a divine retribution for the rapes of peasant women by her knighted ancestors. *Benighted* ancestors, I should say."

Our conversation continued on in the same jovial vein throughout the meal as we found humor in this claimant's tale and that. But when

I pointed out how Adelaide had succeeded in narrowing the investigation down to corroborating or disproving Anne's story of her grandfather having been Iain's younger brother, Adelaide surprised me by suggesting there might be no further investigation—the Scottish court might just take Anne at her word.

"Even if they track down the survivors of the Rourke fire, and they were not named MacDonalde, she may nonetheless inherit the twenty-five million dollars?"

"Anne can argue her grandfather was put in an orphanage *before* the fire—maybe a few years before. That could be close to impossible to disprove."

"I suppose the lessons of *Bleak House* are not far from the solicitors' minds."

Peering cautiously at me over the rim of her wineglass, my granddaughter asked, "Since I didn't expect to be done looking for clues about Mary until tomorrow morning, do you think we could do a small detour on our way home and stop in Treurig?"

"Treurig?"

"Where Dr. Lomond lived."

"Does his daughter have additional records?"

"I wasn't thinking of bothering her—she showed Brad the file. But we could do like we did here: ask around."

"Hoping to find what? I thought Anne's parents were just passing through."

"That's what she said—what they told her. So we probably won't find anything. But what if they stayed a few weeks or longer, and someone remembers something?"

"Tomorrow is a Sunday—what will be open?"

"Churches."

"Didn't Violet's detectives already 'scope out' the area, as the television detectives phrase it?"

"They never knew about Anne. She wasn't born until 1962."

"Yes, yes, that's right. But how far of a detour will that entail?"

"Just a little, south of the Finger Lakes. But we don't have to worry about the time, since we won't be checking into a motel."

"I concur: it is much less worrisome being on the road when our destination is our own apartment. And it is staying light later, this being the week of the summer solstice. However, if we come across a second grave for Mary, I will not know what to believe. Perhaps we should stop in Sleepy Hollow."

CHAPTER 62

ON DAYS LIKE THIS, NORTHERN California could rival Southern in warm, rampant sunshine, fresh air off the Pacific, and sparkling blue water. The florist's was crazy busy, worse than Carson had ever seen it. He stepped to the back to let the elderly women get waited on first.

The owner, a thin middle-aged woman, noticed and insisted on helping him herself. She took him to a table of elegant single-stem flowers in unusual arrangements—even the vases were unusual, artistic-looking. But he went with the large *Summer Bouquet*, a safer bet.

He chose the route to the trolley stop that went by nice pastel-painted houses. Rows like these lined the hills, resembling children's chalk blocks, pink and yellow and green and blue, all soft shades. Arriving at the stop, he felt sleepy standing in the sunshine. That was how he'd felt those weekends in San Diego—you could never get work done living in a place so pleasant. Two ancient-looking Asian women also waiting smiled at him and his bouquet.

The morning telephone conversation with Lucy had accomplished its purpose. For the first ten minutes, they'd just traded investment advice. The judge had insisted she diversify: stocks, mutual funds, T-bills—she rattled off company names Carson recognized. "He had a fit I still put so much in T-bills, but I let him pick the mutual funds and stocks. Is that what you're doing?"

"On a smaller scale. I paid off all my student loans."

Her tone became even more cheerful. "At last! Are you going to celebrate? Take a trip somewhere!"

"Actually, I was going to ask *you* to take a trip. You haven't seen San Francisco. My treat."

"I'd love to. What's a good time of year? Is September nice?"

"I was hoping sooner."

"Hmm—and why would that be? To meet somebody?"

Carson laughed. "No pulling the wool over your eyes. I wouldn't mind a second opinion. *Your* opinion."

"Signe or someone else?"

"Signe."

Lucy made a humming sound. "You know, I might be able to swing it. He's going to some judicial conference in LA in July. I wasn't going to bother—LA in the *summer?* But I could hop up to San Francisco for a day."

"Great!"

"Whose feelings are you not sure about—hers or yours?"

"I'm always not sure of my own—the male fear of commitment."

"Is she head over heels? That's not the worst thing in a wife."

"No, she's nobody's fool. Especially mine. Solid head on her shoulders."

"Problems in the sack?"

"Don't think so. But what do guys ever really know?"

"Want kids?"

"Yep. Worried about her biological clock."

"I thought she was twenty-five."

"Twenty-seven."

"Still, that's—"

"She thinks people should spend two years as a couple before having kids."

"I always told you to find someone who plans!"

"*I* plan. I planned law school—"

"You complained Gloria and Jennifer planned too much."

"The little things. Don't you like spontaneity?"

"In the sack, Car; that's the only place."

SIGNE'S WINDOWS FACED SOUTH, AND being on the sixth floor, the apartment was almost as bright and airy as the outdoors. She was tidy—a "clutter detester"—plus each piece was nice: the small teak dining room set, the low bookcase with glass figurines and pretty pottery, the silvery mobile of fish dangling in the corner over the stereo setup. Now he wondered if the bouquet was the right choice.

"What's the occasion?" she asked after a quick kiss. She had on a navy-blue tank top that draped gracefully.

"None. Or because it's been a month."

"Since what?"

"Since I last brought you flowers."

She stepped into the small kitchen and began unwrapping the paper around the bouquet. Her back was to him, the ends of her blond hair hanging just past the shoulder blades. She turned briefly to take an emerald-green vase from the window shelf, calling through the doorway, "Do you make notations on your calendar?"

Carson was taken aback, either by the comment or tone. "It seemed a while—that's all." He approached the kitchen, vaguely sensing an obligation to make up for some offense.

"Bringing flowers like these to your regular hookup is either an apology or getting ready to ask a favor. I guess it could also be to take the big step, though that's usually roses."

"You sound used to big steps."

She turned; he could see her arched eyebrow. "Are you serious?"

"Why didn't you accept anyone?"

She held the vase at arm's length, examining the stalks, adjusting a petal. "Perhaps I wasn't ready to settle down."

"Now *that's* a romantic response—I'm just happening by at the right time."

"Who says I'd accept you?" She brushed past him and placed the vase at the center of the teak table, smoothing the bamboo mat underneath.

He strolled to the window and looked eastward at the bay. "My sister's coming to visit."

"When?"

"Early July—hasn't told me exactly. She's going to LA with her judge and will fly up for the day."

"What do you think she'd like to see? Fisherman's Wharf and a nice lunch overlooking the bay? Or would she actually like to go out on the water?"

"Probably she's fine with strolling around. I can show her some good views—if you can't get off. And wouldn't need your car."

"I told you: July's a bitch. You can have it all day—just let me know when so I don't schedule a client visit. We should probably go soon."

He watched her pack the blue-and-white-striped canvas bag she liked to take. Her boss's yacht was a thirty-six-foot with a wing keel. The last time, Mike killed the engine, hoisted the sail, and let Carson take the tiller. In *seconds* he felt comfortable, even though the bay was crowded in a way the sound never was. Mike steered them to a spot he liked to drop anchor, and Candace did the whole food-and-wine spread. The females kept the conversation going, Mike and Carson contributing now and then, everyone having a good time. It was in situations like these—and with her parents too—that Signe showed her skill at mixing with different kinds of people. Not just witty and fun, she had a light touch steering people around sensitive subjects. And was unwaveringly loyal to those she considered in her corner. She even stood by Chelsea through all the drama—Chelsea, with an unerring instinct for dating jerks. No question about it: when it came to looking out for her kids, Signe would be a she-bear.

Driving along the Presidio, the top down, Signe's hair blowing every direction, Carson asked himself why had she fallen for *him*? He'd never wondered with Gloria or Jennifer. College girls were eager to please, especially at first. He had liked that, their devotedness—which was so obvious that his friends used to push him to fool around on the side. "Just act contrite if you get caught, say you were drunk. They'll forgive you." But the idea of cheating left a bad taste in his mouth. He looked over at Signe, at her confident profile. *She'd* never put up with bullshit. There was a lot to be said for clear-eyed maturity.

CHAPTER 63

ADELAIDE WAS ANXIOUS THAT WE not miss the eleven-o'clock checkout time, and admittedly I slept in later than usual, perhaps having had a bit too much wine at dinner. But I was willing to postpone breakfast until we had made some headway toward Treurig. "Although," I said, "I feel as though we should detour past Mary's and her son's graves again and confirm for ourselves that they are real—that yesterday was not a dream."

"I was thinking the same thing. But we have the photos. Do I turn at the next light?"

I homed in on the yellow highlighting on the map. Our itinerary started with highway but segued onto smaller roads with scenic views of one of the larger lakes. "Yes, go right."

In consequence of our great discovery the day before, I felt quite lighthearted. To the extent that Adelaide's reputation at Engel Klein required salvaging, locating Mary's and Iain's graves was a more-than-adequate achievement for the purpose—a veritable *coup*. Yet I was reminded of a complaint Olivia had once leveled: that male faculty stintingly praised women academics as 'competent' or 'thorough' while lauding other men with encomia such as 'insightful' or 'brilliant.' The former pair of adjectives spoke more to diligent work than intellectual ability. I suspected there was much truth to her observation. I hoped the partners at Engel Klein would view the discovery of Mary's and her son's graves not simply as the consequence of thoroughness but also of initiative, resourcefulness, and a keenness of mind. Which was not to belittle thoroughness and competence—traits deserving of greater esteem than often accorded!

After a breakfast hearty enough to allow us to postpone our next meal until suppertime, we followed local country roads through the well-known resort area, a picturesque landscape of farms and fields flaunting their early vegetables and berries. The sky was a lovely cerulean blue, adding to the pastoral tableau of alfalfa fields, pastures dotted with haystacks, and silver silos gleaming in the sun. Cows grazed lazily while a mare nuzzled her foal. Pigs crowded a long trough; ducks congregated on a pond—a more scenic idyll could not have been contrived.

"This retreat 'into the land,' my dear, is effectuating a sort of emotional *purification* for me. Of late, our lives have been spattered with falseness. The smell of new-mown grass is *cleansing*."

"What do you mean: falseness?"

"To begin with, the elaborate and devious falsehoods of the MacDonalde claimants. How many cheats and impostors have surfaced to swindle the estate! People with no compunction about lying, spinning intricate fibs. And then, in the personal sphere, Carson's hiding his childhood of poverty."

"He hid a lot more than that. His father used to beat him."

In stunned silence I listened as my granddaughter recited a litany of appalling cruelties, unpredictable assaults by a malicious and often intoxicated father. Several incidents in her narration caused me to wince. And his mother's intoxication and utter indifference to the torment were like so much salt in the wounds. My sense of purity was no more.

Alas, when she had concluded, memories of my own conduct toward the young man surfaced: barbs, clever put-downs, and arrogant, ill-founded opinions that I had so proudly served up during our Saturday-evening dinners. What an astonishing durability and accuracy these memories possessed, a Javert-like doggedness that had all but abandoned me in recent years in other realms of life.

Why had I not recognized that the young man's high-society pretensions arose not from snobbery or opportunistic cunning but from the fictions we each construct to soothe our souls? Why had I harped on the young man's failure to come clean with respect to his poverty, when I forgave Tess *her* concealment of shame? A better man Francis Wallace would have been, surely, had he followed the precept of not casting the first stone.

And yet, despite the young man's sad history, I could not deny my relief that his liaison with Adelaide had come to an end. It would not have led to a marriage of true minds. If I regretted his absence in any way, it was in the loss of an opportunity to apologize, to try to undo whatever hurt I had occasioned. Of course, the impact of my behavior may have been inconsequential—he may have viewed me simply as a tiresome old fogey, an assessment which, in many ways, would have been on the mark.

The abrupt increase in traffic distracted me from these troubling thoughts. Due to some road construction, we were shunted onto smaller byways. A lake briefly came into view, dotted with sails and motorboats and water-skiers, before we were again among fields and woods.

The slowdown became a creeping and then an intermittent start-and-stop and, ultimately, a standstill. In our midst were not only automobiles but recreational vehicles and small trucks, not a few towing small boats. The two lanes of traffic going the opposite direction did not fare as badly, but a culvert between the lanes precluded a U-turn maneuver, even if it had held out promise of a more expeditious escape.

After several minutes of idling, Adelaide said she would turn off the engine to avoid its overheating, a precaution I could not oppose. The woods prevented us from seeing if a restaurant or service station were nearby.

"My dear, in light of the fact that we are not moving, would it distress you terribly if I took a short trip to the cover of trees? Admittedly, my goal will be apparent to the occupants of the other vehicles, but that may be the preferred alternative."

Adelaide was not discouraging and assured me that if the traffic began to move, she would pull onto the shoulder. My ankle fared surprisingly well on the short trip to the woods—I had to take care to pay it some attention and not grow oblivious to my gait.

Traffic did not move, and the sunshine became a source of discomfort. The moisture on the back of my shirt welded the fabric to the car seat. Flies and wasps flitted about the windows and even entered the vehicle, where the atmosphere proved too humid even for them. Finally, after an interminable interval, the brake lights on the vehicles ahead went out. Adelaide restarted the motor, and we recommenced moving along the road, albeit quite slowly.

Once we had passed the last sign for the resorts, however, the traffic eased a little more, and after turning onto a smaller road, we encountered smooth sailing.

IF TREURIG HAD A DOWNTOWN core, we failed to find it. Adelaide pulled into the parking lot of a strip mall and suggested we "grab a snack" at the small restaurant.

The waitresses proved neither talkative nor helpful, the younger and less sullen of the two informing us, between chomps on her chewing gum, "It's not much of a town, if you ask me."

Adelaide inquired as to whether they were familiar with people named MacDonald—she did not specify the spelling. None were. They pointed to a pay telephone in the rear, which had both a white- and yellow-pages directory, and Adelaide spent several minutes perusing the books and making notes on her pad. I attempted to engage the gum-chewer in more general conversation and learned that only she among the staff had grown up in the immediate area.

"If you want to make really good money," she said, "you work at the lakes."

Sitting again, Adelaide informed me that the telephone book contained an entire page of MacDonalds with the common spelling but none with the *e* spelling.

She had even checked the *M-c* spelling—almost another full page of names. She had jotted down the names and addresses of several churches, and when the waitress came with the check, Adelaide asked about their locations. In this matter the waitress proved helpful, and with my granddaughter's quick exit, I was able to leave a much smaller tip than we had in Clopes without risking a rebuke.

ORGAN MUSIC GREETED US IN the parking lot of the First Church of Christ, Scientist, raising the specter of an entire *congregation* to interview, not a happy prospect as I was secretly eager to head back to the city.

"It's still a while till sunset." Adelaide earlier had countered my concern about the delay caused by the traffic standstill. Only to myself did I cavil that our goal on *this* leg of the journey was unclear, Mary's and her son's graves having been discovered.

The church was empty save for the organist, a middle-aged woman, stout but not unkempt. Seeing us approach, she ceased playing and smiled graciously. No, she did not know any MacDonalds, although she had cousins with that name in Milwaukee. Yes, spelled just like the fast-food chain. She seemed surprised but not bothered by Adelaide's request to wander in the adjacent cemetery. The organist also proved helpful in giving us directions to several other churches, warning, however, that most held services only in the morning.

The cemetery yielded nothing of value, and before long we were again in the automobile. Of necessity, roads in undulating countryside do not offer short, direct routes, and we traversed around hillocks and even creditable hills, as well as flat tracts. We saw little in the way of homes, stores, gas stations—Clopes was a veritable metropolis in comparison. The afternoon was looking to be little more than a wild-goose chase as, one by one, Adelaide crossed the churches off the list she had gotten from the organist. Yet gravestones with MacDonalds using the standard spelling abounded, suggesting to me, at least, that the area had been popular among immigrants from Scotland and Ireland. Perhaps poor Mary should have put down roots here instead of in Clopes.

Adelaide pulled into the small lot of a shack advertising *Bait Live Worms*, promising me that this would be the last inquiry. She reported back that while the man inside didn't know of any MacDonalds currently living in the area, he did remember several families by that name when he was a child. A Ralph MacDonald was in his Sunday school class until Ralph's family moved away. There was nothing unusual about the spelling, however. The church that the families had attended was the Episcopal, ten miles farther down the road; if we saw the county sheriff's, we'd gone a mile too far. Yes, he remembered Dr. Lomond; Dr. Lomond had removed a fish hook from his thumb.

Despite the sky already auguring dusk, I acceded to Adelaide's request that we check out one final cemetery. Happily, the bait vendor's mileage approximation to the side road was on the mark, and a short distance after turning we encountered a sign at a parking lot entrance: *St. Andrew and the Redeemer Episcopal Church Welcomes You*. The church was old and had tall, narrow stained-glass windows. The only vehicle in sight was a station wagon at the far end of the lot.

Adelaide tugged at the large wooden doors, which did not budge. She walked a little way toward the station wagon before returning. "There's a sign for the cemetery; it's up that hill. Do you want me to go alone? It might be a little climb."

I said I would attempt to accompany her if she moved the automobile closer to the path. We parked beside the station wagon, which was covered in dust. Adelaide removed the camera from the trunk, slung the strap over the same shoulder bearing her backpack, and the two of us began a slow trek up the worn and fragmented asphalt under a bower of trees. A trill of songbirds in this Hansel-and-Gretel woodland lent an aura of enchantment to the scene.

At the summit, a cemetery spread before us, the gravestones a hodgepodge of different sizes and shapes, easily several hundred in all. Some stones appeared quite old and worn thin as wafers; others shone as if recently polished.

Gesturing discreetly, I said, "Perhaps he can guide us." The groundskeeper trudged toward us, a hefty figure with a forceful step, a large spade resting blade-side-up over his shoulder. I had the sense he became aware of us as we neared, notwithstanding his downward glance.

When we were just a few yards apart, he paused and, eying Adelaide's camera, said, "Not taking my picture."

"No," she quickly responded. "It's just for the headstones. I'm looking for people named MacDonald."

His stolid countenance revealed nothing, and without providing helpful pointers, he continued his trudge, heading over the rim of the knoll in the direction of the parking lot. In order that Adelaide not feel offended by his brusqueness, I commented how that line of work must attract loners. Secretly, I attributed his taciturnity to the ways of rural people, not to his occupation. Marjorie had always mistaken the farmer's lack of gregariousness for a lack of ease.

"If you don't mind," I said, motioning toward a bench, "I'll sit a bit and leave the trekking to you. I am hesitant to overstress His Majesty, whom I must continually serve."

My granddaughter wandered up and down the rows nearest, the camera remaining in its case, her steps slow but not dilatory. She informed me on circling back that there were a number of MacDonalds but none with the *e* spelling. She then departed for the farther rows, beyond the large monuments.

After some minutes, I glanced at my watch, anxious at the latening. As was my wont, I helped the time pass by silently reciting poems.

The curfew tolls the knell of parting day,
The lowing herd wind slowly o'er the lea,
The plowman homeward plods his weary way,
And leaves the world to darkness and to me.

A perspective worth emulating, I realized; instead of decrying daylight's end, I should be embracing the meditative pleasures the hour afforded.

Now I noticed that Adelaide had halted and seemed to be studying an inscription. She removed the lens cap from the camera, slipped it into her back pocket, and held the camera up to her eye. A moment later she moved for a slightly different angle, perhaps taking several photographs. She repeated the motions at the adjacent stone. Had my fantastical prediction proved true: there were *multiple* Mary Agnes MacDonaldes?

Of course my curiosity was piqued. As I rose from the bench, she turned and beckoned with her hand. Perhaps she had found other gravestones containing the *e* spelling—Mary *may* have had additional children!

I arrived in my lumbering stride. "What have you discovered?" Adelaide pointed at two gravestones.

"But there are no *e*'s at the end."

"Read the names."

The first gravestone said *John Patrick MacDonald* and the second, *Lynn Low MacDonald.*

"There are no *e*'s at the end," I repeated.

"But the first and middle names are *identical* to those on Anne's birth certificate—John Patrick and Lynn Low."

"I suppose if we were to visit all the MacDonald gravesites in the country, we would come across such coincidences."

"It's not a coincidence."

443

Adelaide reached inside her backpack and pulled out the manila envelope. She withdrew a piece of paper—the clinic form. *Lynne Lowe MacDonalde*, I silently read.

"Look at the handwriting," she instructed.

"I am." *Lynne Lowe MacDonalde* was written in the space above the typed *Mother*, and *Anne MacDonalde* was written in the space above the typed *Child*.

"Don't you see?"

"See what?"

"The only names that are handwritten are Lynne's and Anne's—not the father's."

"But there is no space for the father's."

"Not on this form, no. You remember saying to me that whoever wrote the names had florid handwriting?"

"It *is* florid." I was still at sea. I sensed, however, that Adelaide had reached dry land.

Slowly she explained, "What if whoever did the writing—whether it was Lynne or a nurse or midwife or some assistant—what if whoever wrote Lynne and Anne's names on the forms put florid curlicues not just at the *beginning* but at the *end* of every word? What if that was just the way they wrote?"

The shadows were lengthening every moment we remained in this isolated park. I tried to banish impatience from my voice. "*And?*"

"I'm saying: What if the names didn't actually have an *e* at the end—what if the *e*'s are just curlicues?"

"All of them?"

"That's right: Lynn and Low and Ann and MacDonald. And what if whoever *typed up* the names for the birth certificate application—someone *else*—didn't realize that? What if the typist thought the curlicues were *e*'s?"

My feeble old brain was beginning to function. "The typist mistook the flourishes for letters, for the letter *e*, you are saying, when in fact *none* of the names on the birth certificate actually ended in an *e*? Not Lynn nor Low nor Ann nor MacDonald."

Adelaide beamed at me expectantly. Perhaps my own face began to smile as her hypothesis took root.

"Yes, yes," I said. "Lynn commonly lacks an *e*, and her maiden name, Low, certainly could lack one. Ann is spelled without an *e* as often as with one. So they all are plain MacDonalds, without a final *e*?"

Her voice became rapid, excited. "It might've been obvious to the typist if the form had had a space for the father's name and John and Patrick had also been handwritten with flourishes. But it didn't. Maybe the typed form, the birth certificate application, was done later, and the typist just asked someone the father's name and spelled it normally."

How long we stood there mulling over this theory, it would be hard to say—there was a marvelous sense of completeness, of tying up of loose ends. Adelaide clearly embraced the idea wholly, declaring Ann a complete fraud who had parlayed a typographical error into a potential bonanza. And, in due course, I arrived at the same conclusion.

"My dear, I believe you are right. Someone who, through a fortuitous accident—a typographical error, as you say—suddenly found herself many years later in a position to masquerade as an heiress. A plan almost *brilliant* in its simplicity."

"She applied for a driver's license," Adelaide said, "and all those other IDs she showed me during the interview, she applied for them using the birth certificate. Maybe in the past she'd gotten it corrected, but for whatever reason, she never threw out the first one."

"Little suspecting it would come in so handy. Until she read in some magazine or newspaper about Violet's will."

We began walking toward the path down to the parking lot.

"So what is the next step?" I inquired.

"Now that we know the proper spelling, Joe can have the paralegals look in this area for documents for John Patrick and Lynn and Ann without the *e*—marriage and driver's licenses, death certificates, vehicle registrations, school records. I'm guessing there will be plenty."

"Are you sure your firm hasn't already performed this investigation?"

"Not for MacDonalds without the *e*—there are tens of thousands."

Dusk had unequivocally descended as we descended the knoll, and Adelaide permitted me to lean on her arm. "The mother may have been the one with the flowery hand," I opined. "In those days, it was not uncommon for the father to be absent when the mother went into labor. Even when women gave birth at home, the father would steer clear of the event—only females, such as sisters and aunts, would be present. So Lynn Low MacDonald may have arrived at the clinic alone and been handed the form and instructed to fill in her name and, once the baby was born and its sex determined, to fill in the child's name as well. Yes, the mother would be requested to write the baby's name herself so Dr. Lomond would not risk the headache of a misspelling—risk a *lawsuit* even—in light of the myriad variations in names. Philip can have one or two *l*'s. Francis can be spelled with an *e* instead of an *i*. But wait: if Lynn was a regular patient, wouldn't Dr. Lomond's assistant already have known the spelling?"

"He didn't have regular patients—only handled emergencies."

Our rental automobile was the sole vehicle in the lot. "And it also stands to reason," I exclaimed, "that the admitting form would omit a space for the father's name. Paternity can be a matter of delicacy or dispute that nurses and the like would prefer to avoid. The government, of course, demands to know paternity, but that issue can be resolved after the mother recuperates."

"There are a lot of ways it could've happened," Adelaide agreed, unlocking the car doors.

She opened the trunk and stowed the camera by the suitcases, and once she started the engine, we lowered the windows, letting in that wonderful fresh scent the mountains exude of a summer evening. Imagining a stop for dinner and a good night's sleep in my own bed, I was 'riding high,' as they say, my only concern that of finding a restroom in the not-too-distant future. I was uncomfortable with the idea of relieving myself on church grounds, particularly in the absence of true urgency.

There were no streetlamps on this offshoot, so Adelaide proceeded cautiously. Up ahead, I could just make out the glow of a lamp at the intersection with the main road.

"I am trying to recall," I said, "if in those days, doctors were such sticklers for insurance information. Certainly not before the war, but by 1962? A woman in the latter stages of labor, say—I suppose the doctor's staff would have been content with the minimum of information before delivery. But wouldn't Lynn or John Patrick have had Ann's birth certificate corrected? I suppose they may have been too distracted by the trials and tribulations of caring for a newborn to even have *read* the certificate once it arrived in the mail. There may have been half a dozen other children keeping them busy. Siblings may all be *in league* with Ann—or perhaps she is hiding the entire scheme from them as well."

"Damn!"

"What's wrong?"

Adelaide pulled the vehicle a little to the right—there was no real shoulder—and turned off the engine. However, she did not dim the lights.

"I think it's a flat."

"Are you sure?"

Without answering, she got out of the car. "Damn!" I heard her repeat.

I leaned over toward her window. "Isn't there a spare? I admit I haven't changed a tire in decades, but I do remember—"

"It's *two* tires. It didn't feel like I drove over anything."

"My goodness. They would not have given us *two* spares, would they?"

"I'll try to get the car up to the main road so we can flag someone down."

She got back in and restarted the motor. It was a painful affair, creeping along with the driver's side sinking lower and lower. However, Adelaide was able to successfully maneuver the vehicle onto the shoulder of the main road, and by a stroke of good fortune, headlights approached.

CHAPTER 64

THE AUTOMOBILE MUST HAVE BEEN going slow, for it pulled onto the opposite shoulder mere seconds after Adelaide had gotten out and begun to wave. The driver emerged and crossed toward us, and I was able to recognize him through the windshield.

"We got two flat tires," Adelaide told the groundskeeper. "I didn't feel like I drove over anything."

He remained some feet away and, without looking directly at her, said, "Construction workers. I can take you to a mechanic. Has spares. All kinds."

After I got out, Adelaide grabbed her backpack and locked up, and we crossed the street and climbed into the middle row of the groundskeeper's station wagon. I duly thanked him, fully aware of how fortunate we were that he had happened by. Indeed, in this minute or two while we discussed our plight, not a single additional vehicle appeared in either direction.

"We may have to stop at a motel tonight," my granddaughter murmured as the man began driving.

"If getting the tires fixed takes time, then yes, that would be a wise move." Despite the possible thwarting of my wish to be home, my mood rallied. You did not grow up on a farm and shrink from adversity. If a blizzard came, or drought, or a neighbor's barn caught fire, you were spurred to action. And, I confess, a mild exhilaration took hold: my granddaughter and I had proven ourselves a crackerjack team. It diminished my satisfaction not one whit that the lion's share of the credit belonged to the lioness and not to me.

Our driver took a fork to the west, where the sunset lingered. The mild air, the turquoise hues of twilight, the blues and greens and indigos in woods and sky, conspired with the easy rhythm of the road to lull me into sleepiness. House lights remained few and far between. Curving around a hill, the land on our left abruptly opened into large flat fields and the faintest paleness on the horizon. Were these farmlands, and if so, what crops grew? Alas, the pressure on my bladder was increasing. How much farther to the mechanic, I wondered. Out in the country, 'nearby' can mean ten miles.

Leaning forward, I said to our Good Samaritan, "Excuse me, but are we near the mechanic's? I am afraid I may have to go on a call of nature, if you understand me."

"Ahead." He slowed and turned onto a dirt road that appeared to head across a vast field. I thought I detected a dim light in the distance.

"Where are you going?" Adelaide asked.

"Shortcut," the man replied.

The land on either side was as flat as parts of Indiana. And although darkness quickly settled on us, the moon was full, a soft golden sphere, not the blazing disk of the harvest moon or hunter's moon. The dim light in the distance did not grow appreciably more intense, but I could see it was not a figment of my imagination. Were those woods beyond?

Again I leaned forward. "I am afraid that even five minutes will be too long a time for me to wait. I am perfectly comfortable with stepping off to the side of the road; I do not require facilities."

Barely a minute later he brought the vehicle to a stop and was considerate enough to turn off the headlights. "There's marsh." He pointed to a clump of stalks to the left.

"Thank you."

I was able to exit the station wagon without assistance, and although wondering at his preference for my relieving myself in the marsh as opposed to on closer ground, I wanted to be obliging. The groundskeeper got out as well, and I assumed he was hearing the same call, but a quick glance over my shoulder showed he went to the rear of his vehicle.

I made my way carefully, and as the soil began to give, the moonlight showed a sharp drop-off, the reeds evidently growing in a depression. The dark night sky seemed immense. Even with the lunar glow, stars were beginning to glitter. No crickets sounded— noiselessness covered all.

I stood at the edge of the slope and did my business. As I pulled up the zipper, a scream pierced the silence. Turning, I saw against the full moon the silhouette of a spade. Reflexively I stepped back and attempted to raise my arms, but the soft soil gave under my bad ankle, and I lost my balance. The spade banged my shoulder as I fell. Hitting the damp earth, I lay panting, awaiting a second blow. Pain shot along my arm.

No second blow came. Despite the pain, I was able to raise my head. The figure had gone. I rolled onto my stomach. And began to crawl and squirm up the incline, pushing forward with my left foot. My hands grasped the soil, at reeds or grass, my fingers seeking anything rooted they could grip. The soil became pebblier, scraping the skin on my palms and wrists. Reaching the crest, I lurched myself onto the flat, dry ground.

The man was by the car, his back to me. He dodged toward the rear—the hatch looked open. He ran again to the front. Then to the rear. He ran to the front and this time around it. Adelaide appeared by the open hatch. The man circled the car, and she did too.

I crawled on my knees. The base of my palms hurt. My shoulder felt on fire. I could hear my own panting but had to keep going, one hand, one knee, one hand, one knee. They kept circling.

My fingers touched something sharp. Metal. The spade. I groped for the handle, the wood. I pulled the handle close and raised it upright and pressed the blade into the ground. I hoisted myself onto a knee. Leaning on the wood, I was able to stand.

The man's back was to me—Adelaide must have been on the far side of the car. He stood stone still. I hobbled toward him, the spade my crutch. My shadow accompanied me.

He placed a shiny object on the roof, close to the front windshield. With both hands, he climbed onto the hood—how had he become so agile? I limped forward and tried to quiet my gasps. I reached the car and rested my weight on the good foot. Every breath seared my lungs.

He was on the roof, holding the shiny object. Where was Adelaide?

And then the laws of physics broke. Eighty-year-old fingers tightly clasped the spade's wooden staff. Eighty-year-old arms lifted the spade. Eighty-year-old arms swung it back and swung it forward.

The metal hitting him knocked the handle from my hands. My legs folded, and I slid along the side of the car onto the ground. My heart drummed painfully.

Leaning with my back against the door, I saw only the ground in front of me. Noises, thud-like noises, came from the opposite side. Undecipherable at first, they had to be, I realized, the sound of assaults to Adelaide's body. Again and again and again. I had no strength; I was sapped empty. Empty of all but the knowledge of God's perfidy. His unspeakable cruelty. Damn you, God, damn you, damn you, damn you.

CHAPTER 65

THE WIND CALLED MY NAME. Not in a long, haunting wail or eerie echo, but clipping the beginning. *Fran*-cis, *Fran*-cis. A shape, ghost-like, ran toward the marsh. It reached the rim. *Fran*-cis, *Fran*-cis. I tried to speak but could not. I tried again. She began to step down into the depression. Once again, a source beyond my voluntary powers took hold, making my voice rumble. A loud "Aaah." She ran back. Her hair in wild strands.

"Can you get up; can you stand? You need to get in the car." I heard the door open. "Is anything broken? I can help you up. Francis, you've got to stop crying and tell me what hurts. What hurts?"

"Nothing, nothing."

She put a hand under my armpit. "Are you bleeding?"

"I don't know."

"Try to lean forward. Can you get on your knees?"

"If you'll help, under the arm. I think I can stand."

Leaning against her and the car, my weight primarily on my left foot, I slowly rose. She helped me into the seat behind the driver's. She got in up front.

"Where's the key?" she yelled.

"Try the rear."

She jumped out, slammed the hatch, and got back in. The motor started; the headlights went on. She made a slow U-turn.

We retraced our way along the dirt road, the bounces shooting sharp knives into my shoulder. I gazed at the back of her head, the tousled hair. Was I dreaming? Dreams give us landscapes from another dimension, from somewhere beyond life. But the scene outside the window was too detailed for a dream.

Now we were on asphalt. Hills appeared. We passed woods but no buildings. No oncoming traffic.

"Look," I cried out, "a house. Lamps are on—stop. We can call the police."

She kept driving. "The bait-shop guy said the county sheriff is just past the turnoff to the church. They could take you to the nearest hospital."

"I don't need a hospital."

We drove through the dark, following the parallel beams. No cars came toward us. Adelaide eased up on the gas pedal. Ahead on the side of the road sat the rental car, with its two flat tires, undisturbed. An emblem of lost innocence, an emblem of who we had been not very long ago.

THE COUNTY SHERIFF'S OFFICE WAS gloriously lit. Dear, kind, precious civilization. The parking lot contained five or six patrol cars, additional reassuring sights. Adelaide pulled into a spot by the front entrance.

"I wish I weren't so caked in mud," I said as she helped me along. "Perhaps I could wash it off before we talk to anyone."

"No, leave it on. And let me do the talking." She spoke with authority, authority commanding acquiescence. I was grateful.

Only after sitting on the varnished bench did I notice her blouse and hair were splattered. Was it mud? Blood? Was *she* hurt?

She went to the counter. The young officer writing barely peered up, his unconcern suggesting he supposed we were lost tourists. The men at desks in the rear of the large room threw perfunctory glances our direction but resumed their work.

Adelaide's voice possessed remarkable self-confidence. "We were attacked by a man who I think worked at the Episcopal Church cemetery. He tried to kill us. I hit him with a shovel."

Her words acted like a vortex. Everyone in the room hurled toward her.

Someone asked if we were injured. Adelaide shook her head no, she wasn't, but I might be. My ankle had been re-sprained, I said, and my shoulder was sore, possibly cut. They would bring someone to examine us.

In short, simple sentences, Adelaide explained our arrival at the cemetery, the groundskeeper disappearing down the hill in the direction of the parking lot, the flat tires, the ride in his station wagon, and then the events on the dirt road. I listened intently as she described the man following me toward the reeds and how his carrying the spade had alarmed her, although she couldn't say why—she also had been bothered by his taking the shortcut through an empty field. Her anxieties had led her to exit the vehicle and watch us, but it wasn't until he lifted the spade that she realized he meant to kill me.

She had jumped in his car, but the key was gone. Next she described the chase around the car and his climbing on the hood and roof, holding either a knife or gun. She had not noticed my approach, her eyes being fixed on him, and when he shouted and fell, she wasn't aware he had been hit. The spade had landed nearby, however, and she grabbed it up and hit him as he started to rise. Her voice grew softer when adding "more than once." At the end of her narrative, she handed an officer the Demon's car keys, saying his station wagon was out front—we had taken it here.

The officers expelled questions like gunfire. What were our names and addresses, which church, at what time did this and that happen, and so forth. They had her describe in more detail the ride to the field, which way the groundskeeper turned to get on the dirt road, how far she estimated we had traveled. They asked us to repeat what had transpired in the field. Some of their inquiries were directed to me, some to her, and some to both of us.

All in all, we must have recounted the episode a half dozen times. In addition to frantic note-taking, a tape recorder was running. The officers were astute listeners, their questions perceptive. I swelled with pride each time Adelaide mentioned having had no idea I was making my way to the car or that I had swung the spade. The only point at which the discussion seemed to veer into tedious minutiae related to Adelaide's use of the spade.

"You say the man and the shovel landed on the ground at about the same time?"

"More or less," she answered. "It all happened fast."

"And you decided to grab the shovel?"

"Before he did—yes."

"And did he try to grab it?"

"I didn't wait to see—I couldn't risk it. Plus, whatever he had in his hand—a gun or knife—I couldn't let him use that either."

"Was he still holding it when he fell?"

"I assumed so—like I said, I assumed he'd jumped. And I didn't see it fall on the ground."

"How many times would you estimate you struck him?"

"Five, six—I don't know. He kept trying to get up."

"And this was on the head?"

"I wasn't really aiming. I guess it hit him on the head, because of where I stood."

"And each time you hit him, he started getting up again?"

"Except the last. Then he didn't get up."

"Did he plead with you to stop?"

"He didn't say anything."

"Did you see the weapon when you were hitting him?"

"No."

"Did you check to see if he had a pulse? When he didn't get up?"

"No, I ran to find my grandfather."

Throughout the course of these recitations, officers came and went—some to desks to make telephone calls, some to speak into what looked like walkie-talkies. A siren flashed by the window. Unlike in the Manhattan precincts depicted on Procrustes's shows, we seemed to constitute the sole crime scene in town.

A woman about Olivia's age and wearing blue plastic gloves asked to examine me. She listened to my heart and lungs and took my pulse and applied one of those blood-pressure cuffs. I watched an officer taking photographs of Adelaide, particularly her face, hair, and clothes. The blue-gloved lady then picked pieces of mud from my scalp, placing them in a small plastic bag, and, using what I at first thought was a piece of glass but later realized was a slide of the kind that went with Richard's microscope, she gently scraped my shoulder. Bless her, she had a gentle touch—Dr. Conti's staff could have used some pointers. She also gently coaxed me into moving my arm this way and that, asking when or if I felt pain. Only when she made the mistake of suggesting I be taken to the hospital to be examined further did my good nature shrivel.

"I have had enough distress for one day and no intention of making myself into a mound of dough to be kneaded by doctors. A little ibuprofen will do."

Adelaide gloriously came to my defense, assuring them that we were fine, and in any event we would see the doctor the following morning. She requested a glass of water for me and reached into her pack for the ibuprofen container. Again, her tone of authority was a wonder to behold, and all discussion of a trip to the hospital ceased. She inquired of the officers about retrieving the rental automobile and our luggage. The vehicle would be towed to the lot outside, we were told.

In short order a good dozen people—some in uniform, some not—rushed into the station and disappeared into back rooms, reemerging with equipment and cameras and what appeared to be enormous flashlights. In a trice, they were back out the door.

At a far desk, an officer holding a telephone receiver shouted across the room, "Chuck, the victim's at county, DOA."

This tidbit of news precipitated in me two very strong—and different—reactions. The first was indignation. How could such a creature—I assumed the officer was referring to the groundskeeper—how could such a creature be denominated a *victim*? I was sorely tempted to lecture the man on the word's denotation! But my second reaction was a spasm of exuberance. I did not openly rejoice—it would have been unseemly—but feigning sorrow at the monster's demise was far beyond my capabilities.

A young officer asked if there was someone we wanted to call—family, perhaps? No; those conversations could wait the morrow, I assured him. My granddaughter was of a different opinion, whispering to me that she wanted to leave Joe a message. The young man was quite obliging and allowed her to use a telephone.

And he retrieved a wheelchair to take me to the restroom to clean up. He washed my shoulder carefully and wrapped it in bandages and assisted me in removing my muddied clothes, furnishing me with a pair of navy-blue uniform pants and matching shirt. I felt quite deputized. Wheeling me back into the main room to where Adelaide sat, he gave firm instructions I was to see my doctor as soon as possible.

"What did you tell Joe?" I inquired when we were left alone on the bench.

"Just that we found graves for Lynn Low and John Patrick without *e*'s, that the birth forms might be typos and maybe Drecker should look for records in and around Treurig for all three of them without *e*'s."

The flurry of activity, of people coming and going, talking on the telephone, typing on computers, continued with no letup. "We must be the first violent-crime victims the police have seen in a long time," I remarked. Someone kindly brought us cups of tea and Danish pastries. The pastries were not particularly fresh, but my goodness, was I hungry!

Typed pages, summaries of our statements, were handed to us to read and sign. I perused mine slowly. The typist had done an exemplary job of adhering to my rendition, and although I would have liked to make some word changes, I decided this was not a situation calling for literary precision. The only actual errors were lapses in punctuation, but again, this was not a report destined for publication. How tempted I was to pen at the bottom *Francis MacDonald* with elaborate curlicues!

Adelaide having performed a parallel act, we were escorted to an adjacent room separated from the main room by windows. Here a large table with magazines was at our disposal, and a young woman brought us packaged sandwiches, sodas, and bags of potato chips. My ravenous appetite had hardly been quelled by the stale pastries, and the two of us dispatched the sandwiches in a matter of minutes, Adelaide no more squeamish about eating than I.

"Considering we had no dinner, this is no cause for shame," I murmured, gesturing at the now-empty tray.

"I heard the officers talking—they said his name was John Blake, and—"

"Blake, of all names!"

"He lived out there, at the end of the road."

What immortal hand or eye had framed his fearful symmetry?

Too exhausted by the day's events, we did not converse further. I could not muster the concentration required for reading and sat inert while Adelaide turned the pages of a *Field & Stream*. It was after eleven when a young officer came in with our luggage and said our rental vehicle had been towed to the lot. There were no motels nearby, but he would escort us to a room with beds. Adelaide, visibly annoyed, asked couldn't we leave, but the officer said apologetically that they would be unable to fit us with new tires until the morning.

"We packed an extra set of clothes for emergencies," I said, "never expecting we would need to make use of them."

Adelaide inquired about taking a shower, and I was wheeled to our quarters, a windowless room resembling a small barracks with metal-frame beds. The instant I rested my head on the starched pillowcase, Morpheus abducted me.

CHAPTER 66

Daylight filtered through gaps between the blinds, and I could make out grated windows and long ceiling lights suspended on chains. Where was I? The sheriff's station.

Adelaide's suitcase sat on the adjacent mattress. Her voice sounded from nearby. "You're awake."

"What time is it?"

"A little after nine. Do you want help up?"

"Yes, it would be safer."

She was dressed in fresh slacks and a clean pale-blue blouse; her hair looked recently brushed. She pulled back the blankets and top sheet and used an arm at my back to guide me to a sitting position. One glance at my face sent her scurrying for the ibuprofen. Returning with the pills and a cup of water, she said we could leave as soon as I was ready as the automobile had brand-new tires.

My ablutions completed, I was rolled in the wheelchair down a corridor to where Adelaide awaited with the suitcases and backpack. The door opened onto morning mist. Both the luggage and I were eased into the rental automobile, the vehicle's interior greeting me like an old friend.

The officer by the gate in the chain-link fence swung it open for us, and as Adelaide pulled even with him, he said through her open window, "If you want to eat breakfast in peace, wait until you turn on 17." What had he meant? I inquired.

"You won't believe what I'm going to tell you. The police got a search warrant last night and searched the guy's property. They found bones—human bones."

"Was he robbing graves?" I shuddered at the ghoulish thought.

"They don't think so. They think"—she shot a momentary look my way—"they think he was a serial killer. They'll have to run tests to be sure. They're getting bulldozers."

To my right was the most quaint, bucolic scene imaginable: cows grazing on long grass near a freshly painted red barn. Songs of innocence side by side with songs of harsh experience. How abruptly the extraordinary can befall each and every one of us.

"He managed his own private cemetery, in other words. Drive on, my dear—I am happy to wait another hour to eat, to get far from here."

"The bit about eating in peace," Adelaide said, "was that the media's going to descend on us, especially if it turns out he was a serial killer. The sheriff can't hold off long on releasing our names."

"Are they *obligated* to reveal our names? And our home address?"

"Yes. At least we'll be seen as heroes."

"Heroes? What I did was in desperation, not courage."

"Same for me."

I would have been hard-pressed to parse my emotions, which ranged from astonishment to revulsion to relief to immense gratitude. Our narrow escape would have filled me with gratitude even *without* its Bluebeard echoes.

WE SELECTED A LARGE, BUSY diner for breakfast. The headlines on the newspapers stacked by the register said nothing of our imbroglio, and by tacit agreement, my granddaughter and I avoided discussing it. And neither of us seemed to mind the obstreperous children at the adjacent table tossing food about; the lukewarm tea was of little moment.

My newfound tolerance preoccupied me as we ate, eventually leading me to wonder: Whence came the penury of soul that had characterized my lifelong temperament ere now? Was it an accident of birth—of genetics—or was it imposed by circumstances? Or worse: Had it been *cultivated*? To what extent did *I* carry the blame for my character? Ah, Scrooge, your ghostly demons numbered far fewer than my own.

"You want more ibuprofen?"

"My dear, the discomfort you discern is moral, not physical. In this extra lease on life, my joy is alloyed with regrets. In taking inventory, I am finding much to fault." Did I dare I bring up my conduct toward Carson? "I suppose, to begin, I was a stern taskmaster to my students. And stinting in praise. To colleagues as well."

This admission garnered merely a shrug. "I appreciated strict professors. I learned more from them."

"Could that goal not have been accomplished in a kindlier fashion?"

"I had a teacher who praised us constantly, so it was meaningless."

"That was my justification—my *rationale*: the view that liberality in bestowing commendations diminishes true praise. Yet the quality of benevolence is not strained! In any case, my harshest judgment is reserved for my role as father."

Adelaide's nonchalance now gave way to solemnity. "We all make mistakes in relationships—wish we'd acted differently."

"With Olivia and even Richard, 'mistakes' might be an acceptable indictment. But with Marcia, the word 'sin' feels more appropriate. I was quite critical of her, of what might be termed a 'frivolity of spirit.'"

"Were you just trying to prepare her in case she'd have to support herself? Wanting her to make the most of her abilities for her own good isn't wrong."

"Perhaps you can be my lawyer when I face the final judgment. No, I do not fault myself for keeping an eye out for her future; an ethic of responsibility and hard work *is* important. You cannot grow up on a farm and turn a blind eye to laziness or a refusal to pitch in and carry one's load. And yet my own children did *not* grow up on a farm. Their environment made its own demands, erected its own obstacles. How could I presume to be cognizant of them? Was I one such obstacle? She became a loyal wife and loving mother. I have felt aggrieved for my own nature not being accorded understanding and respect, and yet I have committed the identical transgression."

Adelaide sipped her tea without further comment.

"My dear, I am reminded of a passage in a novel—perhaps a George Eliot. A curate was quite partial to his palate and relished his dinners in a most un-ascetic manner. Yet the man should not be hastily condemned, the author tells us, for that same leniency of spirit he showed toward himself he showed to his elderly mother and sister. Not all saints have a saintly bearing. Marcia may have routinely and unobtrusively doled out small kindnesses to those in her orbit. Or, benefiting from her mother's tutelage, greased the wheels of human interaction."

THE NEW YORK CITY SKYLINE rises majestically from many angles. Mammoth and gray, silver where the sunlight hits, the first view is of preternaturally colossal monoliths. As one draws nearer, the eye makes out individual buildings—walls of stone, concrete, glass; facades ornate or sleek or simply massive. The city seemed impossibly immense when I arrived as a young teenager bound for England, a bustling hive of activity and excitement. Now it beckoned a glorious welcome home.

Before Adelaide left to return the rental vehicle, she telephoned Dr. Conti's office and wrangled an appointment for me in the late afternoon. Then, using the extension by my chair, she telephoned Olivia.

"Hi, Mom. Sorry to bother you at work, but Francis and I had a pretty strange thing happen you should know about. I have to return the rental car now and go into Engel, so I'll let him tell you. We're both fine, though." With that, she handed me the receiver and departed.

I prefaced my narrative by repeating that we were fine but Olivia should brace herself for a frightening and violent tale. I proceeded chronologically, beginning with our arrival at the cemetery "for reasons having to do with a case Adelaide has been working on."

To be sure, Olivia punctuated my delivery with numerous gasps. At the narrative's conclusion, she required a good deal of reassurance that neither Adelaide nor I had suffered serious physical injury—indeed, her tone became quite sharp when she inquired as to whether I was concealing a sexual assault. There was no need for her to "hop a plane" to come visit, I stressed—for now, a resumption of our ordinary routine was what would do us the most good. No, the creature had never laid a finger on her daughter.

Most generously, Olivia assumed the task of notifying the rest of the family of what had transpired—and given the likelihood the entire incident would be featured on the television news and in newspapers and magazines, she would encourage Marcia and Elliot and Michael to do their own part in contacting friends. Without such a mission to accomplish, I doubt my elder daughter would have ever hung up.

THE THREE HOURS ADELAIDE WAS absent I put to little use. Concentrating on my opus would be an impossible task—even concentrating on a journal article proved futile. The television was not distracting, no news program mentioning the event. Finally, I found one station making vague reference to "how an attempted murder near Elmira led to the death of a serial killer. More details at five o'clock." Was our flirtation with fame about to begin?

Upon her return, Adelaide explained the goings-on at Engel Klein. Joe had arrived in the morning from Edinburgh, and she 'briefed' him on our discoveries of the two sets of gravestones. He was quite excited, immediately retrieving a map of upstate for her to identify more precisely the cemeteries' locations.

As they pored over the map, a secretary rushed in to say that the radio reported an attack on an Engel Klein employee near Treurig. Understandably, Adelaide was compelled to divulge our encounter with the erstwhile Mr. Blake. Joe appeared to doubt the truth of her description—or perhaps he was simply astonished—but when a paralegal burst in with a similar report, Joe said, "the time difference be damned" and placed a telephone call to one of the Scottish solicitors at his home. Using a "speaker phone" apparatus with which I was unfamiliar, Adelaide was made to repeat the entire series of events, to a great many interruptions of "Och!"

The transatlantic call concluded, Joe, Adelaide, and another lawyer had hammered out the wording of a press release about the attack. Adelaide had agreed—in a decision to which I gave enthusiastic endorsement—that all media inquiries made to her or me about the events would be referred to Engel Klein. In other words, Adelaide and I would be spared participating in a public spectacle. "They are considering our trip as on-the-job and paying me," she added. "Plus, we're supposed to send them all medical bills not covered by insurance."

"That is very generous. For, as you pointed out, they did not direct you to conduct the investigation. But what did Joe say the Scottish court ruled?"

"I'm not sure they have."

BEFORE LEAVING FOR DR. CONTI'S, Adelaide went down the hall to retrieve our mail and provide Millie and John with a firsthand description of what she and I now referred to as 'the attack.' She returned with our neighbors in tow, enabling them to see for themselves that I was in fine fettle. They cautioned us to resist answering the telephone for a while as we would be inundated with calls from the media and well-wishers. As if on cue, the telephone rang, and we ignored it. But Adelaide said she would purchase a telephone machine, reassuring me they were not expensive or difficult to operate.

To our inquiries about Robert's funeral, Millie conceded it had been very painful for them. *The Lord giveth and He taketh away* came to mind, followed by a recollection of my blasphemous thoughts in the dark field. Agnosticism and even atheism had supplanted faith, yet I continued to offer thanks and gratitude—to God, the gods, and Fate. Carson had once denominated similar practices "diversifying one's portfolio," a humorous, and perhaps apt, conceptualization. And not that far off from Pascal's.

The visit to Dr. Conti's office of course did not pass without another recitation. Although the X-ray results were not immediately available, the good physician was convinced that my ankle was merely sprained and not broken and that my shoulder might merely be sorely bruised. The cuts and scrapes were insufficiently deep to be troubling.

"My Achilles ankle," I quipped, "may have actually saved us, sparing me from the full brunt of the monster's swing."

DR. CONTI'S OFFICE BEING ON the same block as a Vietnamese restaurant Sam once had effusively praised, we stopped for takeout. I was pleased the bustling full-service establishment provided chairs off to the side for customers awaiting the completion of their orders. We made prompt use of the courtesy.

"Why, speaking of the devil," I said.

It was Sam himself exiting the dining room and walking toward the door. I was about to call out to him from our tucked-away location when a very attractive young woman—perhaps of Japanese extraction—caught up to him. Sam turned and kissed her on the mouth. My glance darted to Adelaide, but her face showed only surprise. The couple left without noticing us.

Fortunately, there was no sign of him or his companion once we emerged onto the sidewalk with our meals. My list of self-deceptions, I realized, would not come to a conclusion anytime soon.

MILLIE AND JOHN'S ADVICE WAS on the mark, for the answering machine received quite a workout, principally from radio and television stations, magazines, and the occasional newspaper, although sometimes from strangers wishing us well. Adelaide dutifully wrote down the name and telephone number of each caller and passed the information on to someone at Engel Klein.

Poor Violet's search for an heir or heiress was the least of the media concerns—the main story initially was the *young woman lawyer* and *elderly grandfather* slaying an ogre, followed by the ghoulish exhumations on the Blake property. Several reporters, including a few with television cameras, camped outside our building for a short period, but the superintendent loaned Adelaide a key to the back door, allowing her undetected ingress and egress. The foulness of the odors emanating from the dumpsters at either end of the alley apparently was sufficient to keep the paparazzi at bay until an amalgamation of matters international, local, and political, along with celebrity folderol, drew their attention elsewhere.

On the MacDonalde front, Engel Klein had no difficulty proving that the woman Adelaide interviewed in Wichita was one and the same as the Ann MacDonald whose parents' gravestones we had discovered—in other words, that Ann's birth certificate harbored a typographical error. The firm also determined that the survivors of the Rourke fire were an older couple and not some second MacDonalde offspring. The Scottish court expeditiously wrapped up the case and, in a fitting but most un-Dickensian conclusion, after paying fees to the Scottish solicitors and Engel Klein, the estate was able to distribute many millions in funds to charity.

I *was* annoyed to learn, however, that the Drecker firm unearthed a newspaper account of the Rourke fire from Mary's time that actually listed the casualties—and this account had spelled Mary's and her son's names without the *e*.

"The correct spelling had to have been known," I exclaimed, "for the stone mason got it right. Imagine the time and effort looking for

Mary that people might have been spared had the reporter written down their names accurately."

"Maybe in a way it was a *good* thing," my granddaughter interposed. "Violet got to hope she'd hear from her sister again."

The wisdom inhering in Adelaide's remark was underscored by the delight I experienced in the coalescence of my own family in the wake of the attack. Richard managed a telephone call from Bangkok; Adelaide's brothers telephoned from the western part of the country; and some of Nathan's siblings, nieces, and nephews got in touch as well. Marcia urged me to acquire a second telephone line, a pressure I resisted, the answering machine proving an excellent screening device.

Olivia, of course, remained a regular caller, every few days seeking reassurance we were emotionally stable. On one such occasion, she handed the receiver to Tony.

"Francis, I mailed you the names of some therapists in Manhattan. In case you and Addy want professional assistance dealing with the lingering effects of the trauma."

"Very kind of you, very kind."

"These are excellent people, and you should make use of their services. If Medicare or Addy's insurance won't pay for them, allow Ollie and me to foot the bill. It's well worth it. And remember, this is Addy's second encounter with senseless violence; she may be more sensitive than you."

"I will not gainsay that she is the more sensitive of the two of us, on any of a number of scales. And know we are grateful even if we do not make use of the information. We have had to repeat the story of the attack so many times—to the police, family, neighbors, Adelaide's colleagues—I cannot count the number. So we have had prodigious quantities of what you therapists like to call 'catharsis.' And Adelaide has thrown herself into her bar review studies, either a sign of resilience or a means of achieving it."

"But if in weeks, even *months* from now, either of you have trouble sleeping, notice unexplained anxieties, don't ignore it. Symptoms can arise *years* after an event."

"I won't be on the planet years after the event. In all seriousness, Tony, I do thank you and am appreciative of your advice. For the nonce, as the old writers say, for the nonce, we are managing. I have even weaned myself off the pain medications the doctor prescribed."

To his credit, Tony did not belabor the point.

OF ALL THE TELEPHONE CALLS we received during the first few weeks following our heroics, my favorite, indisputably, came from Sam. His message on the answering machine urged Adelaide to act quickly "to cement book and movie deals" before the story was no longer "hot." My granddaughter, a chip off her grandfather's block, was quite uninterested in "deals." The mailbox teemed with such offers, which promptly made their way to what I termed "*our* Graveyard drawer."

The most interesting piece of *correspondence* we received was from the county prosecutor. The legalistic letters, Adelaide explained, were essentially determinations that we each had acted in justifiable self-defense in the assault and killing of John Blake, and thus the prosecutor's office would not press charges. To think that this conclusion had ever been in doubt! However, on further reflection, I conceded that the authorities would have been remiss in their obligations if they had failed at least *to entertain* the notion that we had been the aggressors. And, in its own way, the suspicion, however tenuous, was somewhat flattering.

Adelaide made no mention of returning Sam's call, but my hope that we had completely done with the fellow was extinguished when I paid a follow-up visit to Dr. Conti. While we sat in the waiting room, Adelaide tapped me on the wrist and held aloft a magazine article titled "Squaring NY's Bermuda Triangle." The paragraph above her index finger described an interview with *Sam Rosen, a close family friend of the grandfather-granddaughter Mod Squad* and quoted Sam as saying that Adelaide and I hoped the media and public would respect our privacy.

"I hadn't realized you asked him to relay such a message," I whispered.

"I didn't—I haven't spoken to him since before graduation."

"*That*, your father would say, is chutzpah."

CHAPTER 67

SAMUEL JOHNSON FAMOUSLY OBSERVED, "WHEN a man knows he is to be hanged in a fortnight, it concentrates his mind wonderfully." I would pen a corollary: *When a man has just escaped hanging, it concentrates his mind wonderfully.* The result of such concentration is the ability to distinguish between the truly important and the insignificant. And the truly important, paradoxically, may be the very things he had always considered trivial.

Indeed, having escaped hanging, so to speak, I became attuned to the astonishing loveliness of the prosaic. Habit was transformed from a taken-for-granted mistress to a favorite. Thornton Wilder captured this wisdom beautifully in Emily Gibbs's act 3 return. The greatest riches, the most glorious dreams, the most exalted peaks of fulfilled ambition cannot compete with simple, repeated, quotidian pleasures. Gabriel Oak knew it. Jude learned it. Give to others the acclaim of ascending Everest and attaining the Nobel, and leave me exactly as I am.

So there were no regrets when the excitement of our brush with fame faded from both public and our own attentions. What Warren Gamaliel Harding would have termed 'normalcy'—Adelaide attending her bar review classes and me resuming work on my opus—was as welcome as peacetime activities on the heels of war. The familiar sounds of the bathroom door closing and the shower squeaking on that came through my bedroom wall, signifying Adelaide was preparing for the day ahead, whetted my own appetite for the day ahead. The eight or ten minutes I lay in bed until hearing the faucet squeak off were as serene as any I could spend on a tropical island.

On some days, Adelaide went to Engel Klein after her bar review class to assist in winding down the MacDonalde case. Disappointed claimants had to be notified, files organized for storage, and various tasks attended to. She would then stop for takeout for our dinner. On the days she came straight home from her class, she usually cooked something. This was the major variation in our routine. Of course, the people at her firm treated her like a heroine, both on account of the great discoveries and for her 'actions on the field,' one might say.

The resumption of our old life varied in one significant way, other than Robert's absence: we no longer refrained from brief tactile affection. She might rest a hand on my good shoulder while leaning over to peruse a passage in a book I called to her attention. I might give a brief hug before retiring for the night. These actions arose spontaneously and without awkwardness, casual gestures of family intimacy as unself-conscious as if rotely iterating a pattern of several years' duration.

Yet despite my having boasted to Tony and Olivia of renewed energy and ability to focus on my opus, all was not entirely well on that front. I kept putting off work on those sections that required me to reimmerse myself in certain novels, to reread sufficient portions to recapture the *sensations* they engendered. Imagine trying to accurately describe, say, a Vermeer or Rembrandt only from memory. No, one must have the picture or an adequate reproduction squarely before one's eyes. In an analogous vein, to accurately render the feelings conjured up by Isabel's last visit to Ralph, or Henchard's encounter with Farfrae in the barn, or Esther's rain-drenched discovery, one must revisit those scenes not in memory nor by simply rereading one paragraph; one must again become engulfed in the fictional world.

Ultimately, my mind fixed upon this explanation for my procrastination: I feared that the intense emotions experienced in earlier readings could no longer *be* recaptured. I feared that the attack might have permanently emasculated for me the power of the written word.

Years ago, I had tried to steer a student away from the melodramatic tales of escapes from prisons, invading armies, and secret police she so ravenously devoured, for in my estimation, she was capable of appreciating finer works. In the course of our discussions, I was surprised to learn that her parents and siblings had fled El Salvador in harrowing circumstances, a brother perishing in the effort. A life lived amid violence could put melodrama in a new light, I realized, and novels that for me fairly dripped with excess, to a person with violent experiences may have constituted restrained and artistic retellings.

I also was forced to confront the ancillary question: Could a person intimately connected with dire circumstances appreciate the worries of, say, an Emma Woodhouse? The amorous difficulties of an Emma Bovary? Even Dorothea's frustrated efforts to assist Casaubon could seem marked by superficiality. Some veterans found it difficult to resume old pastimes; all that retained meaning was the battlefield. Had the attack rendered me incapable of empathy with Tess and Eustacia and Jude, and perhaps even with Robert Jordan? Did my deliverance from *real* sorrow destroy my capacity to experience fiction's?

"CONGRATULATIONS!" MARCIA'S VOICE VIRTUALLY EXPLODED through the receiver. "You're the great-grandfather of Jarrod Christopher and Caitlin Ann. They didn't waste any time, Alex and Mindy. One of them better get their tubes tied."

"And congratulations to *you*," I responded. "Are you at the hospital?"

"No, Alex is there. I stayed an hour—long enough. They look like hairless guinea pigs."

"I am sorry Adelaide is attending her bar review class and cannot share in the news just yet. The mother, how is she doing?"

"Still groggy—it was a C-section, so they gave her plenty of dope. Boy, she's in for a ride: three under the age of three. And Alex is *drowning* at work, so he'll be useless. Ted and I are springing for a part-time nanny. We don't want Mindy to regret the whole thing and run off with the milkman."

"Do they still make milk deliveries in this day and age?"

The silence at the other end made me worry we had been disconnected, but Marcia a moment later replied, "Isn't that what you call a metaphor or simile or something? Anyway, the babies have ten fingers and ten toes, so we're happy." I said several things of a congratulatory nature and promised to inform Adelaide of the good news the moment she arrived home. To myself I recited Madison, Noah, Jarrod, and Caitlin Ann—I would commit the names to memory. Was Ann with or without an *e*?

Olivia's call came not long after, and for a good ten minutes, she waxed effusive on the new arrivals. Ecclesiastes tells us: *To everything there is a season . . . a time to be born, a time to die*, and fittingly, in counterpoint to its brush with death, the Wallace family brimmed with new life—or lives, to be precise. Yes, I was blessed with abundant simple joys. And if the world of fiction was not as bright a star as before, perhaps the cause of that dimming was not loss but an increased luminescence all around.

CHAPTER 68

"YOU'RE LOOKING GOOD, LUCE. GET your tan in LA?"

Carson leaned to kiss her cheek. She wore a silky dark-brown dress and matching espadrilles; her makeup and hair Signe would probably categorize as 'fashionable,' as opposed to 'professional.' Carson didn't get all the differentiations she and Chelsea bandied about: 'movie-star wannabe,' 'slummer,' 'on the prowl,' 'hip momma.' Whatever category they put Lucy in, though, he knew she didn't reek of money. There was a time he had wished she did, back when he worried people might look down on her, but either he'd outgrown that fear or else become convinced she was too self-confident to care. And he'd stopped worrying the judge would trade her in for someone younger.

"His hotel has a pool, so I've done some sunbathing."

They began walking toward the exit, Lucy clutching her large leather purse under her arm. She smiled up at him happily.

"Unfortunately, Signe can't leave work till four, but we can do an early dinner, if that's okay?"

"Great—my flight back's at nine. Sorry I had to come on a weekday and make you take time off."

"No problem. What would you like to see? Golden Gate Park, the bridge, Fishermen's Wharf? I've got her car, so we can go anywhere."

"You pick."

They started at the Hyde Street Pier, but it was too crowded, so they strolled along the wharf, looking out at Alcatraz and the sailboats and the bridge. His sister was as much of a people-watcher as Signe; Carson was content just to soak in the fresh air. It wasn't one of those fog days, thank God, which could've delayed her flight and taken some of the fun out of sightseeing. Lucy got a kick out of the mime and the silver man's poses and for a minute watched the balloon twister. She bought a blue T-shirt with a picture of the prison for the judge, rolling it up neatly and putting it in her large bag, careful not to scrunch some manila envelope.

They ate in the Mission, at a taqueria with sidewalk tables, and

Carson showed his sister Haight-Ashbury and Castro Street. With all the gays, were the boutiques wonderful, she wanted to know. They stopped at his apartment—she liked the small slice of the Pacific you could see from the kitchen window, and Sydney allowed himself to be petted. Carson took a detour along the ocean on their way to the restaurant.

SIGNE INSISTED THAT LUCY HAVE the seat with the best view of the bay. The place was swanky and popular but at this hour almost empty. Brother and sister happily deferred to Signe on the wine, and the three quickly agreed on mussels and roasted asparagus appetizers. Signe was happy to answer Lucy's questions about San Diego, Carson kept them both amused with crazy court cases, and Lucy told amusing stories about her work.

IT WAS STILL LIGHT WHEN they dropped Signe at her apartment. She apologized to Lucy for not being able to accompany them to the airport, but she had a write-up due on the boss's desk first thing in the morning. The two women waved in parting.

When the car merged onto the highway, Lucy asked Carson when he was planning to pop the question. He made an offhand shrug. "Soon. Why do you think I pushed you to visit?"

"That's what she thinks too."

"I was gone three minutes in the restroom, and you got down to brass tacks?"

"Women can do that. I like her. She won't let you get conceited."

"Don't give her *that* much credit. What else did she say?"

"That *you* said—in so many words—you wouldn't marry anyone without my approval. No, she didn't mean that exactly. She told you her parents liked you and would be pleased if you got engaged, and you said even if our parents were still alive, it was *my* reaction, not theirs, that would matter. But she added that we're all too old to let other people's feelings change our minds."

"True enough. But did you give her your opinion?"

"I said although I didn't know her well, my impression was you're a good fit. She smiled and said too many people downplay compatibility. She dated a vegetarian once and could've lived with separate foods—he didn't care if she fried up bacon to eat with his spinach omelets. But he wanted the *kids* to be vegetarians and never eat processed *anything*—no Hostess cupcakes, no potato chips. Don't worry: It wasn't all compatibility. What she likes best about you is you know who you are, what you want, and how to get it." Lucy laughed. "She said she's done with musicians. And doctors and stockbrokers who *wish* they were musicians. I like her, Car. She's upfront, not secretive."

He said nothing, and Lucy watched his face while he watched the road.

"You were a lot farther along than you let on in Florida. You'd already met her parents."

"I guess."

"That's okay. I haven't been a hundred percent honest with you. But if you'd been honest with me, I would've been spared a grueling day in Norwalk with your ex."

"Ex?"

"Addy. I took her to lunch in Norwalk. Back in the spring."

"Wow, Luce. Why?" His foot eased up on the gas without his realizing it. The car behind honked; Carson signaled and moved into the right lane.

"I thought you were still hung up on her."

He turned toward his sister but quickly looked back at the highway, shaking his head. "Wow."

"I wanted to know why she was keeping her distance but wouldn't break up." Lucy opened her purse and took out a black plastic compact and flicked up the mirror. "I never did find out. But if you'd told me about Signe, I wouldn't have bothered."

"What did you talk about?"

"I gave her a tour of the old neighborhood. Showed her our building. Told her about our lovely parents."

Carson's hands tightened on the steering wheel. "What did she say?"

"Not much. Asked some questions. She's not a great conversationalist."

The truck in front was only doing fifty, but that was all right. "Why didn't you tell me?"

"Guilt, I guess. Are you pissed?"

"No. Just surprised."

"I didn't open old wounds, did I?"

"Not at all. It just seems like a big secret to keep from me."

She snapped the compact shut. "I was annoyed she was dangling you; I wanted to figure out her game. I'm sorry—I won't do anything like that again. I have one more thing about her, but I'll let you read it. I brought some newspaper articles." She put the compact in her purse and took out the manila envelope.

Now he *was* annoyed. Lucy didn't have to bring the wedding announcement from the paper—she could've just told him.

"Maybe you already know," she said, "how the MacDonalde case ended?"

His hands loosened on the wheel. "Should've figured."

"Signe's a great catch," Lucy said when they hugged goodbye. "Your kids will be gorgeous."

Carson found a place to pull over before getting back on the highway. He read every article twice. Then he drove back to the city and the beach.

THE AIR WAS MILD, NOT a given even in summer. The waves slid wide and flat, barely frothing. He headed toward the narrower, emptier part of the beach, taking long strides, getting sand in his shoes, his good shoes—he'd clean them out before getting back in Signe's car. The hedges planted between the road and the beach were taller here, blocking a view of the streets, so he wasn't aware how far he had walked. Up ahead some unsavory-looking characters milled around, so he did a one-eighty. Back and forth he went over the same stretch, looking up from time to time to see the reddening horizon. Sailors' delight.

A thousand thoughts eddied: about love, relationships, life's surprises—about what a slippery concept carpe diem was. Did most people find answers to big questions—not the philosophical or moral or religious questions but the ones having to do with love and simple decency? Dr. Kim had used to needle Carson he was too afraid to live life with some trial and error. But trial and error felt like his normal MO.

On the last laps, he thought about Lucy and her judge and about Gloria and Jennifer, but an image kept imposing itself, an image he would've liked to shake. A man on a car roof above Addy's frightened face.

Why hadn't she phoned? After his letter, how could she? But what choice had *he* had? Being just a friend was impossible—or it had seemed that way. Maybe that was one of those self-constructed barriers that needed tearing down.

The article referred to a *family friend*—was it a euphemism? Yet it didn't call him 'boyfriend.' Was that all Carson had been: a family friend? So many things he could teach her about dealing with brutal memories. Some of it you had to leave to time, but there were strategies. Should he write? Begin with: *I'm sorry for all the lies. One thing I never lied about was how I felt about you.* Felt?

He climbed up the trail to the sidewalk. Before getting in the car, he emptied the sand from his shoes and wiped the soles with a tissue.

CHAPTER 69

"DID I GET THE SEAL of approval?" Signe smiled coyly as she removed a pale-blue sweater from a Nordstrom's bag and held it up by the lamp.

Carson placed her keys on the half-moon glass-top table. "Yes, Lucy likes you—thinks you're great, in fact."

"The picture in the catalog didn't have a greenish tint—maybe this won't go with the gray skirt after all. But will with the black and navy. I love these faux-pearl buttons."

Carson went to the window and gazed at the glittering lights across the bay.

"Sig, I don't know how to say this nicely. There isn't any way. I'm sorry, really sorry, but it's not going to work, you and me." He forced himself to face her.

She laid the sweater on the sofa arm. "What are you talking about? By the way, Chelsea wants to get tickets for *Friday* night, not Saturday."

"We need to break up—I'm serious."

She glanced at him, mildly annoyed. "Stop talking gibberish."

"I've spent the last hour walking on the beach. Thinking. It's not going to work—us as a couple. I'm sorry—sorry to hurt you."

She strode to the side table, opened a drawer, and took out a small pair of scissors. "If this is your idea of a joke, it's not funny."

"I'm not joking. I didn't think the past would stick like this. Old feelings aren't old enough. I'm sorry."

"*Old feelings?*" She glared at him. "You've known about them since our second date. One is married with two kids. The other could be dead." She strode back to the sofa and picked up the sweater. "I didn't lie when I said I haven't been in touch with them for years. To bring them up now!"

"That's not—"

She snipped off the tag and scrunched it in her free hand. "You could have your choice of a *hundred* good-girl types—they'd worship the ground you walk on. But you picked me. Now I'm supposed to be a virgin?" She returned to the side table, dropped the scissors in the drawer, and slammed the drawer shut. "I never expected this double-standard crap from you."

"You've got it all wrong. It's my *own* feelings, old feelings."

She frowned, disbelieving. "You said Gloria moved to Dallas and married some oil tycoon or whatever. Are you secretly—"

"It's not Gloria."

"Who, then? You said she was your last—"

"She was, in a way. But I dated someone after. It stayed casual—she wasn't up for a relationship. We never even—"

"And now she *is*? How long have you been in touch, you slime?"

"We haven't—I haven't heard from her since February—and her letters were just newsy, not romantic." He looked down at his shoes. "She might be going with someone else, for all I know."

The hand with the tag rested on her hip. "Then what are you talking about?"

"I still have feelings for her—*strong* ones. Even though she never was all that keen on me."

"Jesus, Carson! How do you know that when we have sex I'm not picturing Kevin Bacon? You don't, but who cares? Everybody fantasizes." She squinted like he was nuts. "What's this about—cold feet? You could just say so."

"You should marry someone who doesn't still have strong feelings for someone else. You deserve better than I can give you."

She rolled her eyes. "You're saying this for *my* sake!"

"I don't know what else to tell you. I still feel—"

"And you plan to spend your entire life sulking about her?"

This comment seemed to rankle more than the others. "I hope not—I hope I get over her. But if I don't—I guess certain things won't be in the cards."

"What a load of crap. You're fishing for excuses to break up."

Carson gestured helplessly.

"What changed your mind? Your sister? Did you lie about her? Is she two-faced, pretending to like me but—"

"She *does* like you. She thinks we'd be great as—anyway, it doesn't matter."

"Well, I'm not going to plead. You can walk your goddamn cold feet out of here." Signe took purposeful steps to the bedroom.

Carson lingered by the window, waiting for the additional rebukes he felt were his due. The fact that his unkindness was unintended didn't excuse it. Was there some monastery he could join until he got over Addy, assuming he could? Nuns could be teachers—could monks?

Signe returned carrying two large shopping bags. Dropping them beside the front door, she retreated to the kitchen doorjamb and folded her arms. Her mascara was smudged. "I expected more originality from you," she said. "Not just obsessing over the one that got away. We *all* get screwed by love, but you move on. Jeez—why am I bothering. Take your crap and get out."

Carson stepped toward the bags. One had his blue sweater and a white shirt and more clothes piled underneath. The sight of the hand-carved mahogany box in the other bag, and the glass Labrador—which hadn't been cheap—plus the carelessly tossed in silk scarf, the sight of these gifts jolted him. She'd really admired that box at a high-end crafts fair and had had no idea he'd palmed one of the artist's cards.

With one hand Carson grabbed the four bag handles. At the door, he pivoted and tried to frame some phrase of farewell, but she beat him to the punch.

"You're really fucked up."

He couldn't agree more.

CHAPTER 70

SECURED TRANSACTIONS AND COMMERCIAL PAPER, this week's subjects in the bar review class, were near the bottom of Addy's 'enthusiasm list,' a phrase she'd picked up from Zach. Luckily, Francis was open to hearing about *any* subject, so she could review each day's material with him to etch it deeper in her brain. Most of their dinner conversation tonight was about collateral. Maybe it was too tedious even for him—in the past, he used to linger at the table longer. And now he'd gone to bed, and it wasn't even nine. Age might be taking its toll.

Standing by the living room windows, she gazed at the lights of Roosevelt Island reflected in the river. They formed a kind of moving carpet, going on and off, right and left. Again, it struck her how so many people could live in close proximity to one another and yet know nothing of each other's lives. Did bees and ants have the same tunnel vision? Early human societies—the hunter-gatherer ones, at least—had operated as teams, each member alert to the others' whereabouts. Was the evolution to large settlements accompanied by a psychological evolution as well?

The phone ringing startled her. She waited by the answering machine.

"Hi, it's Carson. I'm just calling—"

She grabbed the receiver. "Hi, sorry—I didn't know it was you."

"Is this a bad time?"

"No."

"My sister was visiting and gave me a wad of articles about the MacDonalde case. You solved it!"

"I guess."

"And the Bermuda Triangle guy too."

She sat on the edge of Francis's chair. "That was pretty gruesome."

"Are you okay? It said you weren't hurt, just that—"

"We're okay."

"What about emotionally?"

She moved farther back on the cushion but still sat up straight. "The first week or two felt strange. I didn't have trouble sleeping, but at times during the day, I'd shiver, like it had just hit me what we escaped. The thing is: the whole attack, it only lasted a few minutes. The fear came on suddenly and was over suddenly. I think that helped—helped us bounce back. Plus, I wasn't hurt—he never even touched me. Francis got a bruised shoulder, but amazingly, it wasn't shattered. And his ankle got sprained. We were *really* lucky." Was she talking too much?

"Compared to his other victims, sure, but it's a helluva thing to go through." He paused, and for several seconds, neither of them spoke. "You met Lucy—"

"Yes—she invited—"

"Sorry I'm such a liar, Addy. Telling you all that stuff—I was a real stupid jerk."

"It's okay."

"No, it's not. I'd undo it if I could. I don't know why—it was—"

"It's okay. Really."

He was silent a moment, then asked, "How's the bar review course going?"

"All right."

"Dumb question. Anyway, just curious: one of the articles mentioned some guy named Sam. You dating?"

"No. It was never a big deal. What about you? You wrote you were getting serious about someone."

Almost imperceptibly, his voice quavered. "Would that matter to you?"

Hers didn't quaver. "Yes. I have no business saying so, and I don't expect you to still care—"

"Addy—"

CHAPTER 71

WAS THAT THE SHOWER? MY goodness—the bedside clock said only 6:15, and Adelaide rarely rose before seven. Perhaps Engel Klein had requested she attend an early-morning meeting. I *had* heard the telephone ring last night.

I rolled over, and the next thing I knew, the clock said 7:48. A note lay on the kitchen table. *I'll be home around 2.* Had her class been cancelled? I checked her bedroom. Indeed, her backpack sat by the desk chair. Was that not another of life's little pleasures: the minor mysteries that got cleared up at day's end?

The work on my opus went well, although I continued to procrastinate venturing into sections requiring a deep immersion in what had been my profounder literary experiences. I perused the newspaper while eating lunch and noticed several plays listed in the arts section that I would consider attending, adorned in my still-unworn necktie. Of course Adelaide and I would take a cab each way. Perhaps a Sunday matinee performance would be the least troublesome.

She must have arrived while I was having my nap, for she was just putting on the kettle when I joined her in the kitchen. That she wore nice gray slacks and a nice yellow blouse lent support to my hypothesis of an early-morning meeting at Engel Klein. I took my usual spot.

"You were up and out the door at the break of dawn. Did the firm need you?"

"Actually, I was at Kennedy."

"The airport?"

She set our mugs on the counter and took tea bags from the tin. "Carson flew in. I met him there."

"To visit his sister?"

"No, he just flew back—to San Francisco."

A short laugh escaped me. "He flew *into* New York this morning and then turned right around and flew *out?*"

"Not right away. He was here about five hours."

"Five hours—why?"

She turned toward the stove. "To see me."

This response was—not to put too fine a point on it—nothing less than bewildering. "To see you?"

"Yes, we talked on the phone last night and arranged it." She continued to face away, although the kettle was merely rumbling.

"Does he have so much free time to fly from coast to coast for a few hours' visit?"

She pivoted my direction, her face inscrutable. "We're… dating again." Now the kettle rumbled energetically, and she gave it her attention.

What had prompted this dramatic turn of events? Was Tony right: emotional issues could surface *weeks* after a traumatic event? Had the attack rendered her newly vulnerable?

Adelaide brought the cups to the table and sat across from me.

"I confess I am a little stunned. By the expense of such a cross-country circuit."

"He and his sister came into a bunch of money a few months ago. Their mother was hit by a truck and killed, and the company gave them a large settlement."

The opportunity to dwell on a tangential matter was exceedingly welcome, as it might assist in reestablishing the world as I knew it. "And this is the same mother who turned a blind eye to the father's abuse all those years? To paraphrase Shakespeare, perhaps nothing in her life became her like the leaving of it. The line is from *Macbeth*. Or, as actors prefer to call it, 'the Scottish play.'"

I rambled on a bit about Shakespeare, hoping to shed my uneasiness and confusion, then lapsed into silence, my gaze resting on the floor to one side, unaware of where hers rested. Inwardly, I chanted *Absence makes the heart grow fonder* multiple times. Besides, wasn't the longevity, the *durability* of such a romance, improbable? For even if the young man had acquired untold millions, the cross-country excursions were likely to grow tiresome. Perhaps his new girlfriend had recently given him the boot, and out of a kind of nostalgia he wooed Adelaide. A colleague had once used the phrase "going through the Rolodex" to describe the period right after his divorce. Yes, the odds of a romance enduring across three thousand miles were slim, for hearts are easily distracted by temptations near at hand. I thought of Jude and Arabella.

And of course poor Tess, although temptation in her case came in the form not of personal advantage but of advantages to her impoverished family.

I braved raising my glance; Adelaide was looking at the tabletop. "You must not have run out of things to talk about at the airport," I ventured to say, "catching each other up on events large and small. You told him how the MacDonalde case concluded?"

"Yes, but the thing is"—and here she looked directly at me—"he asked me to marry him."

"Marry him!"

"I know it seems sudden. I guess it *is* sudden."

"And right on the heels of a tumultuous few weeks."

"It wouldn't be right away—"

"Of course not. Even if you were at some future date to entertain such a proposal, you would need ample time to consider its advantages and *dis*advantages."

"Actually, he proposed a long time ago—before he went to San Francisco. This time I said yes."

"You said—"

"The ceremony won't be until—"

"Not for a while—you need time to turn the idea over in your mind fully. That is what engagements are all about, my dear: to see if marriage is *truly* the best step. Consider, your—your romance, its renewal, is not a full day old. Of course it *seems* permanent—that is the nature of romantic feelings. But a long courtship allows a couple to ascertain whether their feelings can stand the test—"

"We're thinking of September."

"September of this year?" Adelaide nodded solemnly.

I was at sixes and sevens. Play along, I told myself, play along; being obstructionist will only stiffen her resolve. With laudable effort I forced cheerfulness into my voice.

"It will be manageable, reconfiguring the living spaces when he is ready to move. You and I are old hands at rearranging this apartment, are we not? It would make the most sense for my office to be reconverted to the master bedroom for the two of you. That is no problem."

"We've decided to live in the Bay Area. We want you to live with us. Carson's going to look for a house, one where you'd have plenty of space and privacy. I know it sounds complicated, but movers can do all the packing—even paintings and fragile stuff."

I did not know what to say.

"The winters are mild," she blithely nattered on. "You wouldn't be housebound like here. Carson was the first to suggest you living with us. He never had much of a family growing up—a happy family—and he likes the idea of us—"

"That's very kind," I mumbled.

"It's a beautiful city—right on the ocean with the bay all around. Most of the buildings are only a few stories, so you get great views everywhere, and it feels open. A lot of firms there do environmental law—I was thinking of trying that."

A lot of firms in *New York* did environmental law! "How does your mother feel about it—have you told her?"

Adelaide nodded, but I could see the question made her uneasy. Bless you, Olivia!

"She thinks some of it makes sense."

"And which part does not?"

"She'd rather you move to Seattle."

"That is *all* she finds fault with?"

We sipped our tea. Adelaide said, "Maybe once Carson finds a good area to focus the house search, we can fly out and see what you think. I know moving seems scary, but like I said, we can hire people to pack everything up. The only real hassle will be deciding what to take. But whatever you leave behind, Aunt Marcia might be able to arrange an estate sale. You wouldn't have to put the apartment on the market until you wanted to."

How I struggled to keep my voice calm! I do know the words came out slowly, deliberately. "This is quite a quantity of decision-making in the space of less than twenty-four hours: that you're in love, that you should get married, and then move from one coast to the other. Particularly following so soon after our escape from mortal danger. Surely you need more time to consider these changes?"

Rising, Adelaide took her cup to the sink. "Nothing's happening right away. And we have all summer to pack. But sure, we can talk about it some more." She squeezed my good shoulder gently. "I know this seems sudden. But it'll work out; the three of us will be sitting around talking about cases like we used to. He's really ashamed of the lies he told—you'll see."

CHAPTER 72

THE TREES ACROSS THE WAY showed their full summer green, the verdant hues of mature foliage. Last year's saplings were now sturdy trunks. The season of ripening had arrived. Even those pedestrians on their way to work slackened their pace, an unusual sight in this so-busy city.

Perhaps Adelaide would prove prescient: it would all "work out," and this marriage in the offing would bring long-lasting happiness. What distinguished the impulsive from the ardent? Austen's *Sense and Sensibility* argued for patience and against the prompt yield to passion. *Persuasion*, penned some years later, taught the opposite: that setting aside passion was perilous. Did the older, wiser author harbor personal regrets?

For Henry James, forbearance was a quintessentially *European* trait; we Americans are too imbued with ambition to let reservations impede our strivings. Thomas Hardy, true Englishman, was careful to temper ambition with steady industry—look at Clym and the reddleman and, eventually, Bathsheba.

But perhaps I was foolish to look for my doppelgangers in Thomas Hardy characters, for they felt thwarted, and I did not. I have had a life of riches in all things personal and professional. Shall I quibble about a father's disapproval? No, not after becoming acquainted with a father's brutality.

THE LATE-AFTERNOON SKY TEASED TINTS of lavender. Adelaide sat on the sofa with the laundry basket beside her, lifting out garments one at a time to fold and set on the adjacent cushion. They gave off that mild pleasant scent of recent washing. She offered a timid smile at my approach. I sat in my chair and lay the crutch on the floor.

"My dear, I listened to you expound on your plans yesterday; today you are going to have to listen to mine. To begin: early impressions can be egregiously erroneous, and I will be the first to admit that I gave undue credence to my own. You should know that I am pleased with your choice of a husband as I now perceive him to be a kind and loyal man. Any disapproval I may have conveyed you should ascribe to my resistance to change, to upheaval in any form."

Putting aside the towel in her hand, she rose from the sofa and came forward as if to hug me, but I held her off with a raised hand.

"I am not done, and not everything I say may be to your liking. My next point is that although I am truly moved by your and Carson's offer to make a home for me within your home, I refuse it. I have given the matter serious consideration—I have given quite a few things serious consideration. And when all is said and done, I believe Seattle will be more to my liking than San Francisco. You yourself have vaunted the virtues of your hometown. How I will arrange such a move I am afraid to contemplate, but as you have said, we have the summer to execute our plans, and I can count on your assistance in the sorting and packing. No, do not protest; my mind is made up. If you find my absence too hard to bear, you can always come visit."

"It's only two hours by plane."

"Yes. That is not *all* I have decided upon. My additional plans, which I will have to rely on you to communicate to the relevant parties, pertain to this." I waved my arm broadly at the rooms. "When you telephone your mother to inform her of my eventual move to Seattle—I do not have the energy right now to be the bearer of news—you shall also explain that the idea of putting all these furnishings on the market does not appeal to me. I have seen many, many estate sales in my lifetime. So I will leave the bulk of the furnishings for Alex and his family. With three children, he and Mandy—Mindy!—he and Mindy will make good use of these rooms.

"There will be details to work out—I want to be fair to everyone—but these are the essential points. I suspect a colleague of yours at Engel Klein can draw up the appropriate documents. As I say, I leave to you the task of notifying your mother and Alex of my plans."

Adelaide made no reply but watched me so intently I felt compelled to murmur that I had writing to do, and I reached for my crutch, stood, and hastened as best I could to my study.

Evening has come. I sit at the desk and take stock of my friends, these oft-perused stories of the human heart, searching with some measure of desperation for meaning and happiness. These books will offer sanctuary, they *must*, they *shall*.

Culling through the volumes to decide which to bring will be the most arduous task—Olivia does not need extra copies. Should I leave the remainder behind, in the event one of Alex's children develops a taste for literature? Yes, I will bequeath this library. A seed may take root.

Marjorie, I am cognizant of how full my cup is. And has been and will be. I am not without gratitude, and I say fie on any who would offer pity. Nor am I insensible to the good fortune that awaits me at Olivia's—our father-daughter relationship is short on neither affection nor shared interests.

Yet to you I cannot pretend that the move pleases me. Not simply the views from the windows, or furniture that will remain behind, but even these walls and floors signal loss, for they have borne witness to my years as husband and father, as professor, as grandfather. The tables and chairs are not simply creature comforts, as the phrase would have it, but comforts to the soul.

Yet my own comfort does not rule; its importance is not paramount. No, not paramount. John Jarndyce and Michael Henchard tutor me, teach me not to delay the step to the side. I shall not resist irrelevance.

Do not for a moment presume I begrudge our granddaughter her happiness. The glow that infuses her features cannot fail to reflect its warmth on me and will help me to abide her absence. But understand my journey. When I lost you, armies of grief and loneliness set up camp, plunging in stakes all around; relentless and implacable, they besieged my heart. How many times did I cry out for you!

Always in vain, always in vain.

Soon after, my career in academia, the principal distraction from grief, halted. To where could I turn? The children, grown and independent, did not need me. I had no students. Continuing to live on was a duty, merely a duty, sustained by the fiction that I would join you in the afterlife.

In this bleakness, merciful Habit graced me. Habit allowed me to endure the exercise of living, the passage of hours. Over time, I was granted another gift: if not of serenity, then of tranquility, of quietude. And with it, an asceticism befitting old age, befitting the body's decline. I was granted some measure of peace.

I can hear, faintly, Adelaide's voice in the hallway. Whom did she call first, Olivia or Alex? Or perhaps Carson, to tell him a smaller house would suffice. A generous man, who waited many moons for her with little in the way of encouragement. Will I ever warm to him? It does not signify.

The hum of her voice ceases. It begins anew. My hearing is not acute enough to pick up the intonations or inflections, just the hum. A few more minutes of episodic sounds, followed by silence, save for the street noises below: a siren, brakes, a horn.

The gods granted me a peace, Marjorie, and I came to treasure that peace as a child treasures a lovely pebble plucked from a creek bed or the first autumn leaf turned crimson. I savored routine, the quiet contemplations, the way the morning sun changes the river from dark to blue. The descent of dusk on the shore opposite.

My appetite for life shrank, but it was sated.

How could I have foreseen how fragile that peace was—that it would easily shatter? Not by misfortune—no, not by misfortune, but by the most-undeserved fluke of good happenstance. She moved in and, with neither artifice nor cunning, wove a spell that turned the day's rote cycle into adventure. She reignited curiosity, enthusiasm, love. Oh, Marjorie, no longer am I reconciled to dying.

SLOWLY, CAREFULLY, I HOBBLE TO the hall. An envelope rests facedown on the vanity. It has not been sealed.

Mom, enclosed is a sketch of the invitation. As I mentioned, Lucy is the only relative on his side, but he's inviting a few people he worked with at Macy's. Hopefully they won't mind coming up to Greenwich. The ceremony's going to be simple; we have a judge.

I like your idea of Francis flying back with you a few days after the wedding. He wouldn't want to remain here alone. He might even admit that—he's begun to let his terrified affections show.

Terrified affections. Dear, dear granddaughter, truth-sayer *and* poet.

I replace the letter in the envelope and leave it faceup.

* * *

ACKNOWLEDGMENTS

I thank Ruth Pettis for her discerning eye and detailed critique of the long manuscript. I thank Vicki Moran Dhingra and Merri M. Monks for their careful reading and numerous insights. A thank-you also to the Honorable Fred W. Kawalski for information about the law practice of tracking down heirs and to Erin Cusick for her thoughtful and painstaking editing. Any errors that made it into the book were my doing, not theirs. And, of course, a thank-you to Dave for his unwavering support.

CPSIA information can be obtained
at www.ICGtesting.com
Printed in the USA
LVHW051547200723
752859LV00002B/90

9 781737 083429